By Dana C Brentson

The Ambient Series: Sam

Salvation's Fall
Ambient Height
Desolate Seasons

HER LATENT CHARM

The Ambience Series:

Book One

Dana C Brentson

www.dcbrentson.com

To my husband, Quinn
For all that you've done to encourage this journey

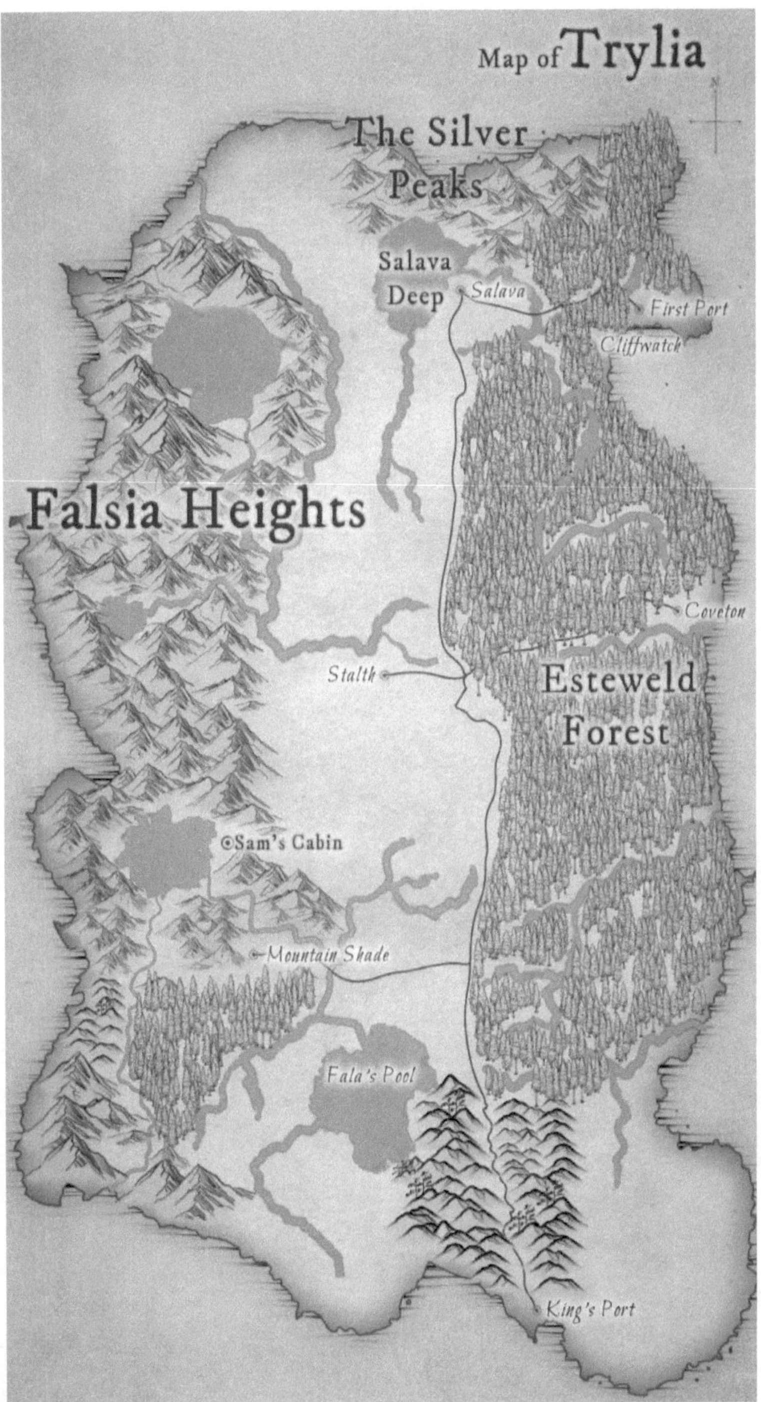

Map of Trylia
The Silver Peaks
Salava Deep
Salava
First Port
Cliffwatch
Falsia Heights
Coveton
Stalth
Esteweld Forest
Sam's Cabin
Mountain Shade
Fala's Pool
King's Port

CHAPTER ONE

My fingers brushed canvas sails and rough hempen rope — just out of my frantic reach — as I hurtled toward the deck of my ship. The wind roared in my ears, pulled my clothes and auburn hair back, and stung my eyes. The sea crashed against the hull again, another large wave rocking the *Catherine* as if to throw the rest of my crew as it threw me.

Above the roar of the wind, voices rose, calling out my name. The deck came closer, inch by torturous inch, as I scrambled for something to grab, some way to save myself from the death I was rushing toward. Louder than the voices, the wind, and my own fear came the echoing voices in my head.

We come.

Incorporeal, translucent hands reached through and above the people trying to catch me. I stopped with a jolt that whipped my head back painfully, a few feet above my shocked crewmates' outstretched arms. Unseen by anyone but me, they were shaped like people shrouded in cloaks, but it was like looking through water filtered with sunlight near the surface. I could see no faces, nothing but the shape of shoulders, heads, arms and hands. I floated in the air like I was lying flat on the deck, but I couldn't feel anything around me. It was as if whatever these incorporeal things were, they were forcing the air to hold me instead of letting me drop. Preventing my body from breaking against the planks below, comforting me as they had since childhood. I stretched my hands towards them.

The faces of the people below blurred as I focused on the cloaked figures, straining my ears above the wind to hear their whispers as I always did. Whispers that teased me with the promise of knowledge I had longed for as long as I could remember.

Hunter's ivy-colored eyes caught mine, but I pulled my gaze away from his creased brow and worried eyes to regard the others that he couldn't see. The heavy wind subsided, whipping my long hair in front of my eyes in a last furious gale, and the figures were gone. I finished my plummet with considerably less force than I should have, and my fingers grasped at Hunter's shoulders, dragging him down to the deck with me.

Marl and Roy rushed forward to pull us upright, identical rich obsidian hands patting my head and back to assure themselves that I was all right, as Captain Morrig's voice rang in my ears, shouting my name. I turned my eyes to his when he shoved between the twins and cupped my face in his large sable hands.

"Lila, child, are you whole? Are you hurt?"

I shook my head as best as I could in his grasp. The fear fell from his face, now crumpled in relief. He pulled me into his embrace and I swung my arms around his back. It reminded me of another time, more than fifteen years ago, when he had paid to release me as a small child from men that intended my sale to make me a slave. Despite my misgivings, I had trusted him then, and I placed my trust in him now, taking a deep breath to calm myself. Murmurs from the crew were drowned in the heavy sigh from the captain.

"The *gift*," Roy whispered. More whispers followed, and soon there was a cacophony of voices all around me, muttering to one another. More than one voice muttered the familiar curse, *blight*.

My breath came out in a huff, my eyes straining past the captain's shoulder for another glimpse of the cloaked figures. As I always did when something brought out my supposed *gift*, I tried to hold onto the feeling that caused it, letting myself feel the fear that falling had elicited, trying to awaken my connection to whomever those people were. Just like every time before, I failed. I cursed the Elders internally, seething with frustration.

A familiar chorus of disbelief, awe, and shock filled my ears. Many of the crew had been with us for years and had witnessed an event like this before; assurances of sanity passed from the mouths of those veterans to some of the newer crew. Yes, they had seen me fall from the main mast, and yes, I had stopped in midair.

Not again, I thought.

Stories were told around campfires and bedsides about a time long ago when the Chosen held sway over the land and her people. Tales of benevolent people who aided anyone in need and served the king loyally abounded, but also those that described something more wicked and foul. Whether or not the crew believed that what I had just done was something to be feared, a familiar litany of questions flooded my mind as I considered the possibilities.

Would people fear me? Would they revere me, try to use me? Could I do it again? *Why* could I only see the people when I wasn't trying?

Time after time, I tried to make them come. To do things like the Chosen in the stories I read as a child. Why couldn't they help us load heavy cargo, or even let me fly? I tried to move cargo with the gift when we were in port last, but instead, I pulled a muscle. And almost fell off the dock when I tried to fly over the water later that day. Years ago, when I became frustrated by Hunter's teasing, I almost set his hair on fire when sparks flew out of my hand.

I had given up on fanciful ideas of flying. If I could just understand what was happening, I could prevent someone from getting hurt when I lost my temper. And maybe, I could use it to help people.

Wary, disbelieving expressions surrounded me, broken by a few that seemed genuinely relieved that I wasn't hurt. Marl and Roy smiled with relief and let out sighs in unison.

The trimmed hair of the captain's black and gray beard prickled my scalp when he tucked my head under his chin. Voices rose around us as the crew talked over each other, my friends trying to calm the newest members who hadn't seen this yet. The captain's kind dark eyes found mine when he pulled away and flashed me a reassuring smile before he turned back to the crew.

"*Silence!*" he bellowed, and silence surely followed. Captain Morrig hesitated, at a loss for words. The planks of the deck creaked as men shifted their feet back and forth. The silence stretched, the wind snapping at the sails overhead.

Finally, the captain shouted, "Back to work!" Everyone lingered, but after a moment and a few more sidelong glances my way, they started to shuffle away to bring us safely to port. Several people curled their left hands into fists, placing them on their chests above their hearts. A sign I had seen many times, a sign to beg the Elders to protect them from evil.

I turned, facing the captain. He looked down at me with his usual kindness, but there was also a hint of apprehension. I didn't miss the flash of his gaze at the members of the crew gesturing toward me, and his brow furrowed. From the corner of my eye, I saw them retreat, their thudding feet receding quickly.

"I'll watch them," he assured me. I nodded with a grimace. This was an uncomfortable routine between us: I prove the impossible gift exists without intention, and he dismisses the most superstitious among the crew in order to protect me. Several weeks of rumors follow us, and then new stories of the gift are dismissed. He gave my shoulders a squeeze and walked aft, barking orders as he went.

Only Hunter remained at my side. His bronze hair waved in the ocean breeze to straighten the slightly curled ends. He reached out to touch my shoulder as he had so many times in our long friendship.

"Again?" His lopsided smile broke me from my irritation. Another uncomfortable routine.

I shrugged. "I think I'm starting to figure it out," I said, hoping to give the impression that I was learning to control it.

"Really?" he asked, his smile widening to show the dimple on his right cheek. "It'll be nice not to worry about you taking another tumble. Maybe you can use it on me the next time I take one."

He turned, laughing at himself, thankfully not noticing the tears welling in my eyes. I blinked them back and turned to take my place with Marl and Roy securing the sails.

A few men chattered at me as they passed, letting me know that they were glad I was all right and how excited they were to see the gift for themselves.

Why do I have this gift if I can't use it? Why only when I'm afraid? Am I broken?

A small voice at the back of my mind replied, *How else do you explain it?*

I lost myself in the physical work of hauling lines, securing sails, and stowing cargo alongside the twins with the sting of rope sliding through my calloused hands to keep my mind from the events of the morning.

After a time, I could see the harbor of Firstport filled with a range of vessels from large, three-masted cargo ships like ours, to small fishing boats. Most of these vessels hadn't seen open water for years. The wear was evident in the splitting wood of masts and decks and the tightly furled sails crusted with salt and stained with age.

I couldn't blame anyone for keeping to shore. We had escaped ships heading north from Vortheim twice. Each time, it had been the Elders' own luck that we had emptied our holds before our encounter and had the speed to stay out of reach. The thrill of fear I felt at the time, wondering whether we would be caught and killed, still ran through me whenever I thought about it.

It must have been nice to sail without having to worry about slavers, thieves, and murderers, I thought.

The city beyond sat on a flat peninsula at the eastern edge of Trylia, protected on all sides by a massive wall of stoic and uninviting gray stone. The dock looked welcoming, if less sturdy with the decline of sea travel, and we slowed to meet it. Men climbed up and over the rail as soon as the lines were secure, and we pulled to a full stop. The captain was the last over the edge and smiled reassuringly before his weathered face disappeared with a murmured "Stay here."

I trudged to the rail, despondent at the reminder that I was different, watching their progress along the weather-beaten pier. Though the men around me did the same, a clear space separated us. The warmth of the sun couldn't penetrate the chill in my body as I was left alone with my thoughts.

They're all staring or talking behind my back. I could be a danger to everyone. Should I leave? Where would I go?

The day faded to evening with words of doubt echoing through my skull, and I followed the others to my berth below. Glances were less than discreet as they tracked my progress and stayed just far enough away that I was touched by no one, despite the cramped nature of this part of the ship. It made me feel lonelier, as though I didn't belong.

My hammock swung beneath me as I climbed inside. I gave myself a moment more to wallow in the knowledge that I was something more – or less – than another member of the crew, and then I pulled it around me like armor. If some of them wanted to keep their distance, that was fine with me. My duties were enough to keep me busy, and I could always spend more time studying with Smitts.

Holding myself apart from the crew was another part of my routine, and I knew it would hurt some. Especially Hunter and the captain, but it was part of the process of calming my self-doubt. If I could detach from the mistrust I saw in others, I could learn to trust myself again. When I gave myself space from anything too personal, I found a way to connect to the people I loved instead of the worry that they only saw what made me different.

I pulled a tattered, leather-bound book from the blanket balled up by my feet. Knowing it would contain no new insights about what I could do didn't deter me from searching for them. Straining my eyes against the meager candlelight, I traced familiar paragraphs as they recounted the myths of the gift in Trylia.

Those with the gift were said to be people that could tear down mountains or raise them from the ground. They were capable of healing grievous wounds or creating them.

We know not whether they ever existed, or if these are tales of fancy created when people spent long winters inside their homes, waiting for spring. The only evidence, which is largely debated, seems to be journals from centuries past recounting the stories which have been mentioned.

I sighed and closed the book. Smitts had given me this volume of Trylia's history years ago, after my first incident with the gift. And this simple passage was the most I had found on the gift in all my years of searching every volume I could find. Even with Smitts' connections to the university in King's Port, we came up empty.

Everything written seemed to be folk tales that mentioned the gift in passing or songs that were very poetic and unhelpful. I shoved the book under my legs and fished around for the only other one I owned.

My fingers closed on a smaller, smoother binding. With the light low, I could barely make out the faded, golden letters on the cover, or the creature with wings and scales flying over an ocean filled with rainbows. I had worn it down over the years, running my fingers over it just as I did now.

I opened the book carefully. The pages were loose, and I didn't want to lose any. This was a gift from the captain, to welcome me to his family here.

My favorite story was near the end. About a woman, Chosen by the Elders, to watch over the entire world with her gift. I scanned the story, clutching the silver key that dangled from a chain around my neck, the only token of whatever life I had before, looking for the passage that had always made me feel like what I could do wasn't a curse.

The darkness had spread to every corner of Celuthia. The entire world was cold, and the people suffered. The sky opened, like a mouth trying to swallow everything.

But she was the Elders' Chosen. She had the light inside her. The light at the heart of Celuthia was for everyone. So she gave it back to everyone.

She let the light out to drive away the darkness. To close the hole in the sky so that the sun could shine again.

I knew it was a story for children, but I let it soothe my anxious mind as I closed my eyes. Steady breathing and snores from people falling asleep surrounded me as I fought to calm enough to join them.

CHAPTER TWO

Around midday the following day the crew returned, and the job of unloading the sold goods and taking on new cargo and deliveries began in a flurry of activity. A recent addition to the crew raced past me with an armful of violet silk, stomping on my foot in his haste. A young boy with sandy hair and a bright, eager smile turned to me. I couldn't help but smile back, his grin so wide that it broke me from my self-imposed isolation.

"Sorry, Lila."

"It's all right, Walter, just watch where you're going or you'll end up over the side. Are you headed to the hold?"

"Aye," he said as he disappeared below.

More silk was brought on board, in a variety of colors. Everyone chattered about the captain's luck in obtaining such a rare cargo to sell.

Marl and Roy stood guarding the gangway to ward off the beggars and thieves. The twins acted as hired muscle but showed promise as sailors. With their arms crossed, their muscles bulged under thin cotton sleeves, and their scowls made a wall of hard menace against intruders.

"Lila," Marl called. I ducked between two women passing bags of grain along a line to the hold and looked up at the twins. "Smitts needs you. Hunter got hurt."

Roy spared me a glance, his eyebrow raised as if expecting a certain reaction at mentioning Hunter.

"Thanks," I said, and turned away before they could see the flush in my cheeks as they chuckled to each other.

Only a little older than I, Hunter shared my predilection for misfortune and, despite his cavalier attitude, my suspicious and cautious nature. That he would be caught off guard surprised me. He stood taller than most of the crew, with a lean, muscular body; he was a handsome man, and he knew it. I certainly knew it.

He came to live on the *Catherine* shortly after I arrived, "adopted" by the captain like I was. Always teasing, smiling, and joking, I didn't think he knew how to be serious. And for a long time, I didn't know how to be anything *but* serious. But we became friends, and when we were a bit older, we almost became something more.

My blush deepened as I remembered the touch of his lips, his hands in my hair. At sixteen, my impulsive desire led to a few stolen kisses in the hold. Occasionally, I would try to shut down after the gift manifested, but Hunter's easy humor and our friendly, joking banter broke through my defenses. After a couple of years, I was tired of telling myself that I had too much to worry about without the complication of an intimate relationship, or because of it. We spent a few days of shore leave stealing away from our duties to find dark corners, where we almost became as intimate as any two people could be.

But, when I was almost stabbed in one of those dark corners by a woman who wanted our money, I threw her against a wall without touching her. And when I withdrew from everyone, as I always did, it hurt both of us more than ever before. My feelings for him hadn't changed, but I knew as long as I couldn't control my episodes, I wouldn't be able to guarantee that I wouldn't close off again.

My progression toward the surgeon's cabin was slow as I reminded myself of all the reasons for my decisions. I ducked to the side rail to avoid being bowled over, sliding across the worn wood of the deck in my bare feet until I was able to dart across to the hatch.

Before disappearing below decks again, I stopped to savor the sunlight and took a deep, steadying breath as the wind tugged at the knot of hair behind my head, teasing me with the cool promise of the ocean.

I hurried down the passage of the berth deck to the surgeon's door. Smitts was the only formally educated member of the crew, having studied in King's Port, and oversaw the education of younger crew in addition to treating injury and illness. He had been with the captain almost as long as I had, a source of comfort and knowledge since the day we met.

As I grew, I was able to take on more physical tasks, but my first years had been spent in the shadow of the willowy surgeon. Now my duties revolved around Smitts with occasional forays into other tasks when needed.

The door swung open silently to Smitts bent over the narrow bunk set into the far wall of the ship. The dim light cast through the small window glinted through his wire glasses and illuminated his furrowed brow as he examined the wound in front of him, his slender fingers gently probing the broken skin. I had always been fascinated with his hands; he possessed none of the calluses most of us sported from rough work, and his fingers were long and slender like the rest of his wiry frame. He had a nervous disposition, so I cleared my throat to announce my arrival.

He seemed startled all the same, and I smiled. "Lila! I didn't hear you come in. Please, come look at this."

I passed to Smitts' side and looked where he indicated. Even injured, Hunter flashed me a cocky, though unconvincing, smile, and my heart leapt. A ragged gash oozed on his arm, ripped rather than sliced, likely by a blade in need of sharpening. "I wasn't watching, Lila," he told me. "Bastard came out of nowhere trying to steal the food I was bringing for Drain. Nearly took my arm off."

Shoving my feelings aside was a huge effort, but I put what I hoped was a benign smile on my face. "Well, you'll have to be more careful next time," I said.

He laid his head back and closed his eyes, his opposite hand clutching at a piece of white stone. Something of his mother's, I knew, that gave him comfort in times of worry.

"This will need to be closed," Smitts told me. "I already gave him some rum for the pain. I want you to get a bit more practice stitching, so I'll hold his arm for you to clean and close it."

I glanced at Hunter as I inched closer. It was easier to ignore the fluttering in my stomach with a task to focus on. "Try not to move too much, and bite down on this," I said, half smiling as I waved an indented leather strip in front of his mouth. "You don't want the others to hear you crying, do you?" I teased.

Hunter groaned as he looked up at me. "As long as you're at my side, Lila, I won't make a sound."

Forgetting my worries in our familiar banter, I rolled my eyes and picked up the diluted rum we used to clean wounds. Smitts handed him the leather strap and grasped his arm. Hunter held it but didn't place it in his mouth, apparently believing he could withstand the pain quietly. I couldn't say the same, as I had put a few of the tooth marks in the strap myself.

I poured the rum into the wound and Hunter inhaled sharply. The muscles under my hand tensed, and I grimaced with a twinge of pity.

"All right, I'm ready to stitch this closed. Hold him still," I said. Smitts pressed Hunter's arm firmly onto the bench in preparation. I picked up the needle and gut and took the first bite of skin. A grunt emerged from the patient.

"That's the worst it's going to get, Hunter. Don't worry, you'll survive," I said with all the empathy I could muster while gritting my teeth. It had taken me a few tries to get over my anxiety with the needle, but my stomach still twisted in knots when I caused other people's pain.

"Great, Lila," he growled. "I had my doubts."

I pushed my nerves aside so I could focus. The rest of the world fell away, and I was done before I knew it. Sweat beaded Hunter's brow and neck. He spat out the strap I hadn't seen him take.

"You'll need to rest the arm. Use your right and leave this one be for a while, or I'll be seeing you again for more," Smitts told him. "Now, Lila, let's get him something for the pain while I get something to wrap that arm."

I picked up the undiluted rum bottle and poured a small amount into a glass. "You can have more later, but for now this is all you get. We need you to keep us afloat, you know."

Hunter downed the rum in one gulp and handed me the glass. "I wouldn't say no to more of that. I could use a kiss for luck, too," he said. His words held the edge of a joke, and Smitts chuckled as he turned away to get the bandages. The desire in his eyes, and the way he angled himself closer when he stood up, told me how much he wanted that kiss.

It hurt to see the pain in his eyes when I silently shook my head, my hand touching the place where the key rested beneath my shirt. "Hold still for the doc." My stomach fluttered as he held my gaze when Smitts came back.

When the wrap was applied, Hunter took his leave of us, stopping himself from waving his injured arm when he noticed my warning scowl. I started to tidy while Smitts took his logbook out. "You know," he called without looking up, "you'll make a fine surgeon one day. You have steady, gentle hands, and you aren't afraid to do what needs to be done."

My cheeks warmed in gratitude at his confidence in me. "Thanks, Smitts. I have to go. I have watch."

"Thank you for the help, Lila. Don't fall out of the sky today," he told me with a rare smile breaking through his clinical expression.

I couldn't help but smile back, and turned out into the hall. Despite the trials of the previous day, I looked forward to my climb into the sky. The feel of the wind snapping my clothing and hair around as I climbed, the unopposed view of the sea for miles all around; I could feel the call of freedom from guarded glances. I emerged from the dim recesses of the ship to the blazing sun and crisp breeze of the world above.

CHAPTER THREE

I arrived on deck to a flurry of activity. Lines snaked and ground against cleats, cargo shifted in a chorus of thudding from below, voices called across the open air, and the ship started to move into the harbor. The first lurch of the mighty beast was an old friend, and I took comfort in the fact that we would be alone on the sea once more. I made my way towards the mainmast with the breeze ruffling my sleeves. I jumped atop the bulwark and started aloft.

My hair whipped out of its holdings and about my face. Twisting and turning all around my head and out into the air like a fire hit by a gust of wind. I smiled, feeling my sweat and exhaustion float away on the breeze even as my muscles warmed with the exercise.

The yard of the main topmast grew closer and I heaved myself atop it. I gripped the smooth surface beneath me and locked my legs in place as well. A wariness that would have served me yesterday weighed on me as I balanced at this height; my heart fluttered with a tingle of anxiety as the ship swayed, remembering Smitts' warning not to fall out of the sky.

It brought to mind the dramatic events of the day before. The strange sensation of being surrounded by air, and the invisible hands that caught me.

Who are those people I keep seeing? Are they *the ones with the gift and I just happen to be prone to danger and need to be saved? Or am I doing these things?*

My litany of questions after each time the gift was used. And with no answers available, just like every other time in my life, I sighed and shook my head.

"Elders, why does this keep happening? If this gift is mine, why can't I use it?" I muttered. Resentment roiled inside me, swirling with the endless spiral of *whys* and *hows.*

While balancing, I looked to the open sea, seeing nothing but the clear, eternal blue-green. The sea was calm, not a cloud in the sky. I shook my head to clear the remembered roar of wind from my ears as I mounted the next height in the rigging.

The hemp rope scraped against the calluses on my hands and feet. Lila's nest, as the crew called it, was situated above the yard at the main topgallant mast. Most of the crew despised watch, but I volunteered. Every small pitch of the ship at sea was amplified up here, but I had never been one to succumb to seasickness, and the height allowed solitude never found on board surrounded by people. The unparalleled view of the sea, reaching for miles, glittering in the sun, didn't hurt either. I hauled myself over the rail, landing with a thud.

Standing in my nest, leaning on the mast with my head back and my face tilted toward the sky, I soaked in the sun and let it burn away the last of my anxiety. It was always a balm to my spirit to relax at the top of my world, alone with my thoughts. I stretched my hands outward, enjoying the flex of my recently warmed muscles.

The wind whistled past my ears, and I imagined voices speaking to me. *We come.*

My hair whipped past my shoulders like the light caress of ethereal hands that caught me the day before. A flash lit the clouds ahead, a drop of rain slid down my cheek. I opened my mouth to shout a warning to the captain.

We come. We come.

I frowned. Those voices seemed close, almost like someone whispering in my ear.

"*We come from seas calm and rough....*"

A strain of music reached me above the wind, distracting me from the storm. As quickly as it appeared, the inclement weather passed on. Another voice, as beautiful and rich as the first, joined the first in a familiar song of homecoming. The twins, singing their favorite song.

I love it when they sing for us, I mused.

More voices joined, winding their way around one another in a dance of distant dots below as I peered over the rail. A full chorus floated up to me. Inhaling deeply and releasing my breath slowly, I allowed the music to calm me.

Looking out at the ocean now, I could see the port quickly shrinking behind. The sea was still calm and serene, with the sun just starting to sink toward the horizon. The crew was distant below, moving with purpose about their tasks.

A smile broke out on my face as I considered the size of the men from my point of view; it reminded me of a time when I had been tiny, and I fondly remembered staring in awe up at the *Catherine*. She was a proud, three-masted ship, and I thought that there was nothing so big in the entire world. Over the years, she had changed a bit; foul weather and recent misfortune had taken their toll on her.

But in my opinion, the flaws made her more beautiful. Part of the hull had been replaced by part of a dismantled ship. Now, she had a large stripe down her side several shades darker than the rest. But the darker wood had a rich, red tint in direct sunlight that made it look like the *Catherine* was blushing.

I had watched from the captain's shadow for months before feeling brave enough to talk to anyone, and months after that asked any question about sailing. I had the benefit of an entire crew's collective knowledge, as well as my lessons from Smitts and the captain in the finer disciplines such as mathematics, charting, reading, and eventually the healing arts.

The process of healing the sick and tending the wounded held a special fascination for me, and I spent many hours in the surgery when I wasn't needed elsewhere. Along with those lessons, he taught me about how our world functioned.

The sun reflected in the sea forced me to squint, but I kept alert while I reflected. The gentle rise and fall of the ocean below the hull was as a hand beckoning me onward into the unknown, and I smiled at the boundless possibilities that it might hold for us.

CHAPTER FOUR

Over the next week, we sailed south, the shoreline barely visible in the distance to the west. The cargo hold had been filled to bursting and all our spirits were high as we envisioned the coin to be made from the unprecedented haul. The course for King's Port was now set; as the largest – and wealthiest – port city in Trylia, it held the best promise of payment for all that we carried. It was home port for many of the crew, and we were promised a few days leave.

The last night before reaching port, we gathered for a meal on deck as the light faded. Drain, our cook, hauled our feast from below, while young Walter, his blonde hair dripping with sweat from the heat of the kitchen, followed in his wake with an armful of stale bread..

"This is the last of it, so eat up!" Drain shouted, plunking one huge pot onto the deck. A small army of other crew members arrived with two more pots and a load of bowls and spoons. "Might as well give us a feast afore we get a fresh load."

The captain slapped Drain on the back, any conversation lost in the clamor of people lining up with bowls and scraping the pot for the heartiest ingredients at the bottom.

Everyone sat and ate, the captain and Drain watching over the rest while they shared stories of home and hopes for the time ashore. Some spoke of their families, children they left behind and how much they might have grown. I sat aft, apart from the crowd so I could listen without having to speak with anyone.

I listened with particular interest as Hunter spoke to Kai, who hoped their girl was still working at a shop, showing him a bauble they had picked up at another port. The lantern light glinted off a small piece of blue glass in a delicate gold chain.

"She'll love it! You said before she loves sea glass," he said, handing it back to them.

"Do you have a girl lined up?" Kai asked, their eyebrows waggling, the silver piercing contrasting against dark skin in the lantern light.

Hunter looked down, and I saw his cheeks flush. His curly hair fell over one eye, and I felt a spike of heat in my lower belly. How could he look more attractive when he was embarrassed?

"Not lined up, no. Just hoping she notices me." The stone was in his hand again, his fingers running over the smooth white surface again and again.

He seemed to sense he was being watched, and he turned to see me staring at the two of them.

"What about you, Lila? Have you got someone waiting?" Kai said.

I flushed, embarrassed that I had been caught staring, and choked on a mouthful of stew. Kai laughed, and Hunter smirked.

"N...no," I sputtered as my hand moved to the key again. "We move too much for that. I've got everything I need here."

"That's probably true," Kai said, smirking back at Hunter as they stowed their gift in a pocket. They stood and grabbed their empty bowl, heading for the nearest pot.

Hunter gestured to their vacant spot on the deck, so I walked over and sat down, my back against the hull.

I was saved from any awkward conversation as the twins started to sing, their song low and sweet, a song of longing and homecoming. Soon others joined, including Hunter's tenor and the captain's bass.

My eyes closed as I listened, letting the warmth and sadness wash over me. My home was the ship, the crew my family. I had no one to go to on the mainland. The lantern light flickered, painting my eyelids red. For a brief moment, it transformed into something moving, almost like hair blowing in the breeze, and a memory teased me of someone else singing this song to me as a little girl.

I started out of my reverie when a loud voice began to sing an irreverent song about the Elders and their teachings, and smiled at the chorus.

Livette is the life, and Woleth destroys it,
Bestell shapes the law, and Elter abhors it,
Anyska loves war, Uonna loves all,
I follow no rules, those Elders can fall!

Not one of the most creative versions I knew, but fun nonetheless. There were scowls here and there, particularly from the few that eyed me with the sign of the Elders clutched against their chests when they noticed me looking their way. But most of the crew enjoyed an irreverent tune. A chorus of voices rang out across the calm water as the sun fell below the horizon.

Just after dawn the next morning, we caught sight of familiar outcroppings of rock guiding the ship around the edge of the bay that enclosed the harbor.

Most of the people seemed to have calmed down about my incident, though I heard the word *curse* muttered here and there. Now I stood at the rail with a handful of people, squinting against the increasing glare of the rising sun in anticipation.

One or two shifted away from me, which gave Marl a chance to join me.

"You all right, Lila?" he asked. He leaned on the rail like me as we looked toward our destination.

"I'm fine," I said. "A few mutters, as usual. Nothing I can't handle."

He nodded and pulled away from the rail. I noticed he was looking down at me, so I looked up at him.

"If it's ever more than that, find Roy or me. It's hard enough out here. I don't want someone accusing you of calling a storm or angering the Elders, inciting someone to hurt you."

He clapped a hand on my shoulder before he turned away. He smiled over his shoulder.

"And please, try to take the slow way down from your nest."

I smiled, thankful for how easy it was to feel safe with the twins around. The smile faded as I caught a glance of Hunter emerging from below, and I turned away to see our destination.

The palace on the hill gleamed as if it were a beacon to guide our way; it was the center of the city and soared toward the sky, its five towers stretching like the fingers of a massive hand. The brilliant white of the marble structure reminded me of Hunter's stone, and the endearing vulnerability he showed when it appeared. The gardens of the palace beckoned me with the memory of the scent of flowers along the paths and in the trees, leaves and grass as green as emeralds, or the color of Hunter's eyes,

"Stop it," I muttered. Our interaction the day before were making it difficult to hold my resolve. My eyes traced the spiraling, cobbled road through the marble wall of the palace downhill toward the sea to distract myself.

Past grand houses and shops whose windows shined like jewels in the sun, the inns, barracks, and houses built into the steep hillside, down to the open marketplace that acted as a bridge between the wealthy and the rest of the citizens. From there, the road went beyond the gates to connect the city to the rest of the continent. Sprawling out from the market were homes and businesses for the majority of the citizens of King's Port.

On such a fine summer day as this, I could see the colorful banners and flags adorning the many carts and stalls within the marketplace fluttering in the breeze.

"Market day!" someone shouted.

"Just in time," another replied. "I can see my house!" A finger pointed to one of the poorer sections of the city where the hill flattened in a gentle slope to the sea.

Captain Morrig shouted over the din of excited voices. "You'll have plenty of time to rest your bodies and exercise your mouths while I find buyers for the cargo. Back to work!"

We arrived in the harbor to a chorus of shouting as we all prepared to set anchor and be on our way to shore, all fear of my "gift" forgotten in the sweet anticipation of all that lay ashore. I helped to lower the longboats the moment we stopped and I smiled as Marl and Roy started to sing, a lively sailing song that lifted my spirit to soar over the ocean toward the city. One by one, the rest of us joined them, our voices lifting on the breeze, accompanying the splash of the boats in the water below and the surge of bodies over the rail.

The worn handle of the longboat's oars felt rough, even to my callused hands. The captain sat in the prow facing the shore with ten of the crew, myself included, pulling at the oars, propelling us swiftly forward.

The water fought against us, choppier the closer to the shore we came, and talk faded as we all pulled that much harder to reach our destination. Hunter was in the row ahead of me, and despite the effort it took for me to keep up, he seemed very much at ease. I gazed at his back as he rowed, admiring his graceful motions, the outline of his muscles as they moved, and the lopsided smile on his face while he spoke with the man next to him.

When we drew alongside the pier, we lifted our oars from the water in one smooth movement and pivoted them skyward, clearing the way for our boat to thud into the planks. Roy and Marl jumped up to tie off the lines and secure us to the pilings of the pier. Two from the other longboat did the same, and the rest of the fifty crew members leapt off the boats and onto the dock.

The captain stood on the cobblestone walk in front of the massive stone wall separating the harbor from the town. City guards patrolled the top, disappearing behind crenellations only to emerge from the other side with the same bland look that belied their readiness. After paying the dockmaster, Captain Morrig looked at his crew with his hands clasped behind his back. I moved through the line and stood in front of him, waiting for the rest to follow suit. As everyone fell into a loose line around me, the captain spoke.

"The next three days are yours. Take your rest, enjoy yourselves. I expect everyone to report at dawn four days from now to unload cargo. Dismissed."

A cheer exploded from everyone around me, and most raced off toward the gate to the city. They piled through the larger gate, wide enough to allow handcarts but still not wide enough to allow our throng to pass in their haste. Vendors stood on either side of said gate, shouting at the sailors who raced by, reaching out to those who became wedged against the stone.

I stood still, letting the last of the men filter around me until it was just Hunter, the captain, and me alone on the pier. I turned to Hunter waiting for him to run off with the rest of them.

"Aren't you going in?" I asked, hoping he would so I could focus on something else.

"If it's all the same with the captain, I thought I'd stick with you two while we're here," he said. "I think the rowing opened my wound, and I was hoping you would see to it, Lila."

"Come here," I sighed as I pulled cloth from the pouch at my waist. His bandage was starting to soak with blood from the inch-long section of open wound, and I wound more cloth around it. "You absolutely pulled these stitches apart; you should have let someone else take the oars!" I growled, exasperated. "We'll have Smitts tend to it when we go back, but this will do. I don't have the tools to do it now."

"You're almost as good a fighter as you are a healer," Hunter smirked, but there was warmth to his words.

"Perhaps if I had a better teacher, I wouldn't be so lacking in skill," I retorted.

Hunter smirked at me when I tucked the ends of the cloth into the wrap and pulled the sleeve of his shirt back into place. I blushed and followed the retreating back of the captain inside the city.

Just inside the wall sat the section of town most frequented by sailors and mercenaries. Two-story houses leaned over the street in the shade cast by the massive stone wall. Children ran barefoot through the muck in alleyways, leaving dirty footprints on the stone lane. Some of the sailors from the *Catherine* were visible when we passed, wandering into shops, low-rent inns, and some to the brothels that made up the businesses in this area. If one didn't know where to go, it seemed all but impossible to navigate the faded signs scrubbed clean of their painted words by the sea air.

A few blocks in, the city changed drastically. The buildings themselves seemed to straighten and reach higher into the sky.

People strolled along the street, looking leisurely into shop windows, walking in and out with bundles under their arms.

We followed the captain into a couple of shops, knowing the best sweet rolls belonged to the baker he needed to talk to about offloading our flour, and the latest news could be heard from the grocer, Malcom, and his wife. I browsed through soaps and combs while they talked, listening to gossip about a young couple that had run away together, and a list of towns along the coast that had seen other young people go missing.

"Just the time of year, I expect," Malcom said. "Spring comes and the young people lose their minds, leaving on romantic adventures."

A short time later, Hunter and I meandered up the street on our own, having accompanied the captain to various seamstress' shops after he negotiated the sale of the myriad bolts of fine cloth taking up part of our hold. The air between us was charged with tension, and the words I knew he wanted to say to me.

We made it a few blocks before he couldn't stand the silence any more.

"Please don't do this again, Lila," he said. I didn't break my stride, skirting a mother herding two small children up the street. I glanced at him out of the corner of my eye to see him looking down at his feet, kicking a stone ahead of him.

"I don't know what else to do," I replied. Already I felt the tears stinging my eyes. I didn't want to have this conversation with him when I couldn't stop thinking about him.

"You don't have to isolate yourself from us," he continued, his voice thick with emotion. "We can help you through it."

"That's not how I feel. I need space from all of it. All I want is to curl up in one of Lottie's chairs and be left alone. To get away from all the noise for a bit."

He halted and put a hand on my arm to turn me toward him. We were just outside the wall separating the palace from the city, blocks away from our destination. Insecurity and hurt flashed in his eyes.

"I'm just noise?" he asked.

"Right now," I said, pulling away, "yes. My thoughts are just noise. Everyone here, everyone on the ship, they're all noise. And I need quiet."

"All right," he said. "I'll stop being so loud."

He turned on his heel and stomped away, his left hand in his pocket, worrying at his mother's stone. I watched until he disappeared around a corner, let out a frustrated sigh, and made my way toward Lottie's.

We spent a few days in King's Port without any responsibilities, and though I knew I was welcome in most of the crew's homes, my favorite place to stay was the home of the twins, Marl and Roy. They had no partners of their own, but Lottie, their elderly mother, was happy to have another woman in the house, having only her boys for company for so many years before they had taken to sea.

She owned a house larger than those around her, as her husband had been a servant to the king and very well-off in the eyes of the common folk. We always walked in to a table full of food – no matter the hour – and the sharp wit of their mother, scolding them for the slightest transgression in her playful way. She knew more stories than anyone, and her jokes were envied and retold by every member of the crew, including the captain.

I never laughed as hard as when I stayed in Lottie's home. She made me feel like a daughter, not someone she had taken in but a child that she had raised herself, and stepping across her doorway with the towering twins in tow was like the warm embrace of a loved one before actually being swept up in a bone-crushing hug.

And on this occasion, knowing me as well as she did, she knew that after that hug, I needed some time to myself. To quiet the noise, as I had told Hunter. It was something Lottie had taught me as a child, to take time to work through my troubles at my own pace.

One day I spent with Smitts, shadowing his steps to apothecaries and doctors in the city to barter for fresh supplies and trade knowledge. He carried his journal with him and often opened it to various pages to recall details about injuries we had treated. The fourth and fifth days the crew and I spent unloading most of our cargo and filling the hold again with fresh supplies and more goods to trade with the distant islands that were our next stop.

Our last day in port we gathered for a large feast at Lottie's home with children running in and out from the street and every inch of the open space filled with laughing and talking, eating and drinking. We spent most of the day and well into the night in the company of everyone that we knew and loved.

Feeling rested and content the next day as the sun began to peek over the horizon, we made our way back to the docks, families in tow. Families cautioned their loved ones to stay safe, looked after one another's children, and wiped inevitable tears from their cheeks at the prospect of parting.

The dock creaked with the weight of everyone taking their leave. Children were fished out of the longboats and sent giggling back to the gate, everyone shed tears of farewell and spoke promises of return and doled out fierce hugs to each member of the crew in turn. Despite their hospitality and love for me, I felt a pang of longing, knowing that I had no one of my own.

Back on deck after the slow trip to the *Catherine,* I looked out at all the people waving to us from the dock, beginning to filter away and back into the city. I felt a squeeze of my shoulder and turned to see that the captain had walked up beside me. He placed his free hand on the rail, looking out at the farewells on the pier as I turned my gaze back.

"You have more here than you think, young one," he said. He looked down at me, the corners of his eyes crinkling as he smiled. "You have the biggest family I've ever seen. And it wasn't like this until you came along." I looked up at him, surprised. "Hard to believe, I know," he said, answering my expression and unspoken words. "They knew each other, but there was no bond until they saw your fiery head and your big hazel eyes. They all fell in love with you, Lila. They came together for *you.*"

My cheeks warmed with embarrassment at my earlier self-pity. I had always thought of myself as an orphan, with no one to go home to, no one to care whether I came or went, lived or died. But, looking back at the dock as our crew climbed on board from the longboats, seeing the rest of their families catch my eye and wave their goodbyes to me, I understood that I *did* belong to these people. And they belonged to me. My wave was even more heartfelt as I came to this realization, and I felt uncommon tears prick the corners of my eyes, drawn by an unexpected font of grateful joy.

We made quick work in finishing the preparations to cast off, and soon sailed out to sea and away from my second home and the large family I hadn't realized that I possessed.

CHAPTER FIVE

I woke before most of the crew from the same dream that persisted after every episode. I had wandered in mist and darkness, following whispered words toward half-remembered faces. They drew me forward, each step bringing me closer to something I was supposed to remember. Toward a light that was always just out of reach. Cold air hit my face when I stepped onto the deck, and my mind cleared as my feet followed familiar pathways across the cold planks in the early morning, leading me to the bow of the ship where I rested my elbows and lifted my gaze to the sea and sky.

Dawn erupted as I watched, the sky ignited with orange and pink as the sun crept closer to the horizon. The last of my dream slid away as the sky and my mood brightened. It finally appeared, and I squinted against the dazzling sparkle over the surface of the sea.

Hunter appeared beside me and leaned against the rail as well. He looked as though he hadn't slept well either, with shadows under his eyes and his hair in disarray. Perhaps the wound on his arm was causing him discomfort after we closed it a second time, more than he would admit.

"Morning, Lila," he said, smiling at me as he smoothed his wayward locks.

"Morning," I said. "You sleep all right? You look rough." His eyes were bloodshot above his smile.

He grimaced slightly and shrugged. "I've been worse. You?"

"Aside from the normal dream, I slept well. It's a beautiful sunrise, isn't it?"

"Yes." He turned to look, his arms on the rail and his back bent as he leaned forward.

I watched him for a moment, not sure if I should say anything. So I turned back to look at the ocean, now flooded with sunlight and almost blinding.

"I want...." Hunter said, and then he trailed off. His eyes were fixed on his hands, now clutched together into a fist and hanging over the rail, his forearms propped on the wood.

"What is it?" I asked, turning toward him. His posture and the firm tone of his voice made my stomach knot with anxiety. For the first time since my latest episode, I didn't know if it was dread or hope.

"Kai asked if I had someone waiting for me, and I said I hoped the girl I wanted noticed me." His eyes darted to me for a moment, and then he looked away again, as if he was afraid to see my reaction. "I was talking about you."

Oh, I thought. My cheeks flushed so hard I could feel the blood pulsing in them, and I could hear it beat a roaring rhythm in my ears when my heart started racing. I opened my mouth to say something, but nothing came out before he continued.

"There's so much I want to say to you," he said. "Things I've wanted to say for years, even though I knew you didn't want to hear it. I understand that you're afraid, and that you have so much to deal with, that the gift is confusing and overwhelming. That's why I've given you space, and hoped that you might decide I'm more than background noise."

He took a deep breath and stood tall, away from the rail, facing me. "But we would be so good together, and I needed you to know that."

He looked nervous, and vulnerable in a way that I hadn't seen in a long time. He tried to smile but only managed an awkward grimace before he turned his face to the sunrise.

This is a mess, I thought. *I'm a mess.*

"Hunter...." I said, pausing when he didn't look at me. "I-I, don't know...." I trailed off. My fingers itched to touch his face, but every instinct I had told me to stop this before I made it worse.

"If this is too much, I'll leave," he said. His vulnerability was still there, but it took on a hard edge of hurt.

"No," I said, reaching for him before he could turn around. He noticed the movement, and I let my hand drop before I touched him.

"Would it be so hard to try to be more? I've seen you staring sometimes, and I always hoped we would try again. But you've been trying so hard to keep your distance. Even though I *know* you still have feelings for me."

"Oh," I mumbled, awkward and unsure. My heart hammered against my chest, and I felt certain that he could hear it.

"Am I wrong?" he asked.

His gaze bored into me. I was taken aback by the amount of feeling I saw there, and my body flushed in reaction. I had never seen a look like this on his face. Desire, hope, and longing at once. This was a look reserved for me alone, that tore down all the walls I had put between us, and I was in love with it.

I shook my head, grasping at the rubble my defenses had been reduced to, but it did nothing to dispel the heat in my cheeks.

"I'm a mess," I said. "There's some curse I can't control that comes out of me at random times. Every moment I seem to be in some kind of trouble. No matter how hard I try to avoid it! And imagine if this doesn't work, would one of us leave? Say we make this work, what happens if I get pregnant? Would we both leave? Would I have to stay on the mainland, alone, while you're out here?" I waved my hand to encompass the ship and the ocean surrounding us. "There's so much that could go wrong. And, even if it didn't, there's so much that could happen that would change *everything.*" I held back a sob. "There's so much that's out of my control. I don't know that I can handle adding to that list."

Hunter touched my arm, offering comfort while giving me room to refuse it. The same as he had all our lives. I moved closer, and he wrapped his arms around my shoulders when I wrapped mine around his waist.

"I'm so worried something will go wrong that I feel like I'm ruining everything I touch. I can see how much I'm hurting you, but I'm so worried I'll hurt you more. In some way I can't come back from."

I laid my head on his shoulder, and it felt like the safest place in the world.

"There's not much you could do that I wouldn't forgive, Lila."

A chuckle escaped my throat, strangled by a sob. "I don't know why."

Hunter pulled away so we could see each other, and smiled as I rambled. "It's endearing, actually. That you don't understand how appealing you are after how many times I've shown you."

"Hunter, I...."

He cut me off with a hand on the back of my neck that pulled me slowly toward him. He gave me all the time in the world to resist, to pull away. But his hand, rough and warm and gentle, melted the last of my resistance. I kissed him.

It was everything I remembered and more than I dreamed it could be. He held me in his strong arms, my body flush against his, his lips soft and urgent. Every moment spent longing for one another made every touch feel like a bolt of lightning running through our bodies. My hands ran down his shirt, feeling the tense muscles beneath.

He pulled back, placing his hand on my cheek. His eyes bored into mine, as if he could see into my soul.

"You have the most amazing eyes I have ever seen," he told me.

Flustered, I replied with the first thing that popped into my head. "Yours aren't bad, either."

He replied with a husky laugh and kissed me again. My tongue traced his bottom lip before being engulfed in his mouth. He wrapped his fingers in the hair at the base of my neck. A shiver of pleasure ran down my spine and I groaned.

Coming up for air, I murmured, "I've missed you."

His kiss was hungry, asking me to stop fighting against our attraction. My body felt hot and cold at the same time, my extremities tingled, and my legs nearly buckled when we crested a swell and came back down.

I responded with a fierce kiss of my own. It felt right, a piece of my life I had denied for so many reasons falling into place. I tightened my grip around his arms.

Hunter sucked in a breath and winced as he pulled away from me. His right hand went to the site of the gash on his left arm.

"I'm so sorry!" I said, the heat between us doused by cold fear of injuring him further. "I completely forgot! Do you need me to get you something? Let me look at the bandage."

"It's fine, Lila," Hunter chuckled.

He folded me into his embrace again, kissing the top of my head, and then my nose, and then my lips again.

"Well, that's interesting," the captain's voice grumbled from behind Hunter.

Hunter stepped back from me quickly, letting his arms fall to his sides. I looked at him, then looked to the captain. He had a look on his face that was part disapproval, part amusement, and part resignation. My stomach flipped, anxiety flooding through me.

"Lila. My cabin, if you would," he said as he stepped back and gestured me forward across the deck.

I entered the captain's cabin alone, taking in the familiar sights and smells of ink, paper and sea air. Natural light filtered in through the large bay of windows aft.

The door thumped closed behind me. I turned to see the captain leaning against it with his arms crossed over his chest.

The captain smiled. "It's about time you two stopped dancing around each other."

My anxiety abated by his warm smile, I replied, "I agree, Sir."

"I thought you two were going to make a go of it a few years back, but you pulled away." His brow furrowed with concern. "I know why you did. Hunter does, too. I want you to know, if you need help, with anything, I'm always here. If it gets to be too much, and you have any trouble, I'll help in whatever way I can."

"I know," I whispered. "I don't know if this will work, but I'm so tired of worrying about everything that could go wrong."

He sighed, nodded to himself, and smiled at me before dropping back into the façade of the stern captain. "Well, if this...relationship... gets in the way of your duties, I will have to discipline you both. And consider the consequences if it doesn't work out. Understood?"

"Aye, sir," I said, grateful and happy that I could always count on him to care for me, even if he did his best to hide it from the crew.

"Join me for breakfast," he said, gesturing to the table.

We sat and ate for a short time as the ship came to life around us and our duties started. I exited the cabin as the sun cleared the horizon, happier than I could remember.

After a day spent climbing in and out of the rigging, securing and hauling lines, retrieving assorted items for Smitts, Drain, and the captain, I was exhausted. I moved to the bow of the ship and leaned on the rail.

The dark blue sky still held traces of sunset. The sea was calm and empty, and I felt at ease. After the press of the city and the bustle of our duties to set sail, I marveled that there could be such serenity anywhere; that there was a place where a crew could be alone, at peace.

A hand grasped my shoulder, startling me from my peaceful reverie. I spun, and a translucent hand covered mine and wrenched the hand from my shoulder farther than I would have on my own.

I come.

"Lila!" cried Hunter.

"Oh!" I said, releasing his hand. "I'm sorry. You surprised me." My heart pounded in my chest, the fear not yet abated, and embarrassment rising. The presence retreated as I took a deep breath to calm myself.

"You would think I might be able to touch you now, without you attacking me. I know this is new, but...." He smiled while he massaged his injured left hand.

"I'm sorry, I was just looking out at the ocean," I replied, gesturing behind me, "and thinking how alone we are, and...well...you startled me." Now embarrassment was all that was left making my heart race.

Hunter bowed slightly. "I apologize, fair maiden, to have frightened you so." He looked up at me with his eyebrows raised and a sardonic grin across his handsome face. I fought the urge to push him.

"Kind sir, you flatter me," I grumbled.

He straightened and pulled me into his arms. My heart raced from anticipation now, and when he tilted my head up so that he could kiss me, I thought my face might spark into flame.

"Is everything all right with the captain?" he murmured against my lips.

"Don't worry about him," I replied. "This is between you and me." People started to move toward us, so I pulled away and yawned. "I'm exhausted, so I'm headed to bed. I'll see you in the morning."

Hunter squeezed my hand and kissed my cheek, and then I walked down into the ship. As I lay in my hammock, the sway of the ship traversing the waves lulling me to sleep, I smiled and let my eyes close.

CHAPTER SIX

Everything was brighter and easier now. Whether it was because of the clear sky, steady wind and cooperative ocean, or the fact that I was finally enjoying my life instead of dreading my next episode, it didn't matter.

Hunter and I decided to take things slow after our failed attempts at a relationship. We weren't impulsive teenagers anymore, and we had been friends for a long time. We could exist comfortably beside one another without pushing our intimacy too far for our comfort. It was a subtle change from friend to partner, with the thrill of his touch making my heart race and my skin tingle. But I knew that Hunter wanted to protect himself from another heartbreak, and I wanted to leave myself a way out if I felt the need to withdraw again.

I didn't have another episode for more than a week, and I started to relax more than I had for as long as I could remember. I sang and laughed with Marl and Roy, teased Kai about their girl as much as they teased Hunter about our relationship, and sat with Hunter at the bow, gazing up at the stars as often as I could.

My self-imposed isolation was over, and the superstitious members of the crew responded well, no longer treating me like the curse I thought I was until recently. They joined us for meals in the mess and in card games when we had downtime. I didn't see the sign of the Elders flashed at me over the next several weeks.

The best outcome was that I had never seen the captain smile so much in all the time I had sailed with him. He was the picture of contentment, and all of us benefited from it with extra rations of food and rum on more than one occasion.

I felt like I was finally putting together pieces of my life that I had deliberately separated from the rest of the puzzle. And they fit so perfectly that I marveled at my idiocy for refusing to see it sooner.

It helped that our last trip to King's Port had been one of the most lucrative I'd ever seen. Those myriad bolts of fine cloth were in high demand amongst the wealthy of the city, and with so few trade vessels willing to risk the trip, the supply came through in a trickle before we arrived. There was more gold in the ship's coffers than I'd seen in my life.

Now, with no clear destination in mind and money to spend, the captain decided to use our good fortune to expand our business. We were headed to a large island east of Trylia, outside the jurisdiction of the king's navy. A place called Rogue's Island, where people from all across the ocean traded goods that couldn't be found in Trylia. Exotic foods, materials, and resources from across Celuthia. Trylia was the world's largest source of lumber and specialty goods carved from that lumber. But there were other things that we needed for everyday life that we couldn't produce.

Vortheim might export slave traders, but they also exported sugar that helped feed the entire world. It was the place for precious metals and gems, teas, various alcohols, and many other goods that grew in the warmer climate. Since direct trade had ceased over the past decades due to the unrest caused by the slavers, the price of necessities like sugar and tea was outrageous. And our captain hoped to find some of these trade goods that could be provided to the people of Trylia without the increased prices other merchants would charge. Since the only other ships willing to brave Vorthe waters were pirates and slavers, he was hopeful we would succeed.

At the end of the third week we were a few days away from Rogue's Island. An undercurrent of trepidation was covered with a thin veneer of excitement for all of us. It was the first trip to the lawless destination for most of us, and while we knew what we might find, we didn't know what to expect of the place and people there.

Staring across the small table in his cabin as Hunter, Smitts and I joined him for the evening meal, I asked the captain what it was like.

He swallowed a bite of bread before he answered. "Keep your wits about you, your hand on your money, and trust no one," he replied with a stern look as he lifted his cup. He took a long draught of water, and then continued. "There are plenty of good people there, or so I've been told. But I didn't meet one either time I visited."

"From what I've read," Smitts added, "it's a common hub for slave traders and pirates, as this is the only place north of the channel where that sort of thing isn't outlawed. And in recent years, the king's forces have been more vigilant along Trylia's coastline, so their supply there has slowed."

"So, they either have to trade here or take the months-long journey to Vortheim," Hunter said. His plate was empty, and he leaned back in his chair to stretch his full stomach. The ship rocked from side to side. It felt like the weather was turning at last.

"I might stay here," I said, using my fork to push a piece of gristle around on my plate to avoid their eyes. Talking about slavers dredged up painful memories that evoked a war between my fear and anger. "If I'm out there, it could trigger the gift, and I don't want to know what people like that would do to me if they saw it. I've gone a few weeks without...." I shrugged as I trailed off. They all knew what I meant.

Hunter reached over to grasp my hand and squeeze. "I'll stay with you. To keep your mind off it."

I looked up from my plate, his reassuring gaze lending me a portion of his casual confidence. I smiled, and watched as his demeanor changed. His eyes lingered on mine as they smoldered with desire, his thumb drew circles on my palm, and he smirked as he saw a blush creep into my cheeks. I wanted to feel his lips against mine. Soon.

"Or," Smitts said, interrupting our silent exchange, "you could accompany the captain, Hunter. Watch his back with the twins. Perhaps a few more, just in case."

"That's a wonderful idea," the captain replied. His eyes bounced back and forth between Hunter and me, lingered on our clasped hands, and then narrowed at Hunter.

I took a sip of water as Hunter cleared his throat.

"Great," he said. "Will we stay on land?"

"No," Captain Morrig replied. "I don't want to be robbed or killed in my sleep. I think it will take a day, perhaps two, to talk to my contacts and negotiate for a few unique cargo items. Another day to load, and then we'll head back to Trylia."

"And then a few days of leave?" Hunter asked hopefully.

"That's likely," the captain replied. He turned to Smitts. "Do I need to procure any supplies for you?"

Smitts shook his head, dabbing at his mouth with a linen napkin. "We haven't had many injuries for the past several weeks. The occasional rope burn here and there, but I have more than enough to see us back to King's Port."

Captain Morrig nodded and put his hands on the table. A signal we knew meant that we were dismissed so he could get back to work. I stood and gathered some of the dishes while Hunter piled the rest for himself to carry back to the galley.

Smitts mumbled his farewell before disappearing as Hunter and I sidled through the door with arms full. Drain was in a foul mood, ordering a young man to take our pile of dishes to clean with the others. We slipped away before Drain could turn his wrath toward us.

On deck, we walked hand-in-hand to the bow. It was our spot, since we were out of the way, and it gave us a view of the ocean and sky.

Hunter pulled me close, brushing his lips against mine. I wrapped my arms around his waist and squeezed him tight, leaning into the kiss to deepen it. The wind whipped my hair around in a sudden gust, and I looked up.

The sky was no longer clear, with thick, fluffy clouds stacked like the pillars of the palace in King's Port. The air changed as we approached where the clouds were thickest, surrounding us with frigid cold. I wrapped my arms around myself to keep it at bay.

"Storm ahead," Hunter said as he squinted up at the clouds. "Big one."

The captain's voice boomed. "Strike the royals!" A distant rumble of thunder accentuated his command.

We all scrambled to obey the order. Everyone could feel the air shifting, pulling toward the clouds, picking up speed. Those of us who could withstand the pitch of the ship at the top of the masts climbed as fast as we could, battling the wind, cold, and list over the angry water.

I pulled with all the strength I had, the rough rope felt like a thorny vine in my icy hands, and the sail began to furl. By the time we finished, the waves were cresting above the rails despite our light weight letting us sit so high in the water.

"Strike the top gallant!" a voice shouted from below as I swung my leg over to begin the long climb down. Glancing between my feet, I saw a few sailors climbing up behind us, ready to strike the other sails in succession. We lurched as the ship struggled to turn away from the storm that worsened by the second. There was no doubt in my mind that it would become a hurricane before the end. Lightning flashed, illuminating the thick clouds and showing the rain that was just behind us. We repeated the process with the next sail from the top and started the climb back to the deck.

The descent was harder as my muscles seized. Wind whipped across the length of the ship, threatening to lift me and toss me into the ocean. My foot slipped a few feet from the deck, and Hunter was there, taking me in his arms to steady me.

Lines of thick rope passed from hand to hand, and we all began the task of tying ourselves to the ship. The mainsail snapped as it caught the wind, and waves crashed against and over the stern. The captain stood at the wheel with Kai, both heaving against the force of the waves and wind to keep the storm behind us.

But it was closing fast, and it didn't look like running would be enough to save us. I pulled the rope around my waist and tied it as the ship rocked again.

"Reef the mainsail!" the captain shouted. His voice was almost lost in the cacophony of wave and wind, so other voices took up the call, and those nearest began the task. Hunter and I balanced near the stern of the ship, one hand on the rail to help us keep our balance.

Another wave crashed over the stern, drenching Kai and the captain. They barely kept their hands on the wheel, or their feet beneath them. Another flash of lightning and immediate boom of thunder heralded a downpour of rain. Frigid wind bit through my clothes and into my skin. Now that all but the mainsail was struck, most of the hands went below to save themselves from being thrown overboard or getting in the way of those of us that stayed.

"We'll have to abandon course soon!" I shouted to Hunter. He nodded and clutched the rail as we listed to port. The water was so close that if I reached out, I could plunge my hand into it. My legs braced, I clutched to the rail, too.

When the *Catherine* righted herself, I watched in horror as another wave loomed above the stern, large enough to plunge it below the surface. Before I could consider the consequences, I grasped the end of my rope and pulled to loose myself.

"What are you doing?' Hunter shouted. He tried to grab my hands, to stop me before I lost my tether to the ship, but I pulled away as the rope came loose and darted up toward Kai and the captain.

My feet slipped on the slick wood when we listed to starboard, and I heaved myself up using the rails on either side of the stairs to the quarter deck.

Please, I thought, my inner voice a desperate cry for help, *if there was ever a time that you came when I called, let it be now!*

The wave crested and began to crash down. But something stirred inside me, and I felt the touch of an ethereal hand on mine. It lifted my arm out, toward the wave.

We come.

A burst of light exploded from my chest, through my arm, and toward the wave. When it separated from me, it split into many cloaked figures, all racing toward the water that threatened to capsize the ship and drown us all. I wanted it to collapse, to split and surge around us, or to disappear altogether.

Instead, the figures splashed into the center of the wave and forced it back, against the wind, toward the storm. I screamed, in delight and surprise, as it churned against the flow of water and lifted the stern, pushing us further away from the hurricane in our wake.

My feet gave way as we listed forward, and I slid a short distance before Hunter appeared and stopped me from crashing into Kai's legs.

"What was that?" he shouted.

"I stopped it!" I replied.

"We're taking on water!" the captain yelled. He pointed to the bow, which was low in the water after the surge astern. A few sailors close enough scrambled to keep their feet. Everyone below was in danger of drowning.

We can't go under! I thought, picturing the bow flying over the waves, and again the figures answered me.

They swarmed around the hull, below the bow, and lifted just enough to avoid being plunged below the next wave. I laughed, feeling the strength of these figures and whatever was glowing inside me. Finally, it wasn't just an episode of the gift. I was using it. Gifted, like the woman in my favorite story.

"Lila, did you do that?" Hunter asked.

I flashed him a smile, savoring the feel of the gift all through my body.

"Your eyes, they're glowing!" he shouted. I worried for a moment that it would scare him, but the answering smile on his face, the look of pride in his eyes, dispelled that worry. And gave me the strength to hold onto the glow before it faded.

I knew we'd only be safe once we escaped the storm, but the *Catherine's* power was limited in the storm. So, I decided to use the ocean to our advantage. If the waves could push us forward without tipping us, we could float faster than the sails could push us.

No sooner did the thought occur to me than the ship jolted forward. Hunter slipped, Kai and the captain clutched the wheel to keep upright. They struggled to keep us on course, not yet realizing that the ocean was doing that for them. And I was pushing it to do so.

It seemed so simple now, to control the gift. I felt what I needed, I asked the figures for help, the glow made it happen. How had I not seen the connection before? This power was intoxicating. I felt like I could do anything if I just decided it should.

The storm fell behind, and my strength faded, the feel of the cold seeping back into my body. I hadn't noticed it was missing until now, and I shivered from head to toe. The shiver broke my concentration as my focus was drawn to my discomfort, and the figures faded with the glow. The ocean receded and the ship dropped, my stomach flipping as my body lurched with her.

Kai and Captain Morrig stared at me, and I smiled up at them, happy to see that they were still with us. Hunter strode forward and lifted me into the air to pull me into a tight embrace.

"That was amazing!" he said, his mouth next to my ear so I didn't have to strain to hear him. The wind was still loud, though nothing like it was on the edge of the hurricane. "I can't believe you just moved the entire ship!"

I laughed, but it was weak as I felt fatigue settle over my body. "I can't either," I replied. I craned my neck to look around him. "Is everyone all right? What about below?"

"I don't know yet," Hunter said. He set me down but kept a hand under my arm for support when I swayed. I felt like I hadn't slept or eaten in a few days. My muscles were weak, my head swam and pounded. "Can you stand so I can help below?"

I nodded and stood a bit straighter so he would feel confident enough about my condition to leave. There were a lot of hands below that were likely bailing the water out already, but they could use all the help they could get.

When he was out of sight, I stumbled toward the nearest rail and slid down the bulwark. My legs were shaking too hard to hold me up any longer.

Kai appeared at my side as the captain called for the mainsail to be unfurled.

"You all right, Lila?" they asked.

I smiled. "I'm fine," I lied. "It was more tiring than I expected."

"That wasn't just an episode this time," Kai said. "That was you. You saved all of us."

I nodded, a surge of pride bubbling out of my chest as a happy sob. "Finally, something useful from this nonsense."

Kai chuckled and rose to their feet. "I'll see if Smitts can come look you over. Just rest." They turned to leave, and I heard them mutter under their breath, shaking their head. "Elders' eyes, that was a sight."

All around me, my crewmates were loosing themselves from their tethers and rushing to unfurl the sails, lest we be pulled back into the storm. Others emerged from below with buckets full of water to rid us of what we took on from the waves. Marl and Roy each hefted a full bucket in each hand before they went to help wind the excess lines.

The captain handed the wheel back to Kai as Smitts rushed toward me. They arrived at the same time, Smitts kneeling at my side and the captain crouching on the opposite side.

"Are you all right, dear one?" the captain asked, his brow furrowed in concern. He looked up at Smitts. "Is she all right?"

Smitts pursed his lips as he searched my face. "Give me a moment," he snapped. I wasn't surprised by his tone. He acted like this when he was worried about one of us. "Lila, how are you feeling?"

"Exhausted. Hungry." I thought about what I had done, and tears pricked the corner of my eyes. All those years of feeling cursed were like a nightmare I had just woken up from. "Like I finally know what I can do."

Captain Morrig smiled, tears in his eyes, too. "You saved the ship and all our lives, dear one. I'm so proud of you."

"What happened?" Smitts asked. "Wait," he said, before I could speak. He put a hand out to stop Walter before he went below with his empty bucket. "Get some food for Lila, please," he said. "Quickly, whatever Drain has ready." Walter scurried away, and Smitts called after him. "And a tot of rum!" He turned back to me, glancing at the captain. "What happened?"

I let the captain tell him, the words lost to me as I let my mind drift and my head rest against the bulwark. The sails were full of wind, pushing us forward, further from the danger we left behind. The sky was clearing, and lightening from black to dark blue as the morning approached. I hadn't realized we'd spent the entire night fighting to escape, but I was thankful it wasn't days on end.

Walter appeared with some dry meat and bread, and a small cup. As tired as I was, I devoured all of it in what felt like moments. As I swallowed the rum, the captain's voice came back into focus.

"We were moving so fast I thought we would list forward again, but she didn't let us. It was... incredible. She was glowing. I thought I would go blind, but then it was gone, and we were clear."

Smitts shook his head as he looked me over once more. "You need rest, Lila, but otherwise you seem fine to me. I'll send Hunter up if we're clear below, and he can help you find a dry place to sleep." He nodded to the captain and left as I leaned back and closed my eyes.

The captain put his hand on my shoulder. I clasped my hand around his and smiled, thinking of all the times he'd placed his massive hand on my shoulder as a child.

"I'll sleep a bit and get to work as soon as I can," I mumbled, half-asleep.

He squeezed my shoulder. "You rest as long as you need. You've done more than your share; we can manage the rest."

I felt my body lifted, but I was asleep before I hit my hammock.

I slept until the sun rose the following day. Over another two days we patched up what we could of the damage from the storm. It was all internal, after a few barrels of water came loose and smashed around the galley and the hold. Drain was in a state for a day, but his irritation subsided as soon as the damage to the galley was repaired.

It felt like the gift needed time before I could use it again, but on the fourth night, as I was lying in my hammock straining to look through my books, I wished I could see the pages more clearly. The ghostly voices answered, and a light materialized in the space above my head. I was so startled that I jerked and fell out of my hammock. The light moved with me, shining into the eyes of Kai in the hammock below me. They grumbled and cursed until I scooted away and woke someone else. Hunter shouted for someone to put out the light, Roy growled nearby, and everyone started to stir.

I scrambled back into my hammock and pulled my blanket over me to shroud the light. As I waved my hand at it, trying to shoo it away and hoping it would stop, it did. It was dark again, and I heaved a sigh of relief.

But then I smiled, realizing I'd done it again. I could use the gift instead of letting it use me. It felt like my curse was broken, and I drifted off to sleep.

CHAPTER SEVEN

Pleasant dreams of sunrises and the ocean and warm lips against mine were shattered by a sharp voice raised in alarm.

"ENEMY SHIP!!" the man bellowed. The entire crew erupted in a flurry of activity; everyone shouted and boots pounded on the deck above my head as my eyes snapped open.

I flipped off my hammock in a flustered heap and bounded up the ladder with the others, into the bright morning sun. It had just cleared the horizon in a blaze of glory and the ocean was a blinding brilliance. I threw myself into the rigging and started to climb, stopping as I reached the yard to sit astride it. With a hand on my brow to shield my eyes from glare, I looked out to the sea beyond the stern, the air oddly still around me. A large vessel was closing in with unimaginable speed.

The captain emerged moments later and climbed the steps to the quarterdeck as I began to descend from the rigging. With his spyglass in hand, he looked out in the direction of the other ship. I couldn't understand how it moved so close in those scant minutes before the captain was on deck. It flowed over the waves as though it were made of quicksilver, closing a distance in moments what should have taken the morning to accomplish.

"Slavers!" the captain bellowed. "They're flying Vortheim colors." In recent years, the slave ships from Vortheim to the south had spread like a plague. Our luck in avoiding them had just run out.

A hurried descent brought me to the deck moments later, coming to a stop near the captain where he peered at the ship. Hunter arrived to stand beside me as the captain lowered the glass.

"The figurehead is one I've not seen. A mermaid with a spear through its chest," he said to his first mate.

All at once, a rush of long-repressed memories came to me. Rough hands herding me along the shore towards a huge ship with the same figurehead. The stench of fear and unwashed people, cold eyes and a vivid scar, a hoop dangling from an ear catching sunlight, the pain of being kicked and slapped and prodded by fat fingers....

Terror long held in abeyance surged through my body, and I broke out in a cold sweat. Swirls of light and dark danced in my vision. I clutched the small silver key dangling from its delicate chain around my neck as the deck swayed beneath me. My free hand grasped the nearest arm to keep myself upright. Hunter's voice rumbled as if from a distance, mirroring echoes of cruel rumbling voices I had forgotten.

"Lila!" he cried, turning at the vice-like grip I had on him. "What is it? What's wrong?!"

I looked at him, fighting the darkness in my vision, trying to put my terror into words. I found I didn't have them.

The captain grasped my shoulder. "Lila." My eyes drifted to his face.

"It's them," I whispered. I tried to find solace in his warm, dark eyes, but there was nothing there that could help me. I forced the feeling of panic down, pushing aside the terror of a little girl and taking hold of the resolve and strength I had found in my new life. It was like pulling the line for a sail pulled loose in a gale, and I heaved with all my might until more hands, that of the captain and Hunter, came to help me secure the wild flapping of my panic.

The crew stared in awe at the speed of the slave ship, evident in the way it slid across the surface of the water with the sails full. Any other vessel that size would have lifted at the keel, creating enough drag to prevent the speed we were seeing. A few voices wondered aloud whether they were seeing more of the gift, and eyes turned in my direction.

"Who are they?" Hunter asked, ignoring the chatter of the others. "How do you know who they are?"

"They're the ones that took her. Before I found her," the captain said to Hunter.

Hunter looked out at the ship, then back at me. "Well, I'll be damned if they'll have you again. Get below, Lila."

His resolve afforded me some measure of strength, and my voice returned, if breathlessly. "What are you going to do?"

"I don't know. But I'd rather fight than let any of us be captured."

I looked at the captain, standing next to us, watching our conversation. With an uncertain look in his eyes, he asked me for the one thing that I wasn't sure I could give him. "Lila, is there anything you can do?" the captain said.

I took a moment for a deep breath to force myself to grab hold of that strength. This is what I had spent all those weeks pushing myself to do, what I had done during the storm. Panic almost loosed itself from the firm grip I had on it, and a hint of a translucent hand reached out toward me.

My hand raised on instinct, and the other disappeared when Hunter grasped mine. I shook my head and tried to keep the panic at bay. "It's not working. I can't think, there's so much noise...." I trailed off, shaking my head. I needed clear purpose to make it happen. And I had no idea what I could do to stop a ship that moved like that, like they had someone better versed in the gift propelling them forward.

The captain placed a hand on my shoulder, and then walked to the middle of the deck. "Attention!" he cried. "Gather the weapons and pass them out. We will not be taken without a fight!"

People started towards the hold, brimming with nervous energy. The sound of metal hitting metal rang in my ears as swords and spears were passed among the crew. I followed, matching their grim expressions as they passed swords up to waiting hands. Several passed through mine before I grasped my slender hand-and-a-half sword.

I walked away from the crowd, moving through a few guards to ready myself. I had spent so much time in these positions that my body moved from one to the other without thought, the sword as much a part of me as my hands and arms. Soft, worn leather wrapped the hilt and warmed in my hand now, as I gripped and regripped in preparation and dread.

A few others with longswords and pikes joined me, spaced apart to let others with shorter blades stand between us. Those with bows stood behind with arrows placed between them by Walter and a few of the other younger crew. If words didn't work to stop the conflict, arrows might. Those of us with longer blades would hold as many boarders at bay as we could, while everyone armed with shorter blades repelled anyone who made it past us. If I couldn't force the gift to help us now, at least I could trust my body to do what I had trained it to do.

Rolling my shoulders, I took a deep, steadying breath. My slender blade glinted in the sunlight, and I admired the slight curve that gave it graceful strength.

I could only hope that that strength would be enough.

Still silence pervaded the air as we watched our fate approach us. The captain stood apart from the rest, standing atop a crate so he could be seen and heard. Hunter stood on one side of me, Marl on the other; they seemed to be preparing to protect me. Their concern touched me, but also terrified me that one or the other would lose his life trying to keep me from harm. I was prepared to fight as well, but this ship seemed to be propelled as mist on a breeze; what else could their crew be capable of?

Again, desperately, I tried to summon the figures that had haunted me throughout my life. They obeyed me once, why not now? Drawing on the confidence having my blade in hand gave me, I looked at the ship closing in, wondering what I could do. If I moved the water like last time, they could glide above it. Could I force the entire ship to stop?

Imagining the ship coming to a halt, I felt a tingle of glowing strength awaken and build. It pulsed, and for a moment, I thought I saw the ship lurch.

An arrow dropped out of the sky with a high whistle and buried itself deep in the main mast, mere feet above our heads. Shapes on the deck of the slaver's ship resolved into figures of men with bows and swords, readying their attack. Something pushed against me, and the connection to the gift shattered like glass.

"Hold," the captain growled as everyone with bows pulled their strings taut, ready to fire. "It was a warning. If they wanted us dead, they would've fired more than one."

The next few moments brought the ship closer as it slowed to position next to our ship, the two figureheads alongside one another. The slaver's ship stopped more quickly than it should have, guided with more precision than could be explained by the man at the helm. The crash of waves against the hull and growls of aggression broke the heavy silence.

Everyone was still for several long moments. And then a voice rose above the grumbles of the other crew.

There was something familiar about it, sending a shiver of fear down my spine.

"Put your weapons down, and we will not harm you. We are here to procure you for sale, not to end your lives. There is no profit in that," he smiled. While his voice was gruff, he spoke with an easy air of someone who is used to getting their way; his words slid over us, leaving me feeling filthy, and I shuddered from head to toe.

"We have little in our hold that would interest you," our captain called out, "but you're welcome to it. There's no need for violence today."

The other man laughed, triggering the rest of his people to join him. Their voices rumbled through the air, reverberating beneath my feet.

"We'll take whatever you have, but that's not why we're here," he answered as the crowd of armed sailors parted, letting him step to the front where we could see him.

The scar above his left eye, the immaculate brown hair now cut close to his scalp, the same easy smile that changed as he gazed over our crew. His expression flashed with a look of disgust I remembered well. The blade of my sword shook with my hand.

Captain Morrig stepped forward. "This is my ship, and you have no right to board. We will not be taken."

The other captain laughed, but his eyes remained cold. "You will not be taken? There is nothing that you will or will not do without my consent from now on. You'd best keep that in mind if you want to keep your head. Please, hold still."

Their ship proceeded to slide aport, above the water, closer until the bulwarks met with a thud. They made to sling lines across to secure the hulls together. I looked over my shoulder to the captain, who had a grim set to his mouth as his eyes scanned the forces arrayed against us. I let out a gasp of breath that sounded more like a sob to my terrified ears.

Our captain bellowed to be heard over the clank of hooks digging into our rail.

"Repel boarders!"

I turned back as arrows loosed above our heads, and we thrust pikes and swords forward to repel the first wave. The tip of my blade slid through the side of one of theirs, and I pulled back long enough to Roy bring an axe down onto one thick length of rope tying the ships together. The blade glistened in the sunlight, as did mine when I thrust forward again, narrowly missing another slaver.

Again and again my blade stabbed forward, drawing blood from the bodies trying to gain ground. Axes slammed against lines, anyone who moved past our first line was pushed back by our second. But they were gaining ground as arrows slammed into others in the first line. More lines were thrown over, the metal of one hook slicing through Kai's calf, sending them toppling back in agony.

An arrow flew through the air, seeming to slow as it neared my chest. A flash of light blinded me as I realized the danger I was in.

We come.

A wall of force pushed me back to slam into Hunter, and my sword dropped from my hand. I felt around as my vision returned and my hand closed on the arrow, buried in the deck, that had narrowly missed me. Next to that was my discarded blade, and I snatched it up as I stood.

Blinking my eyes to clear them, I couldn't see Hunter, but rather the absence of defensive lines and an abundance of chaos. It was a melee now, with more slavers jumping across the small gap between our ships.

A man stepped over, armed with a two-handed sword with a massive black blade. He held it in one hand as if it were no bigger than mine. The man towered over those nearest to him, and sunlight glinted off the silver hoop in his ear and bald head alike. A cold, calculating look danced in his eyes as he surveyed our scrambled movements. My legs trembled and threatened to buckle as I fought against a fresh wave of recognition and fear. The bruises his meaty fingers had left in my small arm ached again when his eyes found mine for a moment before locking onto something behind me.

I turned to see Hunter throw himself to the side to avoid a cutlass slashing at his chest, Roy slamming his axe down once, twice, onto the shoulder of a slaver with a spray of crimson blood. I stepped in front of the man with the black blade as he stepped forward, paying me no attention. My blade swung up, meaning to slash his sword arm, but he slammed his foot into my bent knee, and I stumbled as he continued forward.

Using the momentum for another swing, I was blocked by a different slaver with a shortsword. We traded a few blows, but he slipped in a pool of blood and I took advantage of the opening to bring my sword down in an arc that opened his throat and part of his chest.

"Anyone who wishes to live, please put your weapons down," the slaver captain roared. "No more need die today!"

A roar went up from the battle, but I couldn't tell if it was the encouraged shouts of the attackers or the beleaguered defiance of the defenders. I scanned the crowd, looking for my captain, Hunter, or the man with the black blade. I found the latter stalking aft, pausing to strike one of my crewmates in the head with the pommel of his sword. They crumpled, and he continued walking, toward my captain as he brought his sword up to block. Sparks flew as his opponent's blade slid down and their guards locked together.

"No!" I screamed as I ducked another attack and dove forward with a swipe to deflect an axe from connecting with Roy's exposed side. He parried, and brought his axe around in an arc; his opponent's body wrenched to the side with the force of the slash. My foot slipped and I looked down to see blood pooling all over the deck as people lay dying. I had no time to see whose life drained out of them.

In the time it took for me to force my way through the melee, I lost sight of the black blade. But I spied Captain Morrig lying on the deck, an arrow in his chest and a slash across his belly. He looked at me as I crashed to his side, cradling his head in my lap.

"Lila," he said, reaching for my hand. I grasped his bloodied fingers tight to my chest and called out to anyone that might help me.

"Help! The captain is hurt!"

Roy appeared, his back to us as he became a barrier between us and anyone who might attack. Several others joined him, circling us as I searched the captain's eyes.

He was already fading, trying so hard to cling to life while it was pouring away from him. His other hand gripped at the tear in his abdomen, attempting to hold his insides in place. Blood oozed from his mouth and frothed over his lips when he coughed.

"Sir," I groaned, tears in my eyes. "Hold on, I'll find Smitts. Hold on, we can fix this. Please, hold on." My chest burned with the ache of fear and despair, trying and failing to hold back the sobs that racked me. Above the groans and screams of my injured and dying friends, I heard the graveled, oily voice shout again for our weapons to be surrendered. A weak squeeze of my hand pulled my eyes back to the man dying in my lap.

"Smitts is dead, dear one." His waxy face turned to one side, his eyes grasping for something nearby. It pulled my gaze to the slight frame of Smitts, with his glasses crumpled beneath his face, eyes open and staring at nothing. I choked on a sob and helped the captain turn his head back to look at me. "There's not a hope for me. But you keep fighting. You don't need anyone to save you anymore." His pained smile faded as his eyes closed with a sigh. I had loved this man as a father. He had saved me from slavery and given me my life. It was up to me now.

As I snapped the haft and pushed the arrow from his flesh, the ache in my chest burned away, a calm focus that Smitts taught me replacing it. This was nothing more than a problem that could be solved, as he would say. Air rushed into the hole I created with a sucking sound, and I slapped my palm over the hole. Suction created by the wound pulled at the skin of my hand.

Letting instinct guide me, I closed my eyes and desperately imagined the wound closing, the body healing. Under my breath I intoned, "You can't die, don't leave me, you can't die, don't leave me...."

Something deep within me pulsed and I opened my eyes to see my hands glowing. Blinking to clear my eyes, I realized that it wasn't my hand glowing as much as countless spectral hands that reached to close the wound at my direction.

I felt the world move, and something like a splash of cold water rushed through me at the touch of those hands. Relief exploded from me in an exhaled sob. They were back, and I knew what to do.

My anguish dissipated as the pulse increased in intensity, and a mantle of calm settled over me like a warm blanket on a cold day. The suction on my palm abated and I lifted it to find the skin scarred, but whole. With calm clarity, I guided the contents of his abdomen back inside.

Every diagram Smitts had shown me about the form and function of the human body flashed through my mind, and the ghostly figures understood what they should do. The gash on the captain's belly started to knit together, starkly lit by the light shining from our hands, and I could *feel* the holes closing from the inside of the gap in his chest. I could *feel* the tissue coming together, the blood draining from his lungs in the moment it took me to remember my lessons.

The captain gasped and his eyes popped open.

"Lila."

I gently placed his head on the deck and stood. New purpose filled me, and I only perceived his cries at the edge of my consciousness. My gift was under my control now, the cloaked figures moving with me, awaiting my command. I just had to decide how best to use them.

Beyond the protective circle of my friends I noticed that the battle had ended. Outnumbered, my friends began to surrender; weapons clattered to the wooden planks at their feet and chains were placed on the wrists of the few people that survived. The slaver's crew picked through the corpses of their fallen foes, looking for trinkets. Bodies were heaved overboard to clear the way for men returning from the hold with small crates as others made their way down to steal more of our cargo.

Hunter appeared next to me, blood dripping from slashes on his arms and chest. He swiped a hand at a gash on his head that had blood streaming onto his face.

"Lila, is he dead?"

I placed my hand on his forehead. The gift pulsed again; my glowing hand and thousands of *others* wiped the remainder of the blood away to reveal the closed wound.

Hunter blinked and reached up to feel that he was whole again. Reaching out, I grasped his arms at the site of each wound. *There*, I thought to my invisible allies; the wounds disappeared without a trace, as did those on his chest. Hunter's eyes widened as his fingers probed the even skin of his forehead, smearing the blood left behind.

Without a word, I turned in search of someone I could help, and I didn't stop until Hunter grasped my arm and yanked me around to face him. In that instant I felt myself again. The heat drained out of me as I shook my head; a wave of dizziness washed over me as I blinked. The figures were gone.

"What?" I mumbled.

"What just happened?" Hunter whispered. His eyes strayed behind me, and when they returned to my face, they were still wide. "Is the captain dead?"

"No, he's alive."

"Your eyes were glowing again. Are you all right?"

In shock and exhaustion, I could only shake my head. There was no time to talk about myself when people needed help. I turned my head back and forth, but there was nothing but the heartbreaking scene.

Hunter's eyes were full of awe and grief and rage as he pulled me to his chest, crushing my blood-soaked body against him. I started to push away; our friends needed our help, and I didn't have time for comfort. Before I could move on my own, someone grabbed my wrists and twisted them behind my back. Hunter was restrained as I was wrenched away from him.

An involuntary cry of pain escaped my lips. The man behind Hunter snaked his head around, sneering at me. Hunter's face twisted with rage and fear as he struggled, and I threw my weight backwards into my captor. His grip on my arms faltered and brought space between us, which I used to kick back toward his shins before whirling around to face him.

My eyes found the familiar silver hoop swaying in the bald man's ear when he limped a step backward. His grimace of pain twisted with the same disgust and frightening anticipation for violence that I had seen in my youth. But I wasn't the same terrified little girl anymore.

Time seemed to slow again as I brought my arms up to defend myself. My eyes drifted to Hunter, shoving against his assailant. The captain was still trying to regain his feet, and another pulse spread through me on a wave of unexpected rage. It was a palpable thing; the rage welled inside me, and it had a purpose. That purpose was to destroy these men who would bring to ruin in minutes what it had taken me years to assemble into my life.

I turned the wrathful pulse of the gift to the bald man with the silver hoop. His look of anticipation altered to confusion as he closed on me and perceived a change in his prey. The moment his shoulder connected with my midsection I unleashed the force straining for release.

Cloaked figures unseen by any but myself mimicked my posture when I slid my foot back and shoved my arm against his chest. From there a lethal spout of air and fire tore through him, leaving a hole the size of my open hand. He staggered to his knees, dragging me down with him; one hand braced his body above the deck and the other clutched his wound with a shocked look on his face, his blood adding to that of my fallen comrades.

I regained my feet amid a crowd of men rushing to aid the bald man. My focus turned to them, their hands reaching to restrain my arms and I imagined their bodies flying away from me and over the side. The moment the thought occurred to me, the closest of my assailants flew into the air as a legion of hands grasped each by both arms and tossed them over the side of the ship. The others fell back, afraid of what I might do to them next.

As I stood still to assess the scene, the waves of my rage and power swirled around me. I stood sheathed in cold fire, manifested as I imagined my anger as a shroud of flames to keep my attackers at bay; undulating waves crackled about me, longing to find another target. Hunter was lying motionless on his face nearby, and a wave of hatred gripped me, urging me toward the other ship.

Their captain stood aboard his own vessel and now turned to look at the commotion he heard behind him.

I glared into those eyes, devoid of feeling, devoid of a soul. The pulse began massing again as the faces of the people he had killed, the women and children he had sold, the lives he had destroyed flashed across my vision.

Imagining all the people I hadn't seen, the countless others whose lives he had ruined, called forth the gift again. An army of the spectral figures surrounded me and began moving as one toward him.

Someone slammed into me from behind, sending me stumbling forward. I struggled to maintain my balance and turned, throwing the pulse outward before me into the chest of another of our assailants. The power yearned to be released, and I felt the elation the figures felt as more poured out of me. It was almost alive, with its own intention, out of my control.

Hunter, having regained his feet, rushed in my direction. Knowing he would be caught up in it, the pulse extinguished in a rush. Numbing cold spread from my fingertips inward, but it was too late to stop it slamming into Hunter. He flew through the air and out over the sea. He seemed to hang motionless for a moment before plummeting below the rail; his eyes stood open wide in shock, and then disappeared.

I screamed and sprinted toward the rail. Something heavy landed on the back of my skull and my vision fractured in a starburst that matched a burst of pain from the blow.

My feet stumbled against something rigid in my path and I crashed onto my back to see large hands descend as my vision began to clear. In a daze, I cast about, unable to form a coherent thought, watching black spots waver before my eyes while I blinked against the pain in my head, hands, and hip where it struck the deck. My head lolled back as my stunned body flopped over someone's shoulder.

The pain in my head jolted me with every heavy thump of my captor's feet, even more so when he climbed up and then dropped from the rail to the deck of the other ship. My only recourse was to moan against the agony. My mind searched for purpose.

The sunlight disappeared, blocked by the deck above our heads as I was taken below and dropped in a dark, fetid cabin. My body slumped to the floor to the sound of a slamming door. When my head hit the damp floor, pain flared brilliantly, and darkness enfolded me.

CHAPTER EIGHT

I awoke disoriented; the room swayed and rolled around me, my eyelids felt as though they were made of lead, and my eyes were dry and painful. My right arm tingled painfully from shoulder to fingertips. The other I lifted in the air to the rattle of a chain.

Finally getting my eyelids open wide, I tried to take in my surroundings. Lifting my head increased the sway of the room far beyond what could be explained by the rocking of the ship, so I gently placed it back down, shutting my eyelids once more. I tried to remember what happened; being on board the *Catherine*, the blinding sun, and something about Smitts. Hunter....

Clawing out of my stupor, trying to put the events together to make sense of them, felt like swimming with my hands and feet bound. Pieces of something I'd seen flashed before my eyes – blood, men with the faces that chased me in my nightmares, the captain's pale face – and then I was dragged down into murky depths. Hunter's emerald eyes wide in terror came back again and again, and like a hand hauling me up to the surface, broke through to give me clarity.

My stupor vanished and my skin flushed from head to toe, regret and despair overwhelming as I remembered the events of the attack. The look on his face as he disappeared over the rail of the ship, propelled by the force I had unleashed, haunted me. Tears welled in my eyes and spilled over. Hunter had fallen in the wake of my rampage, and I had been unable to help him. It was my fault he was gone. Losing control meant losing Hunter.

The captain's face came unbidden to my mind, then; the smile before his face relaxed as he started slipping away from me, and the strange calm I had felt as I healed him.

I recalled the rest of the crew, Smitts, the pools of blood. An ache took up residence in my core that throbbed with the beat of my heart, with my every breath. The edges were as knives, twisting and biting deeper with every passing moment. My breathing became ragged, shallow, and fast at the thought of my ruined family, and the knives twisted harder; I couldn't slow them, and my face started to tingle as my body yearned for air.

I instinctively tried to curl into a ball to contain the pain I was feeling, but I was bound hand and foot, and could only manage a small curve. Fighting in vain against the restraints earned me more stabbing pain in my head and bloodied wrists. The rattle of the chains sounded like high-pitched laughter at my fruitless struggle.

"I need you," I said, calling out for whatever gift I might have. I pulled against the agony in my bound limbs and pictured the chains snapping, my skin knitting together. But nothing happened.

Spent by grief and pain, I shook and sobbed for what felt like hours. My entire life was gone, my future and every possibility, gone. Hopeless and helpless, feeling small and alone, I felt myself falling once again into the dark promise of oblivion and let myself drift.

The sound of boots hitting the planks of the deck was the first thing to penetrate my consciousness. The kick to the ribs was the second.

I recoiled as far as I could away from the attack and curled myself into the smallest arc that I could manage, attempting to shield myself from further blows. Another cracked against my spine and sent me flying against the chains in the other direction, brought short by metal digging into my flesh. A pitiful moan escaped my lips.

"Enough," a gravelly voice called from behind me. "Turn her around."

A pair of rough hands wrenched me onto my back and delivered a quick and merciless punch to my midsection. For a few agonizing and fearful seconds, I gasped for air that would not fill my lungs. Mercifully, the seconds passed, and I gasped in a breath. Nausea replaced the need for air, and bile rose in the back of my throat.

Light stabbed painfully at my swollen, crusted eyes when I managed to pry them open. A large man's outline was visible in the doorway, but only the outline. I could make nothing of his features.

He stood there a moment, letting me catch my breath. Then he took a step towards me and the heartless stare of the slave ship's captain materialized out of the darkness. I blinked up at him, and he glared down at me.

"You've caused me no end of trouble," he drawled. While his tone implied menace and anger, he sounded casual about it. That, more than his words, sent a shiver down my spine. "You killed a few of my best, injured more, and would've done the same for me if you hadn't been stopped. I had to kill the rest of your crew to stop them from retaliating. And the damage to your ship was immense. I couldn't salvage it, and that, my dear, has cost me more Malachs than you'd have seen in your lifetime."

He paused and leaned his back against a nearby wall. I gasped and sobbed through the pain in my side, an unrealized hope that *someone* would have survived broken like my ribs. When he pulled a dagger from his belt I flinched; he smirked. He continued while using the dagger's tip to pick dried blood from beneath his fingernails. "Now the question is what to do with you. I've some aboard that would like to see you try to swim with your hands and feet bound. But I think you may be valuable enough to hold on to."

My response was to attempt to control panicked sobs and the bile still threatening to rise, so he continued. "I have a man here that tells me he doesn't think you've learned much about the gift. Says you would've used it sooner if that were the case. And, it makes you easier for him to control. So that puts my mind at ease a bit, knowing you can't just decide to do something I'll regret. But it does make me wonder, what made you able to use it when you did?

"I wonder, was the little girl angry with us?" he asked, smiling without humor. He hunkered down, balancing his large form on the balls of his feet. His face edged closer to mine.

With nothing to say, I could only stare at the man. A few long moments passed with our eyes locked. I wanted to think that I was being defiant, but I couldn't tear my eyes away from his, cold and frightening as they were.

"In any case," he sighed as he stood, "we can't have you walking around without some sort of restraint. Wouldn't want you surprising us, would we?" He chuckled to himself. "I have just the thing in mind. It'll keep you from getting too excited. You'll have just enough of your faculties to be of use."

Without a backward glance he turned and strolled out the door, gesturing to someone I couldn't see in the hall. What was he going to do?

Rising panic overcame reason, and again I yanked against my restraints, cutting into the flesh of my wrists and ankles. My quick gasps burned my lungs, and slick blood accompanied a sharp pain from the edges of the shackles. There wasn't much slack, and there was no hope of slipping free. My panic increased as I realized I couldn't help but lie here and let them do what they would, but the pain finally won over my desperation, and my body stilled against the damp wood.

A lanky, hunched man shuffled into the room. His bright eyes twinkled in the dim light. Though his gait and bearing spoke of age far beyond my own, as he edged closer I could see no wrinkles or other such marks of years on him. A large hump stood out on his back, his right leg turned at an awkward angle to his body. One side of his mouth hung slack, morphing his expression into a permanent sneer.

He gazed at me dispassionately, as if I were no more than a fly. The casual menace of the captain paled in comparison to the malevolence shining through this man's pale blue eyes.

The man limped closer and bent down over me. He smelled as though he had never seen soap and water together in his life; my gorge rose again at his overwhelming stench. His blonde hair framed his sallow face in matted, greasy clumps. I shrank from him, repelled by this filthy, malicious man. He closed his eyes and frowned, lifting his hands in the air, moving them back and forth over my body. Then he moved to place his hands on either side of my head, not quite touching me.

As I peered at this man's face, he seemed to lose his color. Not just him; the whole room and what I could see of the outside of my cell seemed to be fading to a muted shadow of the world as I knew it. The unwashed wheat color of the man's hair changed moment by moment until its hue was dull gray. The light no longer glinted from his blue eyes; they shone a pale gray, nearly white.

Lethargy settled like a large blanket that covered my entire form, but sank deeper into my mind and body. The terror at my circumstances, the sorrow eating away at me, all became insignificant.

Help, I thought, desperate for the figures to keep this feeling at bay.

We come. The reply was strangely muted, as if they responded through a wall. One started to reach out, to place a hand against my head where this strange person was. But they stopped short, and began to fade.

A vital part of myself faded with them and I let out an anguished cry as it was finally wrenched away, leaving me blank.

My eyes blinked once, looking again at the man hunched over me. I no longer felt revulsion at seeing him. I felt nothing. The smell he emitted and the sounds of his rasping breath faded as well, as if my senses were dulled along with my feelings. Complete apathy surrounded me.

The man struggled to his feet and shuffled out of the room. I watched him leave, and then turned my head back to look at the ceiling of my small cell. His rough voice drifted in as he spoke with someone outside.

"It's done, sir," the man rasped.

"Are you sure she's safe?" I could make out the captain's voice. It seemed he had waited for the strange man to be finished.

"Her mind still works, she can still think and react. But the spirits will no longer answer her call."

"How can you be certain, Derth?" the captain grumbled.

"Because, *sir,* the talent she possesses is erratic. She pushed against the ship before the battle, but it was weak. Her demonstration was impressive, but would have been more so if it hadn't taken so long for her to begin." He paused, and when he spoke again his voice became a growl. "Or do you doubt my ability to do what I was put here to do?"

"You're sure?"

"Yes, *sir*, Captain Roglin," the man growled again. "This is something I've done before, and I am confident that even were she able to use the Ambience well, she wouldn't be able to now."

"All right then, dismissed."

"Aye aye, sir." Shuffling steps receded as Derth moved away from my cell.

The information passed over me with little notice. A moment later the captain sauntered back into my cell. "How are you feeling?" he asked me as he walked to my side.

I looked at him, confused by the question. "I don't know," I replied.

"Well, that's fine. Try not to worry about it," he said with a grin. "I'm going to unchain you. Will you behave?"

"I don't understand," I said.

"Don't move when you're free," he warned. He hunched next to my feet and produced a key from his pocket to unlock first my right ankle, then my left. I moved them in circles and flexed my feet.

He looked at my face as he bent over the manacles holding my wrists. "How does that feel?"

"There's less pain," I told him.

He smiled to himself and unlocked my wrists. I pulled them to my chest and rubbed them each in turn. My fingers stuck to the painful rings around my wrists and I looked down. The drying blood clung to my fingers, dark gray, the color of iron.

"You can sit up if you like," the captain told me. "Best do it slowly; you've been down there for a while."

I obeyed and sat up slowly. My vision darkened for a moment with black spots and the room swayed again. Captain Roglin remained at my level, glaring at me, waiting for me to move.

"You going to give me trouble?" he asked.

"Why would I give you trouble?"

"Why indeed. Stand up," he commanded. He rose to his feet, blocking the light from the doorway.

My arm buckled when I braced my hand on the floor to push myself up. Pain shot up my arm and I gasped.

The captain looked down upon me with disdain and exasperation. I attempted again to stand, without the use of my arms for leverage, but my legs were far too cramped and I fell to the floor. The captain turned and moved to the door, pausing with his hand on the handle.

"We'll take this slow, then," he sneered. "I hope you like your accommodations, because you'll be spending quite some time here." With that, he slammed and bolted the door and I was left alone, sitting on the floor, cradling my wrist.

I spent what seemed like weeks in my prison cell, sitting and staring at a spot on the wall. It could have been less time, it could have been more time, but with no view of the sky, I wasn't able to count the passing days. Occasionally, a man brought food and water without saying a word, or emptied the bucket in the corner, though that was less frequent.

An interminable gray cloud of apathy surrounded me, with only food or the need to relieve myself to break up the hours, I sat staring, my mind blank. I wondered at nothing, I asked for nothing, I felt *nothing*.

One day, the captain came to my cell and covered his nose, glaring at me and gasping as the door creaked open to illuminate my otherwise lightless room.

"Well, you *are* a mess, aren't you, little lady?" he mocked. My staring gaze moved from the wall opposite my position to the captain's face. He scowled. "You are also very disconcerting. Stop staring at me."

My head turned and my eyes resumed their spot on the wall. He passed in and out of view, walking around my still form where I sat on the floor. He sighed. "We'll need to do something about your state. You are disgusting."

He stomped by again in the direction of the door and shouted, "*Bryn!*" More booted feet thundered on the wood of the corridor in our direction.

"Yes, sir?" the second man asked, winded after his run. This new voice held a smooth quality unlike the bark or growl of the captain's.

"Fetch me a bucket of water, a rag, and some fresh clothes for the lady," the captain grumbled. "We can't have her falling ill because she's covered in filth."

The second man hesitated for a moment before moving away at a swift pace as the captain closed and bolted the door, leaving me in dim silence. When that door swung open again, light poured in from the torches in the corridor. The second man had returned, with a bucket of water sloshing in his hand.

He stooped and placed it at my side, then placed a gown on the floor beside it. He started to rise, but paused, instead squatting in front of me so that his face came into view.

He grasped my wrists, turning them over to look at the dried blood and the healing gashes I had made in my futile attempt to fight my restraints. Without a word, he took the rag from the bucket, soaked it in the water, and started to clean my wrists. His touch was gentle, but the wounds were painful. When I flinched, he continued with less force, and my wrists were soon clean. He placed the rag back in the bucket and stood.

"This is for you to clean yourself. There is a comb as well," he intoned as he turned and closed the door behind him. The bolt clicked into place, and I leaned to take the rag out of the bucket.

I removed my torn and stiff clothes, placing them on the floor. It took a long time and a lot of effort, but I removed all the grime before I started to comb through the thick tangles in my hair.

The gown hung from my frame when it settled onto my shoulders. It smelled very strongly of sweat and whomever had worn it previously, showing signs of heavy use. I folded my legs under to sit on a section of the floor that was cleaner than the blood soaked planks near the chains and waited.

Some time later, Bryn returned with Derth and Captain Roglin at his side. Derth moved into my cell first, placing his hands at my temples. He frowned as he concentrated. Like a shadow in the corner, I perceived him in my mind.

For a brief moment, I shuddered with revulsion at this connection, sensing something very wrong with this man in front of me. I felt the figures just out of reach, Derth called them spirits, straining to get to me, to help me use the gift to stop what was happening. Whatever spirit Derth was using felt *different*, somehow painful or pained.

The gray fog that enshrouded me receded, allowing color to push at the gray. I glanced at the doorway, seeing Bryn's eyes start to change from gray to dazzling blue, mouth frowning in what might have been disapproval or sympathy.

A grunt from Derth pulled my eyes to his face and the gray shroud returned. The shift was less subtle, more akin to a door slamming in my face. I stared at Derth with blank, unfeeling eyes again.

Stepping away from me and letting his arms fall to his sides, Derth turned to the captain. "She started to come out of it for a moment, but I've reasserted my control. She should pose no threat, but I'll need to watch more closely from now on."

"If she snaps out of this, it's on *your* head, *gifted* man," the captain fumed. He strode into my cell and peered down at me. "She's cleaner, at least." He sighed. "You'll have to make sure she stays that way. It's a long journey, and she needs to survive long enough for me to get paid."

CHAPTER NINE

The next weeks would have been monotonous if I had had any notion of what that would feel like. It was decided that I would make myself useful by waiting on Roglin hand and foot over the long journey. I fetched things from the galley and the surgeon, from all members of the crew. I delivered messages and summoned men to Roglin's cabin. When he had no task for me, I was relegated to my cell.

Roglin told the crew I was off limits. Under no circumstances were any of them allowed to lay a hand on me. If pushed, he assured the men that I could kill every one of them, and he would personally skin any man alive that tried and pin him to the main mast as a lesson to the rest of them. To ensure his edict was followed, Bryn acted as my shadow and the first line of defense for me, and as a measure of protection for the ship and crew if I were to regain my senses.

One of the crew, a small man by the name of Seth, shadowed my movements throughout the ship for more than a week. Every day I overheard his mutterings about the death of his friends at my hands and what he would do to me if my guard dog were to leave me alone.

One day, as I carried food on a wooden tray someone called, Bryn's name. When his attention was diverted, Seth stepped between us and thrust his blade toward my midsection. In one fluid movement, Bryn grasped his wrist while his other hand slammed the pommel of his dirk into the overextended elbow. Howls of anguish followed the resounding crack of the bones breaking and summoned the attention of the captain near the helm.

Roglin was sincere about his threats.

After being apprised of the situation, he went straight to work. Claiming Seth's knife for himself, he used it to skin the man, who screamed until the life finally drained out of him. The captain singled out Seth's friends and forced them to swab the decks clean of the blood and sinew left behind.

I was not attacked again.

With a dispassionate eye, I marked the passage of time by the slow emaciation of my body. My food and water rations were only just sufficient to keep me alive, and I no longer used my muscles to climb and haul lines, so they wasted away. My movements became clumsy, and my strength waned with every passing day.

The gray, lethargic haze that overshadowed me prevented my interest in anything around me. I woke every morning to see Bryn standing just inside my door with orders for the day. Every day I would emerge above decks to see the gray sun peeking over the horizon.

For moments alone in my cell, Bryn gifted me a candle and lit it every night to stave off the darkness. I would focus on the flame as the only point of interest in the room. Once I felt my mind still as I repeated the word *come* over and over, a plea to the spirits to help me free myself from this nightmare. I pictured myself moving toward them, hand outstretched, before pressing against something solid that I couldn't see. After that, I fell into the haze again.

One morning began as the others, with Bryn summoning me to the galley to fetch the captain's breakfast and watching while I shuffled along the corridors with my hands full. As usual, I waited for Bryn to climb the ladder to the deck to hand him the tray so that I could fumble my way up behind. Crossing the deck, the men gave us a wide berth in response to Bryn's scowls and my feet followed their normal path toward the door to the captain's cabin.

Today, however, my foot slipped on the rain-slick deck, and I stumbled. The tray tipped out of my hands and I lurched forward to grasp at it instead of trying to steady myself, but my reflexes had dulled over time and I fell atop it instead.

Sharp pain burned in my right side when I moved to lift myself from the tray. I crumpled and the burning worsened. An involuntary cry burst from my lips and I thrust myself onto my back to lessen the pressure on my wound. The short blade of the knife supplied to slice the captain's ham was buried into my abdomen, surrounded by a dull red ooze that spread along my skin and soaked the fabric of my loose gown.

The door to the cabin opened and Captain Roglin stood over me, disgusted at the display at his feet even as Bryn swept down to assess my injury and place his hand near the wound to staunch the bleeding.

"Clumsy bitch," Roglin grumbled. "Get that knife out of your side before you do more damage."

"No, wait," Bryn breathed, taking his red-stained hands from my side to stop me from following orders. He failed, as I wrenched the knife out at an angle; fresh blood gushed from the wound in copious amounts and I screamed as I tore something further.

Bryn turned to flash an angry blue glare at the captain and grumbled something that I couldn't understand over the pounding blood in my ears and my pitiful mewling sobs. My hands grasped the wound, pulling the stained fabric of my gown into a ball around the gash as I recalled something Smitts told me about leaving a stab wound alone until a surgeon could assess the damage.

The thought of Smitts' open eyes staring at me from a pool of blood brought further tears for a moment before the memory faded behind a hazy curtain of gray.

Bryn turned back and spoke, but I heard nothing over my pain; when I didn't react, he sighed and slid his left arm under my shoulders and helped me into a sitting position. I winced as pain shot through my side, and curled into a ball with my hands over the wound.

"You, dear nephew, are too caring for my liking. Take the woman back to Derth's to be patched up." With that, he turned and stalked back into his cabin, slamming the door behind him.

Bryn tried to help me to my feet, but the pain flared and I was unable to stand. When I moved my hand from the wound, blood began to flow freely from it, soaking my fingers. Bryn cursed under his breath and lifted me bodily from the deck. I cried out and Bryn's lips tightened.

"I apologize for that, miss," Bryn said as he stalked across the deck towards the hatch. "I have to put you down now. We can't climb the ladder like this."

He placed me carefully on my feet and started down. I turned to face the ladder and stretched my right foot down into the opening. My side screamed with pain, and for a moment, I could see the russet and tan of the wood in front of me. My eyes turned to my side, and crimson blood stained my filthy dress where my wound bled. I lost my footing on the first rung of the ladder and fell the few feet to the lower deck.

Bryn tried to catch me, but only succeeded in breaking my fall. My body dragged him to the ground with me; my limbs tangled with his, and we sat sprawled with me half on top of him.

"Are you all right? What happened?" Bryn grunted as he helped me to my feet.

"I was trying to climb down the ladder, but I think I tore something in my side. It's bleeding more now," I hissed through gritted teeth.

Bryn studied my face for a moment, and I looked into his. In the light from the hatch above, his features stood out as they couldn't in the confines of my cell, and my breathing halted, my pain forgotten as I realized that I could *see* him.

His dark golden hair shone like wheat in the noonday sun. His eyes widened, as blue as the sea on a clear day, the color of sapphires around the edges and fading to a lighter opalescent blue surrounding his pupils. Full lips frowned with concern and confusion. His nose sat slightly crooked, but it added to the overall impression of a hardworking, genuine man. I perceived none of the wanton cruelty displayed by the captain or Derth in this moment, and realized though he hadn't been kind, he hadn't gone out of his way to punish me like the others.

He studied my face, noticed the flush I felt creeping over my countenance. He looked more closely at my eyes. His confusion faded to astonishment.

"How are you feeling?" he whispered.

"I...I am in a lot of pain," I stammered. "And I'm a little confused," I told him. I couldn't pry my eyes from his face, especially when he blushed, noticing my ardent attention. My fingers twitched, and it took a gargantuan effort not to reach up and rub them against the heavy stubble on his cheeks where the blush disappeared. I started to reach up, but it pulled the wound in my side and I looked down, clutching at it. Blood was continuing to ooze from the large gash.

"Confused?" he asked.

"Yes...I feel like I've been asleep...." I trailed off, feeling the lethargy that had enveloped me for weeks starting to settle over me again. My eyes sought the clear blue of Bryn's in a bid for the last moments of color in my gray prison, and I silently wished that he could help me, somehow. I touched my side, and the flare of pain held the lethargy at bay.

"Miss?" Bryn asked, worried again.

"My name is Lila," I said, seeing the world around me change from the vivid colors of life to the dull blacks and whites of my altered state. The brilliant hues in Bryn's eyes faded back to gray. I clutched at my wound, wincing as the pain flared, but it didn't help. I struggled to stay alert, to fight the fatigue, to fight the hazy curtain. "Please, call me Lila."

My struggle ended in defeat, and I watched Derth shamble out of his cabin. The world held no color, gray once more. My clarity had lasted only moments.

"What happened, Bryn?" Derth croaked.

Bryn looked down at me, then back to Derth. He hesitated for a moment before saying, "She fell and impaled herself on a knife. My uncle ordered her to remove it; the wound is deep, and has been bleeding freely."

"Get her into my cabin, then. It will only take a moment to mend." He looked irritated, but there was an excited gleam in his eyes that sent shivers down my spine.

Bryn knelt next to me and lifted me with slow, calculating movements. His eyes gazed into mine, seeming to search for something. In Derth's cabin, he placed me on the bunk.

"Step back, now," Derth commanded. Bryn, with his eyes still glued to mine, took a step to the rear. "You," he said to me, "lie down, with your injury facing me. Place your right arm above your head, out of the way."

Derth moved closer to me as I obeyed, pulling the torn edges of the gown away from the wound. He placed his hands over it, and then pressed down hard enough to make me gasp in pain. I flinched away from his hands, but he quickly and none too gently replaced them.

"What are you doing, Derth? You're hurting her!" Bryn shouted, taking a step in our direction. The pressure on my wound did not lessen.

Derth looked over his shoulder at Bryn. "You haven't been with us long, and you haven't been in my care yet. I will tell you only once. Do not interrupt me, and do not presume to tell me how to do my job. You will never understand the forces I can command, and I will never explain them to you."

It was the longest speech I had heard from him in my weeks aboard the ship. It served to halt Bryn in his tracks, glowering at the man with his hands on my wound.

Derth returned his attention to me, closing his eyes and increasing the pressure. Veins in his head stood out, his mouth twisted in a grimace, and the muscles in his neck bulged as he strained against unseen forces. The pain in my side sharpened, and I screamed. It was as sharp as thousands of needles being plunged through my skin and into my vital parts all at once.

My eyes shot wide open in agony, riveted on Derth's face hovering over me. Color came back into the world with the pain as it had mere minutes before. Derth's lank yellow hair matched the color of his teeth, bared with his effort. I tried to move away from him, but it felt as though I were tethered to him through my wound and his hands upon it. The pain was red hot, and I could not escape it.

Emotion once again flooded through me, and rage flared from deep within, grasping my heart in a vice. That anger stoked a fire, and that heat began to pulse outward. Through the pain I focused that heat, letting instinct guide it into the palm of my hand. The hand of a spirit coaxed the flame higher.

We come. White hot fire manifested where I directed it, and I reached out to place my hand on Derth's chest.

Bryn's shout of surprise distracted me, pulling my eyes away from my target and locking them on his startled face. Time seemed to slow while Bryn took the steps to reach the bunk; the space between my palm and Derth's chest diminished at an agonizingly slow pace. Derth grunted when my hand came close enough to burn the fabric of his shirt.

As the skin beneath began to redden, Bryn's fingers closed around my wrist, wrenching it away. I screamed again, this time with unbridled fury. My fingers spread, and I unleashed the summoned fire in Bryn's direction.

He ducked and pushed my hand up in one swift movement, and the fire hissed and spat as it burned through the wood of a cabinet mounted on the wall.

Derth grunted, and something inside me twisted. My eyes lost focus and my mind was drawn inward to witness Derth's efforts to repair the damage in my side. My muscles grasped the space between the severed ends, as hands searching in the dark for one another. The vessels draining my life's blood knitted themselves together, drawing the lost blood I still possessed back into themselves. All layers were mending as though it was their dearest wish, as if they couldn't wait to be reunited.

But they were driven by a dark version of the spirits I saw. I reached out to that twisted presence, compelled to aid it in some way.

As the work finished, I turned to see Bryn's face. In that moment, I loathed him. He had stopped my effort to break free of my imprisonment. But where I expected to find my loathing reciprocated, I saw only concern and kindness, his hands on Derth, his voice cautioning against harming me. My hatred slithered away, and in its place I found hope of an ally. Rather than face the strange and confusing feelings, I closed my eyes and retreated into my thoughts. Instead of the peace I sought, I found myself in a vision of things that I had felt before, but never seen. Like a world made up of the feelings and power inside me, and came up short in front of a large barrier.

It appeared as the same hazy curtain I had been living with, rippling as if in a light breeze that I couldn't feel. When I placed my hands upon it, the apathy of the past weeks started to creep into the tips of my fingers, inching its way up my arm. I recoiled immediately, backing away a few paces to gain some space between myself and this awful edifice.

A tiny burst of light caught my attention far to the right of where I stood. The light beckoned me and I moved, first walking and then sprinting in its direction. I stopped as I reached the source: a tiny gap in the haze, standing still amidst the shifting curtain, and I felt vibrations as if something were searching for the seam, trying to part it. My hand reached up to touch the sliver of light and it widened an infinitesimal amount.

I removed my hand and crouched down to peer into the wider space. On the other side of this curtain, a large pool of water that reflected and radiated light and color like a sunbeam shone through a crystal.

Something seemed so familiar about this pool, a dream half-remembered on the edge of waking thought. Figures bathed in the pool and lounged around it; I could see no features of any but noticed the vaguely human silhouettes in the dazzle. The spirits! As I tried to grasp what I was seeing, the opening became larger, just enough for my hand to fit through.

The spirits moved in my direction as my fingers stretched to touch them and bathed in the light, soaking in the warmth to drive away the cool lethargy. Before my fingers could brush against whoever approached, they shrank back as one and waited, turning their heads to peer beyond where I stood.

I whipped around to find Derth with me in this void, standing tall and thin with a dark shadow clinging to him. He considered the folds, shuffling along the length of this thing that stretched out into the distance that separated me from what lay beyond. With him here, I could feel the connection between the gray haze and the gift he wielded.

"What are you?" he muttered. He stopped and turned, fixing me with an odd look, and something in my head shifted.

The curtain slid into place as if thrust along a metal rod, and the light and color faded, though the curtain still swung back and forth to let a small weak light through. Another shift occurred, and I felt the hard bunk beneath me, my world becoming the muted mockery I had lived these past weeks. My eyes focused again on the gray room that held the two men and my emaciated frame.

My head rolled to the side as Roglin entered and glanced at the cabinet still smoldering in the wake of my rage. A dull roar filled my ears, my vision darkened on the edge of consciousness.

Derth turned to the captain. "It is holding, but she is starting to make holes in the barrier containing the Ambience. I fear my control is waning. It may hold for some time, but as I have never done something like this long term and she is not normal, I don't know when it will come down," Derth wheezed. "We must be rid of her, by any means necessary. Soon."

CHAPTER TEN

Flickering light from a candle flame silhouetted my feet and lit the nearby table when I opened my eyes. The smell of wood smoke and burnt flesh pervaded the air in Derth's cabin. I was alone. I sat up slowly, tensing my muscles against the pain I expected from my wound and clutching my skin, but my fingers found no trace of the gash. Muffled voices caught my attention and I looked to a door slightly ajar where faint light filtered through.

"The veil is breaking down," Derth insisted. "If I place a new one, it will eventually break down as well." He paused, and when he continued he spoke as if to himself. "She has strength I've not encountered before. I wonder what drives it...."

"You said she would comply through pain," Roglin snapped. "You didn't say anything about pain waking her up."

"I told you I didn't know what exactly would happen," Derth hissed. "This restraint has not been attempted over an extended timeline, or with such a complicated case. We need to keep her isolated until we can be rid of her. I don't know what will set off a chain reaction that could result in our destruction."

"We have three days until we make port. We should find someone who'll take her on Rogue's Island. We'll say nothing about her condition, and she'll be a prize for anyone."

"You know what we have to do with someone like her," Derth protested. "Either we deliver her as ordered, risking months at sea with a tenuous hold on the Ambience, or we kill her and pretend this never happened. Whichever we choose, there will be consequences. And if we choose to dispose of her elsewhere, the consequences will be worse."

Their voices faded when I rolled onto my side and felt a sharp bite of pain in my head. Awareness flared with the pain, and I recalled a pool reflecting brilliant light, but the pain subsided and so did the memory.

Footsteps approached and the two men in the hall fell silent. "What happened in there?" Bryn demanded. "She almost killed us and set the ship on fire!"

"She is more capable than I expected," Derth replied. "Her talent is stronger than any I have faced before. And standard measures of control aren't strong enough to contain it."

"What does that mean?" Bryn insisted. "Can you keep her from attacking us or not?"

"Easy, nephew," Roglin warned. "We'll be rid of her soon enough."

None of the men spoke, leaving the hall in silence that Roglin eventually broke. "She will be confined to her quarters until we reach port and I need you to keep her fed until then. I want constant guard on her door; I'll assign some men to relieve you. You bring her food, but do not engage her otherwise. Understood?"

"Yes, captain," Bryn sighed.

"I'll decide what to do with her by then."

Heavy footfalls receded down the hall. Moments later, Bryn and Derth crossed the threshold to the cabin.

"Bryn will escort you to your cell. Do not exert yourself," Derth informed me. He stared at me for a few seconds, that gleam in his eyes again before he turned away, dismissing me.

Bryn stood silent as I entered my cell. I walked to the far wall, turned, and sat on the small pile of blankets serving as my bed. When I looked back toward the door, Bryn stood in the same place.

He searched my face for a few moments; his mouth opened once as if about to speak, but he closed it and stalked out. The key clicked in the lock, and I sat alone in darkness.

A short time later the door opened, revealing Bryn holding a single candle in one hand and a crust of bread in the other. He closed the door behind him and crossed the room to place the bread in my upturned palm.

I took a bite, the dry bread scratching my raw throat when I swallowed. Bryn's eyes never left my face while he took a seat against the far wall. My small meal finished, I waited in silence as he studied me.

"What are you, Lila?" he whispered.

"A woman," I replied.

"There's more to it than that," he insisted. He scrubbed a hand over his face and sighed. "Derth says that you have some strange gift that he's never seen. I think the gift is strange enough, but for you to have something that he hasn't seen...." He trailed off and finally pulled his eyes away from mine. "This is too much."

He stood and strode through the door, leaving the candle in the spot he had vacated. It closed with a thud, and the key rotated in the lock again, leaving me with the flickering light of the candle to ward off the darkness. I stared at the flame that wavered in the draft from gaps in the door. The occasional creak of boards beneath Bryn's feet drifted to my ears when he shifted his weight. Waves lapping against the hull were the only other sounds that reached me.

Hours later, Bryn's relief arrived. A few gruff words were exchanged, and then Bryn shuffled off to find his rest. By this time my eyes burned from exhaustion, and I decided to lie down to sleep. My eyes closed, and images of the day's events flickered at the edge of my mind.

Half seen pictures of people and places, fire and burning fabric floated in and out of my consciousness. With those pictures came fleeting images of a beautiful pool surrounded by figures shadowed in mist, but it faded as I let myself drift into sleep.

Dreams visited my slumber for the first time in months. Always running, I stumbled through swaths of fabric that stretched so high they blocked out the sky as they reached out to entangle me. Blue sapphires sparkled in the light of the sun reflected off the ocean but fell beneath the surface as a heavy fog rolled in and blotted out the radiant light. Roglin stood laughing as I tried to fight my way free of gauzy fabric twisting round my arms and legs.

The curtain loomed above me again; a crack in the gray edifice caught my eye and I halted my attempts to break free. The crack spread and prismatic light flickered; voices whispered from behind the gray veil, calling my name. My hand reached toward them of its own accord while I twisted and slipped free of the substance containing my limbs. In a frantic rush, I threw myself forward toward the curtain, tearing at the fabric to shove it aside in large fistfuls. Though it abated, it began to surround me as soon as I turned my back.

Lethargy bloomed whenever the curtain caressed my skin, but the growing light blossoming from the larger opening helped to push it away, beckoning me onward. The breach became as big as my torso, and still I continued. Light and color swelled, beating away the apathy.

I lashed out with my arms to grasp a section of the barrier with both hands and pulled with all my might; it collapsed in a heap, disconnecting from somewhere in the endless void above my head to reveal a clear path forward. Panting, I stood gazing at the results of my efforts, bathed in light more brilliant than the sun at its peak, more colorful than the sky at sunset. It warmed me and called me forward.

Without hesitation, I stepped forward into the embrace of something entirely strange and yet familiar. It blinded me for a moment before everything that had been separated from me became whole. My memories, my emotions, and my will to live free and escape this waking nightmare became part of me again. This barrier had held them all back, and now I had broken through.

I awoke with a start, sitting upright in my cell. With my eyes wide, I surveyed my surroundings, noticing again how filthy the floor was. My hands, my face, my hair and my clothes all stank with weeks of unwashed grime.

Along with the grime, the light from my dream bathed my body in a faint glow, as if I were in water reflecting the noonday sun. My hands rotated back and forth, illuminating the otherwise dark cell. More than light, they were outlined by one of the spectral figures, a spirit. Nodding in thanks, I cast my eyes around the room.

My search stopped at the door, and I leapt to my feet. That door marked my path to freedom, and the desperate need to follow it gripped me. My bare feet crept silently across the floor until I came near enough to press my ear against the damp wood.

The guard cleared his throat and stomped his feet, but the thick door muffled sound from farther away. I concentrated, trying to discern whether anyone else moved along the corridor. My shroud of light intensified as I strained to hear more. The spirit touched my ear, and voices from above became audible. At first I heard only garbled conversation, but the words became clear enough for me to follow as I turned my intent to interpreting the conversation.

"We have to be rid of her if she's gonna burn up the ship," a man grumbled.

"That's my decision," Derth replied.

Someone else shouted, "Then get us moving!"

"I'm otherwise occupied," Derth said. Everyone was silent for a moment, waiting for him to elaborate. When he didn't, the objections continued.

"We should just kill her and be done with it," another interjected. "Before she kills us!"

I pulled away from the door. Any pleasure I felt at the successful use of the gift paled in comparison to the fear of being killed by an angry mob, and I started to pace.

Three days from port. I couldn't swim that far or stay ahead of the ship. My only recourse would be to get to the longboat and somehow sneak away without anyone noticing. With a guard on my door, and the crew working themselves into a frenzy, that sounded as fatal as an ocean swim. With every step of my pacing, the glow around me faded as the spirit pulled away. The grip I had on whatever allowed me to listen through the decks faded with it, and I was left feeling empty and alone.

Without the aid of the gift, I could just make out raised voices as they moved from the deck above to the crew quarters at the end of the corridor. A large group of the men that had been between me and the longboat had just gone to their rest for the night.

I pressed my ear flush with the wood of the door again and strained to listen to the sounds above as I had minutes before. The guard still shifted his weight on the other side of the door, but no other sounds reached me. Whether this was the result of the deck emptying or the thick door preventing me from hearing, I had no way of knowing.

Inch by inch, I lifted the latch holding the door closed, hoping to avoid notice. Every click forced me to halt and wait for the guard to hear evidence of my efforts while I held my breath, my heart pounding against my ribs. The metal slipped free of its boundary and I let out my held breath before I realized that the door wouldn't budge; the bolt still held firm. The guard held the key to my freedom, but he would be more likely to gut me than anything else. With a soft click, I placed the latch back and looked around the room for something I could use. The flame guttered in the wax of the candle at that moment, and my eyes found the metal candlestick.

Tiptoeing across the room, I stooped to grasp it. The whole thing measured as long as my palm with a wide, circular base and a thick, blunt edge about as wide as my thumb. It was heavier than I expected.

I stood in the darkness, wondering what to do next. To leave, I would need to get the guard's attention and have him open the door. In doing so, he would likely alert someone else in the process, and my chance of sneaking out would be gone.

If I hadn't been so attuned to the noises outside my door I wouldn't have noticed, but a slight metallic hiss alerted me that the bolt was being slid out of its bracket. I sprinted silently across the room, my heart in my throat, to the space next to the doorframe as the key turned the lock and the latch slowly clicked open as well. With the room in darkness, I hoped there would be little chance of someone seeing me when they crossed the threshold. Just in time, I flattened myself against the wall. The door swung open with a creak and a large man poked his head in.

"Where are you, cursed whore?" a deep voice rumbled.

The rest of his body followed his head, and he shut the door behind him. In the gloom, his shape was barely visible as he stalked across the small space in a crouch. Before he slunk three paces, I lunged.

He turned as I swept the candlestick down, aiming for his head. His temple pivoted into the direct path of my weapon; the edge of the candlestick cracked against his skull. He fell with a grunt, sprawling in an awkward position on his side. Wary, I swung the candlestick again with another sickening crack, and again with a grunt of fear and anger as he groaned on the floor, until he lay prone and still at my feet, dark blood oozing from his split skin.

A dagger stuck through his belt, so I discarded my candlestick in favor of the small blade. It was a considerable improvement, something I was familiar with. But my arms were shaking after swinging the candlestick, so I realized I might only be able to stab reliably once or twice before I wouldn't be able to lift it again.

He had no other weapons, so I unbuckled his belt and pulled it through the loops of his pants. Once free, I rolled his large frame over onto his stomach, my feet slipping on the floor, and pulled his hands behind his back. Wrapping the belt around and between his wrists, I made sure he wouldn't be able to free himself quickly and come after me if he ever stirred again. Now armed, I marched to the door.

I need help, I begged the spirits. *A way out, something!* I imagined myself disappearing, and then reappearing behind the longboat. And then flying, followed by setting the ship on fire. But the spirits didn't come. It felt like they were gone, but I'd just seen them, hadn't I? Why were they ignoring me?

With my head inclined beyond the doorframe, the corridor became visible. No one was in sight, and I could hear nothing beyond the creaking of wood and the snap of the sails in the night wind.

In wary silence I stepped into the hall, pausing to close the door and slide the bolt home. Alone in the silent passage, I began the torturous and slow journey to the hatch and the deck above.

Low candles sputtered in silent witness to my unhindered movements. With the dagger clutched in my hand, I climbed up a few rungs of the ladder until the top of my head broke the surface of the ship. No movement drew my eye, and I dared not wait long in case someone emerged from the crew cabin to find me escaping. I pulled myself up the last few rungs and into the night air.

A crescent moon reflected little light off the black water, and lanterns hung dormant and dark all around. A small sound startled me, and I jumped back, holding the dagger at the ready.

A loose length of hempen rope flapped against the rail in the ocean breeze in front of me, unconcerned about the weapon I wielded. My heart hammered in my chest, my breathing came in rapid pulls as I struggled to think clearly. Where I gripped the dagger, my knuckles stood out white in the darkness. My nerves and fear stood on high alert, spiraling out of control. I took a deep breath, filling my lungs with the familiar scent of the sea air to steady myself.

My heart rate slowed and the fear lessened as I stood alone on the deck. The longboat creaked, swaying in the wind on the starboard side, and I rushed toward it.

The rope scraped my hands as I worked the lines to lower it to the water. Back and forth I rushed in the dark, keeping the boat even in its descent. Every creak of the line or thump of the boat against the side of the ship caught my breath and heightened my fear of being found, pushing me to move faster.

One end of the boat hit the water with a distant splash. The rope at the other side pulled against the fading calluses on my hand, but a voice froze me in place before I could finish the task.

"More tenacious than I thought, to break free of my binding." My hand still on the rope, I peered over my shoulder to where Derth stood, a few paces from the hatch opening. His hands hung from his sides at different lengths, his lank hair floated away from his face in the breeze. His face transformed into something foul with the mock grin he wore.

I lowered the boat the rest of the way to the water with renewed haste. It crashed to the ocean's surface and bobbed in blissful serenity against the waves.

"If you think you will escape, you are mistaken," Derth continued. His voice croaked above the sound of the wind in my ears. I ignored him and lunged for the rail, trying to heave myself overboard before he could act.

His words rang true as my body locked up in mid leap and hung in the air suspended above the water. When I struggled to move, my limbs refused to respond; my head whipped around, but I had no control of any other body part. My hair hung down in a greasy curtain over my face, so I shook it back, flinging the mess behind me to see the twisted man preventing my descent.

"Let me go, you monster," I hissed. This felt too similar. I'd made some progress, fought to make my life what I'd made it, and as soon as I made some progress, these animals were going to take it away again. Anger flared like a beacon to call the spirits from wherever they had disappeared to, and I felt the gift stir. I wanted to knock Derth down, fling him overboard to give myself time to escape. A pale semblance of the spirits surged forward and pushed against him. He dismissed them with a wave of his hand, and I felt weaker than before.

"Monster?" he replied, as if nothing had happened. "I suppose if I were in your place I might feel the same. But I don't think I would be stupid enough to think I could escape, either."

"What do you mean?" I demanded.

"I knew the instant my hold on you ceased," he chuckled. "That connection we have is deep. And you were days away from leaving us; now, I'll need to kill you since I can't control you." His humor faded and he shook his head, regretful. "I could have learned so much from you."

With a flick of his wrist, Derth brought me back to the deck at his feet in a painful crash. The dagger fell from my hand and spun away, a cry escaped my lips, and Derth chuckled again.

"I would have made this painless, but for your attempt to kill me," he sighed. His hand sought the place on his chest where hours ago a burn had eaten through his shirt and skin. "Don't worry," he said, seeing my eyes following his hand. "The burn is gone. But you were close."

Derth wrenched his hands, as if wringing out a wet cloth, and my insides twisted with them. Writhing in anguish, all I could do was scream. The sound rent the air, shattering the peaceful silence.

Shouting erupted from below, and Bryn appeared from the hatch, his face twisted in anger.

"What are you doing!" he raged. He grasped Derth's arm and yanked it down. My torment ceased as his arm descended; my body curled up in a futile attempt to protect myself from further torture. I groaned, still in a ball, unable to force my muscles to respond to my attempt to move. Aftershocks of pain made my head feel like it was full of water. I thought about the spirits, but couldn't find a way to call them.

"My control of her has failed, and it's time for her to die," Derth said. I peeked out from behind my arms, shaken again by the dead tone of Derth's voice. He looked lost in his intent to kill me in the most painful way imagined, and I began to pull myself, trembling, toward the longboat in a fit of desperation. My mind cleared a bit, and I called out to the spirits.

Please, help me move. It felt like soft hands pushed against my bare feet, letting me slide a bit farther than I could on my own. But as soon as I moved, they fled again, and I felt like they were being pulled away from me.

Bryn threw him to the side, forcing him to break his eye contact with me. "So kill her, but stop this. This is monstrous!"

With Derth distracted, I continued to drag myself away from the argument. In the back of my mind, I knew that one of them could see me at any moment, but it was all I could do to escape. The spirits wouldn't answer me, so I searched for the dagger.

"You do not dictate her fate to me, boy," Derth hissed. Light glinted off of the blade of the dagger, an arms-length ahead of me. "She is my responsibility, and I will dispose of her as I see fit!" His eager gaze narrowed on me, as if we were the only two people in existence. "There is more to learn before she dies."

"Your responsibility is crawling away," Roglin stated with cold malice. His boot thumped to a stop next to my outstretched hand as it brushed the cold blade. He kicked the dagger away. "You might want to see to that."

"Sir, I need to protest this treatment of the prisoner," Bryn insisted. I rolled onto my back, and our eyes locked for a brief moment. His face held fleeting sympathy that disappeared the moment he looked back at his uncle. "If the time has come to kill her, so be it, but he needs to end it, not play with her." He gestured to Derth, who stood still, staring at me.

"As much as I despise the sentimentality this springs from, I have to agree," he replied. "Derth.... Derth!" He shouted to gain the man's attention, which Derth reluctantly transferred from me to the captain.

Men streamed up and piled around the spectacle of the four of us, leering down at me with avid expressions as the captain decided my fate. I shrank away from him, all hope of escape extinguished. My mind turned to the spirits again. If I was going to die, maybe I could bring a few of these monsters with me.

"Kill her, Derth, and don't take your time with it. I would like to get some rest tonight."

Derth nodded, but when he turned his gaze back to me, I could see that he had no intention of ending it quickly. I took a deep breath, trying to feel the gift and reach out to the spirits.

Help me, I thought.

As the first wave of pain hit, I screamed and began to thrash about in an attempt to move away from the pain. When the pain intensified, I tried to throw myself backwards, only to land at the feet of one of the crew. Sharp kicks peppered my back, adding to the torment. One man kicked me hard enough to launch me back into the space I had just vacated.

"Help me!" I screeched, not knowing who I was calling out to anymore. My eyes locked onto Bryn's again. I reached a hand in his direction.

We come.

Spirits surged from my hand to encircle Bryn, called by my pain and my belief that I would die if they didn't answer. My body began to glow with an intensity that forced the spectators to squint. Derth and Bryn alone left their eyes open wide to the glare. A tendril of the light that surrounded me reached out to Bryn along a path of connected spirits, lancing through his middle. His back arched, and his head fell back.

For a moment I saw the pool again, the spirits reaching out to me. And then I saw spirits scattered all over the world as brilliant lines of light that connected it all.

The moment lasted for an eternity as I stared at his bent form but lasted only seconds to those around us. The tendril severed, and some of the light outlined Bryn for the briefest of moments before disappearing from both of us. The spirits around him touched his chest above his heart and vanished.

Another wave of pain wracked my body, and two screams echoed over the water. Men turned to Bryn where he crouched, in agony.

"Derth, I said to end it!" Roglin pushed through the men nearest Derth, shouting above our cries. "Derth!"

My limbs unfolded, unresponsive when I tried to move them, and I realized that the pain had ceased. Whatever the spirits did, it hadn't stopped Derth. As I lay there panting, wrung out and wishing that I could die before the agony began anew, I turned my head to see Bryn straightening. He looked to Derth, and then back at me as if wondering whether the man was punishing him for speaking out. The captain reached the hunched man and grabbed him roughly to gain his attention.

An argument broke out between the two of them, and the men became restless. One of them pulled a knife and moved to stab me. I kicked to the side, making contact with his wrist, so he was only able to slice a small line in my leg. Bryn cried out, more in anger than pain, and blood soaked through his pant leg in the exact place that blood flowed from my wound. My mind cycled through all the ways I was trained to protect myself, unable to make my muscles respond as they spasmed in the wake of Derth's attention.

"Enough!" Roglin roared. Derth stumbled back as Roglin shoved him. "This has gone on long enough! Back away from her," he commanded, pointing at another man that was moving to stab me. He let the blade drag across my arm, and I moaned as it joined the rest of my pain. Bryn looked down at his arm with a horrified expression, watching blood soak the sleeve of his shirt.

Roglin pulled his sword, the metal ringing as it slid out of its scabbard.

"If you won't follow orders, I'll turn to you when I'm done with her." He glared at Derth, challenging him to disobey such an overt threat.

Derth glared right back, but when Roglin took a step in his direction, he backed away and held his hands up in defeat. Roglin nodded and turned to the middle of the deck. The crew backed away, giving their captain more space to advance on my prone form.

Fury lit Roglin's eyes, and he crossed the short distance with a few angry strides. I stretched my arms to grasp for purchase, something to pull my body away, but he grasped the hair at the back of my head to stop me in my tracks. His knees popped when he crouched at my side and drew his sword to place it at my throat, cool against the heat of my desperation.

I reached up to grasp his wrist, and he yanked my head back and upward with savage force that forced me up to my feet as he stood, a reluctant cry escaping my throat. From the corner of my eye I saw Bryn's hand fly to the back of his head, and then he began to push through the men around him. My attention drew back to Roglin as he pressed the sharp point of the sword into my flesh. The stinging nick dribbled blood down my neck and to the hem of my ragged dress.

"You brought this on yourself," Roglin whispered.

The pain receded as his body lurched to the side after a blur of movement. A few grunts, and then sailors hauled Bryn away from his uncle as he thrashed and shouted.

"Stop!" he screamed. "Lila!"

Roglin wiped blood from the corner of his mouth, and knelt down again. Looking over his shoulder at Bryn, he placed the blade at my neck again, and increased the pressure with the sword; the stinging sensation changed to outright pain and my blood began to flow freely. In another moment, my throat would be severed completely.

Help, I pleaded, turning my eyes to Bryn and to the spirits that I could see surging past him to answer my call.

We come.

My body began to glow with brilliant light again, and I felt a bit of myself break through the pain and hopelessness of my situation, and Roglin paused as I lashed out at him. I wasn't this helpless creature. I had worked too hard to feel this way again. My ears popped with sudden, massive pressure, and a pulse of thunder slammed into Roglin's chest. He hurtled through the air, tumbling end over end before crashing down beyond the wall of his crew. Every man assembled turned to watch their captain's flight.

Bryn called out again, and I turned to see him pulling against the arms restraining him, blood pouring from a wound in his neck. Derth stepped between us, and knelt down with his face almost touching mine.

"You should have let him kill you," he said through a malicious grin. "Now, you'll feel the Ambience pulled from you as you die."

He touched my forehead as I grasped his wrist, letting my anger burn through me like the fire that ignited over his flesh. His grin widened into a full smile, and my vision blurred as he forced his way into my head. He rooted around, looking for the source of my glow, in that same inner space where I had found my way past his barrier. It felt like my head would explode, and as he went deeper, the pain followed until it spread throughout my body.

The pain intensified, and a small part of my mind wondered how my body was still intact. It felt like every muscle was being torn apart, every bit of me squeezed in a giant vice tightened to its maximum. When my muscles went slack, the pain remained, and I felt my life draining away. My body flopped with the force of Derth's malicious intent; my mind now detached from the body, I realized I must look like a fish flopping out of water to everyone around me.

My glow retreated, and I let go, releasing myself from the pain that still gripped my useless body. My vision began to fade to darkness, and I welcomed it.

As I felt myself drifting, my life all but gone, my glow pulsed once, as if in a last effort to push Derth away. As it did, it pushed the darkness away, bringing welcome relief to the pain. A shockwave of air followed, bringing everyone nearby to their knees. Derth fell over, and the pain stopped altogether. Still on the brink of darkness, I coaxed the glow like a burgeoning flame, and pictured the destruction of the ship that would at least take all these monsters with me into the arms of death.

Opening my hand, I stretched it up toward the sail on the mainmast. With my fingers curled into claws, I pulled my hand down, and the heavy canvas tore in lines to mimic me. The ship shuddered, creaking when I placed my hands palm down on the deck and pushed.

Creaks turned to snaps as the planks all around tore free and flew into the night sky. My screaming had ceased, but the screams of the crew replaced it.

Another burst of naked force radiated out from me, and the ship crumbled around my prone form. A series of deafening explosions followed, and the mainmast crashed into the rail feet from where I lay. The weight of the beam tore through the rail, pulling large pieces of the starboard side with it. Lines and sails tangled around fleeing men, pulling them to a watery grave.

Something heavy crashed to the deck nearby, and the portion holding me gave way. Air rushed around me as I fell with the rest of the men into the cold ocean water.

The small section of the deck I lay on remained, and my head cracked against it when I hit the water. Salt water poured into my nose and mouth as I plunged below the surface, burning my raw throat. My limbs flailed in a feeble attempt to orient myself in the churning ocean.

The makeshift raft surfaced the next moment, and I sputtered and coughed; I rolled onto my side to let the water pour out, numb to anything but the air pulling into my lungs through jagged breaths.

When I could breathe again, I looked around. Pieces of the shattered ship bobbed in the water surrounding me. The aft section teetered above me; the remaining mast still stood with lines draped down, pulling it first one way and then another as pieces of sail descended below the surface. Men screamed in the night as they bled and drowned with no one to help them. Above the cries of pain and fear I thought I heard someone call me by name, but another moment passed and the voice didn't come again.

I rolled onto the flat of my back, staring up at the stars and the moon, listening to men wailing around me, horrified and relieved. I lay still and let the water rock me into a trance, a faint glow still outlining my body to add to the glow of the moon and stars.

A loud groan issued from the aft portion of the ship, and it began to tip. The mast leaned out over the ocean where I floated, blocking out the moon and stars. A shout echoed from somewhere nearby, but over the sound of the water rushing to claim the rest of its prize, I couldn't hear the words.

Abandoning my raft in a last burst of desperate survival instinct, I rolled over into the freezing water and forced my weak arms and legs to propel me deeper and hopefully out of the path of the falling beams. The water pulled me toward the sinking mass, my furious struggle like that of a gnat against a swatting hand.

I tumbled over and over; up became down and then up again as I lost track of the surface. My lungs burned in need of air and my arms and legs screamed with the effort of moving myself in any direction.

The salt water burned my eyes as they cast about in search of something to show me the way to the surface. The bulk of the ship at last fell to the depths, and the water stopped churning. Seeing the ship falling below my feet, I now knew the way to the surface, and I swam as hard as I could. The moon at last became a dim light far above my head, and I fought even harder as the lack of air caused black spots to dance in front of my eyes.

Water rushed into my open mouth and nose, and my arms and legs stopped moving. I floated just beneath the surface, unable to pull myself up the remaining distance. Well past the last vestiges of strength I possessed, I fell back into darkness and the cold embrace of the sea.

CHAPTER ELEVEN

Oblivion loosened its hold on me in sporadic bursts; a man cursing my name, the rhythmic splash of oars breaking the surface of water, the creaking of a boat all came and went as I drifted below the surface of consciousness. My body bobbed in a familiar fashion and any time I neared the edge of consciousness, the sensation lulled me back into a peaceful slumber.

The sun shone red through my closed eyelids, dreaming of Hunter's warm hands grasping the back of my neck to pull me in close for a kiss. When his lips touched mine I was surprised to feel cool water sluice over my lips and into my mouth. My throat convulsed in protest, and I tried to wrench away from the unexpected contact as I recalled that I was drowning.

"Easy," a voice urged. "Calm down."

The water stopped, but I began to cough; it escalated until I could no longer catch my breath. My throat and lungs burned, and my eyes refused to open, lids stuck together with salt and sleep. I was wrenched up into a sitting position, and then the large hand pushed my head forward and down between my legs. It held me there even though I flailed, trying to escape the iron grip.

"Calm down!" it snapped, more angry than consoling now. "Breathe, damn you!"

Blood rushed to my head while my forehead scraped against the hard wood beneath me as all the water was expelled from my chest. The pounding of my heart slowed and the cough subsided after a few agonizing moments. Breaths came in ragged gasps, and I forced my eyes open. I pushed against the hand and it released me, allowing me to sit up and take a deep breath. The air burned in my lungs, but I relished the pain as I realized that I had survived drowning.

A longboat held me, bobbing in the choppy water under a sun at its peak. I blinked against the glare to clear tears.

"Are you all right?" the man asked. Turning, I saw Bryn taking a seat on the other bench of the longboat. His scowl belied the concerned words.

"I'm..." My voice came out in a croak that threatened to choke me again. I cleared my throat and tried again. "What happened?" I asked.

Bryn stared for an uncomfortable minute, and then shrugged with a huff.

"Not much," he stated with a nonchalant air that was again betrayed by the hostile set of his mouth. "You only killed the crew and blew apart the ship."

Blood rushed to my cheeks as I bristled at his obvious anger. "I killed men holding me captive, trying to murder me," I retorted, coughing. "And escaped a bunch of monsters that watched while I was being tortured to death."

His finger jabbed at me accusingly and I hesitated. "And what did you do to me?"

Confusion furrowed my brow. "You?"

"You were lying there, and I tried to get Derth to end it, and then there was so much pain...." He shook his head as if to expel the memory. "I felt it, whatever he was doing to you. I *felt* it."

His desperate, angry gaze bored into me and I could only shake my head in reply, baffled. The boat continued to sway and the sun continued to blaze, baking my skin. Sweat rolled into my eyes so I swiped it away with a hasty gesture, grasping any excuse to look away from his penetrating azure eyes.

"What did you do to me?" he whispered.

"I don't know," I croaked.

Bryn sighed in frustration and fell silent. While he stewed, I took stock of my injuries. The scars on my wrists had faded in the first weeks; Derth hadn't seen fit to heal those wounds completely. A bandage had been wrapped around my leg to cover the gash; a piece of sail repurposed to stop the bleeding. The puncture on my arm was open to the air, but the bleeding had stopped and it looked clean. The gift that Derth had used on me in those final moments left no further marks on my body. Stretching my arms, legs, and back, I found that aside from a few sore muscles, I felt no lingering effects, either.

"I don't think what he did to us is lasting," Bryn grumbled behind me as if reading my mind.

"Good." In every direction the interminable sea stretched out to the horizon. With the sun at its peak, I had no way of knowing the direction Bryn was taking us. I also had no way of knowing what he was doing here, helping me. With a suspicious glare, I picked myself out of the hull and turned to face Bryn. "Why did you save me?"

"I had no choice in the matter," he replied. "You should know."

"Whatever happened to us, it was Derth's doing," I snapped, incensed anew. "I know nothing about it."

"This didn't happen until you started screaming for help!" he shouted.

"And I didn't do anything *but* scream for help!" My shout tore at my swollen throat. "There was nothing else I *could* do, surrounded by you and your vile friends!"

"You certainly seemed capable of killing them when it suited you," he said, his shout echoing across the open water. "You have the gift!"

"I was only just learning to control it!" I screamed. This infuriating man had the nerve to look skeptical. "But after what Derth did to me, it seems like I've lost that, too! And you seem to have forgotten all the men that you and your crew murdered when your uncle attacked my ship. Stop acting like there's no blood on your hands!"

We fumed in silence, our chests heaving with the stress of the argument. Tears pricked the corners of my eyes, so I turned my head away and stared at the endless sea.

Bryn sighed again. "I'm sorry," he mumbled.

"What?" I turned back to see him staring into his lap as he wrung his hands.

"I'm sorry," he repeated. When he looked up, I could see he was sincere, though still furious. "All of those men are dead, and you've been through hell." He paused, and when he continued, he seemed reluctant. "Those people weren't my friends, but seeing them die in all that destruction...." He trailed off and shook his head, and his fingers gripped his leg just above a bloody patch on his pants.

"You have a wound there, too?" I asked, still angry but starting to recall some of the details from the events before the ship exploded. He nodded, and some of the anger blazed back into his eyes. "And on your arm? If I'm hurt, you get hurt?"

"It seems that way," he said.

"When I was drowning?"

"I couldn't breathe, and I had no idea why until I saw you in the water."

"You saw me in all of that?" My hand waved out, gesturing to indicate the destruction we had left behind.

"You were glowing," he stated. "I was thrown overboard with the first blow, and then the ship came apart. When parts started to rain down all around me, I dove beneath the surface to avoid it. I saw you, floating on a piece of the ship right before the rest of it sank. When you didn't come up, and I felt like I couldn't catch my breath, I started to swim. The light went out right before you surfaced, and I was able to grab you and pull you out. This beauty," he patted the longboat bench, "wasn't far away."

"Thank you," I said, my voice a reluctant grumble. "You saved my life."

"Well, you can repay me by helping me row," Bryn replied. He slid over and gestured to the seat next to him. "I have no idea where land is."

In the time that we had been shouting at one another, the sun had begun its descent to the west. I lifted my arm and pointed in its direction.

"Follow the sun for now, and when it's down I can show you a cluster of stars that shows where North lies, since you don't seem to know. And I can do more than help row," I climbed over the bench to the stern. Pulling on a line, I freed the small mast and let the end fall to the hull with a thump. Behind the round beam, a sail sat neatly folded. An empty waterskin and a small stash of dry rations were tucked next to it.

"That might help," Bryn agreed with a terse nod.

After showing him how to place the mast and helping to attach the sail, our longboat nearly flew along the surface of the choppy water. We took turns manning the rudder until night fell. With the sail furled, we settled down into the hull to rest. Though exhausted, my mind reeled with thoughts of the past and the loss of my family.

Images of their faces grieved me and wrenched my heart and gut with pain; with every breath, the pain stabbed deeper and twisted. With no time to grieve and no connection to myself for months, everything flooded in at once, like a giant wave overtaking a ship at sea.

My eyes burned with tears I fought not to shed. Bryn's breathing evened out when he finally fell asleep, and I didn't want to wake him so that he could witness my breakdown.

Along with my family, I grieved for the death of my former self, the life I had finally begun to build, and the scar it left on me now. The complete loss of control of the path my life was taking made my skin crawl; in years past, I strove for control over anything that I could, in defiance of my lost past. The only control I had now was over my tears.

The stars blinked overhead and reflected up at me from the black surface of the sea. So many years had passed where they provided comfort as I considered how vast the world must be beyond what I could see. Looking up at the endless sky now only emphasized how alone I had become. When I turned my gaze to Bryn's sleeping form, the loneliness became punctuated by anger that out of all the people that could have survived, the man that had helped to keep me in line was the one that I was inexplicably tethered to.

My mind wandered to the men I killed, whether in defense of myself or not. Though I told myself that most of them had likely killed and brought many people to ruin over the years, their lives were over because of my actions. They had cheered and helped to torture me, but the terror they wore in their final moments haunted me as much as the faces of the men I loved.

Guilt weighed as heavily on me as the chains I had worn.

The night continued, unaware of my personal plight. The sky began to brighten from black to purple, and then to pink and lavender with the imminent sunrise. While turmoil still raged inside, my tears were long since dry when Bryn stirred; I hoped my face showed my exhaustion and little else. He blinked against the first rays of sunlight that peeked over the horizon and glinted against the gold in his tousled hair.

He considered me once he had rubbed the sleep from his eyes. "Did you get any sleep?"

Sighing, I replied, "I feel like I've been asleep for a long time. I want to spend some time awake."

"All right," he said. "I can understand that."

"Thanks," I replied, an edge to my voice.

Bryn ignored my tone and lifted himself from the hull with a grunt before starting to pull at the lines on the sail. When it became clear that he had no idea how to untie the knot, I sighed and lugged myself out of the hull.

I slapped his hands aside with more force than intended and untangled his mess. In minutes, the sail was unfurled and secured, and picked up the small breeze to propel us toward where I hoped land lay. I glanced his way as I moved to take my seat, unable to wipe the glare from my face.

"What have I done now?" he muttered.

"Nothing," I sighed, angry with him and myself. I plopped down next to the tiller and pulled it to steer us away from the sunrise. Tense silence descended between us again, and in my foul mood, I had no desire to break it.

As the boat rose over the waves and crashed into valleys between, the sun continued to ascend and the wind increased. The waves heightened, creating larger and larger swells that our tiny boat traversed with great effort. The sails pulled taut against the small mast, and the wind picked my matted hair from my neck. For the first time in a long time, I relished the feeling. The wind also blew away some of my exhaustion and grief, and I sighed as I let my shoulders relax. Bryn sat in the prow, facing away from me and looking out to the sea ahead. Nothing but the distant horizon was visible, especially in the glare of the sun.

The heat began to rise, exposed as we were in the middle of the ocean with no shelter to keep the sun's rays off of us. Sweat beaded my brow and cooled on the back of my neck, blown away by the breeze. I wiped again and again at the rivulets that tickled their way from my head down the front and back of my battered dress.

Bryn fared no better, and plucked at the front of his shirt often to give himself some relief until the sun set.

Another night passed with me at the tiller, taking full advantage of the continued wind to move at a swift pace. While Bryn slumbered, the moon and stars kept me company.

Land became visible on the horizon with the dawn of the next day a short time after Bryn awoke. He leaned forward, looking eager to get his feet on the earth again while I wondered in silence what would become of me.

CHAPTER TWELVE

The hull scraped against the loose rocks in the shallows, the boards groaning in protest, as the sun reached its zenith the next day. We scrambled out into the cold water, the soaked hem of my ruined dress dragging against my legs and onto the rocky beach in a desperate bid for land and the possibility of food and fresh water. Both had run out the day before when Bryn had given me the last of it. I had tried to protest, but he insisted I needed it more than he did. Now, my lips were dry and cracked from the sun and wind.

Rocks clacked against one another, shifting beneath my feet, and I struggled to keep my balance. A fine tremor ran through my entire body from the cold water and the wind that bit through my soaked skirt.

Bryn heaved a sigh of relief as he gained the shore and the finer gravel above the waterline. I focused on my feet until I passed the treacherous footing and could spare a glance at our surroundings.

Smooth pebbles formed the bulk of the beach, with speckled black and white stones hiding the occasional translucent pink poking through the masses of plain neighbors. Hulking driftwood trunks, white in the morning sun, rested in varying distances from the water. Kelp clung to some of these and dwelled in waterlogged clumps closer to the sea. Bleached driftwood gave way to fallen trees as the land rose in a steep ascent from the gravel of the beach to moss and tall grass interspersed with brush and ferns growing in the shadow of towering trees.

From the boat, we had spied a harbor in the distance with several ships at anchor. With the tide against us, this remote part of the coastline was the closest we could come to civilization. Picturing the distance to the town in my mind, I blew out a frustrated breath. There was no way to figure out where we were unless we moved. My stomach rumbled in agreement.

Bryn stood with one hand on his hip, the other scratching at the light growth of stubble along his chin, surveying the forest.

"We should get there by sundown if we hurry," Bryn informed me. He lifted his arm and pointed down the beach to the northwest. Glancing over his shoulder, he quirked an eyebrow at me. "Think you're up to it?"

I nodded and sighed after he turned, and wrung out the hem of my skirt while he walked away. My toes sank between the pebbles as I followed in Bryn's wake. He angled toward the trees and away from the shifting stones closer to the water. The ground was littered with branches and I hissed as a thorn stabbed into the bottom of my foot. Bryn lifted his foot at the same time, as if he had stepped on a thorn, too.

After pulling the thorn out, I stayed on the edge of the beach, trailing behind Bryn to his right. He set a pace that had me panting with the effort within an hour. My legs burned and my feet cramped from maintaining my balance. Every so often I saw Bryn shake one of his legs, like I was doing to ease my cramped muscles. At this far edge of the trees, only occasional shade broke the monotonous heat of the progressing day. The ocean taunted me; it lapped at the shore nearby with the promise of water that could only further my misery.

When I could stand no more, I plopped down onto a round of driftwood below an overhanging bough and called to Bryn.

"I need a break!"

He turned and trudged back to me. He looked as exhausted as I felt and plopped down behind me on the round and slumped back. I straightened and scooted from the touch of his back against mine, revolted by the contact. He failed to notice, and sighed.

"Sorry, I didn't think about how hard this exercise is for you. We need to find some water," he stated as he fumbled with the empty waterskin tied to his belt. With a determined huff, he slapped his hands on his thighs and stood. "I'll be back soon."

I felt wrung out and shaky, too exhausted to respond. Closing my eyes, I let the breeze cool my heated skin. The sweat droplets evaporated, and the branches above lent a helpful hand to block the sun's rays.

I allowed myself to relax a small degree while I waited for Bryn to return. I dug my thumbs into my aching feet and massaged my calves to work out some of the tension.

It seemed only minutes had passed when I heard sticks breaking with the weight of a booted foot upon them. Out of the darkness Bryn emerged, holding up a full waterskin. Water dripped from his hand as he held it aloft like some grand trophy. He smiled with triumph as my mouth dropped open in delight in spite of myself.

Rising from my perch, I rushed to meet him, kicking stones up in my wake. As his feet crunched at the edge of the beach, I snatched the skin from his hand and poured a mouthful of the crisp, sweet water into my mouth. Swallowing, I poured more down my throat before Bryn snatched the skin away again.

"Slow down!" he scolded. "You'll make yourself sick and use all the water." I wiped a hand across my chin to dry it. Though I wanted to argue, his words rang with truth. The concept had been taught to me at a young age; every sailor learned how to survive at sea with no water in case of shipwreck.

"Thank you," I replied with a nod. "For finding the water."

"Where there are this many plants, some kind of water source exists. Thank the Elders it wasn't far away, or I might not have returned."

"You believe in the six Elders?" I asked. At his nod, I raised my eyebrows in wonder. "I wouldn't have guessed that."

"A man can't believe in something greater than himself?"

"A man, yes. A slaver...?" I let my words trail off. His eyes narrowed at me, and his anger flared.

"I'm no slaver." He exuded righteous indignation at my assumption, which silenced any reply I might have made. "I told you those people weren't my friends. My reasons for agreeing to sign on with them are my own, but I assure you it was not because I sought that profession."

He shook his head and turned from me. The angry set to his shoulders slumped and regret crept into his voice, though it still held its edge. My indignation flared again at his tone; what right did he have to be angry with my assumption?

"In the months I spent on that ship with my uncle I saw people treated so shamefully that it shocked me, more than anything I've seen in this world. And after what they did to you and your people...." He glanced over his shoulder at me, light spilling through a break in the trees to illuminate the gravity in his eyes.

"There is nothing I wouldn't give to rewrite my own history, so that I wouldn't have to live through that. If I could go back and stop them..." He shook his head. "...but it's done, and I can't change it. Know that I am not my uncle."

I nodded, still suspicious. Most of the people I trusted were dead because of the people he sailed with, but I needed Bryn's help and I wanted to trust him. He tied the waterskin to his belt and nodded his head along the path toward the town. I followed in silence, considering what I thought I knew about this man in front of me.

I studied him as he moved through the edge of the forest. He moved like a cat, slinking between obstacles whenever he could avoid them. His feet found quieter places to step that avoided rustling the leaves and pine needles underfoot that I failed to emulate.

Tired of the silence, I asked, "How did you come to be on the ship, if you aren't a slave trader?" He spared a glance over his shoulder that looked equal parts disdain and surprise.

"Does it really matter?" he grumbled.

"I want to believe you, since it seems like we're stuck with each other for a while."

Bryn grunted in reply and we passed a long part of our trek in silence, with only the constant crunch of stones beneath us to break the monotony. While our tension faded with the exertion, I could tell it sat just below the surface for each of us. Bound by something neither of us could understand, our only choice seemed to stay together.

Night fell, and lights became visible in the distance. Scrapes and gouges covered my feet, and I winced with every step, but my pace increased seeing our destination so close.

The forest gave way to packed earth surrounding a wooden palisade. The trunks of many trees formed the wall, torchlight making the sharpened stakes at the top seem to waver in the darkness. Men marched behind with a head above the points to stare down at passersby and those looking to enter. We circled around to the southwest where a gate stood open despite the late hour. A small group wandered down the dirt road toward the town, and we came out of the trees behind them to trail in their wake.

A few raised eyebrows turned our way, but little comment was made about our sudden presence. They gossiped about people they knew, spoke of hardships they endured, and spoke of the town we now entered.

"Coveton," I murmured to Bryn.

"At least we know where we are now," he replied.

The doors of the gate were flung wide to allow latecomers entry into town; large planks of thick oak hung just above the ground. Huge metal brackets lined the inside of the doors to hold the bar leaning against the palisade on the other side.

Guards stood ready, surveying our group as we strolled inside. Bows hung from their shoulders, and quivers from their backs. None of the bows were to hand, but the threat was clear from the expressions on their faces.

The walls of the palisade disappeared into the gloom of night to either side, with only the torches to mark the outline of the walls. Streets of packed earth ran inward; the street leading from the gate to the center of town stood widest of the others, with buildings lining it into the distance and more torches to light the way. Smaller roads led along the outer wall and into sections with smaller buildings than those on the main thoroughfare.

Only a few people aside from the group we followed were on the street after dark. These disappeared down alleyways and made their way silently to their homes.

The street widened as we approached the center of town. Torchlight illuminated a square at the foot of a cluster of buildings two and three stories high with smaller alleyways separating them. A crowd stood and laughed in front of the door to the largest building, with a sign swinging above the door depicting a mug and a bed. Raucous laughter poured out of the open doorway along with a copious amount of light and the smell of smoke and ale.

The men eyed me as I sidled past them through the door. When they spotted Bryn's glare, they turned and laughed, paying me no further mind.

Inside, the merriment increased. All around, men gathered in large numbers at tables filled with mugs of half-drunk ale and plates of food. Women in knee-length skirts, tight bodices and shirts that covered most of their bosoms flitted from table to table, dancing away from grasping hands with smiles and good-natured admonishments.

More than one of these women's eyes widened at the sight of me in my ruined gown but didn't halt their brisk pace in serving their customers. Candelabras illuminated the heads of deer and a bear on the walls, along with large fish mounted on plaques with brass squares beneath. I stood just inside the door, overwhelmed by all the noise and crush of people, until Bryn grasped my hand and tugged me forward, toward the bar.

A burly man with close-cropped black hair and bushy black and gray mustache stood with his arms crossed as he argued with a man that leaned heavily on the bar. His scowl looked like it was etched on, with wrinkles borne of long use.

With a slight nod, the bartender signaled to a man that appeared out of the corner of the room to escort the leaner outside. When Bryn and I approached, his scowl deepened, exaggerating the wrinkles around his mouth.

"We'd like a room," Bryn informed him, his voice authoritative over the din.

"Is that so?" the bartender asked. His eyes roamed my form, taking in my bedraggled state, inciting embarrassment and anxiety in the pit of my stomach before turning back to Bryn. "Can't stay for free." I clutched at a large rent in the skirt where the blade had cut my thigh to close it.

"I didn't think we would," Bryn replied with a scowl of his own. Reaching into a pocket, he pulled out a silver Aelios and slapped it onto the bar's clean surface. I hadn't realized he had any money with him. "That enough?" he demanded.

"Not enough for a week, but you could stay four nights."

"With food?" Bryn asked, his hand still covering the coin.

The bartender considered for a moment, glancing at me before he answered. "Two nights, plus food," he replied.

Bryn lifted his hand to reveal the coin, which the bartender promptly covered with his own. It scraped against the wood of the bar as he slid it toward himself and placed it in his pocket. A screeching whistle erupted unannounced from his lips, startling me with the sudden explosion of sound that carried far above the voices of the men in the room. After an apologetic pursing of his lips to me, he waved his arm above his head to summon one of the barmaids.

"Yeah?" she shouted. She stood a head below me, with thick blond hair piled atop her head.

"Cass here will show you to your room," he told us. Looking back to the woman he said, "Top of the stairs on the right."

Cass nodded and waved at us to follow. Despite her size, she cleared a path through the men around the bar with a shove here and a smile there that led from the main tavern to a hall in the back.

The cacophony became muffled as we walked away from the tavern, giving my ears a needed rest. The walls were plain wood and unadorned, lit with sconces that held white candles. Flames flickered in the breeze made by the brisk pace Cass set for us. At the end of the hall, a narrow staircase rose to the next level of the building. Without a word, she started to climb the stairs, expecting us to follow.

A window across from the top of the stairs let in the warm breeze from outside, causing the thick curtain to wave as we passed. After the stale smell of ale and the crush of sweaty men below, the ocean breeze smelled wonderful.

"Here we are," Cass lilted with a smile, opening the door for us. "Would you like your meal here?"

"Yes, please," I replied, smiling at the prospect of a hot meal.

She nodded, and pulled the door shut in her wake. The noise of the tavern below became a muted hum in the closed sanctuary of the room. I let out a deep sigh, glad that I could get some rest at last, when Bryn cleared his throat behind me.

"We need to get a few things straight," he informed me as I turned to face him. He looked determined and unsure all at once.

"We do," I agreed. Moving to a chair in the corner of the room, I sank down onto the hard wood and sat with my back straight, bracing myself for another argument. I rested my hands in my lap and ran the crusted fabric of my gown between my fingers.

Bryn pulled a wooden stool away from the wall next to the chair I sat perched on, and plunked it down a few feet from me. He sat facing me, his hands braced on his thighs, his eyes locked on mine.

"First, I want to know if you can undo whatever you did to me."

I blinked and sighed and kept my eyes on his. "No," I stated in a brisk tone, irritated to have to repeat myself. "That would require knowing what I did in the first place, and I can assure you I do not."

He sighed and nodded, his disappointment and reluctance to accept my words clear on his face. "Then we need to figure out our next move."

"I don't know that it needs to be *our* next move, Bryn." His brow furrowed, and he opened his mouth to protest. I held my hand up, and his mouth closed. "You saved my life, and I thank you for that, but we don't know one another, and there is no reason for us to stay together." It felt satisfying to say, to hope there might be an end to our brief and painful acquaintance.

Bryn sat in silence, staring at me as if considering his words carefully before he spoke. "And if something happens to you, and there's no one to save your life next time, I die as well. Am I supposed to live my life never knowing if I could die the next moment because you did something reckless?"

I fought to control my rising ire. "We don't know that this will last, or that it will be a problem if we're apart."

"And we don't know that it won't," Bryn growled. "I'm not willing to risk my life because you refuse to trust me."

"Can you fault me for not trusting you?" I asked, the edge in my voice mimicking his as I lost the hold on my temper. "When I met you, I was a slave to your uncle and that monster, Derth. You said that you wanted no part of that life, but you still chose it. That either makes you a liar," Bryn's back straightened as I spoke, and his frustration turned to anger. "Or you're not squeamish about where you get your money, even if your actions to earn it are against your moral standards. Honestly, there's not much of a difference in my mind."

Before Bryn could respond, a sharp rap at our door turned both of our heads. Cass peeked inside before we beckoned her to enter, balancing a tray with plates piled high with food.

She smiled but kept her eyes on her burden as she placed the tray on the small side table near the door.

"Some hot lamb and fresh baked bread, and cooked vegetables from our garden out back. I hope you like it...." She trailed off when she looked up and noticed the tension between Bryn and me. Her eyes shifted back and forth between the two of us for a long and awkward moment.

I stood and approached her, shaking her hand in gratitude for the food. "It smells delicious," I assured her, my stomach grumbling.

She chuckled at the noise, and the tension broke. Smiling up at me, she nodded and made for the door. Just before I closed it, she popped her head back in and beckoned for me to lean closer, murmuring so as not to be heard by Bryn.

"Hoping I'm not being presumptuous, ma'am, but there is a fine seamstress in town, about a block over. Tell her I sent you, and she'll make you a fine gown."

My eyes left her face and looked down at the dress, barely more than rags hanging off of my bony frame. I smiled and nodded, whispering my thanks for the information.

The door clicked closed and the stool creaked beneath Bryn's weight when he stood. His boots thumped across the wooden floor until he stood next to me, eyeing the food heaped on the tin plates. When he noticed me looking, he gave me a brief and begrudging smile and gestured for me to gather my food first.

Surprised by the chivalrous behavior after our conversation moments before, I paused only long enough for my stomach to growl again. Picking up the plate, I carried it back to the chair and placed it in my lap. The heat from the slab of meat warmed my legs through the thin metal. The smell of rosemary and baked bread made my mouth water. Tearing a chunk of bread from the heel on my plate, I swirled it around the sauce trailing from the meat and placed it in my mouth.

After so long without food, it was the best meal I had ever tasted. In what seemed a matter of moments, my plate was clean. I wiped a finger through the remaining sauce and sucked on the tip to savor the last of my meal.

When the plate touched my lap again, I looked up to see Bryn watching me, his plate on the floor next to him. His arms were crossed over his chest and it seemed obvious he was waiting for me to finish so he could continue our argument. I sighed, weary and agitated, and closed my eyes, attempting to gather my strength for the battle ahead.

"I don't think it's a good idea for us to part ways," he stated simply. Most of the heat had dissipated, and his tone rang with forced civility. Some of the tension in my shoulders eased when I realized that he wasn't shouting at me. "There's too much we don't know."

"Where are we going to find answers?" I asked. Though still irritated, I attempted to force my tone into a semblance of civility.

Bryn's fingers raked his hair back from his forehead; it flopped back into disordered pieces, leaving portions of his forehead exposed. "I don't know, but it still seems safer to stick together for now."

"To what end? The chosen and their gift are a myth," I insisted. "I doubt there's anyone in the world that could help us. Are we supposed to spend the rest of our days wandering around Trylia hoping for someone to show up with the information we need?"

Bryn stared at me, frustration evident on his face. His eyes slid closed, and he heaved a long-suffering sigh.

"You've told me that you don't trust me or my gift. I'm telling you that I don't trust your motives." Bryn's eyes popped open, their blue depths issuing a look of warning for my line of argument. "We have no reason to believe that a solution exists to our problem, and no way to find it if it does. I'm sure you have people to go home to, so why not end whatever this is and go our separate ways?"

"Everything you've said makes sense," he admitted. "But I'm having a hard time making sense of our situation. In all the time I sailed with him, I wondered whether Derth was some sort of Elders-cursed monster. But the gift exists," he stated, "all of those men are dead because of it, and my life is tied to yours."

"I've had my whole life to get used to it, and I still haven't," I agreed.

"Where will you go?" he asked.

I opened my mouth to answer, to tell him that I have people in King's Port that I would find, but thought better of it and shut my mouth. If I couldn't trust this man with my life, why should I trust that he wouldn't do something to the people I love?

"I know some people that might be able to help me," I stated.

We sat facing one another in silence as we considered the decision before us. The choice was clear to me; to put my life in his hands seemed the height of folly. Though he appeared passionate and sincere about his belief that his uncle and his people were reprehensible, I had no way to know for sure.

After a few moments, Bryn sighed and stood with sudden resignation. "Fine, we'll part ways." He took three long strides to the door, the floorboards reverberating under his heavy footfalls. Grasping the doorknob in his hand, he turned his head to peer over his shoulder at me. "I'm going down for a drink, and I'll find out where we can get supplies in the morning. Just keep in mind that my life is in your hands." He yanked the door open with a screech of the hinges. "Try not to get yourself killed."

The door thumped shut behind him, and his retreating footsteps fell just as heavily as he stomped away from the room.

Staring at the door, I felt confused at his sudden acquiescence to my wishes. I shook my head in frustration and sighed. Now alone in the room, I felt uncomfortable. This separation was exactly what I had argued for, but now that I had it, it disturbed me.

My solitude reminded me too much of the time spent in my cell, alone without even the comfort of my thoughts and feelings. Tears brimmed in my eyes as I fought against despair that threatened to overwhelm me. Too many people were gone. Why was I still here? To dispel the creeping disquiet, I stood and began to examine the room around me.

My fingers ran along the rough blue and green quilt on the end of the bed and pushed at the lumpy straw mattress. With nothing else to do, I sat on the edge of the bed. It felt surprisingly comfortable, and I swung my legs up, sliding them under the sheet. As soon as my limbs stretched out, my exhaustion began to overtake me. Scooting my feet toward the end of the bed, I was able to lie down at full length with my head on the soft pillow. My eyelids became heavy, and my mind began to drift. I spared only a passing thought to where Bryn would spend the night before sleep took me.

CHAPTER THIRTEEN

Struggling from the depths of dark dreams of loss and terror, a sudden slam woke me. My eyes flew open and I sat upright, searching for the source of the noise, tensing for an attack.

Bryn stood near the door with a bundle in his arms; his eyes wide, frozen mid-stride. "Are you all right?" he asked, wary.

Blinking to clear my bleary eyes, I nodded. I felt disoriented after my rude awakening, and not as rested as I should have been. "You startled me," I yawned, waving a hand at the door.

"I'm sorry about that," he replied. He set the bundle on the table next to our dirty plates from the night before. "The door got away from me."

"Have you been gone all night?"

Bryn shrugged. "No, but you were dead to the world. It's near midday." When I only blinked in response, he gestured to the table with the cloth-wrapped lump atop it. "I bought some supplies and some clothes for you. I hope they fit, but they'll certainly be better than what you have on."

"I have no doubt," I yawned again. A dingy lock of hair fell into my face. Reaching up to run my fingers through it, I became entangled in the gnarled mass and yanked them out. My eyes watered as a group of hairs tore free of my scalp. "Is there a comb, by any chance?"

Bryn smiled at my struggle and obvious distress with my head. It lit his face, erasing the frustration and exhaustion of the past few days we had spent together. A smile came unbidden to my own face at seeing his expression and then my cheeks reddened, the flush warming my skin as it crept down my neck.

"I thought that might come up," he assured me. With deft movements, he untied the string around the cloth and extricated the comb from the pile of clothing beneath as I plopped my feet onto the floor and stood with the blanket clutched to my chest. He handed it to me, still smiling, and crossed the room to sit in the chair.

The war against the mass of knotted hair raged for a time that seemed like hours as I tugged and teased my thick hair into submission. Bryn busied himself by dividing up various foodstuffs into small canvas sacks. When he finished and I still stood nearby, tugging at the latest section of my wild mane, he departed with a word about a plate from below. Grimacing and grunting against the pain, I refused to give in, and a few minutes more granted me success.

I let out a triumphant breath and ran the comb through my ordered locks with ease to remove some of the grime.

Moving to the table, I found a plain gray linen dress with matching bodice in much better condition than the one currently sticking to my skin. The fabric felt soft as I rubbed it between my fingertips, and I pulled my reeking garment off over my head with haste.

Mindful that Bryn would return any moment, I found a basin with water behind the sacks and used a rag draped over the side to wash some of the dirt and salt from my skin. The water now filthy, I set the rag down and pulled the gray dress over my head. With the recent washing, the dress felt like satin as it slid down the length of me to pool on the ground.

The cuffs of the sleeves stopped short of my wrists and the neckline drooped lower than I would have liked. The waistline fell loose around my hips, but it was a vast improvement over the pile of fabric on the floor. The bodice cinched it closer to my skin so that it wouldn't fall. I pulled the string out from beneath the package and repurposed it to hold back my soiled hair.

Soft leather shoes were on the table as well, so I sat on the chair and slid them onto my battered feet. They cramped my toes but they would protect me, so I couldn't complain. I stood and paced back and forth across the room, testing the shoes while I waited for Bryn to bring food.

He appeared minutes later with a tray holding fruits and lamb from the night before, and another loaf of bread. We devoured the food in silence and divided the remains of the loaf into portions that we could take with us.

A sturdy canvas bag with shoulder straps bulged beneath the pile of clothes. When I examined the contents, I found a blanket covering a large, filled waterskin and a lot of food. A small leather purse also held a few silver and copper coins.

"It's not much, but it should see you to wherever you're going," Bryn explained with a shrug.

"Thank you," I replied, genuinely thankful for the thought he had given to my travel.

He shrugged again. "It's not only your life you're keeping safe now."

With everything gathered and my new pack's reassuring weight on my shoulder, we left the small room and descended the stairs to the main room of the inn. I heard raised voices as we reached the end of the hall that led to the tavern. Bryn slowed in front of me and held a hand out behind to stop me in my tracks.

"Didn't think you'd come back here, Harry," a voice grumbled. I recognized it as the voice of the bartender, and he sounded less pleased than he had when addressing us the night before. "Not after what you did to me. There are other inns in town."

"There are," another man growled. Anxiety blossomed in the pit of my stomach. The voice was familiar, and my mind raced to place him. "But none are run by a man that used to serve with me, Stephen."

"You look like you've been to the land of the dead and back," Stephen replied.

"We have," the gravelly voice replied. "And we need a bed and a meal. Also looking for someone; perhaps you've seen them."

"I see a lot of people," Stephen replied. "Anyone in particular?"

"A woman with red hair."

I started, realizing who the other man in the tavern could be. Bryn's uncle stood around the corner from where we waited in shadows, and he was looking for me.

"Try the whorehouse," Stephen scoffed. "Out on the harbor."

A loud retort of a large hand slamming against the bar exploded in the room.

"I'm not looking for a whore!" Roglin bellowed. "I'm looking for the bitch that sank my ship and almost killed me!"

"One woman did all of that?" Stephen whistled. "Must be some woman."

"I saw someone like that," a woman's voice interrupted. The voice belonged to Cass, and I groaned inwardly. Bryn began to shift backward, pushing me along behind him to move away from his uncle. "She's upstairs, with a man."

"You see, Stephen?" Roglin's tone lightened, with a heavy overtone of mocking menace. "This young lady has a head on her shoulders. And she's more likely to keep it than you are, you worthless whoreson. She's upstairs now?" he asked, his voice sweet and foul, like rotten fruit.

"Yes sir," Cass murmured. "That way."

Bryn turned and shoved me back along the hall, in the direction of the stairs. I stumbled, and the voices fell silent as I regained my footing and began to move.

A few murmured words echoed down the hall as we turned the corner and Bryn sprinted silently to a door in the back wall I hadn't known was there. The bolt slid free with a squeal. He wrenched it open, shoving me out in front of him. As soon as he shut the door behind him, he turned and grasped my arm, urging me to run.

I needed no help and sprinted away from our pursuers into a wide clearing behind the inn, with nowhere to hide. An alley stood between two buildings nearby, but we were exposed in the meantime. When I checked behind, the door was still closed, and I saw a curtain flutter by a window on the second floor, just outside the room we had stayed in.

My steps faltered for a moment when a face appeared, haggard, and covered in healing cuts and bruises. Roglin stopped and turned to face the window as a wide, evil smile broke out on his face. He shouted something over his shoulder and disappeared. I turned away and ran faster.

"Bryn," I yelled, "Roglin saw me!"

"Keep running!" he shouted over his shoulder.

A few heartbeats, and then I heard something slam in the direction of the inn, followed by several shouts. Bryn looked behind us, skidded to a stop and reached for as I heard a whistling sound nearing me. His hand closed around mine and *pulled* me forward, just as an arrow thunked into the ground where my leg had been a moment before.

I stumbled, and as I picked myself up, Bryn's hands grasping my arms to get me on my feet, I saw Derth emerge from the open door of the inn. In front of him were several people pulling arrows from quivers slung on their backs, starting to nock them on longbows.

"Lila, come *on*!" Bryn insisted, heaving me the rest of the way to my feet. He kept hold of my hand, but I didn't need the help to keep up with him. My fear was enough to lend me speed.

The alley swallowed us as another arrow clattered off the stone wall of the small house next to us. A few turns, and the gate came into view. We pushed harder, moved a bit faster, as voices echoed behind us, raised in pursuit.

"They went this way!" a pursuer shouted.

We made it to the edge of town, and out through the western gate. Bryn led us along the road for a few steps, and I looked over my shoulder to see whether we were being followed. All I saw was a confused man pushing his cart toward the town, watching as Bryn ducked off the road and into the trees. I didn't hesitate to follow him.

CHAPTER FOURTEEN

By the fourth day away from Coveton, our nerves were raw and our tempers to the point of breaking. Every word spoken held a razor's edge, no matter how trivial the issue. Fear shadowed our every action and thought, adding to the tension. When my foot snapped a branch, I imagined pursuing footsteps. Every branch that snagged my dress or hair felt like a hand trying to drag me back to Roglin.

When we slept for the first time since Coveton the night before, nightmares plagued me, keeping me from the rest I desperately needed. I felt Derth's foul touch, like he was scratching at my mind. He tried to smother me with that curtain again. The world grayed at the edges, but I always fought free and woke with a start.

I fought the urge to walk off into the forest, leaving Bryn behind to make my way south alone. Bryn chose a path that led north, cutting west for a few hours every day to throw them off our trail. We had climbed steadily for several days up the gentle slope of the land leading away from the coastline. Through breaks in the trees, I spied valleys ahead where the evergreens stretched toward the horizon like a sea of green waves.

When night fell, we took shelter under the branches of a tree with a massive trunk. A clearing of sorts spread out from the behemoth, though the sky still eluded us through the boughs above.

Years ago, I marveled at my first sight of a forest. So many trees huddled in one place with varied plants at their feet sheltered from the world by their tall counterparts, the wildlife that called these places home; all of it fascinated me. In my current situation, I kicked aside shrubs and plants and bounced off of the trunks of trees, heedless of the damage in my wake.

Every tree looked alike and vindictive; the small branches at my feet clawed at my legs and skirt to slow me down and draw my blood. Old, rotting tree trunks barred my passage and slowed me down, forcing me to climb over and scrape my palms again and again.

The risk of being seen through the thick growth of trees had lessened – we hoped – and we decided to build a fire to cook a hot meal. The higher altitude sapped my strength and stole my breath. Conversation was thankfully avoided as we cleared a space of leaf litter and dug a pit for a fire in the soft, moist dirt. Bryn gathered dry twigs and fallen branches, breaking them with a resounding crack that echoed far beyond where we sat.

I leveled a glare at him and stacked the twigs and pieces of wood in the pit, throwing a handful of pine needles beneath for good measure. Small clicks issued forth in more abundance than sparks as Bryn struck the steel dagger against a rock to catch the kindling aflame.

One spark took hold in the kindling beneath the tent of branches, and Bryn set the rock and dagger aside to blow through pursed lips at the infant flame to coax it to maturity. As the twigs caught, and then the branches, he began feeding larger pieces of fallen wood to the pile, and a small blaze lit our faces and warmed our hands. After so many days spent shivering, the warmth felt blissful, and I scooted as close to the pit as I dared to soak it in.

Bryn did the same on the other side of the flames, and bit by bit he seemed to relax until he sprawled out lengthwise next to the fire with his head resting on his arm.

Rummaging in my bag, I found some dried meat to chew while I stared at the dancing orange flames. They crackled and spat as they found pockets of moisture in the wood, flashing wavering light on Bryn's serene face across the way.

"Where are we going?" I asked. His eyes opened, reflecting the flames. He considered me for a moment, and then sat up with a grunt. With his legs crossed underneath him he leaned back onto his hands planted on the ground.

"Stalth," he replied. "I know the place, and I know some people that will help us if I ask."

"You spent time there?"

"I grew up there," he stated. "I was born outside the city and lived there when I was older."

"I've never been there," I informed him.

"It's in the middle of Trylia; a center of trade." His gaze moved to the fire. A weak smile crossed his face, and then faded. "It will be strange to go home."

"Why did you leave?" He looked up at me with his eyebrow raised.

"You want to know?" I nodded, and he hesitated. When I continued to stare at him, he shrugged. "I worked with some people who made decisions I didn't agree with. They informed me that I could leave town or else something could happen to me."

"What kind of work did you do?" I asked absently, focused on the heat of the fire and drowsiness it inspired.

"Why do you want to hear about my life now? After spending so long arguing with me and telling me that you'd be better off on your own, why the change?"

"I'm just making conversation," I replied, some of the anger returning. "And you were right; we need to stick together. At least for now, with your uncle so set on my demise. If you would rather continue in silence, knowing nothing about one another, that's fine with me. But it's my experience that getting to know someone makes it easier to live day-to-day with them."

Bryn's eyes seemed to gauge me as I spoke. When I finished, he nodded.

"Apologies," he sighed. "It's been a while since I've talked about myself. I'll answer your questions, but only if you'll answer mine."

"Seems fair," I agreed. "We can start with you answering my last question."

"Before I signed on with my uncle, I worked escorting traders from one city to the next as an armed guard. Before that, I worked in a shop with a friend. Before that, I was a thief."

"Thief? You've had quite a past."

"It was necessary," Bryn shrugged. "My mother died when I was young, and my father left before that. I had no option but to take what I needed if I wanted to eat. The only reason I stopped was that I broke a window in a shop, trying to steal money, and the owner caught me. He took pity on me and told me that I could work off the cost of replacing the glass. We became close, and he kept me on until I was old enough to find other work."

"I'm sorry about your parents," I said, hoping he could see my sincerity.

"Thank you," he replied. "What about your parents?"

It was my turn to shrug. "I don't know."

"What?"

"I was alone when I was very young, and I don't know where or who I came from before I washed up on a beach somewhere along the coast. My captain rescued me from slavers and adopted me. I spent most of my life on that ship." I paused, trying to fight an emptiness that threatened to overwhelm me. "If anyone could be called my family, it was the people that died when your uncle attacked." I paused to fight tears that I thought long spent from falling.

"Lila," he said, sitting up and rustling the leaf litter beneath him. His concern was plain on his face, making it harder to fight the tears. "I'm so sorry."

I sniffed and rubbed the back of my hand across my eyes, mopping up the moisture. Nodding, I took a deep breath before continuing. "Thank you. The strange thing is, that wasn't the first time I met your uncle." Confusion furrowed Bryn's brow as I looked up at him, and I let out a mirthless chuckle, my grief ebbing. "When I washed up on that beach years ago, it was his men that found me and sold me into slavery."

Bryn's eyes widened in shock and stared at me. The flames popped when they found a pocket of sap in the wood, and the noise seemed to shake Bryn from his silence.

"That is too much of a coincidence. How can that happen?"

"How could I link your life to mine? How could Derth torture me without laying a hand on me?" Again I shrugged. A stout stick sat at the edge of the fire, and I picked it up to poke at the charred wood at its heart. "Too many things are happening that don't seem real." I pulled the stick out of the fire and considered the sharpened point for a moment. Lifting the point to the thumb of my left hand, I pushed it into my skin until it began to hurt.

"What are you doing?" Bryn asked across the fire, peering at his thumb and then at mine as I let the end of the stick fall to the ground.

I shrugged. "Just checking."

"Don't," he warned, sucking on the resultant wound on his thumb. "Your captain bought you, then?" Bryn asked after a few moments.

Nodding, I replied. "If it hadn't been for him, I would have ended up in a brothel, or worse. Even so, I was afraid of him. He towered over me, and I thought he was a giant. He told me that I was safe with him, and that if I chose to leave he would honor it, but he warned me that there were more people in the world like those he saved me from. In the end, I chose to go with him." Grief welled up again as I pictured Captain Morrig's warm smile.

"He sounds like a good man," Bryn sighed.

A tear rolled down my cheek as my gaze wandered back to the fire. Staring into the fire and beyond it, I nodded. "He was."

CHAPTER FIFTEEN

With no sign of Roglin, Derth, and the others hunting us, some of the tension eased between us. The land continued to climb for the next few days, the towering trees sheltering us from the heat of the summer sun. Bryn set a quick pace, but it was no longer fueled by a desperate fear to escape as it had been. I stopped, resenting my surroundings and the difficult nature of moving through the underbrush since I now had time to move more carefully. A hushed serenity settled over everything in the forest below the canopy of branches; the golden rays of sunlight that filtered through illuminated the ferns and moss, and everything sparkled with emerald brilliance.

Bryn slid like a shadow between branches and bushes while I was still ensnared in every wayward branch and crushing every fallen leaf beneath my clumsy feet. After such a long time with only enough food to keep me alive, my muscles had wasted away. Walking for more than a few hours left me winded and the rising altitude only added to my fatigue.

Try as I might, I couldn't keep up with Bryn's pace for long without resting. Though impatient, Bryn didn't try to keep me moving. He would often trot off into the distance instead, to check for any sign of his uncle or any other potential danger.

Every day I regained a small portion of my strength, and every day I could cover more ground before collapsing against the nearest tree with my lungs afire. Every day Bryn appeared a little more relaxed as he continued to assure me that we were alone for now.

But my nightmares still plagued me. And they started to get more realistic, and specific. I watched figures wielding bows stalking through the forest, along paths that we had walked down the day before. And Derth watched it all, though he was seated, being jostled, with the smell of horses in his nose and Roglin's voice grumbling nearby.

I didn't know if I was seeing real events, but I felt, with every bit of intuition that I possessed, that I was watching the pursuit as it happened whenever I slept. That Derth was still a part of me, and that he was coming. When I told Bryn what I had seen, he grunted, and increased our pace.

We walked as long as there was light enough to see in the dense forest, fearing that any wasted time would bring those following us closer. The moment the sun began to brighten the trees, looming all around like silent sentries, Bryn nudged me awake if I wasn't. Each night I prepared a fire and arranged some small meal from our lightening packs while Bryn stalked around the perimeter of our small refuge.

One such night, with the fire crackling and a blanket spread over a pile of fallen needles and leaves, I separated out a small pile of berries I had literally stumbled upon earlier in the day. The branches of the plant, snaking out from between a small bush at the base of a tree in a patch of rare sunlight, snagged at my skirt and made me lose my footing. Landing on my elbow stung, but the small bounty of sweet berries was a balm.

My teeth sank into the plump fruit, releasing a burst of juice in my mouth. After so many days of nothing but weeds and salted pork, my taste buds sang and I moaned with pleasure. Nearby, Bryn chuckled as he popped his handful of berries into his mouth and sat on a pile of pine needles covered by a thin blanket.

"I agree," he mumbled around the mouthful of fruit. "This is the best thing I've tasted all week."

Nodding, I elected to place another of the berries, this one tart, into my mouth to savor rather than reply.

"We'll turn to the northwest in another few days, and then it should take us a couple of weeks to reach Stalth on foot. I still can't find any evidence of it, but I don't doubt that they are following us. I'm not foolish enough to underestimate Derth's abilities."

I paused with my hand halfway to my mouth. "There's not much we can do about it, except keep moving."

"True," Bryn nodded as I continued to eat. "And we will. If they're following us no matter where we go, we may as well go to a place that I know well. But we shouldn't stay in Stalth longer than it takes to gather some supplies and weapons. I have some things there, and I feel lost without my bow in my hand."

"Did you lose it when the ship went down?"

"No," he replied with a shake of his head. "It's in Stalth, with a friend of mine. I didn't want to risk it being lost or broken. And I have some money saved up, so we can buy what we need and get out of there in a hurry."

"Roglin knows you lived in Stalth?" Bryn nodded. "And that you would go there if you had nowhere to go?"

He nodded again. "That's where he found me and offered me a job."

"After you were a mercenary?"

"Yes."

I frowned, suspicious again. "Did you know that he traded in slaves?"

"Not at the time. I knew whatever he was doing wasn't legal, but I had no options. He visited town a few years before and offered work that I eventually had to accept."

"And now he's hunting us both. It's hard to believe that he would kill his own nephew."

"We aren't related by blood, as far as I'm aware," Bryn replied. "He knew my father and owed him some sort of debt. After my father died, I was his only way to make good on that debt. He gave me a job when I needed one, which puts him in the clear. As far as he's concerned, I'm sure my life means nothing."

"And the lives of your friends would mean less than that." I nodded, sympathetic. "We could avoid the town altogether; keep your people safe."

"I wish we could," Bryn sighed. He turned a genuine smile my way, the firelight glinting in his eyes. "Stalth's the closest place with everything we might need. I've got a decent amount of money saved up, but it's with my friend. And from there, we can find somewhere out of the way so that we have time to think. Thank you for thinking of their safety, though."

A small smile of my own answered his gratitude. It felt good not to bicker. "I wouldn't want to be the cause of more of Roglin's wrath."

"I'm hopeful that we have a large enough lead that we can spend at least a night in town," Bryn groaned after a long silence. He shifted his weight on his blanket to pick up a large branch just out of reach at the edge of our campsite. He held it up to measure against me, as long as I was tall, and then grasped his dagger in one hand to cut the smaller branches off of it. "I haven't slept this rough in a long time."

I chuckled. "Sleeping in a hammock on a ship *is* sleeping rough," I reminded him. "After we find everything we need in Stalth, what's the plan? Do we run all over Trylia for the rest of our lives, hoping never to run into Roglin again?"

"To be honest," he shrugged, his mouth pulling to one side as he carved off a stubborn branch, "I haven't thought that far ahead. Right now, all I want to do is get away from him."

"If he knows where you'll go, why do you think we can get there ahead of him? What if he's waiting for us when we get there? We could be walking into an ambush." This thought had been nagging at me over the past couple of days. How could we find safety in a city Roglin knew Bryn would be drawn to?

With a firm shake of his head, he rejected the idea. "He doesn't know the land like I do. Even if he's following our direct path, they won't move as quickly as we can. I've traveled most of this country over the years, and I know the shortest routes to every major hub. We'll make a more direct line to Stalth than he can if he's following the roads, and from what I know of him, he'll want to follow the roads. They wind through the foothills, but we can go north and cut around them.

"I know these mountains," Bryn nodded, looking skyward. "I know these trees, and I know my way home." He looked at me again, radiating determination that gave me confidence. "We'll get there before him."

Panting with the effort of keeping myself upright, I slogged in Bryn's wake as he wove through a tangle of underbrush. The thick branch he cut for me the night before bore more of my weight than my burning legs could.

Sensing my pause, Bryn turned. He looked winded himself, standing with his hands on his hips and taking deep breaths.

"Why don't you rest for a moment," Bryn said. Raising an arm, he pointed to our right at a short dip in the hill. "There's a stream that runs in that direction. I'll fill our waterskins."

I unfastened the strap holding my waterskin to the bottom of my pack and upended it into my dry mouth before handing it over. With a nod and a brief smile, Bryn disappeared over the edge of the hill. The crunch of his steps faded quickly, and I was alone in the quiet forest, save the chirping of birds overhead and the buzz of a gnat flying past my ear.

I plopped to the ground in what I hoped was a dry spot and dropped my pack to the ground to stretch my back and shoulders. Moments passed in relative silence and my mind turned to larger concerns with no physical task to occupy me.

Roglin and Derth were certainly trying to find us. Though I felt more confident about our chances of evading him, at least until Stalth, I wondered whether we would ever be able to stop running. My nightmares had become less frequent, like I was leaving Derth behind, but they left me feeling like he could find me if I stopped moving.

I certainly couldn't return to King's Port and lead him to the families of my departed crew, nor did I trust Bryn enough to inform him that they existed. And if Bryn and I remained linked by whatever I had done to him, I doubted he would let me leave his sight. Even if I tried to make my way from Stalth on my own, he would likely follow me; after watching him move through the forest, I knew I would never be able to evade him if he came after me.

This line of thinking reminded me that, above my other problems, I couldn't fathom the limits of my gift, or how to separate myself from Bryn. No matter what happened with Roglin, or whether we stayed together, the shadow of this tether still hung over us. The lack of options chafed almost as much as my shackles had.

As my mind considered all of this, I stared at my hands, willing them to glow again. There had been a few quiet moments while we traveled where I tried to summon the spirits, but it seemed they weren't answering again. I squinted, I widened my eyes, and I closed my eyes, all the while picturing the luminescence surrounding me. Straining my eyes and gritting my teeth brought no results and I sighed, dropping my hands to my lap in frustration.

I had fought so hard to understand this devastating power, pushed through pain and what should have been my death to destroy an entire ship. But now, as I tried to imagine the spirits or the glow that preceded my gift, it felt like they were behind that gray curtain again. Cut off from me, unable to hear me call.

Diving into that space within myself, where the glow waited behind this curtain, I screamed for the spirits to answer me. My inner struggle manifested in a cold sweat, a clenching of hands, jaw, and a tightening of all of my muscles one by one. I strained for an answer to my summons, and tears began to roll down my cheeks from my eyes, from behind eyelids clenched tight. It felt like I had lost a piece of myself that I had fought to claim, as if, on top of losing my home and family, I had failed.

What had been a peaceful moment alone now changed to a spiral of shame and fear that consumed me. The loss I had endured filtered in to add overwhelming grief to the churning maelstrom.

Tears fell from my closed eyes to drip off the end of my nose and into my upturned palms below as I hung my head and sobbed. A red glow behind my eyelids disrupted my thoughts, and my eyes popped open. My hands beamed with bright, white light that seemed to swirl and pulse to mirror my inner turmoil. A myriad of translucent hands gripped mine.

We come.

In that moment, I was filled with the certainty that if I willed it, I could burn the forest to ash or send the trees around me flying into the distance. The light gleamed brighter, like a star in my hand.

The world around me seemed to drop away, as if I had been drawn behind the curtain to the place where the spirits were waiting; all that existed was me and this power that blossomed from within. It was as if I had crossed through the worst of the storm, to its heart where I could find some respite. All of the danger and doubt remained, surrounding me, waiting for me to wander into it again. In spite of that danger, a smile broke out of my face. I couldn't control the rest, but I could work to reclaim control over my power.

In the distance, I heard Bryn call my name. My eyes turned in the direction of the sound, and the glow began to fade. My smile faded with it until both were gone and Bryn came crashing through the trees.

"What happened?" he demanded, sword in one hand and waterskins, still dripping from the stream, in the other. "Are you hurt?" His eyes scanned me, and then the forest around us.

"I'm all right," I drawled as the world came back into focus.

"I felt something," Bryn snapped, still alert for danger. His eyes found mine again and stayed focused on me. "What happened?"

"The gift."

CHAPTER SIXTEEN

"What do you mean?" Bryn demanded, a dangerous glint in his eyes as he returned his sword to its scabbard.

I blinked as the waning gift left me feeling empty and confused. It was shuttered away again, as if it didn't exist. I frowned as I found Bryn's face.

"I felt something...strange," he explained, "and then the forest started to glow. And when I came back here to get you there was no one around but you, glowing like you did right before you made the ship explode."

"I was trying...." I shook my head, not sure exactly what I wanted to say, still confused as to why the spirits came, but were still separated from me. On the *Catherine,* I could feel them like a constant vibration in my chest, even when I didn't need them. Now, that vibration was gone.

"You were *trying* to make yourself glow? It was a beacon!" He took a deep breath to calm himself. "We can't afford to be seen. And what would have happened if you hurt yourself?"

My brow furrowed in frustration and irritation seeing Bryn's obvious anger.

"Meddling with the gift could get us killed," he said. His tone was even, but it was a bit too controlled. And his nostrils flared as he huffed out a breath.

"I'm not," I assured him, an edge to my voice. "I'm trying to get some control back so that I *don't* get us killed. Or, a better outcome, I can keep Derth from killing or maiming us."

He looked at his feet and chuckled, but it was without humor. "I've seen that man kill people with no warning. If you can find a way to stop him, I won't argue." Without moving his head, he lifted his eyes to me, his brow wrinkling and his gaze intense. "Everything I've seen you do has been unintentional or explosive. How, exactly, do you plan to get control over that?"

"I won't know unless I try," I said. "Derth's influence is still there. Sometimes I can get past it, but most of the time I feel like I'm cut off."

He walked forward and knelt before me, our faces hovered mere inches from one another. His eyes narrowed, and his voice lowered. It wasn't a menacing look, but something in his countenance sent a shiver down my spine.

"I'm going to trust your instinct about this because I don't know how it works. But I need you to understand that I can't save us from you."

Rather than match his smoldering intensity, I nodded and forced myself to relax bit by bit, starting with my gritted teeth.

"I know it's dangerous," I said. "It's been dangerous for as long as I can remember. But I think it's more dangerous to leave it sitting beneath the surface with no idea when I might kill us both. After everything that's happened to me, the one thing I've been able to count on was how I reacted to things. Now, my body is betraying me in every possible way, and I... I can't stand it."

Exhaustion ate at me; my eyelids felt heavy, and my head drooped down near my chest. A long moment passed, and Bryn passed me a full waterskin, which I accepted with a nod. Holding it up, I let the water trickle into my dry mouth to slide down my throat.

"I think I understand," Bryn said when I was finished. I wiped my hand over my mouth to dry the stray droplets. "If I'd been through what you have, I think I would feel the same as you. Please, for both our sakes, be careful Lila."

"I will."

As the sunlight began to fade, we made it to the top of a steep rise. Following in Bryn's footsteps, I was able to climb with the aid of the branch, bracing it against the ground behind me to push myself up to the next root or rock that aided my ascent while avoiding the scree that threatened to send me sliding back down the slope. When he reached the top, Bryn turned to offer me his hand. Accepting gratefully, we heaved the rest of my body over the top of the ledge.

Looking back the way we had come, I marveled at the distance traveled, and that I had made it this far. The land dropped in a steep slope to the forest beneath. Littered with loose rocks and jutting roots, it looked like an impossible climb from my current perspective.

Bryn's light touch on my shoulder made me turn to follow. At this crest of the hill, the trees thinned enough to see the sky between the branches above. The fading sun lit the evening sky with a vivid mix of orange and pink clouds, looking like mountains against the pale blue backdrop. It reminded me of sunset at sea and brought a smile to my face.

Our tense exchange earlier in the day had finally brought to surface some of our lingering doubts about one another. In the wake of our newfound understanding, we were able to walk in a comfortable silence that had eluded us while only a shaky truce had held us together.

As the sunset began to fade into darkness, Bryn found a spot beneath a large tree. He slid his pack from his shoulders and set it next to the trunk before he walked away into the distance in his nightly routine and I began the task of clearing a space for a fire.

The fire crackled under the open sky while I waited for Bryn to return from his patrol around the perimeter of our encampment, which he assured me couldn't be seen through the leagues of forest all around, and I sat chewing on a piece of dried meat. A twig snapped to my left as Bryn ducked under the low branch of a nearby spruce. He flopped down on the blanket I had spread out for him and smiled when I handed him food. He tore off a chunk of the meat and chewed as he stared at the fire.

"All clear," Bryn announced, as he did every night. I smiled to myself, amused that he would still seek to reassure me that there was no danger around after also insisting that there was no way for his uncle to follow us. "I can't help feeling like we're being watched, but there's no sign of anyone. It looks like we'll have rain in the next day or so."

My eyes turned skyward, searching for a sign of impending foul weather. A few clouds in the distance loomed dark and ominous in the last of the day's light, but looked nothing like what I was used to at sea.

"I'll trust that you know what you're talking about," I smirked.

An answering smirk formed as he chewed. The stubble had grown, forming a small growth of beard shot through with some white and some red patches to augment the tawny whiskers on his face. "You should," he replied after swallowing his mouthful of dried beef. "We don't have cloaks, so we'll need to stick to the thicker parts of the forest for now. It should pass in a few days."

Those few days of rain turned into a weeklong downpour, soaking us to our skins as it fell from branches above our heads. It was a miserable slog through the undergrowth each day, slowing our progress as we picked through deepening muck and rivulets of rainwater that wound their way downhill with us.

Bryn led me down into the valley between the surrounding hills, though we still stuck to a straight path in the direction that he intended. When we were lucky, Bryn would find an outcropping of rock jutting out from one of the hills that we could use as a shelter from the rain when we could no longer see. Some only allowed us to sit with our backs against the cold rock while huddled together behind hastily stacked branches to keep out the worst of the rain.

Conversation was sparse as we blinked against the water that dripped from our heads day and night; our only interest was covering as much ground as possible each day and trying to rest and stay warm at night. Our strength waned a little every day that we walked through the wet and every night that we weren't able to build a fire to ward off the chill of the breeze that cut through the trunks of the trees. Even with the small amount restored by our one restful and warm night spent in what could generously be called a cave, I could feel myself slipping into a lethargic haze as I shivered with bone deep cold.

The chill of autumn swept through the forest, propelled by the distant ocean breeze. At first stubbornly insisting that I was strong enough to bear the cold, I lost my will to fight as lethargy rooted deeper with every passing day.

On more than one occasion, Bryn remarked that he could feel my discomfort and it added to his own; we took to sleeping side by side under a single pile of blankets at his advice one night when my hesitation was overshadowed by my chattering teeth.

Despite being soaking wet, Bryn radiated constant heat that seeped into my spare frame and allowed me to sleep and recover some of my strength. Though still uneasy about his proximity, I swallowed my pride and realized the wisdom of his suggestion. To his credit and my immense relief, he did nothing more than lend me his heat.

When the rain ceased one night, we woke to the sun filtering once again through the trees above, and we each let out a sigh of relief as we soaked up the warmth. Our spirits rose along with our bodies' temperatures, and we set off with a spring in our steps that had been absent these long, wet days.

Each day that passed brought us closer to our goal, and closer to food and shelter. Our supplies ran dangerously low, despite Bryn's preparedness and his ability to forage for the last of the summer berries and greens. If we didn't arrive in Stalth soon, we might not make it all.

CHAPTER SEVENTEEN

One night, after I had chattered myself to sleep, I was wrenched awake by a hand hauling me away from the warmth of Bryn's body, into the frigid cold.

"Ah!" I shouted as arms hooked under mine, and hands wrapped around my ankles to lift me into the air. Reminded of being chained in Roglin's ship, I thrashed against hands that acted like manacles in a startled panic. "Bryn!"

His grunt was muffled, and I twisted far enough to watch the silhouettes of two large people grapple Bryn to the ground and strike him across the face. I twisted back, kicking my legs with all my strength while I reached up behind me to claw at my captor's face.

"Elders!" the one holding my upper body shouted as I dug my fingernails into what I thought was his cheek. He dropped me moments before the other one dropped my legs and I fell, my head slamming against a tree root before the rest of me thumped to the forest floor. A shock of pain raced through the back of my head where it lay against the rough bark, and my head swam. The cold and wet started to seep through my clothes again as I rolled onto my side. "Bitch gouged me!"

The other one laughed as I tried to get to my knees, dizziness making my gorge rise. Before I could move further, I felt a boot in the small of my back as it shoved me down onto my face in the mud. The foot pressed harder, compressing my chest as whomever was above me leaned forward. I turned my face to the side, spitting the mud out and struggling to take a breath.

"Hold her down," the person restraining me said. The pressure on my back let up as a hand shoved my face sideways into the wet ground and another put pressure between my shoulders. My right arm was wrenched painfully back as another heavy weight settled onto my back and legs. The rope tightened around my wrist as I reached up toward the man holding my head down.

"Get off me!" I shouted, trying to force the gift to shove this man, burn him, or something that would get me out of his grasp before my other arm was bound. I felt a stirring of the spirits, but the curtain was in the way, as if the spirits were tangled in it and unable to free themselves. Instead, I clawed at his leg, feeling for the arm holding my head down.

He grasped a handful of my hair, lifted my head, and slammed it down again. I let out a pained cry, and heard Bryn's muffled voice yell in pain and rage.

A hand grasped my left arm and pulled as I fought against it. Again, I strained to draw on the gift, at the same moment pushing against the curtain in my inner space that separated me from the spirits and the glow. I found a crack, tried to use the small light that touched me to throw the man off of my back, and he stumbled to the side for a moment.

"She's moving too much," he grumbled. "Get her arm!"

I tried to get my feet to the side, but the one behind me laid across my back as the other one released my shoulders and scrambled to grab my arm. With a grunt, I shoved against the ground, trying to buck the one on top of me. It wasn't enough; even as my assailants cursed me and grunted with the effort of keeping me still, my left wrist was wrapped with rope, the line tightened, and it jerked back to slam into my other wrist. I kicked out, and the two men worked to bind my ankles.

It felt like my shoulders would pull free from the force with which they were bound. But I didn't want to give in. I hadn't had much choice on the ship when Derth shrouded me in apathy, but I had a choice now. I pushed myself toward the sound of a pained grunt from Bryn, digging my toes into the soft earth to propel myself forward. One of them kicked me in the ribs, and my breath exploded out of my lungs. I curled into a ball, still pushing with my toes as I gasped in a breath.

"Go help the others," one of them demanded. The one still behind me hauled on the rope binding my wrists, and I let out another agonized cry as my shoulders protested. I flopped onto my back, my arms pinned beneath me, facing the man standing above me.

His outline was visible, but with no light, I couldn't make out his features. He leaned over and grabbed my arm, pulling me up.

"You can fight all you want, but it'll cost your man's life." His voice was smooth and deep, and his words were direct, with no hint of malice, just a statement of fact. I kicked, trying to turn, to see what was happening to Bryn. The man reached down and hauled me to my feet, spinning me around to aid my endeavor.

There were four people struggling to hold a fifth to the ground. Bryn's grunts sent chills down my spine as I watched one person kick him, and another punched down. The figures stilled, and then stood, and Bryn was still. I heard a blade being pulled from a sheath, and one of the shadowy figures turned toward the man standing with me.

"We should kill this one," the woman said. "He'd be more trouble to move to port than he's worth."

"Then he'll be worth more," the man beside me said. "For now, we bring him. To keep this one in line. When he wakes up, we'll use her to motivate him. And if he's still too much trouble, we'll kill him."

They hauled us for almost an hour, and in the darkness I had no idea which direction we were headed. Bryn groaned as the light of a fire came into view between the trees. We emerged into a clearing, equipped with several lean-tos and tents, stacks of crates, and three more men.

"Put him in here with this one," the man holding me said, as he dumped me onto my side beneath one lean-to. There were a few large sacks and a barrel in here with me, and the ground was dry. The two carrying Bryn threw him down on his side facing me, and he groaned again.

They walked away, leaving Bryn and me alone, bound hand and foot, with a gag in Bryn's mouth. I scooted toward Bryn, seeing that he had a swollen cut on the right side of his jaw as his eyes opened. They were unfocused for too long as he mumbled something.

"Bryn?" I whispered, looking toward the campfire where the group was assembled. Several of them had similar injuries to Bryn's. "Bryn, look at me."

He mumbled something unintelligible behind the gag. His eyes focused as he heard me and found mine. He tried to say something again.

"I'm all right. Are you?"

He nodded, and winced in pain. After the beating he'd taken, I wasn't surprised. He lifted his head, trying to look around, and found the group near the fire.

"It looks like they've been here a while," I whispered. One of the group looked over toward us, and I leaned away from Bryn, not wanting to provoke a reaction. The man looked away. "I'm not sure where we are, but we were walking for almost an hour. If we're anywhere near the road...." I trailed off, the thought of Roglin and Derth nearby making my heart race.

Bryn strained his arms, and then his legs, trying to see if he could free himself. I did the same, but the ropes were too tight. Bryn gave up a moment later, letting his muscles go slack as his eyes met mine again. His eyes were watering as he moved the gag around in his mouth, it looked like he might choke.

"He's choking!" I yelled, watching the figures turn away from the fire to peer at us. One of them sneered, one made a rude gesture, and they turned away. "Elders," I cursed, and wiggled toward Bryn.

He watched me come closer, confusion evident in his furrowed brow. Once I was close enough, my chest pressed against his, and our faces were all but touching. I leaned forward to grab the gag between my teeth, and pulled it down toward his chin. It took a bit of maneuvering, but I was able to pull it free, and Bryn cleared his throat.

"Thank you," he said, his voice low and hoarse. He cleared his throat a few more times as I pushed away from him, rolling awkwardly to the side away from him.

The group around the fire had dispersed, a few moving off to bedrolls while two walked into the forest, disappearing into the darkness between the trees. The last walked toward us, and when he spoke, I recognized the man who'd carried me here. I sat up and scooted back.

"Your woman is resourceful," he said, towering over us, looking down at the gag around Bryn's neck. He was clean shaven, with the right side of his head shaved as well, and a flop of bright red hair tucked behind his left ear. He had a handsome face, with a charming smile that made me want to punch him in the mouth.

"She is," Bryn replied, his voice full of menace.

"I don't normally go for the slave trade. It's complicated, and there aren't many places you can get paid without leaving the continent. But when I found two people in the middle of nowhere, sleeping so peacefully, it seemed like too good an opportunity to pass up. But, if one of you moves from this place before morning, or we find that you've slipped your bonds, we will hurt the other." He peered at me. "You wouldn't want me to cut off one of his fingers, would you?" I glared at him, and he smirked before moving his gaze to Bryn. "Let's see what we have here."

He crouched and pulled the collar of my dress down between my breasts, exposing the skin over my midline. He trailed a finger from my neck down to where he held my dress. I went rigid, disgusted by the touch, and pushed myself backward until my back touched the barrel. He let go of my collar when I did. Bryn sat up, trying to scoot between this man and me.

"It would be a shame to cut that soft skin," the man said, "especially before I've finished threatening you properly." He stood again, planted a foot in Bryn's chest, and shoved him backward. Bryn landed with his head on my leg. The man winked at me, smiled at Bryn, and walked away.

When we were alone, Bryn sat up again, and scooted back until our shoulders were touching.

"Why are there so many people here that can make a living selling people?" I fumed. "It's like there's no one enforcing the law."

"It seems that way," Bryn muttered. "And we keep getting caught in it. We must be Elder cursed."

"I thought I was for most of my life. It seems like I was right."

We huddled close to keep the cold at bay, watching as our captors went about the business of settling down for a few hours of rest. Every few minutes, a figure appeared on the edge of the camp, watched us for a few moments, and blended back into the shadows. Bryn shifted his hands, trying to stretch the rope around his wrists to give him room to slip it. When he didn't make progress, I felt along his hands and found that they had bound him down to the fingers. And it was so tight that the skin around the rope was swelling.

Several times, I tried to use the gift to burn or cut the rope around my wrists or Bryn's, but it felt like I had drained whatever reserve of strength I had gained when I failed to free myself earlier. Finding that I couldn't use that method to free us, I pivoted a bit, putting my back against Bryn's so that I could try to work the knot binding his wrists loose. While the sentries were in sight, I stopped picking at Bryn's rope, but as soon as they disappeared, I started up again.

My fingertips were raw, and still I pulled at the knot. It felt like I was making a bit of progress. It looked like there wouldn't be much time before dawn, and I wanted to be far from here before we saw any sign of the people I was most afraid of.

Dawn came too soon, and though I had succeeded in loosening the knot, I could tell that Bryn was in a lot of pain, and we wouldn't be able to escape as I'd hoped. The gift was still out of reach, and I felt like every moment brought us closer to being found by Roglin and Derth.

One of the sentries flew into the camp, and made straight for the leader who had threatened us hours earlier. They exchanged a few hushed words, and then the leader smiled, clapped the sentry on the back, and turned to the rest, who were all watching the exchange like I was.

"It seems our luck is continuing!" he announced with a huge smile. "A wagon carrying a bounty of supplies, guarded by a few sentries and a couple of gentlemen who look like they've had a rough time of it lately. Gather your weapons, we take the sentries out, and there's a bounty waiting. Even a wagon to transport our other cargo!" He laughed, nodding in our direction, and the rest chuckled as they started moving with more purpose.

I shared a look with Bryn as we watched our captors fetch bows, swords, clubs, rope, and empty bags. "Do you think it's them?" I asked him.

"One of them is hunched so bad, I doubt he could lift a sword," the sentry was telling another as he walked back in the direction he had come from.

"I think it's likely," Bryn replied, his tone tight with anger. "We'll have to slip out while they're distracted. They won't survive this, but if any of Roglin's new crew come through here looking for stragglers, we won't survive it either."

I scooted closer to Bryn again, and furtively tried to pull his knot free. We couldn't wait for everyone to be out of sight any more. We needed to leave as soon as possible.

Most of the bandits filed out of camp, moving as silently as Bryn did. They left one man behind, and he busied himself with packing some of their belongings, as if preparing for a journey. I supposed they planned on striking camp to take us to wherever they thought they could sell us after their business with Roglin was concluded. But I knew they wouldn't get the chance.

"Come on," I muttered, feeling the rope pull a bit more, the knot come a bit looser. Bryn flexed his arms, trying to twist his wrists to help loosen the rope. "This isn't going to work," I hissed.

"Just keep going," Bryn murmured. "You're making progress. I can wiggle my fingers, and I'm getting a bit of feeling back in them. Elders, they hurt."

I cursed under my breath when my own pained fingers slipped off of the knot. The sentry looked up as he walked closer, his eyes narrowing suspiciously as I tugged at Bryn's rope.

"Knock it off," the man called, "or I'll have to take a finger."

I went still, frustrated and not wanting to push our already terrible luck. The man reached past us for a few heavy sacks, and walked away, into the tree line opposite where his companions had gone. He reappeared in seconds, and I let my hands drop before they touched the rope again.

"Spirits," I cursed under my breath. "You're useless."

"I know I said you shouldn't mess around with it, but this might be exactly the circumstance where the gift would be useful," Bryn whispered.

"I know!" I said. The sentry glanced at us but didn't move in our direction. "I've been trying," I hissed. "It won't come. It's like it's just out of reach, or needs time to regain its strength?" I shook my head. "I don't know how to explain it, I'm not even sure what it is."

Bryn sighed. "Then keep at the rope," he said.

I did, and felt as the rope started to slide. Bryn flexed again, and I tugged on the end, giving him even more room. A distant shout made the sentry pause, and I pulled faster, knowing that our time was almost out. Another shout as Bryn pulled again, and one hand's fingers came loose. The sentry moved to the edge of camp, his back to us, as the rope unraveled from Bryn's other hand.

Bryn pushed, and I felt the rope loosen around his wrists and slide off. He turned with a grunt as the sentry ran from camp. "We have to leave," he said, pulling the looser rope from his ankles before trying to untie my hands. "My fingers don't want to work," he growled.

I looked around, finding our packs under another lean-to, and lifted my chin in that direction. "Over there, check to see if you can find a dagger or something. You can cut me loose."

He stood, and I could see how bruised and swollen his hands were. He struggled to lift the packs, and couldn't close his fingers around the hilt of the dagger. But he could still hold it, and sawed through the rope at my wrist furiously as the shouts turned to screams. Something crashed in the forest nearby, and the screams came closer.

"Derth," Bryn said as the rope snapped and I could move my hands. He tore through the rope around my ankles and helped me to my feet, handing me a pack. A body flew through the air, as if hurtled by a giant hand, and slammed sideways into a tree at the edge of camp. It bent backward around the trunk, and then fell in a heap to the ground. The sentry that had just left was sprinting toward us, a look of terror on his face, before he hurtled backward through the air by an invisible force that jerked him like a fish on a hook. "We need to go, *now!*" Bryn insisted. He turned with a hand on my back, and pushed me ahead of him, opposite the carnage.

We crashed through the trees, leaving the screams behind us. With terrified glances behind us, we watched for pursuers that never came. But my heart pounded for the rest of the day and through the night as we disregarded our exhausted pain in favor of putting more distance between ourselves and Derth.

For a few days after our encounter, we squelched through mud hidden beneath the leaf litter. It was miserable, with the trees dropping the last vestiges of rain on us, almost as a reminder of the frigid rain we had already dealt with. And now that we were past the foothills, the downhill slope of the trees sent me sliding a bit too quickly in the direction we were heading in. My palms were scraped from catching myself against so many rough tree trunks.

My only solace in my pain and frustration was that it would be much harder for anyone to follow us if they were slowed as well. I hoped that meant that we were gaining some ground, especially since I kept skidding downhill at breakneck speeds. They had been so close, and the few hours of sleep I had managed to take over the past few nights had been fraught with nightmares of being bound, seeing Roglin or Derth looming over me.

Bryn's hands recovered in time, though they were still bruised and stiff. We said little, both of us lost in our thoughts, as I considered how little time we would have in Stalth'before we needed to leave again.

One day dawned bright and serene when the ground was dry again; birds chirped above us where we lay at the foot of a spruce and an errant ray of sunlight fell onto my upturned face. Blinking against the radiance, I rolled onto my side. My muscles ached from a steep descent the day before, and I moaned as I stood and stretched.

I felt eager to be on the move; Bryn insisted that we were

about a day away from Stalth and I couldn't wait. Hunger gnawed at my insides, and my stomach gurgled in protest as I rummaged through my pack for anything to eat.

When he stirred a few moments later, a similar groan escaped Bryn's lips as he sat upright with bleary eyes and a pained grimace.

"Do we have any food?" he asked as he shucked off his blanket and turned toward me.

Shaking my head, I replied. "Not much. Small pieces of stale bread." I stretched out my arm, offering him one of the two remaining hunks. With a grunt, he shifted himself around to my side and wearily grasped the hard heel. He grunted again when his teeth clicked against the nearly petrified bread. After a few moments of chewing and sawing at it with my own teeth, I broke a piece free and sucked on it to moisten it enough to chew further.

I ran my hand through my long tangles of hair that dangled in front of my face. Despite my efforts each night with the small comb Bryn had bought, my hair seemed determined to twist itself into knots while I slept, almost as if the strands plotted against me. As my fingers became ensnared, I huffed and extricated them with prejudice before rummaging through my pack for the comb. A triumphant grin spread across my mouth as my fingers found the wooden teeth and I freed it from the canvas holding it captive.

While Bryn gnawed at his stale bread, I teased my unruly mass of hair back into order and tied the lot of it behind my head with a narrow strip of leather. After a few more attempts to saw through his rock-hard bread, he gave up with a disgusted sigh and tossed the remainder away.

"We're close enough that we should be there by nightfall," he assured me when I leveled a look of disbelief his way. "I won't be hungry for long."

CHAPTER EIGHTEEN

The forest ended abruptly, leaving a clear space for tracts of land holding fields of grain that sustained Stalth and its people. A large river ran west to east from the mountains, and trickled out in small streams south toward Stalth, which sustained the farmlands for leagues in every direction. The time for harvest had passed, and the golden fields held only a ghost of the growth that these large spaces would have contained a month earlier. To the southeast, the forest we had traversed continued unbroken to the horizon.

The city sat arranged like a large wheel, the roads its spokes lancing straight into the heart of the city to culminate in a large, open square. At regular intervals from the outer wall to the center were streets forming circles around the town, also intersected by the larger roads leading out. Buildings lined every road; larger houses sat tall at the edge near the wall where they had more space between them. While not as large as King's Port, Stalth sprawled over a piece of ground larger than Coveton and other port towns I had visited.

We strolled into the city as the sun sank behind the stone walls encircling the city without incident, though we did elicit more than a few questioning glances from guards and travelers alike. Travel-worn and filthy, with scrapes and bruises discoloring our arms and legs, I couldn't blame the people around us for staring. Alert and on edge, Bryn spared a brief glance at each of the people around us as his eyes sought any sign of danger.

Slogging along next to him, I did my best to remain alert. Weariness ate at me, weighing my limbs like the tide pulling debris down into the ocean, like the sinking ship almost had after I destroyed it.

Trusting Bryn to lead me somewhere safe, fighting the ache in my legs that threatened to leave me collapsed in a pile on the hard earth of the street below me, I willed myself to keep moving, drawing on the reserves of my strength as I had for weeks to keep moving. In the depths of the city, we passed smaller circular lanes that wove around the town in tighter arcs.

Small paddocks held hens and goats near the edge. The closer we came to the center of the town, the less space the buildings had to either side, and the smaller those buildings became until they seemed huddled together against the chill of the autumn breeze that rustled the ruined hem of my skirt and sent prickles along my exposed calves.

These gave way to storefronts and stalls that dominated the smallest circle surrounding a large square that opened at the end of the street we followed. To my right, a long and low building spread, the curve of the street leaving space enough for several benches in the faded sunlight where a few men lounged, mugs in hand and smiles on their faces. Light bloomed from behind glass windows as a few young women flitted in and out of sight with long tapers illuminating groups of candles.

Every person in sight, from the women lighting candles inside a tavern, to the men lounging outside and those wandering the streets, were dressed with a functional grace that led me to believe that Stalth was a prosperous town. Only people who I had seen wandering the palace ground in King's Port, or certain wealthy ship owners the captain interacted with dressed in better finery or held themselves more erect.

We turned right, past the tavern, and halted in front of a two-story building with a sign above the door depicting a needle and spool of thread. Drapes were drawn against the evening, but the flicker of candlelight spoke to someone inside. Curious as to the reason for this stop but relieved at the thought of finding something that could finally cover my exposed skin, I stepped across the threshold as Bryn held the wooden door for me. Along the walls, mannequins stood sporting gowns and suits, plain dresses and work wear for everyday use. Bodices of linen, satin, and leather, along with chemises and shirts of varying colors were displayed artfully along tables trailing in a line from the door to the counter. Different styles of trousers were neatly folded on shelves in the middle of the shop.

A middle-aged and plump woman stepped out of the back of the shop as I looked around. She wore her blond hair piled high on her head and one of the gowns I had seen on display hugged her moderate curves. The light blue linen complemented her flaxen hair and blue eyes, the belled sleeves falling gracefully to her skirt as she clasped her hands together. A look of disdain settled on her face as she took in my attire, and my heart sank with unease.

"I don't know if this is the place for you, my dear," she purred with mock sweetness. The corners of my mouth turned down in a frown as she continued. "The price may not be... right. Do you have any money? If not, I'll have to ask you to leave."

"With an attitude like that, I'm surprised you sell anything at all, Maude," Bryn grumbled as he moved to my side.

The woman named Maude seemed taken aback by his words and choked back a scathing reply before she stopped, scrutinizing Bryn's face. Her eyes widened in recognition as he scowled at her through his thick growth of beard and long, lank locks of hair that he shook away from his face with an irritated flip of his head.

"Bryn!" she exclaimed, at once embarrassed and pleasantly surprised. "This young lady is with you? Why didn't you say so?" She turned her head toward the back room and shouted, "Arthur! Get up here and see who just walked in!"

A man stepped through the doorway with an expectant look on his face. His brow furrowed in confusion as he looked at me, then shot up near his hairline, his eyes lighting up as he noticed the man next to me.

"Bryn! How good to see you, my boy! How have you been?"

"Arthur, it's wonderful to see you, too." Bryn's voice softened with affection, and he strolled forward to embrace Arthur in a friendly hug, parting with amiable slaps to each other's backs.

Arthur stood almost as tall as Bryn. His long, black hair was streaked with gray at the temples and neatly plaited down his back. He wore a plain white shirt over a pair of black breeches, under a light blue vest to match Maude's dress. Wrinkles fanned out from his kind brown eyes as he smiled broadly.

"I've been well enough, Arthur. I found my uncle. I've been sailing with his crew the past six months."

"You look like you've had an interesting journey." Arthur looked at me, then back to Bryn. "Is this lovely young woman with you?" At Bryn's hesitant nod, Arthur turned his friendly smile to me. I felt myself grinning in return, my unease gone in the warmth of his demeanor, replaced by relief. "What's your name?" he asked.

"Lila," I replied. His hand was warm and rough, his grip strong and sure as I shook it. "It's nice to meet you."

"And you as well. You've met my wife, Maude?"

"Yes," I said, hiding any lingering insecurity caused by the woman who had moments ago tried to shun me. I turned my warm smile to Maude, who had the good manners to look mildly ashamed.

"Well, anything they want they shall have. We both know Bryn's done more than enough for us to deserve that much." He smiled warmly at his wife before telling Bryn to take whatever he needed and find him after, and returned to the back room.

Maude watched Arthur leave and turned a worried face to Bryn. After a moment, she faced me. "I'm sorry about that, my dear. I just assumed..." she trailed off, gesturing to my dress.

Bryn frowned, but I instinctively placed my hand on his arm to calm him. While I understood his feeling, I knew that this woman was not the right outlet. The crease between his brow and the hard line of his mouth disappeared when he saw me shake my head, and he moved away to peruse the cloaks along the back wall.

I waved my hand, making a 'think nothing of it' gesture, and asked Maude for her help choosing something more appropriate to wear.

I was now ensconced in a small room in the back of the shop, a wooden cup of water and plate now devoid of fruit and bread on a table nearby. A floor-length mirror adorned one of the pale blue walls and a small padded bench ran along another. Maude offered the use of a comb and mirror to fix my hair and a place to wash up, for which I was genuinely grateful. A small moan of satisfaction escaped me as I used a rag soaked with warm water to wipe the grime from every visible part of my body and dried off with a soft cloth before getting dressed. In the back of my mind, I worried about how close Roglin and Derth might be, but it felt so good to be clean that I couldn't focus on the possibility of danger.

A short time later, I stood properly outfitted for travel once again. A green linen bodice hugged my torso over a crisp, white shirt. My trousers were made of soft brown leather, with sturdy boots to match on my feet. A deep green cloak, the color of pine needles, completed my ensemble. Maude also recommended I take a full-length chemise and green skirt to match my bodice as well as a leather bodice to match my trousers. I tried to protest, insisting I would have little use for the skirt while walking through the wilderness, but she insisted with a fervor that implied an attempt to atone for her earlier behavior.

Bryn had picked out a new shirt and a brown wool cloak and now sat in the office across the hall from the small changing room, speaking quietly with Arthur. When Maude took her leave and made her way up the stairs to their apartment above, I padded to the door before it closed and strained to hear the men's discussion as Maude's footsteps faded.

"…'ve been taking more jobs as thugs for hire. After you left, they started stealing from anyone and everyone, myself included. Some of the merchants were close to involving the guard, so I told them they needed to lay low for a while. They chose to leave, but we hear things from people who come to trade about several young men waylaying caravans in the countryside."

Bryn sighed heavily. "Those two were always reckless, but I didn't think they would stoop to terrorizing the whole city."

Arthur chuckled. "At least *you* had the decency to steal from men who deserved it. *Most* of the time," he added wryly.

"I made amends for your broken window long ago," Bryn chuckled.

"That you did, my boy. And you more than made up for it by helping me with that little problem we had."

Silence fell across the hall, and I was about to close the door when Arthur spoke again.

"So, who is that young woman you're with? I can see she's a beauty, even through all the grime." I heard a low whistle, and my cheeks flushed. "What are you two up to?"

I pressed my face against the opening in the door, straining to see inside the office through the small crack. Arthur sat at his desk, Bryn directly across from him, showing off both men's profiles. Bryn brushed the dark blond mop of hair off of his face in a flustered manner as he considered Arthur's questions, a flush reddening the tip of his ear.

With a shake of his head, he leaned forward on the edge of his chair and braced his elbows on his knees. "I had no idea who my uncle was when I went to work for him, Arthur." Arthur's face lost its humor as he listened to Bryn. "He's dangerous, and we have something he wants. The man is hunting us. If he finds out we were here...."

Before I could hear any more of their conversation, I heard Maude's footsteps on the stairs above me and ducked back into the room. Maude knocked on the door.

"Come in," I called, and she slipped inside. She nodded approvingly at my clean face and motioned for me to sit in a chair that she placed in the center of the room.

"If you don't object, I thought I could help you with your hair," she said tentatively.

Surprised by her offer, I simply replied, "I would be grateful." Maude smiled as I sat in the chair facing the mirror.

She wielded a comb with a deft tenderness I hadn't expected, coaxing the tangles from my hair. Where I usually tugged at the knots, wincing all the while, she eased them out slowly. At first nervous about the contact, I slowly relaxed as fingers and comb worked together to massage my scalp. When all of the snarls were gone, she produced a soft bristled brush that slid through with a soft whisper, adding body enough to make it float around my face in soft waves.

Maude gestured for me to look in the mirror when she was finished, and I was astounded by the creature who stared back at me. The weeks on Roglin's ship had given my cheeks a hollow look, my weight drastically reduced. My eyes seemed more prominent in my gaunt and pale face, especially with the bruised quality of the skin beneath them. They came to a stop as I noticed how my hair framed my face and fell past my shoulders in a cloud of copper and russet.

"Thank you," I beamed. "It looks wonderful!"

"You're welcome, dear. You have beautiful hair. And you look lovely in that color; it suits you."

Maude opened the door when Bryn knocked. He stared at me as I rose from the chair. I lifted my hands out to the side to showcase my attire, and he nodded with a brief smile.

"Where to now?" I asked. A leather strap crossed the white shirt on his chest; speckled feathers of arrows jutted up past his left ear where they rested in a quiver, and the hilts of a longsword and dirk rested against opposite hips. He clasped a long bow in his hand, his fingers tightening and caressing the smooth grain lovingly, distractedly as he answered my question.

"We're going to see an old friend of mine and get a place to stay for the night."

"Who is this friend?"

"An old man that helped me after my mother died. His name is Samuel."

We said our farewells to Maude and Arthur and made our way back to the square, bundles of clothing taking the place of food in our ragged packs. The large, open space ringed with buildings held eight streets that led out into the countryside. Trees shaded the corners of each; shadows of leaves danced in the flickering light from lamps in every corner that had been lit after sunset.

A large fountain dominated the center of the square with one large column rising above Bryn's height, the water cascading down from three progressively larger tiers until it collected in a pool with a scalloped edge. Made of white marble with gray veins woven through it, it absorbed the ambient lantern light to create its own soft glow. A small, fenced garden held thin trees and flowerbeds.

"For a man who spent a long time stealing from the people of this city you have some loyal friends," I observed as I stood waiting for a direction to follow. A warm breeze blew through the streets between the buildings, carrying the scent of flowers that grew in front of people's homes.

Bryn shrugged. "I didn't steal from everyone; I mostly stole from people too wealthy to notice the pittance I. And once I was able to make a living hunting big game or as a guard for hire, I stole even less. It was only a survival tool, and a lot of people around here knew that."

Bryn led me to the large, wooden building nearby with a sign that read 'Crossroads Inn' above the door. I hesitated, remembering the last time we were in a place like this.

"Bryn," I called, and he turned back before he reached the door. "Do you think this is a good idea? The last time we were in a tavern, it was easy for your uncle to find us. Don't you have a place we can stay?"

His eyes scanned the area as his brows drew down, a look of uncertainty flashing over his face as he shook his head. He walked back to stand closer, so that we wouldn't be overheard.

He looked around the open space, but people were passing by without looking at us. "This is a much bigger city than Coveton, and people pass through all the time. I doubt anyone would take much notice of us if we stayed here. And we'll be gone in a day, two at the most."

"I hope we have that kind of time," I muttered, following as he turned away.

He held the door open and I stepped inside, the smell of ale and cooked meat overlying a musky aroma that I associated with large groups of people. The interior was clean and bright, with polished wooden tables and chairs arranged in a dining area, and a bar at the far end. Customers filled the space around tables and along the bar, and a young woman rushed from table to table placing and clearing food, replacing mugs, and taking orders.

Bryn's eyes scanned the crowd and fastened on the bar where several men leaned against the dark wood. With a gesture he led me forward, taking a seat next to a hunched old man with lank white hair. Sitting at Bryn's side, I waited.

"How can I help you folks?" A man stood up from behind the bar, polishing a glass as he smiled at us.

"My wife and I are passing through, and need a room," Bryn said cheerfully.

I looked at him, trying to hide the shock that I felt. *Wife?!*

The man behind the bar didn't notice anything amiss, and asked, "How long will the two of you be staying, sir?"

"Oh, I think just a couple of nights."

"Well, we have a few rooms available; at the end of the hall, there's a staircase. At the top of the stairs, turn right, and at the end of *that* hall is a room you should find suitable. And it's a silver a night. I take payment up front, if you would be so kind, sir."

Bryn produced two silver Aelios from his pocket and placed them into the man's waiting hand. "If we stay any longer than two nights, I'll pay you then."

The man nodded. "Dinner is served at dusk, but as you just arrived, I can have plates made."

"Thank you," Bryn said. He leaned past me to look at the old man seated next to me. "Allow me to buy this man his next drink as well." Bryn placed a few copper coins on the bar as the old man looked up from nursing his beer. He nodded in thanks, his eyes keen on my face for a long moment before raising his glass to his lips.

We made our way to the room the innkeeper described, and found that it was large, with windows overlooking the square. The pale yellow curtains matched the bedclothes. A small square table with a white porcelain basin and a large ewer were provided for washing, as well as a mirror situated on one wall. A plain wooden chair sat just below the windowsill. The windows were open wide, letting in a slight breeze that made the gauzy curtains float in the air.

People milled about in the square, vendors packing their carts as darkness fell in earnest. A candle's small flame lit our room with wavering light, flickering as the breeze caressed it.

After removing the harness holding his weapons and a small purse that clinked with the sound of coins, Bryn sat in the chair and looked up at me. "I'm sorry I didn't discuss that with you first, Lila. I thought it would be less suspicious to tell people we were married; my uncle isn't looking for a married couple." An uneasy grimace twisted his face as he scratched at his chin under the beard. "It's hard enough to keep people from noticing you."

"If we leave tomorrow, he won't have time to find us."

"Hopefully," Bryn said. He smiled and reached into the pocket of his trousers. With a shy smile, he opened his hand to reveal the silver chain holding my small key. "I've had this since the ship..." He paused, and shrugged. "I meant to give it to you, but with everything that's happened, I forgot."

Tears stung my eyes as I grasped it with my fingers and slipped the loop over my head. I turned the small silver key over in my hands, feeling the familiar contours as I often did when thinking or distracted.

A knock at the door startled me as Bryn surged to his feet. His weapons appeared in his hands as if they had been there all along.

Bryn gestured for me to stay back as he moved to the door. I nodded, my heart racing as Bryn placed his free hand on the doorknob.

He wrenched the door open and thrust his dirk out. The old man from the bar stood outside. As I watched, he unfolded himself from his hunched posture to stand straight. He stood almost a foot shorter than Bryn but held himself with the air of a man twice his height.

Bryn lowered his dirk, the wariness leaving him in a gush of relief. "I *thought* that was you at the bar. You've let your hair grow out since I saw you last, Sam."

The man stepped into the room, and I glared despite Bryn's sudden loss of tension. He looked me over, and then turned back to Bryn. "I haven't seen you for over a year, boy. And you come back with a wife?"

"I'd have thought you of all people could tell when I was bluffing," Bryn said. He held his hand out to me. "This is Lila. And we need your help."

"You always do, boy."

CHAPTER NINETEEN

Just before dusk, and after brief introductions, Bryn called for a meal to be brought to our room. We were provided with beef, fresh bread, roasted potatoes, and various other cooked vegetables. Sam and Bryn sat at our small table, and I was content to set my plate next to me on the bed. I ate until I felt I would burst, my stomach stretching to accommodate my overindulgence and then sat back while the two men talked, fighting drowsy happiness at having my belly full in order to satiate my curiosity.

My eyes rarely left Samuel's face as he listened to our tale and then told his own. His warm umber complexion held deep wrinkles of age, but his eyes were clear and focused, a light shade of brown with flecks of green, intent on his young friend.

Bryn told Samuel of the events of the last year of his life, leaving out all mention of the gift and the details of our escape. Samuel told Bryn about the happenings around town; the latest gossip, and the latest news on Bryn's former partners. He said much the same thing that Arthur had told him.

Bryn shook his head, and his knife and fork clattered onto his empty plate. "I'm not surprised. They were always more open with their talents than I was. I used to think they had more courage; now I'm beginning to think they just had less brains."

"I've been telling you that since I met you," Samuel insisted, smirking at Bryn. He leaned forward to place his elbows on the table, his fingers steepled together. "I'm glad you got out when you did. Though it sounds like your uncle's worse than those two."

"He is," Bryn admitted. "I'm glad I was able to leave."

"How *were* you able to leave so suddenly?" Samuel asked. "All you've told me is that you left, not what happened. I have a hard time believing your uncle would just let you go."

Bryn and I shared a look as he wiped a smear of food from his face, not sure how he would respond. The curiosity from the old man across the scarred wooden table served to grate nerves I had only just soothed with warmth, clean clothes, and a hot meal. Bryn stood and gestured for me to join him. I set my plate atop his on the table and stood at his side.

"I haven't told you everything, but it's not something I want to say where we might be overheard," Bryn said. As if to accentuate his point, we heard a man laugh as he passed our door. "Are you still living at the edge of town?" At Samuel's nod he continued. "Shall we take a walk, then?"

Samuel led the way through the city to the outer ring of houses. As dusk neared, the town was lit by flickering lanterns, illuminating people wandering home after a day's work. We stopped at a one-story stone house with a thatched roof that was falling into disrepair. It was tucked between two larger houses on either side, with hedgerows that threatened to swallow the fence at the front, as if to hide it from view of the grander houses the hedges belonged to.

The fence that surrounded what used to be a garden leaned back and forth like a drunk man trying to walk straight ahead. Weeds crowded the cracked paving stones leading from the packed earth of the street through what might have been a lawn in years past. The sad state of the approach only served to heighten the sense of sad neglect the faded, chipped blue paint of the door spoke to. Cobwebs clung to the darkened glass of a large window to the right of the door, hiding the interior from view.

When Samuel opened the door to lead us inside, we halted just inside the doorframe, unable to see through the crushing darkness.

Samuel's shuffling footsteps were the only clue to his location. A spark flashed as flint struck, and then a small flame bloomed. Matched, plush furniture greeted me when my eyes adjusted; they filled the room with a cozy quality that belied the outer shell of the house.

Books teetered on the edge of filled bookshelves and perched in piles on a small table beside an armchair near the hearth. A round, faded rug covered the bare floorboards between chair and sofas and held the moving shadows as a fire took hold in the small fireplace set in the wall to our left.

A doorway at my right led to a dining room that held a mahogany table and chairs. Large drapes shut out the night where they covered the picture window I had glimpsed from outside.

Samuel shoved himself off his knees with a groan and backed a few paces to the armchair. For a moment when the light flickered, I thought I saw something move around Sam. When I blinked, it was gone. With a sigh he sank onto the seat and gestured toward the sofas.

"Have a seat," he smiled.

My booted feet clicked on the hardwood floor. When I sank into the overstuffed couch, it felt as though the cushions embraced me, and I sighed at such comfort after so long spent sleeping on the ground.

Samuel's eyes bored into mine. "So.... I'm guessing that many of the missing parts to this story revolve around you. Care to fill me in?"

A quick glance at Bryn's wary face confirmed that I should hold back most of the details. My mind sought something I could relate without putting Samuel in danger, and I settled on a simple truth.

"Bryn's uncle is dangerous, and we have something he wants. Since we can't give it to him, he's hunting us. We need to find somewhere remote to hide."

Samuel's silvered, bushy eyebrow quirked with skepticism. "What do you have that could be valuable enough for him to abandon his ship?" His gaze slid to Bryn, and his brow furrowed as he awaited the answer.

"I don't want to give you any more information than that, Sam. If he comes here and learns that you know me, he could ask you questions that you don't want to answer. And believe me when I tell you, it's better not to know the answers than to try and hide them from him."

"Keep your secrets, then," Samuel huffed, turning his gaze back to me. "My part in this is to tell you where you can hide from this man who sounds like he's willing to abandon everything to follow you across the world." He let out a dry, wheezy chuckle and shook his head, his eyes wide in disbelief. "What makes you think you can hide from him? And why would you assume that *I* know of any such place?"

Bryn shrugged. "You know I don't trust easily, Sam. Of the few people I would entrust my life with, you are the best traveled. You're my best and only hope."

A glare replaced the wide-eyed stare. "And guilt is your only recourse," he grumbled. After a long silence, he let out a huff and shook his head again. "I may know of a place, but it's not close, and you're not going alone. If he's as dangerous as you say, I don't want to be around when he comes asking questions. I'll take you there myself."

His face relaxing in relief, Bryn scrubbed his hands through his hair. "Thanks, Sam." He sank further into the sofa's cushion, the tension leaving him in a rush. "We need to get some supplies together and leave tomorrow if we can. I don't know how long it will take Roglin to get here, but I'd rather be long gone by the time he arrives."

"Plenty of time, boy," Samuel replied. "Meet me at the south gate at midday and we can begin our journey south."

I looked back and forth between the two men, wary about the arrangements being made for me. While the prospect of finding a place where Roglin couldn't find us seemed tempting, I would be alone with another strange man that Bryn trusted. Over the past weeks, some of my fear about Bryn's intentions had faded, but I was still a long way from trusting him implicitly.

When Bryn rose and offered me his hand, I accepted, not knowing what to say to prevent Samuel from traveling with us. If seen with us, it could put him in harm's way. If he saw me using the gift, what would he do?

Lost in fresh worries, I followed Bryn in silence as he bid Samuel farewell and led me out the door. Dimly aware of the shadowed stones in the dirt beneath my feet, I stumbled more than once on the hidden obstacles in my path while Bryn discussed the supplies we would need. He spoke of arrows and food, and a sword that I could easily wield. When I didn't respond to his inquiries about the type of blade I felt most comfortable with, he grasped my hand to stop me in the street.

"Lila, are you all right?"

Concern carved a line between his brows, his eyes peering into mine as if he could read my thoughts.

"Yes," I replied. "But I'm worried about your friend traveling with us."

"Sam?" He glanced in the direction of the house disappearing behind us. "He can take care of himself, and he won't slow us down. That old man moves much faster than you would think he could."

"I'm more concerned that he may see something he shouldn't."

Comprehension lit his eyes, and he nodded. "Don't try to use the gift while we're with him," he stated, as if it were a simple matter.

"And if it's not something I can control?"

He dismissed the idea with a casual shrug.

"Sam is a man that you can trust. With everything that's happened, I can understand you might not see it that way, and it must be difficult for you to agree based on nothing but the word of a man that held you captive." Again, his brow furrowed, and his eyes bored into mine as his tone changed, becoming more serious. "So remember that I am also acting on self-interest in keeping you safe. If you can't trust me, trust that."

I considered him for a long moment, matching his intent stare as I attempted to gauge his sincerity. The moment passed and I nodded my agreement, following again as he led me back to the inn. The tavern held only the most resolute drinkers; most of the crowd had dispersed to find their beds for the night and a hushed atmosphere was settled over the remaining patrons.

The candlelight flickered with our arrival and the opening door. Rivulets of melted wax ran the length and settled in the base, the excess flowing over the lip to cool against the wood surface.

"I'll take the floor," Bryn offered, sliding the bolt home with a snap. "If I could borrow your cloak."

"That's fine with me," I replied, relieved to avoid discussion of the sleeping arrangement.

Bryn set about the task of making himself a bed of cloaks and blankets by the door. With his back turned, I took the opportunity to loosen the cords holding my bodice tight against my chest and slide beneath the blankets on the bed before removing it and dropping it to the floor. After shuffling out of the trousers and dropping them next to the bodice, only my short chemise and the blankets piled atop me sheltered my body.

I closed my eyes and sighed as I relaxed into the mattress, Bryn's shuffling noises subsiding as he settled into his makeshift bed.

With a smile on my lips, I drifted off into a peaceful night's sleep.

CHAPTER TWENTY

With the sun peeking over the horizon and the city rising reluctantly from its slumber, Bryn and I exited the inn in search of supplies to sustain us on our journey to an unknown haven. We visited Arthur and Maude, explaining that we would need a pack to carry extra clothes and supplies for the road. They were generous, insisting we take their best leather packs at no charge. Bryn tried to pay them, but they pushed his hand away every time. Arthur only asked that we pay him a visit the next time we found ourselves in the area.

The fletcher stood next to the bladesmith in the square, across from the inn. There, Bryn spent over an hour discussing the merits of this type of feather over that type of feather. I had never learned to use a bow, and my mind wandered as I looked around the room.

Long and short bows adorned the walls and shelves, and arrows fletched with feathers of all colors and shapes mingled among them. Most arrowheads were flat, but some held barbs designed to dig into the flesh of an enemy and prevent removal. When Bryn's long conversation with the man behind the counter finished, he held a set with hawk feather flights that he stuck into his quiver and led me to the bladesmith next door.

A variety of swords and knives were arrayed on the walls and in display cases around the shop. Through a back door, a small room opened into a covered yard where the forge was located. A large, burly man pounded a piece of steel into a work of art, impervious to the loud clangs he was producing. My eyes strayed to the longer swords near the counter.

"Do you have a preference?" Bryn asked, noting my interest.

"I used to have a slim hand-and-a-half sword that I trained with. It had a simple, leather-bound grip and straight guard. I can use a short sword too, but I prefer the longer blade." My hands trailed over the cold steel of a simple blade with a wire-bound hilt, a faint smile on my lips.

Bryn seemed impressed. "I expect anyone who knows their preference of blades so specifically should be able to use one just as well."

"Hunter and I used to spar almost daily after we learned the basics from our crew."

"Hunter?" Bryn frowned, and I realized that we had never spoken of him.

"He was a...friend," I finished, not sure how I should describe the man I had cared for and lost, and not sure that I wanted to try. The thought of his mussed brown hair and his emerald-green eyes made my breath catch, so I took a deep breath and shoved the grief away.

"You felt something strong for him," Bryn drawled, his eyes focused beyond me as if listening to something I couldn't hear. My brow furrowed, confused, and put off by his distant look and uncanny description of my feelings.

"I've noticed a pained look on your face sometimes, talking about your crew. But it's different when you mentioned Hunter." He lowered his voice and leaned closer. "I can actually *feel* how you felt around him. I think it's because it's so strong; I can feel your pain."

I backed away from him a step, staggered by what he was telling me.

"Have you felt anything else from me?"

"The last time you used the gift, your fear was blinding. I think that's why I reacted like I did; I was sure that something happened to you and we were both about to die. And whenever you talk about your captain, it's like reliving the day my mother died."

His eyes held tenderness, and sympathy and remorse flooded through me as I considered what he was going through. At what *I* had put him through.

"I'm sorry, Bryn. If I could stop this and let you live your own life, I would."

"I know, Lila. And I'm even beginning to believe that it's not entirely your fault." A lopsided grin spread across his lips, one that I couldn't help answering. Over the weeks that we had traveled together and relied on one another, this moment was the first time I felt I could understand him.

"Can I help you?" a polite voice asked, breaking our gazes away from one another to regard the burly smith wiping his hands on a dingy rag.

"Yes," Bryn replied. "The lady would like a new sword. Preferably a hand-and-a-half sword with a light, slim blade."

The blacksmith eyed me with curiosity. "Sure, Bryn," he said. "I have a few blades that you might be interested in, miss. Most here are reserved for the guard or the King's army, but I've a few set aside for trade." He slid out from behind the counter to stand next to me. A few claymores and longswords with large, heavy blades dominated the wall to my left while a couple of swords at the end looked to be slim enough for me to handle.

"Both of these I made with high-quality steel. They're slightly more flexible than the wider blades, but I can assure you, they are just as strong. Would you like to feel the balance?"

"Thank you," I replied with a smile.

He grasped one of the swords from the wall and handed it to me hilt first. The leather-wrapped grip warmed in my hand, reminding of my lost blade, and was long enough for both of my hands to grip it with about an inch to spare.

I rotated my wrist, feeling the weight of the sword for a moment before I spied another at the end of the row. The same basic shape and size as the other, it looked as if it had been used before, with a slight notch in the blade near the guard. The guard was straight, as mine had been, but the pommel was molded into the shape of a rose in mid-bloom.

"The pommel is plated in copper, to show off the design," he informed me, following my gaze. I nodded, impressed by the craftsmanship. "This isn't one that I made, but it was traded to me years back and no one has bought it."

Carefully I handed the sword in my hand back to the blacksmith and waited for him to offer me the hilt of the rose-pommeled blade. The leather was worn, with lines that showed where someone had gripped many times before, but it felt as if that hand had been mine.

The blacksmith pointed to the door in the back. "If you'd like to step outside, you can give it a swing or two."

Following his suggestion, I moved through the back room and out into the yard. I noticed along the side of the forge a wide area that looked to be set aside for customers to test the wares. A wooden dummy stood in the middle with gouges and scratches marring the surface.

I gripped the sword with both hands, not trusting that I was strong enough to handle a blade like this with one hand yet. My body flowed through a few of the practice forms Captain Morrig had taught me with loud thumps as the sword connected to the wood. My muscles warmed, my breathing and pulse quickened, and my arms and legs moved faster as they remembered their purpose. I had lost a lot of the strength I built up sparring with Hunter, but the technique was something I couldn't forget if I tried.

This blade felt as though it was made for me, and I grew accustomed to it in a way that I hadn't with my old sword. In mere moments it had become an extension of me, connecting to the target with little more than a thought.

I put a few more notches into the blacksmith's dummy before I let my arms fall. My muscles screamed with the effort, my breathing came harsh and quick, and my brow was slick with sweat.

Bryn and the smith stood near the doorway, watching as I went through my exercises testing the blade.

"It looks like it suits you, Miss," the smith said.

"Thank you," I panted, drained from the exercise.

"I think I need to take you up on that offer to spar," Bryn said.

"I wouldn't say no to the practice," I admitted with a chuckle. "I am very out of shape."

I followed the men back into the shop and laid the sword on the counter. The smith pulled a leather-wrapped wooden scabbard and matching leather belt from a shelf behind the counter and slid the sword inside.

"This is one of my favorites. I named it Desire, for the copper rose. My wife told me that's what those roses symbolize, and I named it with her in mind." He buffed the pommel with a cloth as he spoke. "Normally, I'd charge a small fortune for a piece like this. But since you're with Bryn, I'll let her go for five gold pieces."

"Done," Bryn agreed. "I appreciate it, Peter. Give my regards to Sara and the kids. And please, if anyone asks after me that you don't know, be careful."

The belt around my waist, Desire rested at my left hip.

"She really *does* suit you," Bryn said, nodding his appreciation.

Smiling again, I flushed with pleasure and pivoted to hide my reddened cheeks from Bryn.

Before returning to the inn, we visited a grocer to stock up on food for the trip, filling our packs with as much bread, dried meat, and cheese as we could. A bag of apples made it into the pile. Bryn assured me that he would find us plants along the way to add to our meals while we traversed the continent.

After a hasty meal of beef stew made from the leftover meat served the night before, we collected our packs from our rooms and exited the inn in the bright sun of midday to find Samuel.

CHAPTER TWENTY-ONE

The city buzzed with streets full of people. Constant streams of them flowed into and out of all the shops along our path. The water cascading from the upper tiers of the fountain sparkled in the light of the sun that shone in a clear blue sky.

After bobbing in and out of the path of several wagons and carts on their way to the square, we arrived at the open gate a short time later. Two massive wooden doors on iron hinges, the gate stood wide enough for two wagons to pass through side by side; Samuel stood in his affected wizened old man's hunch, talking to one of the guards.

As we arrived, a steady line of people wandered in and out of the city. Some looked up at the thick stone walls with guards patrolling along the ramparts in awe; likely farmers from the surrounding area coming to the city for a day. Most seemed not to notice the fortifications, chatting with one another as they strolled beneath the shadow of their protection from the outside world.

Several people on horses, armed with bows strapped to their saddles and dirks at their belts, rode in behind the stream of people on foot. They were alert, scanning faces and the area as if looking for danger. We stepped aside to let them pass, and they came to a stop just inside the gate and dismounted.

They watched the flow of people moving in as Sam finished his conversation and hoisted his pack onto his shoulders, shuffling into step with a group on their way out.

Bryn and I started to follow, but were forced aside by another few people on horseback. Also armed to the teeth, they preceded a wagon carrying a load of supplies and several more people. More armed mercenary-types, and two very familiar faces.

I spun away and pulled my hood farther forward to hide my face, and pulled Bryn along with me.

"Put your hood up," I hissed under my breath. Confused, Bryn followed my instruction, turning away like I did.

"What is it?" he murmured. He tried to look around, but I stopped him with a hand on his arm.

"Your uncle is in that wagon," I whispered. "With Derth, and a bunch of people bristling with weapons."

"Elder's eyes!" Bryn quietly cursed. His nostrils flared, and he ran his fingers through his hair under the hood. "I didn't think they'd get here so fast. We have to go. Wait until they're past us, and then we'll move with the next crowd."

We waited, listening to the clopping horse hooves and the rumble of the wagon as it rolled by. The wagon came to a creaking stop, the horses snorted, and the sound of voices rose over the rest of the crowd. My heart was pounding so hard that it pulsed in my ears, and each beat seemed to make my vision narrow. I took a deep breath to steady my nerves when I heard Roglin's graveled voice and Derth's terse reply. I couldn't quite make out the words, but the sound of their voices was enough to rattle me.

Bryn took my hand in his and started to walk away. My shoulder bumped against the person next to me, and I mumbled an apology. A hand wrapped around my arm and whirled me toward the city. I looked up into Roglin's angry eyes and eager smile.

When he spoke, his voice was low enough to avoid being heard by the guards that were standing on either side of the gate, full of eager malice. "Stay for a while," he insisted, "we have so much to talk about."

I pulled against his grip, but it tightened, and tugged me closer. Bryn appeared, trying to interpose himself between Roglin and me by shoving against his uncle's chest. While Bryn tried to wrest me from Roglin, Roglin pulled harder, making me feel like a sail being tugged by a heavy wind, about to snap.

"Let go," Bryn growled. I looked over his shoulder toward the wagon, where Derth was sitting in the bed, staring down at me. As our eyes met, I felt a wave of lethargy crash into me. My legs wobbled, and I pulled my gaze from Derth, the lethargy falling away like water dripping down.

"You took everything from me," Roglin said to me. "My nephew, my livelihood, my *ship*. He's not worth as much as I thought," he spat, glaring at Bryn, "and I have stores of gold. As much as I wish I could let Derth tear you apart for the inconvenience you've caused, it can be rectified. But, if I don't deliver you to where you need to go, I can't let you, or anyone who knew I had you, live."

His words were no less forceful for the fact that he was whispering. Several of the mercenaries that had accompanied the wagon were circling us now, and the crowd was moving around us, forming a circular perimeter around our altercation. I kept my eyes away from Derth, though I could see him shuffling toward us from the corner of my eye.

He glanced over my shoulder, toward the guards I knew were behind me. I tried to look their way, to catch their attention, but Roglin yanked on my arm to keep my focus on him. Bryn tugged me backward, and something inside me snapped. I twisted my arms, pulling them free from each man in the same motion, and took a step back.

I was so angry, and so terrified, I wanted to get out of here, and I didn't want Roglin and the others to follow. "The consequences of your failure are not my problem!" I yelled, turning away again and looking toward the gate, where a number of guards had noticed the commotion and were heading toward us. "Leave me alone!" I yelled, taking a few more steps back.

"What's happening here?" a guard asked, her voice loud and authoritative. Three guards filed in around her, putting themselves between the mercenaries and Roglin, while two more made sure the crowd moved in a different direction.

Roglin opened his mouth, but I was prepared. "This man just grabbed me, he threatened me!" I shouted, letting my terror break the surface, tears rolling down my face. "Please don't let him hurt me!"

The guard stepped between Roglin and me. "Sir, did you threaten this woman?"

Bryn grasped my hand again, and started to edge back from the crowd. I risked a glance at Derth, who was smiling directly at me. A spike of pain stabbed into my head, and my knees buckled again. Bryn held me up, and turned to walk away.

"Keep that maniac away from my wife!" he demanded.

"This is a misunderstanding," Roglin said, his voice smooth and charming again. "I was speaking to the young woman, nothing more."

"When a woman says that she's feeling threatened, I tend to believe her," the guard said. She turned to us with a warm smile. "Please, take your wife to the gate and wait for me there. I'll need a bit more information once she's ready."

"Thank you," Bryn said, helping me move forward as the woman turned back to Roglin.

The malevolent glare transformed into a smile as the guard's attention came to rest on Roglin again. We were moving through the crowd, escorted by one of the guards, and I caught his smooth words.

"We can sort this out if you take me to your captain. He's an old friend of mine, and he can vouch for my character. I assume Joulis Urigh is still the captain here?"

"We won't have long," I whispered to Bryn.

"I wouldn't be surprised if he's paid the captain to look the other way," Bryn said. "We need to get away from this guard."

We arrived at the gate and the guard tried to usher us inside the gatehouse. Bryn stopped short of the door and gestured back toward Roglin. "Before that man grabbed my wife, I heard the mercenaries with him talking about killing people on the road a few days ago. I'm worried they might cause more trouble if they think they'll be detained."

The guard with us stared at Bryn as if trying to feel the truth in his words. He glanced back toward his fellow guards, and the mercenaries bristling with weapons.

"Go inside, please," he said, pointing toward the door, "and wait for us in there. No one will bother you." He walked back through the crowd, and before he had gone too far, Bryn ducked into the crowd, towing me behind him.

On the other side of the gate the crowd dispersed, most heading east or west, with only a few moving south. I wanted to run, to dash into the trees a small distance from the road on my left, but I kept my pace even, my hand still in Bryn's. Sam stood in the distance, waiting at the side of the road as people strolled past him.

"We need to get to the trees," Bryn growled. His rage and fear were palpable, the same as my own. "We'll send Sam ahead, or back... away from us. He can't be part of this." He cursed under his breath again.

"We'll get to the trees," I assured him. "We'll tell Sam to turn back, and hope that they don't realize he's with us. If it comes to it, we can try to fight in the forest. You have your bow, I can try to use the gift...." I trailed off, shrugging as I ran out of suggestions and reassurances.

Sam watched us hurry toward him, his face a mask of confusion and concern.

"Boy," he started, "what...?"

Bryn held up a hand to stall him, and then waved him away, holding his hand close to his chest so that anyone following us might not see him. We walked past without a glance as Bryn spoke under his breath to Sam.

"They've found us. Leave."

"Bryn...." Sam said, clearly torn about whether to listen to Bryn.

We didn't wait for him to continue his thought, but pushed past him, moving faster. I risked a glance back, but I didn't see anyone coming for us. I wasn't naïve enough to think that meant we would escape so easily. It took too long to reach the bend in the road that skirted the edge of the forest. Every moment I expected Derth to cause me unbearable pain again, or for one of Roglin's thugs to send an arrow flying for my back.

But they didn't come, so we cut away from the packed dirt road, and into the trees.

The morning sun fell in patches through the canopy above to warm my face one moment and leave it in shade the next. The trees became thicker and thicker, until cool darkness engulfed us when we plunged between two tall oaks and into the forest itself.

We darted between massive trunks and skirted shrubs that clutched at our legs and threatened to pull us down. It seemed the very forest wanted to slow us as the underbrush became too thick to run through. Bryn pulled aside thorny growths to allow me to pass with my cloak clutched against my side.

Bryn dropped my hand when the forest became too thick for us to walk side-by-side. He led me east for a ways, and then turned south after we'd been walking for a while. I couldn't tell how much time had passed, since I didn't have the sun to reference. We didn't talk, Bryn moved quietly through the trees despite our speed, and I did my best to emulate him.

I started to relax as even more time passed and no attack came. Not enough to slow my pace, but it didn't feel like my heart was going to beat through my chest anymore. I leapt over a large root sticking out of the ground, but my foot caught, and I tumbled to the forest floor. When I tried to stand, my foot caught on something, and I couldn't pull it free.

"Bryn," I called, my voice still low, "I'm stuck." I didn't want him to get too far ahead of me. Turning to take a look at what had my foot, I was shocked to see a root wrapped *around* my foot.

"What...." I muttered, twisting my foot to free it. The root twisted with it, tightening around my ankle. The pressure was almost painful, and I inhaled sharply as Bryn grunted next to me.

He knelt with his face next to the root, examining it as I pulled again.

"This isn't natural," he muttered. He straightened, his eyes searching the trees as I did the same.

"Derth," I whispered.

As if acknowledging something I had felt when I heard his voice again, I felt pressure on the inside of my head, threatening to overwhelm me. Like Derth was wrapping his fingers around my neck, suffocating me.

I tried to call the spirits, but the pressure increased. Derth knew what I was trying to do, and I could feel him tugging at a remnant of the curtain he used to separate me from my gift. A small scrap in the corner of my mind, like a thought half-forgotten, brought to the forefront of my consciousness. I pushed against it, calling for the spirits, reaching out to the gift.

But Derth's presence was smothering me, and I couldn't get through. Something slammed against the root around my ankle, and I cried out in pain as the root recoiled, wrenching my ankle away.

"Lila, this is going to hurt!" Bryn shouted. His voice pulled me from my internal conflict. My eyes focused on his arm as it swung overhead, and the hatchet in his hand. It came down in a flash, splintering the root from the rest of the tree as it twisted tighter, and jarring my ankle again.

"Ah!" I yelled as my ankle turned again. The root still encircled my ankle, but I could now scoot away from the tree. The sharp bite of pain from the root as I dragged my heavy foot helped to clear Derth from my mind, and I could feel the glow of the gift start to push through his interference.

Someone rushed through the trees toward me, sword drawn to stab down at my prone form. I reached for my sword, but I could see that I couldn't draw it in time. Just before it connected, Bryn's dirk deflected it. He hurled himself at this person, one of Roglin's mercenaries, but she parried his thrust and spun around, letting his momentum carry him into the nearest tree.

She turned back to me, but this time I was ready. I brought Desire up to block her downward swing and pushed against her as I got to my feet, twisting my ankle free of the root. She lunged, and I leaned aside, batting her blade away. She spun into the deflection, with the top of her sword aimed for my chest. I ducked, bringing my sword up at an angle, and she impaled herself on the blade.

I wrenched the blade free, and felt the spirits approaching as if wading through water toward me. Their progress was slow, but they were coming. An arrow thudded into the ground next to me as another flew toward Bryn. He shouted as the arrow sliced through his arm.

"Bryn!" I yelled. *Faster!* I shouted to the spirits.

"Just a graze!" Bryn said through gritted teeth. "Come on!" He reached down and hauled me to my feet. I yelped when I put weight on my ankle. "Damn the Elders!" Bryn yelled.

I took a deep breath against the pain, and felt the spirits surge forward, toward the source of my pain. I reached down and grasped the root, wanting to shatter it. A myriad of spectral hands spread along the bark, and each of them grasped it. When I squeezed, the other hands squeezed. The wood groaned, and then it seemed to break into splinters all at once.

Derth's voice found me through the trees. "We are connected. You can't escape."

The pressure increased, becoming a physical pain in my head, and the spirits began to retreat from it. But I wouldn't let them, clutching the gift as I limped away from where the arrows were flying between the trees. I pushed it down to my ankle to ease the pain, and my limp changed to a jog.

Another arrow whistled through the air and disappeared in a bush to my right. I searched for a way to stop our pursuers, knowing my grasp of the gift was waning with every passing moment. If I could get the arrows to stop, I could focus on Derth.

We needed a barrier between us, I decided. More than the sporadic placement of the trees, which they could get around as fast as we were. My cloak pulled as an arrow flew through it. Imagining the trees twisting together, like Derth had done with the root, I sent the spirits away from me. Glancing back, I watched as several tall trees swayed closer, like they were gripped by a strong wind. They didn't straighten back up, but leaned toward each other and remained there. All the way to the ground, the trunks bent inward to form a wall between us and the figures raising their bows in our direction.

I tried to pull another tree, much larger, to join the wall. My control slipped, and I flung the tree too hard at the others. With a loud crack, it fell into the wall. It dragged the outer edge of the wall down, away from us, with a clamor of noise that echoed through the forest. A cry of pain sounded out of sight, and I hoped it was Roglin. I *knew* it wasn't Derth, because I still felt him trying to dig into my head.

The spirits pulled away from his twisted gift as it inched a bit further into me. His darkness surrounded my glow. For a moment, it threatened to smother it, and I felt the spirits begin to fade. Not just cutting me off from my gift, but severing my connection to it. Like he would engulf what I had and take it for his own.

"No!" I screamed, in my head and out loud. My glow brightened, and it felt more powerful than ever. I pulled more trees into my barrier to replace those that had fallen and clear the path ahead of us. Feeling more spirits rush to my side, to do what I commanded, I decided that I was tired of being chased, and that I could end it now. I sought the darkness that I recognized as Derth, and the people around him. They were trapped beneath the fallen trees, Derth's gift the only thing keeping them from being crushed.

I wrapped my glow around his darkness and squeezed, trying to cut him off from *his* gift. If he could do it to me, why couldn't I reciprocate? Why couldn't I destroy this menace to the world right now? I pushed on the fallen tree, trying to crush all of them. The spirits swarmed, as if they were enticing me to reach for more power, that I couldn't do what I wanted without more of the gift in my control.

As I did what they asked, I felt the glow start to overwhelm me as trees uprooted themselves and were flung towards our pursuers. It felt like my power was the only thing that existed, and that it wanted to take control of me. I tried to let it go, to make the spirits go away, but more came.

"Stop!" I screamed. The gift drained out of me in a rush, the trees I was pushing twisting in the air, and one of the branches slammed into Bryn, sending him flying behind me. More screams from the people with Roglin, and Derth's dark presence blinked out. I gasped at the relief, so much like pulling a splinter from my hand, and stumbled forward to where Bryn was getting back on his feet.

"We have to go," I said, hooking my arm through Bryn's. Blood dripped down his temple from a large gash at his hairline, and he blinked a few times, clearly disoriented. Pulling gently on his arm, I urged him up. "Can you stand? We need to go while we can."

It only took a few moments for Bryn to come around, and then I led him forward, away from the danger that might still be lurking behind.

CHAPTER TWENTY-TWO

We paused long enough to bandage the gash on Bryn's arm and head, and then he led us through the trees for a while before cutting back in the direction of the road. As the light began to fade, we found ourselves near the edge of the forest, and Bryn stopped before we could be seen.

I sat down with my back against a pine tree and pulled out a waterskin. While he searched our surroundings I drank, and then passed it to him when he came to sit next to me.

He gulped down a few mouthfuls and wiped his mouth on the back of his sleeve.

"I don't see anyone," he said.

"I hope Samuel got home all right. Or out of sight, at least."

"He'll be fine," Bryn said with confidence. "How are you? We both need rest, but I don't know how long we can. I don't want to assume we're clear of Derth and Roglin."

I shook my head. "I know what you mean. I need sleep, but I don't want them to catch up to us. I'm more tired than I should be.

Whatever Derth was doing to me, whatever I almost did to myself, it drained me."

Bryn fumbled in his pack and brought out a couple of apples. He handed one to me and bit into his with a crunch. He spoke while he chewed.

"We can cut east, and maybe we'll get lucky, find a little town where we can rest, resupply, and figure out what to do next. For now, we'll eat, walk a bit longer, and then bed down for the night. No fire. Sorry." He shrugged and took another bite.

After a bit of bread and some more water, we got to our feet and walked further south. Bryn kept us within shouting distance of the road, but the trees were too thick for anyone to see us. That was the hope, at least.

"What you did back there," Bryn said with a glance over his shoulder, "was pretty dangerous." I waited for him to scold me, but he smirked instead. "And probably saved our lives. Well done."

"Thanks," I said. "It was just instinct, at first. After that, I think I almost did too much. The gift tried to take over."

"Whatever it was, I hope you did some damage to them. It would be nice not to look over our shoulders anymore."

I smiled to myself when he looked away. That would have turned into an argument not long ago. But he didn't understand how close I'd come to losing myself, and my smile faded.

When it was so dark that we couldn't see, Bryn stopped us. We shrugged off our packs, had a bit more food, and I laid down atop my unfurled bedroll. We would sleep in shifts, and Bryn insisted he take the first so that I could rest. Both of us could feel how exhausted I was.

I was asleep in seconds. And it felt like I had only just closed my eyes when Bryn shook my shoulder to wake me. His eyes were bleary as I sat up.

"Thanks," I yawned. "I'll wake you in a few hours."

He nodded and fell onto my bedroll face first. In a few moments he was snoring softly. I pulled my blanket over him to stave off the night's chill and walked a short distance away.

My eyelids were heavy with sleep, but my mind was alert as I moved in a tight circle around where Bryn slept. I heard the sound of creatures moving through the trees in the distance, as well as the crunch of plants beneath my feet. But nothing alarming, which I was thankful for.

Bryn was on his side when I came back to where I started. Wanting to watch the road for a while, I moved in that direction. The trees thinned as I came to the forest's edge, so I pulled the hood of my cloak forward, hoping to blend in with the shadows. Nothing moved along or around the road, and I leaned against a trunk to wait and watch.

Every so often, I walked back to check on Bryn before heading back to the road. I couldn't imagine Roglin giving up the chase, but I didn't think they'd move through the trees if they could avoid it. If I was going to see them anywhere, it should be along the road. I didn't think we were lucky enough to have killed them when the trees fell, so I kept my eyes on the clear space beyond the forest.

When the sky started to lighten, I decided it was time to wake Bryn. I looked north along the road once more before plunging back into the trees. I shook Bryn awake as he had done for me. We shared a cold meal and some water and packed what little we had taken out the night before. Tired and resolved to move fast today, we headed for the road to check it once more.

A lone figure moved along the road, hunched and cloaked. For a moment, I was sure it was Derth. I clutched Bryn's hand, ready to pull him away, but I noticed that despite the dim light, I could see a difference between this person and the man that haunted my dreams. This person was moving much faster than I'd ever seen Derth move. They peered back the way they had come, and then ahead on the road. And then they straightened out of their hunch and began to run.

"Samuel," I said in an exhale of relief. "He looks fine."

Bryn put his fingers in his mouth and whistled. Samuel's head snapped in the direction of the sound, and he veered left, toward us. When he reached us, Bryn clasped his back, smiling.

"You're all right, old man," he said in a murmur. "We were worried about you."

Samuel smiled back at Bryn. "They didn't notice me, they were intent on you two."

"Did they get back to the road?" I asked.

Samuel shrugged. "I've been walking since you left. If they did, they're behind me somewhere. Did they catch up to you?"

"Yeah," Bryn said. He turned into the trees and we all followed as he walked southward. "We got away from them, but it was close."

"Let's hope we can stay ahead of them," Samuel said.

We traveled for a few days without any sign of pursuit, staying deep in the forest to hide our progress. As night fell on the third day, we stopped next to an overhang of rock on the side of a hill. Situated near the edge of a clearing, I could look skyward to see stars twinkling in the deep night sky. All around, a thick growth of bushes grew with fat purple berries; we plucked handfuls at a time, wrapping as many in a cloth to keep as we stuffed into our mouths. Sweet juice exploded against my tongue as my teeth punctured the fragile skin.

The remains of a fire pit suggested we were not the only ones to have found this shelter. Stones placed in a ring sat scattered by the years, plants overtaking the space cleared long ago.

I dropped my pack on the ground under the overhang against the rock face and went to work reconstructing the fire pit. Grasses and ferns tore free of the dirt by the handful and I stacked them to the side, outside the ring of stones. Bryn stalked into the trees, nocking an arrow, and Samuel ambled in the opposite direction, stooping to collect small branches in his path.

As I finished with the pit, Samuel walked back into view with an armload of wood. The dried twigs and small branches clattered to the ground nearby in a heap before he started to arrange them neatly in preparation for starting a fire.

With a small fire crackling beneath the rock a short time later, the peaceful still of the forest and twitter of birds announcing our intrusion, I felt at more at ease than I had in a while. Sighing, I leaned my head back to watch the stars blink in and out above our heads as I had so many times on board the *Catherine*. After a time, Sam shifted his weight, breaking the spell. Looking around, I could see that Bryn had not yet returned, and wondered where he was.

"Bryn's been gone a while," I commented. Sam looked up from gazing at the flames with a faint smile.

"He can take care of himself," he replied. "Tends to lose track of time when he's hunting."

"How can he be hunting in the dark?" I wondered aloud. Sam shrugged in response and turned his eyes back to the fire, dismissing my concern.

I rose to my feet with an irritated sigh, a niggling worry that Roglin may have caught up with us feeding blossoming anxiety in the pit of my empty stomach. Pacing to the edge of the forest in the direction Bryn had taken, I stood in the faint light of the fire behind me to gaze into the black depths between the trees.

I considered plunging into the forest to search for Bryn but dismissed the idea as soon as it occurred to me. With no indication of his location, I would only get lost in my search. The most sensible course of action would be to stay with Sam by the fire and wait for Bryn to come back to us, but my worry only grew with the realization that I could do nothing to help if Roglin was lurking somewhere out of sight.

To calm my fraying nerves, I closed my eyes and heaved a deep sigh. My fingers found Desire's hilt, the leather creaking as I gripped it. Having a sword at my hip brought some comfort, but not nearly enough to dispel my disquiet. The leather groaned again as my hand tightened on the hilt, itching to face an imagined enemy.

I realized in that moment that somehow, friendship and trust had formed between us without my knowledge or desire to allow it. When I pictured Bryn's face, I no longer felt the same accompanying rage and shame. His lopsided grin and clear blue eyes engendered a warm glow I associated with friends that died when the *Catherine* sank. That warm glow grew, bringing a flush of pleasant surprise that shuddered throughout my body and cast my mind *outward* in search of Bryn by ethereal hands.

The knife snicked home into the sheath at his belt, the smell of warm blood filling his nostrils from the kill at his feet. In the gloom beneath the trees only a sliver of light illuminated the ground, the large rabbit barely visible in the leaf litter.

He still couldn't shake the feeling that they were being watched. The same feeling that had followed since Coveton, like there were eyes in the trees wherever they went.

Tying a piece of twine around the rabbit's skinned legs, he tied it next to the other at the bottom of his pack and buried the organs and skin. If he had time and space in his pack, he would have liked to keep the skins to make something warm. With winter on its way, it would get cold fast, and he couldn't have Lila freezing in the snow. Not if he wanted to avoid freezing himself.

A smile tugged at the corner of his mouth as he picked up a handful of leaves to scrape the drying blood from his hands, thinking of her slashing the blacksmith's practice dummy. The sun lit her hair, making it look like nothing so much as a writhing mass of flames as her fluid movements threw it out into the afternoon air.

That look of satisfaction stirred something he thought long dead within him. The trouble she had put him through faded when he recalled the way she looked with that sword.

The hairs on the back of his neck stood suddenly erect as he sensed something...different. One fluid movement brought him upright, sword in hand and body tensed to strike. Hearing and seeing no movement, he glanced up and around, pacing a slow circle around the spruce tree at his back. When he could find no threat, he replaced his sword, the steel hissing along the scabbard.

Awareness tugged at the back of his mind, the sense of something different persisting, teasing him. He stooped to retrieve his pack, slinging it onto a shoulder and turning in the direction of the camp. Suddenly feeling guilty about his prolonged absence, he hoped that Lila wouldn't fear the worst and come after him in the dark.

Picturing the look of disapproval on her face, he felt it again, that sense that something had changed. Focusing on it, he thought again of Lila, and realization struck. This felt like her anger in the woods, when she had used her gift and sent him scrambling to reach her.

With his eyes wide, he stared into the darkness, his eyes fixed in the direction where she stood, staring into the same darkness in search of him.

With a start I staggered back a step as the connection broke. Everything he had seen, felt, and touched; I had experienced as if I were him. I looked down to my own hands to reassure myself that they weren't streaked with dried blood, and found my fist gripped around the hilt of my sword, my knuckles white. It took a gargantuan effort, but I released it.

"Is something wrong, Lila?" Sam's voice called me back into myself.

"No," I stammered, trying to calm my racing heart and bewilderment. "Everything is fine." When I turned back to the fire,

Sam stood poised to move in my direction as if he didn't believe me. I tried to smile to reassure him, but the muscles in my face felt wrong, like they weren't mine. My legs felt stiff and alien and my first steps were halting and clumsy. I shuffled back to the fire and plopped down across from Sam, my back to the rock and my eyes on the tree line.

Our eyes locked when Bryn appeared out of the darkness, each of us knowing where the other would be. Sam asked him a question that I didn't hear, and Bryn nodded in response, handing his pack and the skinned rabbits to the older man. Wary, he lowered himself to the ground close to me, his back against the rock. His eyes wide and his mouth set in a firm line, he seemed ready to run if I moved in his direction.

My heart hammered in my chest like a caged animal trying to break free. Despite the fear evident on his face I could feel he was drawn to me, as I felt drawn to him.

"Were you...." His voice came out in a hoarse whisper, his eyes flitted to Sam and back as he assured himself that his friend couldn't hear us. To make certain of that, he scooted closer, our knees brushing together.

"It felt like you were inside my head just now," he murmured. "And your heart is *racing*. I can feel it."

"I don't know what happened. You were gone for so long, and I was worried," I finished lamely. How could I describe what that was, and how strange it felt to be in my skin again?

"There was more to it." His eyes bored into mine, and I knew in that instant that he heard my thoughts as clearly as I had heard his.

Bryn shook his head as he released me from his gaze to look at the fire. An unbidden sigh of relief escaped me as he murmured, "This just keeps getting stranger."

"I'm sorry. It's strange for me, too."

We sat in silence until Sam handed us wooden bowls with bits of greens and roasted rabbit. With my thoughts in turmoil and my eyes fixed on nothing, my jaw moved mechanically as I ate my meal and sipped water from the leather skin. Sam and Bryn talked for a time, each of them glancing at me infrequently, but I heard none of the conversation.

Sometime later, with the fire banked and bedrolls spread around the warm coals, Sam and I lay down while Bryn moved like a shadow to the edge of the trees to stand watch. The light of the fire gone, only the stars above offered their meager light. Even so, I could see the gleam of Bryn's eyes fixed on me again before I closed mine and drifted into an uneasy sleep.

CHAPTER TWENTY-THREE

The hills gave way to flatland as the first week passed. Oaks and birch trees replaced the evergreens of the higher altitudes; green leaves gave way to bright yellow, orange, and red that grew in numbers over the course of another week.

I had dreamed of the *Catherine* most nights. No Derth, and the feeling that he was closing in was gone.

When we came close to a town on the road from Stalth to King's Port, Sam angled us toward the road. He would shuffle into town to buy food and supplies while Bryn and I stayed in the shelter of the forest. Bryn assured us that there was no sign of pursuit and that the feeling of something watching us had passed. Still, we all agreed that it was foolhardy to show our faces in public areas when we could avoid it.

In one small town, Sam informed us that after a discreet inquiry about any rumors in the area, someone had heard that there was a price on the heads of a young man and woman involved in a theft.

No details about the couple were known, but someone important wanted them alive. Our caution was warranted.

I decided it was time for me to continue to practice calling on the gift out of Sam's sight in case it was needed. I stole small moments during our days. Whispering to the spirits to come while we walked, trying to force a rock to move in my hand by staring at it, falling into old patterns from my life before. Nothing worked, feeling like it was blocked again after my encounter with Derth. And worse, I was interrupted almost every time I tried.

Samuel would turn to ask me a question while I muttered to myself, Bryn would offer some insight about our surroundings while I stared at a rock, and whenever we had a quiet moment in camp, one of them always had something to say to me.

I succeeded once when I tried to light a fire; a burst of flame shot out of my hand when I became frustrated after long minutes of failed attempts, singeing a nearby tree.

Bryn scolded me about summoning a wildfire in the middle of a forest, and I told him I wouldn't try again, though I swore to myself that I wouldn't give up completely.

The interaction held none of the heat that it once did. It was a suggestion from one friend to another, to show concern in the face of danger. He was still concerned about the gift, but we understood each other now. While I harbored doubt about the true nature of this understanding, thinking that it was fueled by what the gift had formed between us, I welcomed the change. The animosity had consumed too much of my time and strength.

Bryn and I became closer as a result. When he asked how I used the gift, I confessed that it seemed to use me more often than I controlled it. With a knowing smile, he nodded and changed the subject.

"Tell me about how you learned to use a sword."

"The crew taught me," I replied. A warm breeze rustled the leaves, falling to the ground around us. I released the clasp of my cloak, letting the wool fall from my shoulders to puddle around my hips where I sat with my back braced against a tree trunk. Samuel had left for town hours ago and we suspected he would spend the night there, so we made ourselves comfortable. We were enjoying the unusual warmth of the day, before the sun set. The risk of someone seeing the smoke was too great this close to a town.

"When the captain decided I was old enough, he told some of the better fighters to train me. When one of them handed me a wooden sword, I had no idea what to do with it. He lunged at me, and I screamed and ran. And when I saw that everyone was laughing at me, I turned and stabbed the man in the knee." I laughed. "He went down *hard*, and then all of them laughed at him."

Bryn laughed with me, sounding carefree for the first time since we met.

"After that, they decided I might be worth the time to train. A short time later, they paired me with Hunter, and we grew up sparring whenever we could."

Grief and guilt threatened to overwhelm me as it did whenever I thought of Hunter. My smile faded and I looked away from Bryn.

Preventing me from wallowing, Bryn spoke up.

"It sounds like they were good people," he offered a hand to help me up. I grasped it and forcibly pushed away my grim thoughts. His hair shone golden in the sunlight, a lopsided and sympathetic grin making me smile.

"For the most part they were. We had our share that didn't work out."

"Why?"

"There was one man, years ago, that the captain ordered put to death for attacking one of the crew."

"What happened?" Bryn asked.

"He tried to rape me," I answered, my voice flat with suppressed horror as I recalled the hungry look in his dull eyes. "No one thought much of him. One night, he attacked me while I slept in one of the hammocks in the crew berth. Put his meaty fist over my mouth to keep me from crying out and started undoing the laces on my trousers.

"I couldn't breathe, and I flailed, trying to hit him hard enough to make him let go, but I hit one of the men and he woke the rest of the crew. When they pulled him off me, my hammock dumped me onto the ground and my wrist snapped." I flexed my left wrist against the ghost of remembered pain.

"Hunter might have killed him, if he hadn't been helping me. I had never seen such a look of murderous hatred on his face, even when *he* was attacked. But the men only restrained my attacker and hauled him on deck for the captain to judge. When he saw my broken wrist and the way that man was staring at me, even bloodied by the crew, he ordered him hung on the spot."

Silence fell between us. A few long minutes ticked by until I could stand it no longer.

"When did *you* first learn to use a sword?" I asked.

His lopsided grin resurfaced. "When my father brought me a wooden sword and I vanquished a lamp," he chuckled. "My father was gone for months at a time, but he always came back with gifts for my mother and me."

Grief colored his features as he spoke of his mother and father. "I saw him once after she died. He found me working in Arthur's store and asked what had happened. I told him, and then I told him to leave. He died a few years later."

We lapsed into lasting silence as both of our stories turned to memories of grief. When night fell, we arranged our bedrolls close together to fight the chill of the autumn evening. The warm breeze cooled, and though the wool of my cloak was drawn tight against me, the wind bit through it to chill me to my core. We didn't speak through dinner or when we laid down to sleep.

The weeks of travel with Bryn and the subsequent trek through the hill-covered forest had rejuvenated me, strengthened me. Without the aid of the walking stick, I could now keep pace with his long strides. After another week traveling with Sam at our sides, I caught sight of my reflection in a shallow stream as I washed and refilled the waterskins. The haunted, hollow look was gone; a healthy flush spread across my cheekbones and the bruising beneath my eyes had disappeared. My hazel eyes sparkled with speckles of sunlight dancing on the surface of the stream as it trickled between rocks and roots.

Bryn repurposed my walking stick into a makeshift sword, hacking off a short length with his blade before finding another stout stick for his own use, suggesting that we spar to keep our minds and bodies sharp.

He was gentle, but he pushed me to my limit all the same. Bryn fought with more grace and control of his body than I had seen in any of my crew. In the early days of our sparring, I found it difficult to avoid his reach. As time went on, I found that my flexibility often helped me to avoid his blows and find new openings in his defense to exploit. Whether through his skill and experience or the bond between us, he seemed to guess how hard he could push and how long before I felt ready to collapse on the ground.

With every passing day, my arms acclimated to the exertions a bit more. Stretching and rubbing cramped muscles as we walked allowed me to continue each night. And each night I fell into my bedroll, my last thoughts on the gift and the spirits. It scared me now, every time I looked for the glow. I knew the importance of finding my control over it again, but after feeling how close I came to being overwhelmed, I couldn't bring myself to do more than visualize myself in that space within, pushing past the barrier to bask in the glow a little longer each time.

CHAPTER TWENTY-FOUR

Branches pulled at my tattered dress and scratched my cheeks, leaving bloody furrows in my skin as I fled through the dark forest. A sense of terror gripped me; I couldn't remember if I was running from something or towards it. My breathing became harsh and my lungs burned as I greedily gulped air.

I glanced at my feet as I ran, trying to see in the dark any roots that would trip me and end my reckless flight through the forest. When I looked up, the trees had vanished, leaving me standing still on the deck of my ship, chest still heaving and lungs on fire. Roglin stood holding a blade to Hunter's throat.

"You destroyed my ship," Roglin snarled.

"I know," I said, rising panic creeping into my voice, little more than a terrified squeak as I looked at Hunter kneeling with his head bowed. "I had to."

"You'll pay for that," Roglin snarled.

From the shadows at his left, Derth limped into view. He raised his hands and pain coursed through me, all too familiar. My knees buckled as I seized uncontrollably, helpless to stop my crashing to the planks of the deck. Hot, metallic blood flowed into my mouth when my teeth clamped down on my tongue.

"You will feel more pain than you can fathom," Roglin growled.

After what seemed an eternity, the current running through my body abruptly ceased, and left me panting on the deck. Blinking my eyes open, I peered through sodden strands of hair plastered to my face at Roglin and Derth's sneers. Unable to gaze into the raw hatred hovering above my prone form, my head lolled to one side.

Hunter's body lay sprawled nearby, his hands tied behind his back and his face turned in my direction. A look of terror and desperation crossed his features when Roglin stepped over him and clutched his hair, wrenching his head back to expose the pale flesh of his throat.

Brown hair faded to gold, and green eyes shifted to a clear blue I had seen on only one person. My terror rose, freeing my mind from the sluggish grip of pain as a blade rose above Bryn's exposed neck.

With the force of unbridled hatred behind it, the blade streaked silver through the air.

I screamed.

I woke to a hand on my cheek. A scream wrenched the air, filled with terror and sorrow. My eyes popped open to find Bryn kneeling over me, shaking my shoulders while he shouted my name.

"Lila! Wake up!" he insisted. He searched my face; a worried crease marred the space between his brows.

The screaming stopped as Bryn levered me upright and I woke fully. I winced as I cleared my throat, the tissue raw and painful. The screaming had come from me.

"Bryn?" I croaked. He sighed, his warm hand on the small of my back for support, rubbing in small circles. I could feel his hand shaking.

"I've been trying to wake you; you've been screaming and thrashing in your sleep. And I could feel that you were in pain."

I blinked as I looked around, noticing that the light was wrong; it was night, why was it so bright?

"Bryn!" Sam screamed from across the banked fire. All the surrounding trees blazed, consumed by flames. Samuel paced before the trees, his hands on his hips.

"Did *I* do this?" I shrieked. In a panic, I scrambled to my feet, my hands rising on their own to clutch the thick mass of hair at my scalp.

"I think so," Bryn coughed. "The first tree caught just as you started screaming. Can you stop it?"

"No!" I screamed. "I wasn't even awake!"

As my fear and frustration rose, the fire rose. The smoldering coals suddenly flared into life in the center of our refuge, quickly becoming a large blaze. A searing gust of air hit me in the face.

There seemed to be no gap in the conflagration as I cast about for an escape. Squinting against the glare and the smoke, I searched in vain for some sign that Sam had succeeded where I failed.

"Sam hasn't found a way through, and we don't have enough water to put out the flames. We tried smothering one of the trees, but the fire keeps burning, no matter how much dirt we throw at it."

I closed my eyes and tried to call the spirits. *Come, damn you! I need you!* But I was left in silence, alone and powerless.

"I'm sorry," I breathed, stepping closer to Bryn to be heard over the crackle of burning leaves and branches crashing to the ground. Despair consumed me and I closed my eyes to shut out the harsh light of my failure.

"I know," Bryn murmured. Strong arms folded around me, sheltering me from the fire.

Where are you when I need you?

The bright glare against my eyelids dimmed, and Bryn's body stiffened against me, his hands grasping my shoulders painfully. When I opened my eyes, the section of trees behind Bryn had stopped burning all at once. In one sweeping movement, the flames disappeared as if doused by a sudden downpour.

Sam still paced along the edge of the trees, but with his hands outstretched and body tensed. Surrounding him like a shroud was a translucent figure. The same figure that had followed me throughout my life. Connected to him.

Flames were extinguished wherever his hands moved. When the last licks of flame were gone, darkness surrounded us as completely as had the flames. Smoke dissipated, and I inhaled a deep lungful of fresh air that burned all along my throat. Sam's shoulders sagged and his muscles relaxed; sweat dripped along the curve of his cheek and disappeared into his growth of beard, leaving a streak of skin through the soot marring his face.

Bryn's arms felt locked in place around me, and I could feel his muscles tensed against my arms and back, hard as iron.

Samuel grinned and said, "I haven't been entirely honest with the two of you."

Bryn and I stood still as stone, at a loss for words.

In the moonlight that was now able to shine through the utter lack of a canopy over our heads, we watched in silence as Samuel stretched his back and went to his bedroll, folding himself into a seated position.

My eyes wide with shock, I could only stare. The old man gazed first at me, and then at the young man holding me in his iron embrace. When Samuel cleared his throat and gestured toward the fire pit, the spirit glowed and a small burst of flames took hold of the singed wood.

I shook myself, dispelling the shock and turning my gaze to Bryn. His eyes narrowed, he regarded his friend with a hard and angry set to his mouth.

"Bryn," I rasped, stifling a cough. He tore his eyes away from Samuel and looked down at me, the angry, fearful look transferred to me. "Let go, please."

His arms fell to his side, and I turned back to Sam. Coughing, my throat sore from the smoke, I sidled back to my bedroll beside the rekindled fire.

"You have some questions for me, I'd wager," Sam said as I sank to the ground. He wheezed through a rueful smile.

"Only one right now," I replied. "How long have you known about me?"

"The moment you walked through the door to the tavern, I knew." My breath came out in a snort as my ire rose. "Do you *know* what you are?"

Taken aback, my eyes narrowed. "What do you mean?"

"Calm down, Lila," Samuel demanded. "You wouldn't want to start another fire."

I opened my mouth to argue, but Sam's raised hand and scathing expression stalled me.

He looked over my shoulder at Bryn and gestured for him to come forward. "Now, you have been very quiet, boy. Don't *you* have any questions for me?"

Bryn's only reply was to shuffle closer and plop down next to me, facing Samuel with a scowl of distrust I had seen many times in the last couple months.

I grasped his shoulder in sympathy and support, my eyes on Samuel. He frowned as he gazed at Bryn's face.

"I'm sorry I kept this from you, Bryn. I had no choice."

At Bryn's continued silence, Samuel sighed and turned back to me.

"How long have you been using the Ambience?" he asked me.

"You assume I know what I'm doing," I retorted, a sharp edge on my words to match the indignance I felt.

"I didn't," he responded. "The state of the trees speaks to that. I meant, how long has it been since it manifested?"

"Off and on for as long as I can remember. I was making progress, and then Derth did something to cut me off. It's still there, and the last time I used it, it was overwhelming. And it's getting worse."

"It's spiraling out of control," Sam declared. "The more often it's used, the stronger it gets. And I've not seen anything as strong as what you've done to this young man."

Bryn stirred beside me. "What do you know about it?"

"Only that you are bound together, and that it originates with Lila. What happened?"

"Roglin has a man that can use the gift," I replied. Sam's eyes widened for a moment, but he remained silent, letting me continue. "I was in a gray haze for months, I guess; I'm not sure how long I was there. I wasn't myself," I finished with an angry shrug.

"You were a shell of a person," Bryn grumbled.

"Go on, Lila," Sam coaxed.

"Somehow, I freed myself and I tried to escape. The man, Derth, caught me and tortured me. He was going to kill me, and I couldn't make it stop." My hand fell away from Bryn's shoulder. "I screamed for Bryn to help me, and a strange light flew out of me and surrounded him. The people, Derth called them spirits, grabbed him at the same time."

"And you used the Ambience to destroy the ship?"

"She started to glow, Sam. And then everything exploded. She was floating in the water, still glowing, and when she sank beneath the surface and started to drown, *I* couldn't breathe. A few seconds more and we would have died."

"You feel her pain?" Bryn nodded. "And it seems that you would follow her in death if it took her." Sam dropped his gaze to the fire, his brow furrowed in thought as he scratched at the wiry beard along his chin.

"It seems that you possess a unique ability, Lila," he stated. His eyes locked onto mine, and I could feel silent appraisal in his penetrating gaze.

"What does that mean?" I demanded. "I thought the gift, or *Ambience,* was a myth. I struggled for a long time to figure out what it was, and that I wasn't cursed. As soon as I started to accept it, it was taken away. And now, I'm afraid to do much with it. It almost killed me." A small tendril of panic began to work its way from the pit of my stomach up my spine.

"I think it's *saved* you," Sam corrected. "You would have been killed or worse if you didn't possess the skill to defend yourself in such a way. You have little control over it, true, but it has saved you, nonetheless. Consider Bryn," he waved a hand in Bryn's direction, and my gaze followed. "If your lives weren't bound together and you had escaped on your own, would you have been able to survive alone in the forest without any assistance?"

"No," I admitted. "But neither would his life be in danger."

A sad smile spread on Sam's face, and Bryn's hand came to rest on my shoulder to offer me comfort as I had done for him.

"You have a kind heart, Lila. And I doubt there are many that could find friendship with someone after meeting as you two did."

I nodded because Sam saw the truth. Bryn and I had become friends, despite the circumstances of our meeting and subsequent mistrust.

"You haven't explained what you meant when you said that I have unique power. And you haven't explained anything about yourself, Samuel." My tone insistent, I refused to be distracted.

"True," he nodded with a brief smile. "I can wield the Ambience, as it is called, but more importantly, you can; and you have no idea what you're capable of. My skill was gained through practice and study and is entirely under my control. With little

more than a thought, I can exert my will on the world around me."
He nodded at the fire, which grew in intensity to brighten the
clearing. Hot air licked my face for a moment before the flames
settled back into the small fire.

"Control is gained through years of study and careful direction
until it becomes second nature to anyone who's tethered to a spirit.
You, though," he frowned, "possess a talent that hasn't been seen in
ages. You must not learn to control the world around you, but to
control yourself if you wish to harness the Ambience."

"That doesn't make any sense," Bryn insisted.

"Doesn't it?" Sam retorted. "You've seen and felt it yourself.
Only when she loses control of herself has the Ambience manifested
in such violent ways. Through panic, anger, despair, she finds her
strength. These emotions, by their nature, tend to overwhelm and
therefore her strength is also a liability." His penetrating gaze
settled on me once again, and the force of his next words sent a
shiver down my spine. "If you don't learn to harness your emotions,
rather than be ruled by them, you will be consumed by your own
power."

"Consumed?" Bryn barked.

Sam's eyes remained locked on mine, though he addressed
Bryn. "Yes. Rumors about this kind of rare talent spoke more of the
danger surrounding the people who wielded it. In moments of great
suffering, anger, or fear, even the most powerful and disciplined
found themselves overwhelmed by the sheer force of their power
and were lost to it."

Considering the crushing grief still haunting my vulnerable
moments, this seemed a real possibility.

"There have been a few times that I've used the gift for small
things, but only when I felt like I was in control." I paused, and
knowing that I had been dangerously close to losing my grip more
than once, asked, "What can I do to prevent that happening to me?"

"You can learn to control your emotions and hone your intent.
Other than that, I can't say. I don't possess the kind of skill that you
have, and I'm not sure that I can help you beyond basic instruction."

"You said tethered to a spirit." I pointed at the spirit that still
enshrouded him. "I can *see* it, like you're wearing a cloak. And
when you use the... Ambience?" Sam nodded. "It moves or glows.
But I've only seen them in large numbers, and they aren't connected
to me."

"Such is the nature of the power you wield. You interact with the Ambience differently than I do. Than most like me would."

"But you *will* help her?" Bryn asked sternly.

"Yes," Samuel replied, quirking an eyebrow at me. "I have to think about the best way to proceed, but I will help. If only to save myself the trouble of being set on fire in the middle of the night again."

An angry and shameful flush crept onto my face as Sam chuckled at my expense.

"Sam..." Bryn warned, feeling my shoulder tense beneath his touch. Sam's smile faded when he noticed my obvious distress.

"I'm sorry, Lila. I can't imagine what you've been through. Know that I will help you, and you *will* learn to control this."

It would be the answer to my biggest problem, if he was right. But at the moment, I didn't feel like it *could* be true. My dream still haunted me, lingering at the edges of my mind. Slumping forward, my head dropped into my hands. My lungs and throat burned, and Samuel's revelations had left me spinning.

The ground rustled at my side as Bryn scooted in front of me to steady my swaying.

"Lila are you all right?" he asked, concern evident in his tone.

"No," I said, my voice muffled by my hands. "It's too much. I've done too much." Shame and guilt increased, and a small voice inside berated me for not being able to stop the whirlwind of emotion that could spell destruction for us all. Not since I was a girl, shoved in a pen to be sold in the street, had I felt so helpless.

"Calm down, Lila," Samuel warned.

The admonishment only served to compound my guilt. Tremors ran through me, whether from exhaustion or the emotional storm coursing through me, I couldn't tell.

"That's not helping," Bryn growled. "She's panicking, and you're making it worse by reminding her that she's almost out of control."

"How do you know that?" Samuel asked.

"Because I can *feel* it," Bryn replied, exasperated. "You said yourself that this bond between us is strong; I can feel when she's about to lose control."

Both men fell silent as I shook and sobbed. A moment passed before Bryn plucked me from the ground and, sitting with his legs crossed beneath him, lowered me onto his lap, tucking my head under his chin.

With his left arm wrapped around me, he murmured gently into my ear, stroking my hair as one would a child. "Everything will be fine, Lila. I won't let you lose control. Sam will help you, and I'll keep you safe."

His words directly addressed my fears, as if my soul were laid bare for him to see and influence. Still, it took several minutes for my sobbing to calm, more from my exhaustion than anything else.

The storm ebbed, and I was left feeling drained on the edge of sleep. Bryn's hand continued to stroke my hair as my body relaxed into him. The words in my ear became muted as I began to drift, but Sam's voice kept me on this side of consciousness as he spoke.

"You have a way with her, boy."

"It's not hard," he huffed. "She's practically shouting; I can feel most of what she does. But it's not all that difficult to see that you weren't helping, even without the benefit of experiencing her pain. And it's like I can hear a voice whispering in my ear when she's like this. Or when she uses the gift. Why didn't you say something sooner if you knew what she was? You could've prevented this."

Bryn's chest vibrated against my ear as he spoke, and my body rose and fell with the even rhythm of his breathing. Comfort and safety. A deep voice rumbling against my ear while big arms held me tight and rocked me. This reminded me of something....

Sam's voice cut through my wandering thought. "The world is larger and more dangerous than you realize. People like me don't walk freely in Trylia." He paused. "There's more between you two than the Ambience, boy. A blind man could see that."

"I don't know what it is, Sam. I pitied her as my uncle's slave, I hated her after watching her kill all those men, and I've been so afraid of what she might do to us. Lately, though..." His voice trailed off, and after a moment of silence Sam spoke up.

"She's beautiful," Sam offered.

Bryn sighed. "She is. But it must be the gift. I feel completely out of control sometimes...." I felt his chin brush against the top of my head when he shook his. "I don't know what I feel, Sam. Confusion, mostly. There's one thing I'm certain of; I would die if anything happened to her. And I'm not sure if that's only because of the bond."

Samuel's reply was lost to me as I finally drifted off to sleep, protected from the world and my gift by Bryn's strong arms and compassionate words.

CHAPTER TWENTY-FIVE

The next morning I woke to find myself lying on a pile of blankets, covered by my cloak. Bryn lay on his side facing me with an arm draped across my middle. His head lay on his outstretched arm, snoring as he slumbered.

I smiled as I looked at his face, carefree in the peace of his dreams. His hair fell over his forehead, fanning out and sparkling with bits of gold in the sunlight. He had long, dark lashes that faded to a lighter brown near his eyelids. He mumbled something I couldn't understand and stilled again.

Loath to disturb him, I lifted his arm by the wrist and placed it in front of him before I slid out from under my cloak. My joints popped as I stretched with arms above my head, and my lungs burned from the insult of the smoke the night before; I stifled a cough.

The charred circle of trees mocked me in the daylight. While some of the trunks looked merely singed, all the branches were mounds of charcoal on the ground. Stark, skeletal trunks stretched toward the open sky.

Sam crouched beyond the ring of desolation at the edge of a nearby stream. Leaning over with his sleeves pushed past his elbows and his arms thrust beneath the surface of the water, I could see by the set of his shoulders that he was deep in concentration. In an attempt not to disturb him, I crept toward the water using rocks and roots jutting out of the leaves and charred wood to silence my steps as Bryn had taught me.

The surface of the stream began to ripple outward from Sam's arms. The spirit pulsed, and I felt something move toward them. As I watched, first one and then another fish appeared in the small area between Sam's hands. A moment more and another swam up beside its fellows. In one swift, smooth motion, Sam's hands rose out of the water, and the writhing fish followed them, suspended in midair.

With a quick, twisting motion and the sound of bones cracking, all the fish suddenly went limp. Samuel lowered his hands and the fish so that they rested on a large, flat rock next to the stream.

He made a horizontal slashing motion with his right hand, and the bellies of the fish were laid open, exposing their innards. Another few motions had the fish deboned and gutted, ready to cook. He hooked them with his fingers and stood, turning toward the camp and me.

He paused when he saw me, and a smile appeared on his face as he started walking again.

"Good morning, Lila," he beamed. "I hope you're feeling well."

"A little worse for the smoke, but I'm fine, thank you."

He stopped just in front of me and looked me over, searching my face. "Well, you seem to need a wash, but otherwise you appear unscathed. I'm glad." He looked over my shoulder to our camp before looking back at me. "Bryn is still asleep?"

"Yes, he was when I got up a moment ago."

"Perhaps the smell of breakfast will wake him up. You go and wash up; I'll start on these." He raised the fish and wiggled them close to his face, grinning. He chuckled to himself as he moved past me and into camp.

I wandered the rest of the way to the stream and knelt at the water's edge, in the same spot that Samuel had been. Rolling up the sleeves of my soot-covered shirt, I dipped my arms in the cool water, scrubbing at the grime. Dark drops of water fell from my face as I splashed and rubbed it. I followed this by scooping water over my head and drenching my hair as best I could. When this seemed insufficient, I bent forward so that I leaned into the river, submerging the top of my head in the cool water.

My fingers tugged at the sodden strands, teasing the tangles and ash from my grimy locks while swishing my head back and forth. Gooseflesh prickled along my skin as the wind picked up and bit through the cloth of my shirt. When I felt satisfied that I could do no more to clean my hair, I flipped my head, flinging a spray of water backward as my hair flew out and over my head.

"Hey!" someone cried from behind me, startling me. Jumping back, I whipped my head around, sending my sodden hair in a whirlwind around my face before it came to rest plastered against my neck with a wet slap.

Bryn stood spluttering close behind me, his face and chest drenched. With one eye closed, his face bore a hilarious grimace as he spit some of the water out of his mouth and glared at me.

Hard as I tried, I was unable to stifle the giggle summoned by his countenance. I placed a hand over my mouth, but the giggles continued to emerge, making Bryn frown for a moment before he too was unable to stifle a smile.

He shook his head and wiped a hand across his face to remove some of the moisture as he strolled to the stream. He plopped to his knees on my left, laughing as he plunged his hands into the water and rubbed them back and forth, trying to remove the dirt.

"At least you've saved me the trouble of washing my face," he said. He glanced at me out of the corner of his eye, small rivulets of water streaking soot down his face. I shook my head.

"You missed a bit," I giggled, at once horrified to hear such a sound issuing from me and delighted that I could feel happy enough to do so.

He smeared his right hand along his cheek, dragging the soot with it. "Did I get it?" he asked.

I shook my head again, giggles threatening to turn into full laughter at any moment. "No."

He swiped his hands along his face, swirling the grime around his eyes and pulling it into lines down his cheeks. "Now?" he asked.

"I'll help you," I laughed. I dipped my cupped right hand into the water and splashed it at Bryn's face before he could turn his head.

He looked shocked for a beat before he returned the favor. With a shriek I scrambled away, trying to regain my feet and retreat to the camp. For my efforts, I was rewarded by Bryn's arm around my waist, lifting me bodily off the ground and hauling me backwards against him as he turned and trudged toward the stream.

I squealed. Bryn waded into the cold water of the stream, carrying me with him as I kicked and protested.

At its deepest, the stream was only deep enough to submerge Bryn to his waist, but when he came to that point, he fell backward into the water. The cold water surged up around me and I gasped a quick breath before my head plunged below the surface.

We were only under for a few heartbeats before Bryn placed his feet under him and stood. I spluttered as we came up for air, my hair plastered to my face and dripping water down my soaked body.

Setting me on my feet in the stream, Bryn asked: "Did I get it?"

"You missed a spot," I growled, turning to face him.

Bryn laughed, and I lunged. Placing my hands on his chest I drove him back into the water, dunking his head beneath the surface before retreating out of his reach. I slogged my way to the bank with my clothing dragging against the slow current as he came up for air, spluttering.

Sam stood on the bank above us, looking amused. Bryn splashed for a moment longer as he regained his balance and followed me out of the water. Wary, I eyed him, ready for retaliation.

"The food is ready, if you two are," Samuel said, smiling.

"We'll be right there, Sam," Bryn said. He seemed more at ease than he had been last night.

A fleeting memory of words spoken as I drifted to sleep in Bryn's arms teased me, but the smell of cooked fish distracted me. My mouth started to water, but the leather trousers hugged my legs in an uncomfortable way. Upon retrieving my pack with replacement clothes, I waddled to the opposite end of the camp.

As I made to weave through the charred branches, Bryn shouted, "Where are you going?"

"I'm not going to eat in these clothes, I'm soaking wet! And I am *not* going to change in front of you two, so I'm going to find some privacy. I won't go far."

Before he could protest, I spun on my heel and walked between the skeletal trees.

Throughout our meal, Bryn badgered Sam with questions about his life. Taciturn as usual, Sam responded with vague answers that forced Bryn to lapse into a sullen silence when he realized that Sam would remain tight-lipped despite the events of the night before.

"I've been wondering something, Sam," I interrupted. Sam quirked an eyebrow and turned to look at me. "For as long as I've had incidents with the Ambience, I've been looking for information when I could. Even at the university in King's Port I found nothing. Songs and a few brief stories, discussion of the possibility of the gift in history books. Why couldn't I find anything else?"

Sam smiled a sad smile. "There wasn't a need for that information to be spread around when the Ambient were around. And when they were gone, there was no way to make sure the idea of the Ambience survived apart from the stories I wrote."

"You wrote the stories I read as a kid?" Bryn asked.

Sam scowled in his direction, and I could see that the time for questions had passed. "I did. And I'd rather this interrogation not continue. It's dredging up old, unwelcome memories."

We set about breaking camp in silence. Once we set off to the south, Bryn leaned close to me and murmured to prevent Sam from hearing him.

"He's always been like this," he admitted. "For as long as I've known him, I haven't been able to get any information out of him."

"Why do you trust him?" I wondered. "It sounds as if you barely know him."

Bryn shot me a wry grin. "Knowing where he comes from and knowing that he's a friend are two different things, Lila."

"If I've learned anything from traveling with you, it's the truth of that." He beamed at me, and I flushed.

"It all feels...better, somehow," Bryn sighed. "Like there's finally an answer for *something*, even if it brings more questions."

Nodding, I replied, "It does. I've had no idea what to do about the Ambience. That there's some truth to the myth and real information to learn makes me feel like I might be able to do something about it."

CHAPTER TWENTY-SIX

Sam didn't offer any more information about himself or the use of the Ambience over the next few days. Bryn asked every few hours why he wasn't teaching me something. Sam replied the first time by saying he was preparing, but every time after, he just grumbled.

Not wanting to push, I let him gather his thoughts, watching him pore through a small notebook night after night, flipping back and forth between pages as if they might contain new information the more he searched. I kept my efforts to reconnect with my gift to myself, seeing no need to involve the others when I was too nervous to do anything but search every night as I fell asleep. Bryn and I continued to spar every evening. As well as being wonderful exercise, it helped to keep my emotions at bay. Exhausted by the brutal standard he set, I slept like the dead, with fewer nightmares that might release my power.

This far south, the forest that spanned the entire eastern edge of Trylia began to thin. More prevalent clearings offered a view of the clear autumn sky, the thick shrubs giving way to tall grasses that swayed in the crisp breeze. A bite of winter's cold settled over us at night; though wary of our fire being seen, we agreed that the warmth was worth the risk.

A rotating watch schedule became routine each night since civilization grew nearer with every passing day. Bryn reported he couldn't find evidence of being followed, but that had been the case on our way to Stalth, and they had been so close. There weren't any nightmares to convince me that they were directly on our trail, but I knew that somewhere, Roglin and Derth were looking for us. After what he'd told me, I didn't think anything short of death would stop him. Though we encountered nothing but animals skirting the edge of our camp, we remained vigilant.

The edge of the forest appeared a few days later, forcing us to hurry across the open, flat land toward the mountains in the west. Tall grass dominated the landscape, bending and rustling from a slight breeze and our passage. For leagues all around, the sight broke only for the road that cut toward King's Port.

I stepped out from the shelter of a massive oak and sighed; the sun warmed my face and a few vibrant, beautiful flowers refusing to give way to the change of season warmed my heart. Samuel muttered something under his breath as we neared the road. A wagon surrounded by a few men ambled down the dirt path; beyond that a small group of people were obscured by the distance. Sam pulled the hood of his cloak low over his face and affected a limp and hunched appearance as soon as we were exposed.

Though Sam had heard nothing further about the price on our heads, I pulled the hood of my cloak over my hair. My ears warmed instantly, sheltered from the cool autumn air. Sam nodded when he glanced back to see that I had done so and muttered something about my hair.

"Like fire?" I teased.

"At a distance, with the sun shining, yes," Samuel grumbled.

The sun had begun the descent from its peak by the time we reached the road. The sound of my feet crunching on years of hard packed dirt and stones replaced the soft footfalls and swish of our passage through the grass. Though Sam still grumbled to himself about being too visible, we stood alone near the well-used ruts.

"How far is King's Port?" I asked.

"About a week's walk," Samuel replied.

"That close?" I asked, astonished. Sam nodded. "We're going west?" Sam pointed at the distant mountain peaks that rose into the sky until they were obscured by clouds.

"Our destination is a canyon between two of those peaks. You can't see from here, but there is a break in the mountains that holds a small forest and a lake. That's where my cabin is."

"If you're so against being seen, why are you out in the world?" Bryn chuckled. "I've never heard so much muttering from you."

Samuel sighed. "I was in seclusion for a time. When I started to crave companionship again, I set out for a city large enough to become lost in. If I had known that *you* would be the one I would find, boy, I would have stayed where I was."

Bryn laughed aloud. "You love me, old man. Don't fool yourself."

Sam muttered something under his breath, and Bryn laughed harder.

"Where did you learn how to use the Ambience, Sam?" I asked, hopeful for an answer in light of how many words Sam had spoken just now. "It's nothing but a legend for most people; is there a group of gifted somewhere hidden away?"

"No," he grumbled. "I'd thought I was the last in Trylia. The Ambience hasn't been used for an exceedingly long time."

My brow furrowed as I considered his words. "How old are you, Sam? You talk as if you've lived long enough for generations to pass."

"I am old enough to have seen this land when the Ambient were many," Sam sighed. He waved an impatient hand back at us, urging us forward as he strode through the tall grass on the far side of the road.

Bryn and I shared a look of astonishment.

"Sam, that was over a hundred years ago!" Bryn exclaimed.

"Four hundred and eighty-seven, to be exact," Sam replied.

"How is that possible?" I choked.

"With the Ambience, of course," Samuel huffed.

"Did you do this to yourself?"

"No, it was a collection of people that allowed me to live for so long."

"But why would they do that?" Bryn pressed.

"Because someone needed to be here when the Ambient returned to guide the new generation. I used to be somewhat of an expert about teaching control and skill, so I was chosen to live as long as it took.”

“That's incredible!” I shouted. “Can I live for that long, once I've learned how to use it?”

Samuel halted and wheeled around to scowl at me. “No, you can't. It takes the combined power of several well-trained and powerful masters to accomplish this sort of thing. And I wouldn't wish its effects on anyone.”

Taken aback at the unexpected heat in his voice, I stammered, “What effects?”

The look on Samuel's face faltered for an instant before he composed himself. That instant showed me a depth of despair I couldn't fathom. “Imagine never aging as everyone around you grows old and withers away. To see the entire lifespan of a human being is a sobering thing. Even more so when you see someone close to you fade away as you remain the same.”

“I'm sorry, Sam. I didn't know,” I said.

Sam gazed impassively at me for a few seconds before he seemed to shake himself and turned back to the west, waving an angry hand to propel us onward.

CHAPTER TWENTY-SEVEN

We followed the road for a time, heading south toward King's Port. I longed to continue to the only home I had left. I could only imagine what all the families were feeling; there was no one to bring word of what happened. The thought of Lottie sitting in her kitchen, wringing her hands with worry when the twins didn't come home haunted my dreams.

Our path led us past the odd group of travelers, or merchants with wagons full of goods. Each time, Sam insisted we duck out of sight, or, lacking anywhere to hide, pull our hoods and cloaks close and hurry along without a word.

Roglin and Derth would still be looking for us, and could ask after us all the way to our destination if we weren't careful. But there seemed to be more to it than that. Sam muttered constantly when we were visible, even if the road was the fastest way to travel.

It grated on my nerves, but as the days wore on I began to feel the same. After all, we had been followed before, and Roglin and Derth could hire another wagon, or horses, and find us at any time.

We camped well off the roads, as often as we could behind whatever cover we could find. The occasional hill, a small copse of trees, the boulders surrounding a bend in a river, as long as it provided cover from the road, we could spend the night with a little less tension. If we were completely obscured, Bryn and I took the opportunity to spar.

I cherished the exercise, and the effect it was having on my body. Along with the interminable walking, I felt stronger than I had when I lived on the ship, constantly climbing and exerting myself to keep the ship running. Each block and parry felt like a release from the anxiety hanging over me. When I worked up a sweat and the evening air cooled my skin, it felt like my worries evaporated with the moisture. Some of them, anyway.

We were forced to sleep close to the road on occasion, when the river ran too close, or there was nothing else for leagues in any direction. And on one of those occasions, a few travelers heading north stopped nearby, a bit close for our comfort. Rather than move away from them, which seemed more conspicuous, we kept our place and went about our nightly routines with our cloaks in place. We could hear everything they said, so we refrained from saying much.

Bryn and I didn't spar, and without its benefit, my thoughts churned. Would the people nearby be able to describe us? What if Roglin and Derth were closing in? There were too many problems that I couldn't solve, and that was too much to bear.

So, I turned to the Ambience, something I hadn't been able to draw on in so long. It still felt distant, the spirits unable to hear me. The Ambient light I visualized refracted like the sun through a fog, so that it was diluted when I sat next to Bryn as he tried to ignite a small piece of wool in his hands for our fire. I let my mind drift in my inner glow, feeling it brighten as I let down my guard. It was so inviting, it was hard to believe that I'd been afraid of it, that it had felt like it would use me up if I let it.

I wish I could start the fire, I thought. *It's so easy for Sam, why can't it be that easy for me?*

A couple of people from the other camp walked past ours, talking to one another as they gathered a few pieces of kindling.

"...said they're offering a hundred gold Aelios for information leading to the capture of those two. Something about stealing from the guards in Stalth."

"Stole from some well-off merchant too, if what I heard is right," the other one answered. "You have to be stupid to steal from a merchant that has the ear of the guards there." They glanced toward me, smiled and nodded in a polite, dismissive way, and continued to walk further from the campsites. "I've never seen so much gold in my life. That would see me through another year...."

A thrill of fear shot through me, and I felt the spirits move, toward the fire pit and the spark that Bryn made from his flint. I felt the glow brighten inside me, and before Bryn struck the flint, a spark lit the starter, and the heart of it was illuminated with my prismatic glow. The wool blossomed into flame that licked at the kindling. Gasping, I pushed the Ambience down, and the flame dimmed to its normal, yellow-orange color.

Surprised, Bryn blew on it until the rest of the kindling caught, and he coaxed it into a full fire. When the flames were licking the large branch above, he sat back on his haunches and smiled his lopsided grin at me.

"Handy," he said.

I took a deep breath, and let it out slowly, nervous about the eager invitation to do more that I felt from within. "It was," I said. "I didn't quite mean it, but at least it was helpful."

"And reckless," Sam grumbled. "Please refrain from more of *that,*" he said, looking pointedly at the fire, "while we're in public."

One of our neighbors cleared his throat and moved away from their burgeoning fire as the two I had heard talking came back and tossed their sticks nearby. When I glanced at the noise, he was staring at me. His look was intense, and after a long few moments with our eyes locked, I looked away. I helped Bryn get a small meal together, and we all ate in silence. Every time I looked in the direction of the other camp, the same man's eyes were watching me.

"That man is still staring at me," I whispered to Bryn and Sam as we banked the fire. "Since I started the fire."

"Elders' eyes," Sam cursed.

"We can leave while they're sleeping," Bryn suggested.

Sam shook his head. "We need the rest," he said. "And the damage has been done. Lila, wake us before dawn, and we'll try to leave before they do. With any luck, we'll be far enough ahead of them to prevent them seeing where we've gone."

Bryn woke me from a restless sleep to take the last watch. I sat up and gave him my bedroll, pulling my cloak tight around me for warmth. As Bryn settled in and began to snore, I looked toward the other camp. Their fire was a pit of glowing embers, and a pair of eyes glinted as they turned to catch mine again.

That man had seen me use the Ambience. And would likely be able to describe us. I'd lit a new beacon for Roglin and Derth, and a shiver ran down my spine at the thought.

I woke them when the black of night began to change to keep blue, before the sun began to rise. The man in the other camp watched us go, but didn't rise to follow, and we were soon swallowed by the foothills surrounding the road. Sam set a brisk pace for us throughout the day. By unspoken consent, we rested for a few hours before we walked through the night and into the following morning, leaving the road far behind as the mountains loomed larger and larger.

We forded a wide, shallow stream late in the morning. Splashing through the cold water felt like putting another barrier between us and the man that had seen me use the Ambience. Now that we knew there was a bounty, more dangerous for the lie that we had stolen from the guards, it was only a matter of time before someone came looking for us. We needed to be far away when they did.

When the sun was high in the sky, we happened upon a small stand of birch trees. One large birch provided welcome shelter from the bright sun, and Bryn and I shucked our packs and flopped with relief to the ground against the trunk of one of the trees at right angles to one another.

Samuel stood over us, rummaging in his pack. He fished out a loaf of bread and handed it to me. I tore a piece of it off before handing it over to Bryn, who ate without a word. As I was happy to let the silence remain, I followed his example.

After our short respite we set off again, drawing nearer to the mountains. More trees, jutting out between boulders at odd angles through breaks in the overlapping rock shelves, looked stark compared to the tall oaks of the forest in the east.

When dusk settled over the land, the sky flushed in ruddy shades. As the sky darkened, the temperature began to fall and I clutched my cloak close around me. Finding a suitable place along the river, which had steadily increased in size the further upstream we traveled, we stopped for the night, all of us weary. Our camp sat nestled between one massive boulder that had been split into many pieces over the years and now lay in a jumble of jagged rock and the pebble strewn beach near the river's edge.

I gathered some rocks from the beach for the fire pit. I found one that fit in the center of my palm, white and smooth as the stone Hunter used to have, and I sighed. I missed all of them, but there was a jagged hole inside me that pulsed as I thought about Hunter. I set the stone aside, not wanting to use it for the fire, and went about my task. Bryn squatted next to his pack and started to gather his knife, bow and arrows to hunt.

"No need, my boy," Samuel said. His better humor had returned once the road faded behind and the land became wilder, with no indication of human civilization. "I'll catch us some fish."

Bryn stayed next to his pack, lowering his bow and looking after Sam as he walked to the river. Shooting me a perplexed look, he said, "He doesn't have a pole or a line. How does he expect to catch anything?"

I looked up from my work. "Go and watch. It's fascinating."

He narrowed his eyes at me, obviously thinking that Sam and I were going mad, and then leapt to his feet and trotted off in the direction of the river.

When I finished lining the pit with enough stones to keep the fire contained, I stood and brushed off my hands and my skirt.

With only hardened weeds growing this close to the water, I had to stray from the campsite to find kindling for the fire. When the roaring of the river was only a whisper in my ear, I found another stand of trees with branches and twigs littering the ground beneath and filled my arms with enough wood to keep us through the cold night.

I dumped my haul next to the pit with a crash and knelt, gathering the kindling and handfuls of dry grass. The sound of bootheels clicking against stone caught my attention and I looked up to see the two men returning from the river. Bryn had an astonished look on his face as he held two large trout in his hands.

"You were right, Lila," he said, stunned.

Sam flashed a smug smile at Bryn as he laid two of the gutted and boned fish on one of the thin, flat rocks from the jumble near the boulder's remains. "It was nothing," he said.

"You need to teach Lila how to do that," Bryn said. "I'll never have to fish again."

"That will be a while yet," Sam said. He removed a small box of herbs from his pack and began rubbing the fish with a small handful each. "Specific skills will come later. First, she needs to learn control."

"When will you start to teach me?" I probed, rummaging in my pack for flint and steel.

Sam finished with the last of the fish and looked up at me. "Now that we've gotten more distance between ourselves and civilization, I don't see why we can't start now. Let's get the fish cooking first, and then we'll begin." Sam stared at the fire pit for a second before the wood burst into flame. I envied how little effort it had taken and stared at the high flames and sparks that danced into the sky before winking out of existence.

"Lila, I want you to know that this is one of the hardest things to learn. Controlling the shape and flow of your talent takes great patience. With your added strength it may be even more difficult. I have not had the pleasure of teaching a Conduit before, so this will be new for both of us."

"A Conduit?" I asked.

"Yes. Some say they are descended from the founders of Celuthia. That is why they call the spirits to them in great number, rather than being tethered to one. And why they can create when we can only manipulate.

"I want you to start by breathing steadily, in and out. Breathe in and hold it for a heartbeat, then release all the air in your lungs for another three. This will help to calm your mind and heart. It is essential to stay calm when first learning control. If your thoughts and emotions get out of hand, you'll have to start from the beginning."

I nodded and inhaled. With my lungs full of air, I held my breath before slowly exhaling. Looking at Bryn's eager face with his eyes wide as he breathed in time with me, I exhaled in one gust and smirked.

"Lila..." Sam scolded.

"I'm sorry, but Bryn is staring at me, and it's distracting."

Bryn's face flushed and he looked away. He tried and failed to hide a small smile as he considered his hands.

"Close your eyes, if you find him distracting," Sam said.

My cheeks flushed with embarrassed denial as my eyes darted to Bryn's grin and back to Sam.

"Close your eyes," Sam insisted.

With a sigh, my eyelids dropped and I began to breathe as Sam instructed. The roar of the river and sizzle of the fish as it heated on a flat stone above the fire rang in my ears. My mind raced as I attempted to still it, trying to force my way through the fog around the Ambience as I always did. I focused on the rise and fall of my chest until my heart began to slow and my shoulders relaxed.

"Good," Sam said. "I want you to look deep within yourself. Describe to me what you've seen when you use the gift."

"For a long time, it was just the spirits, sometimes a glow," I said. "After Derth's hold broke, I was in a bright, colorful light. Now, it's like there's something blocking me from it. The spirits are always far, and it's like they can't hear me."

"Hmm," Sam said. "Tell me about your experience with Derth."

I related every detail I could remember from that time. The lack of feeling, the barrier like a thick curtain in my head, all of it. Sam waited for me to finish, and then I heard him take another deep breath.

"If you'll allow it, I'd like to try something," Sam said. I nodded, and he placed his hands on either side of my head, fingers touching my brow and temples. He nudged at my mind, like he was knocking on a door, asking permission to enter. I was hesitant, but there was no malicious intent behind his request. And it *was* a request that I could deny.

So, I took a deep breath and let him in. It felt a lot like when Bryn and I shared thoughts, but duller, less defined. I pictured my mind as a room, and Sam walking around it, inspecting the corners for a rat with Derth's greasy hair.

Something pulled inside me, and the room I visualized Sam in grew brighter. I knew he was testing whatever remnants of Derth were still inside me. When he pulled again, I could feel it throughout my physical body, too. Like a cord wrapped around my heart, my head, and something deeper, where I knew the glow lived.

Sam retreated from the contact as I opened my eyes. "He put a sort of tether on you, likely stronger from placing the barrier in your mind," he said. "Something like what you and Bryn share. I think it allowed him to try to reassert his control when he was close enough."

"Can you do anything?" I asked. "I had nightmares between Coveton and Stalth and felt like he was getting closer. I don't feel like he's close anymore – maybe he's dead, or so injured that he can't affect me – but if they catch up, I don't want to be under his control. I don't want to feel that way ever again."

Sam shook his head. "The connection between you and Derth is personal. And I think it's why they've been able to find you so quickly. He would be the one to sever it, or you, if you found the strength to do so. I can try to guide you, as I did for many of my students, to the core of your connection to the Ambience. From there, it would be up to you."

I rolled my shoulders and stretched my neck. "I'm ready," I said.

"Focus on your breathing again," Sam began. "In…and out. Slowly, let your body relax bit by bit, starting with your head. Now your neck…your shoulders, let the tension go. If it helps, imagine each part of your body like a closed fist. The tension is the fist, and opening your hand is like letting the tension go."

I took solace in his words, in the soothing tone of his voice, trusting him. My heart slowed as I focused on the glow as I had first seen it when I broke through Derth's barrier to touch the warm light. Something brushed against my mind as I moved forward in that imagined space, and I felt Sam's presence. It was faint, but he seemed to be guiding me, encouraging my search. I approached a veil, the manifestation of Derth's hold on me, blocking the light from me. Sam used his power to pull it aside like a heavy curtain.

The light danced again, ethereal hands reached out for mine and pulled me forward, beyond the veil that had once kept me from realizing the power that I held. My feet moved forward, the hands in mine felt warm and familiar. Whispers welcomed me. The spirits called my name.

You came.

The light resolved into a brilliant pool, like a still lake lit from within and without. A smile broke out on my face when my feet touched the pool. This was home.

Taller than the rest, a figure rose out of the center of the Pool and strode across its surface toward me. My head was no higher than the waist of this spirit. A large hand reached toward me and touched a taloned finger to my forehead.

Daughter.

A small light that throbbed to the beat of my heart glowed before my eyes, flickering like sunlight on the ocean. It circled me, became a cloak, and settled into my body. Anchored in my heart, I could feel the Ambience and the spirits that waited for my call.

I found myself looking at my memories again in the mirror-like surface of the Pool, but this time, all of them clearly showed the specific point in time that the Ambience had flowed freely into the world. Falling from the mast, I was able to witness as it burst forth from my mind, heart, and arms all at once, saving my life. Recalling the battle with Roglin's forces on my ship and Captain Morrig as he lay dying in my lap, I saw it as an inner glow that started from my heart, infusing my hands with the healing power that repaired his broken body. A tear fell from my cheek, and the Ambience sparkled within as it fell to his upturned face.

It showed me images of Bryn. All were represented more clearly than my eyes could have seen. The blue of his eyes was as bright as a clear sky, as rich and deep as the ocean. His hair sparkled like gold in the sun, waving in the breeze as we walked across Trylia. Lastly, it showed me the moment I had placed the shackle upon him, and in that moment, he too was lit with the brilliance of the Ambience. It seemed to take root in his soul, and I could see an almost invisible tether between us.

Tears rimmed my eyes and fell to my cheeks; I was lost in the glow. It danced within and throughout me, leaving traces of joy in its wake. It felt as though my body had been asleep before this moment, that I had never felt the rough stones at my fingertips or felt the warmth of the fire on my face. It embodied elation, wrath, despair, and serenity, and it was the deepest essence that made me who I was. Every choice, every path, had led me to this glittering pool and these figures with their arms outstretched to embrace me.

I opened my eyes as it faded. The Ambience was still with me and when I closed my eyes, it flowed through me again, greeting me as an old friend. I let it go and opened my eyes once more, staring through the blur of my tears at Sam's kind smile.

"Well done, Lila. That's the first step to control."

CHAPTER TWENTY-EIGHT

All of that had taken only a few minutes, though detached from my body, it had felt like a lifetime. Sam reached over and turned the fish, exposing a rich, golden color. Each one sizzled as the new side hit the hot rock. It smelled delicious, but I was so overcome by my experience that I only registered this fact in the back of my mind.

Bryn looked back and forth between Sam and me, confused. "What happened?" he finally asked me.

"I found it," I replied as I wiped tears from my eyes, overcome with satisfaction and acceptance.

"That quickly? It's only been a few minutes!"

"She has some experience," Sam replied, still tending to our meal. "She just had to remember the way."

"I've been working toward this for as long as I could remember," I said. "I thought what Derth did broke that connection, but I just needed some help to find it again. And what you said, Samuel, about it being tied to my emotions.... It was an emotional experience. But I could feel you guiding me. Thank you."

"What did you see?" Sam asked.

"It looked like a still lake, lit by the sun, but also from beneath the surface. And there were people, or what looked like people, standing around it, waiting for me. They almost seemed…happy to see me." I looked at Sam. "Did that happen for you?"

Sam lifted the corners of the stone holding the cooked fish and placed it quickly on the ground, flapping his hands to dispel the heat.

"No," he replied, almost to himself. "What you are describing sounds like an actual manifestation of the Ambient Pool. It is a force from Celuthia herself, part of the world around us. It was often described as a pool from which we draw the talent to affect the world, and which we feed when we leave the world of the living. The figures you saw may have been spirits, which also makes sense as they allow us to access our power, but most of us don't see what you saw.

"Most like me were called Tethers, tethered to a spirit, which in turn became tethered to us. They are made of and are fueled by the Ambience, which is how they allow us to access it. Every time a Tether accesses the Ambience, traces of that power spill from whatever we do, to feed the spirit and allow it to linger."

"Spirits?" I asked. "I never knew what to call them before Derth called them that. Are they spirits of the dead?"

"Yes," Sam nodded. "Spirits of tethers who have passed from the living world to Celuthia, where they fuel the pool of Ambience that is essential to all life, whether Ambient or not. The Ambient Pool that exists in Celuthia is what brings life to death, spring from winter. Each person, plant, and animal feeds the pool when they die. Tethers become spirits who linger in it and add to it.

"What you describe is something that I have only read about. Rather than relying upon a spirit to access the Pool, they can use it in whatever way their intent and emotional state shape it, and spirits are "called" to them. Conduits access great stores of the Ambience all at once, rather than what one spirit can siphon off for a Tether. This creates a wellspring of sorts for spirits whether they are tethered or not. A Conduit could feed the Ambient Pool by using it because spirits would be 'fed,' more or less, from the runoff of whatever a Conduit was doing."

"I am so confused," Bryn groaned. "This is a lot to learn in one sitting, Sam."

Sam sighed and narrowed his eyes at Bryn. "This is but a fraction of what she needs to learn, and it wouldn't hurt you to learn, either." Bryn narrowed his eyes right back at Sam, but they shared a grin that made me think this banter was normal for them.

To me, Sam smiled and continued. "The danger for a Conduit is that their emotion and intent in the moment of accessing the Ambience shapes their use of it, and errant thoughts or feelings can derail their intent. Spirits that are summoned to the wellspring of Ambience will follow any whim of the summoner due to the overwhelming nature of what they are given."

"So..." I drawled, "the fire happened because I accessed it while I was in a state of panic and pain? Like on the ship...." I trailed off for a moment, and then another question occurred to me. "Why fire? I can understand why Roglin's ship was destroyed, and to some extent what I did to Bryn: I was looking for an escape and to punish them and was desperate for help from the only person who wasn't an overt sadist, but I wasn't dreaming of fire."

"Violent reactions tend to evoke violent responses. Spirits are beings of Ambience; though they were people once, their existence is raw and elemental, more like a storm. They can only interpret our world through connection to the living; if there is no direction to draw from as with a tether, they embody the essence of what we intend and feel. Thus, panic and pain can be interpreted as fire, lightning or wind that can tear the world apart as those emotions tear at the person experiencing them."

"So why not keep me in a state like Derth did?" I asked. "It was awful, but at least I wouldn't be able to destroy everything around me. It's easy to lose control—"

Sam cut me off with a shake of his head. "That is a poor solution for whomever the subject might be. When a person is cut off, they lose a vital part of who they are. In my case, using the Ambience is like an extra muscle, and I wouldn't feel whole without it, but I would survive. Much like I should survive if I lost a limb. Being separated from *your* talent, you would likely lose a vital piece of your soul."

"That's encouraging," Bryn intoned.

"We did something similar to people who wanted nothing to do with the Ambience – or were incapable of controlling it – in my time. It is a process by which someone who is experienced with spirits gives some sign that a Tether is not suited to draw upon the

Ambience, cutting off their access to it. For a Conduit it is different, and much more painful. It is a matter of severing them from their emotions and preventing their ability to feel." He smiled reassuringly. "I doubt that there is a person alive that has the talent for such a feat. *I* certainly couldn't achieve it."

"What about what Derth did to me? Didn't he separate me from the Ambience?"

"No," Sam replied. "That barrier prevented you from feeling any emotion. And could provide a way for him to follow. Were you able to break that connection?"

"I'll try," I said. I closed my eyes, took a few deep breaths like Sam taught me, and looked inward. Visualizing the room again, I searched until I found that small shred of the thing that had kept me prisoner for so long. It was a piece of the larger curtain I had seen in my dream, dark, and full of Derth's twisted form of Ambient power. Knowing what I needed, the spirits came, illuminating the space in a light so bright that the shred recoiled.

They grasped it and pulled, and I felt it come free from somewhere in my head, and somewhere near my core, where my connection to the Ambience resided. With a twist of their hands, they wrenched it asunder, and the last vestige of Derth's influence was gone.

I felt lighter, as if I had shrugged off a weight I hadn't entirely felt. And when I looked inward again, all I saw was the light.

"He's gone," I sighed. "I didn't realize how much he was still affecting me."

Sam nodded. "He went to a lot of trouble to place that tether within you, and it must have drained him every moment he kept it intact. I doubt he could've controlled you without it." He frowned. "He must have realized that you possessed greater power than most and did what he could to prevent you from using it. I wonder how he could know that...." Sam trailed off, looking lost in thought.

As he pondered the answer to his question, Bryn moved forward and took a piece of fish off the stone. Following his example, I pulled apart a small section of the meat. It tasted divine, the herbs blending with the flavor of the fish in perfect harmony. As I started in on the third piece of fish, I looked up to see Sam and Bryn watching me, smiling.

"I'm sorry," I said around a mouthful of fish. "I'm starving."

"That's to be expected," Sam said. "What you've just accomplished is almost equal to a vigorous workout. You wouldn't believe me if I told you how much I ate during my first weeks after my Tethering." He grabbed one of the two remaining piles of fish and gestured to me. "I think you should finish that. You'll need it, especially if you're planning on sparring tonight."

When Bryn nodded his approval, I finished off the remainder. I sighed, feeling replete, and laid back on my cloak, looking up at the sky. Night had fallen and the stars were out in force.

"Do you want to spar?" asked Bryn. I lifted my head off the ground to look at him. "Do you need to rest?"

"I feel fine," I replied, sitting up. "Though I don't know how much use we're getting out of these sticks anymore. Besides, when it comes to a fight, I'm not going to be using a stick, and I won't be prepared to use mine like I should be."

"I can help with that," Sam said. I lifted an eyebrow in question, and he chuckled. "I can place barriers around the blades of each of your weapons to prevent any injury. It will feel like you're crossing blades when in fact, there'll be less than a finger's width between them. Just don't tire yourself too much. You'll need your strength to keep up with the lessons I have planned."

"Can you teach me how to guard our swords?"

"In good time," Sam replied. "You've only just begun."

CHAPTER TWENTY-NINE

By the light of the fire, armed with our non-lethal blades, Bryn and I panted as we circled one another. Only a short time had passed since we began, but I was tiring quickly.

"You can submit at any time, my lady," Bryn teased with a wicked grin.

"Why, good sir, your offer is too gracious. I couldn't possibly impose upon your good will."

I lunged forward, expecting Bryn to block downward with his sword, as he had done many times to counter such a move. Instead, he leapt to the side and brought his sword around, slapping it against my left leg as I passed, just above the back of my knee.

The blow knocked me sideways and I fell to the ground, wincing as I ran my hand down my thigh. A lump was already forming, and I hissed at the pain.

Bryn sucked in a sharp breath and grasped his leg, in the same spot that I was holding mine.

"Serves me right, I suppose," he said. He limped to my side and extended a hand to help me to my feet. Pain shot up my leg as I put weight on it, and it nearly buckled.

With Bryn supporting me, we hobbled to camp and lowered ourselves to the ground near the fire. The cold of the stone seeped through my clothing, and I rolled my injured leg to one side to soothe my growing bruise.

Sitting on his bedroll near the fire, Sam shook his head witnessing our matching limps. "You should be more careful. You could break a bone with those, and then we'll be in a sorry state."

"I know," I said. I wiped my brow with the back of my hand, wrinkling my nose at the sweat and grime left behind.

"You also need a bath," Sam said. "Why don't you clean up before we bank the fire for the night?"

I considered this for a moment but shook my head due to the throbbing in my leg. "I'll do it in the morning," I said.

"How much pain are you in?" Sam asked, cocking his head to one side.

"I'm fine," I lied through gritted teeth.

"A lot," said Bryn at the same time.

Samuel stood and moved the short distance around the fire to kneel at my side. Placing his hands with his palms parallel to my leg, he moved them back and forth, finally settling just above the backside of my knee where Bryn's sword had struck.

He closed his eyes and his brow furrowed. Sharp pain in my leg made me gasp, and I heard it echoed from Bryn.

"You almost broke the bone, boy," Samuel said through a grimace. "It's a very deep bruise, and it should heal on its own. We don't have the time to waste limping through the wilderness, however...." He trailed off as his hands started to shake above my leg.

The wound burned as Sam worked, though less intense than when I was healed by Derth. I suspected that was largely due to the man that now tended me. The burning became a faint itch and then mild warmth spread through my leg as he finished. He sat back on his heels and let out a deep breath, his face relaxing.

"Thank you," I smiled.

He smiled back. "Think nothing of it, my dear."

Bryn stretched his leg back and forth, rising to test it as he bounced on the balls of his feet. Sam made his way back to his place by the fire.

"I'm going to follow your suggestion, Sam. I'll only be a few minutes." I strolled a short distance south to a bend in the river, sitting down on a rock and dangling my feet in the cold water. Leaning back on my hands, I gazed up at the stars.

After a while of sitting still in the cool autumn breeze, I roused myself and began washing my face and hands. Footsteps clicked on the stone behind me, and I didn't have to turn to see who it was. Now familiar to me, Bryn's gait slowed and halted when he knelt next to me, splashing his face.

Wiping at the water sluicing off his high cheeks, he turned to me. "I'm sorry, Lila."

"My leg is fine, Bryn." I wiggled my leg back and forth to emphasize my point, and his eyes drew down to gaze at it for a moment. "Knowing Derth was so close for so long, and trying to do that to me again..." I shook my head. "It makes me feel like I need to wash over and over. But it's done now."

When Bryn looked up, the starlight reflected in his eyes, filled with emotions I couldn't describe. For some reason, that look sent a jolt through me, and my heartbeat quickened.

A flush rose in my cheeks, hot enough for me to wonder whether Bryn could feel it, and I looked away, grateful for the darkness. We finished washing in silence, and then made for our beds.

CHAPTER THIRTY

Stark white trunks amid yellowing birch leaves gave way to a large stretch of green pines as we climbed higher into the foothills guarding the passage to the soaring peaks. Hawks circled in the sky above the tips of the green giants, piercing calls echoing through the clear autumn days.

The roar of the river intensified as we followed its twisting route ever higher, climbing over small rises in the stone as it crashed in the other direction over small waterfalls. The rushing water deepened where it widened; small pools carved by years of passing current held swirling eddies before the river found its way back into the mass descending to the grasslands below. Fish became lost in the strong current, pulled into the pools for Sam and Bryn to easily collect while they fought to free themselves.

The snowcapped mountains drew us onward with their promise of seclusion and safety. Though we maintained our watch through the night and Bryn often disappeared into the forest to circle back and ensure we were not pursued, I felt a tingling on the back of my neck that made me feel watched in the darkness, even this far removed from any cities.

Sam led us to the northwest, his eyes often straying to a pass through the impenetrable edifice of the mountains ahead that only he could see. Beyond the hills and the trees, he assured us, an entrance to his sanctuary waited to allow us passage and would deter anyone who searched for it. Though I harbored doubts, staring up in awe of these giants reaching into the sky, I trusted Sam and his desire to escape from prying eyes.

We passed through a small town named Mountain's Shade situated along the river in the shadow of the nearby mountains. A large section of rapids spanned from the edge of the town for a league downriver, preventing the use of fishing vessels of any sort or travel along the water. People old and young waded through shallow water with nets and poles; large groups hauled nets teeming with flapping fish out of pools such as those we had seen farther east. The water carried their shouts of warning and triumphant laughter to us long before they came into view.

The two-story buildings of Mountain's Shade stood dwarfed by the dark and foreboding mountains in the background. Despite this, the town itself radiated a feeling of warmth as we strolled along the dirt road not often used. No wall or fence penned in the town or its people. Distance provided safety this far from civilization, and Sam assured me that there was little in the way of dangerous wildlife in the shadow of the mountain.

Pine logs, stacked and stripped by skilled hands, formed the walls of every house and shop in sight. Shingled roofs and low eaves topped each; moss crept between the shingles and gaps broke between logs after years of expanding and settling with the shifting weather. One small structure near the center of town sat swarmed with men on the roof replacing old shingles in a desperate rush before the first snow. A gust of wind howled through the town, sending a shower of old shingles raining down on the heads of those below, followed by bellows of surprise. A snap of winter air billowed my cloak out behind me as the men atop the building dove for piles of shingles to prevent their escape.

After a quick sojourn to the general supply store to stock up on food essentials, we exited the town on the western side. Despite the friendly nature of the people here, Sam became agitated, more so with Bryn and I in tow. Among the rocks and trees of the pine forest, his shoulders relaxed and his grumbling mutters ceased.

Inside the shelter of the trees, Sam found another stream coursing with cold water from somewhere deep in the mountains. In order to grow my skill with the Ambience, Sam urged me to help start the fire every evening. I found an affinity with the volatile element, especially after my explosive experience in the ring of trees, and what started as a spark to ignite the starter soon became a tiny flame that caught the kindling. It was a brilliant experience, and so similar to what I'd been able to do on the *Catherine* before it was all taken away from me. There was still an element of fear, as the tiny spark called on me to do more, make the fire brighter, taller. But I resisted, keeping the draw small, and the spirits couldn't pull anything more from me.

That night, with a small fire glowing to keep the night at bay, Bryn and I sparred. The warmth of the exertion fought the cold of the clear evening as the last light of the sun faded. With all the ferocity I could muster, I parried and thrust, blocking and swiping at him until I could no longer hold my arms upright.

"My arms are shaking.... I think it's high time I forfeited," I panted, wiping my brow with my sleeve to remove the droplets of sweat that dripped down to sting my eyes.

Bryn replaced his sword in its scabbard. "Sure."

"I'm going to go take a quick dip in the river. Will you tell Sam I'll be along in a few minutes?"

Bryn nodded and strolled into the camp as I moved in the opposite direction. I placed Desire in its scabbard, removed my sword belt, and undressed on the rocks overlooking the water. This smaller stream's current, while inexorably pulling away from the mountain and into the foothills below, didn't threaten to drag me with it. A gasp escaped my throat when I waded into the waist-deep stream. All my muscles tensed and my skin rippled with gooseflesh, but I refused to relent due to frigid water.

It took a short time for my body to adjust and the cold water continued to flow around me, but I shivered and scrubbed the grime and sweat from my prickled skin. For most of the journey, I had bathed only the visible parts of my body, cleaning my face and arms after sparring. I longed for the hot water of Lottie's bath in King's Port. The thought of the fragrant soaps made me groan.

My body floated along the surface of the water, the current pulling at me, a silent force attempting to coax me away. My hair flowed around me in waves; I rubbed at my scalp with fingers and fingernails, a small moan of pleasure escaping my chattering lips. I scrambled out onto the stone near the edge of the pool where I had laid a dry blanket and wrapped myself at once. My arms shook as I rubbed them dry and hurriedly continued with the rest of my skin so that I could dress as quickly as possible.

I pulled my green skirt and bodice as well as my full-length chemise from my pack and dressed. The soft leather of my boots slid over my bare feet with a hiss, and after lacing them I strode back in the direction of the camp. The beacon of the campfire appeared after ducking from behind a few trees.

My nostrils twitched at the scent of fish cooking over the fire. They were laid out on a flat stone again, and Sam stirred dark liquid in the pot set near the flames. With a smile, I nodded at Bryn, who had spied my approach.

"What's in there?" I inquired with a nod at the pot. Bryn waved a hand at the log he perched on, and I took a seat with my lower back braced against it next to his outstretched legs.

"Bryn found some mushrooms and plants from the river, and I threw some of the fish in there. I thought it would be nice to finish off the stale bread by soaking it in something savory."

"It smells delicious, Sam. Thank you."

"While we wait for dinner to finish, let's continue your exercises."

I sighed. My exercises over the past days consisted of immersing myself in the Ambience to familiarize myself with it. While in direct contact with it, he had me practice the controlled breathing I used before so that I could accustom myself to using it in a calm state. It was supposed to decrease the likelihood of my emotions overriding my clear intent. It bored me.

"When will you teach me how to actually *use* it?" I implored, wringing out the water from my hair and then plaiting it with practiced movements. "For something more than a spark?"

"When I am confident that you can use it without interference. We need to know that you can harness your intent with a thought, and not always a feeling."

"How will you know when I'm ready for that?"

"I've had to adapt your training to our situation and to the fact that you are a Conduit," Sam replied. "With that in mind, I think it would be safer for everyone to have you meditate while you become accustomed to your power. That way, I hope to have you using it without evoking strong emotions. This should allow you to direct the Ambience as you see fit, not to have it direct you. But," he added, "I have never done this before. It's likely our results will differ from what I'm used to."

With a reluctant nod, I closed my eyes and began my steady breathing. Within a few moments, my heartbeat slowed, and I followed the pulse inward to the Pool.

Like before, it seemed calm. I pictured myself sitting there for a time, aware of faint sounds of Sam cooking and Bryn's steady breathing beside me on the log. A lifetime of breathing and concentrating flew by in an instant. My mind wandered to thoughts of men pursuing us and a secret haven in the mountains, and then to the uncertain future. The Pool rippled. Could I travel with these men forever? My thoughts turned to Bryn, his warmth radiating from his body like the warmth from the crackling fire, and I opened my eyes in search of him.

The dark night exploded with more vibrancy than my eyes alone had seen. The flames danced, flashing orange, white, and blue, undulating with the breeze I hadn't noticed on my own. Sam's cloak, askew on his bony shoulders, flared the color of honey in the firelight. Not the dull brown I knew it to be. His gray and white hair glowed in the light cast by the flames.

My skirt flared around me on the bed of pine needles, the color reminding me of ivy-colored eyes gazing into mine. With a stab of pain, my heart clenched, and my eyes shot upward to escape the painful reminder of a man I had only begun to love.

Stars winked in and out, more fire than distant light, and beckoned to me. Closer now with the Ambience enshrouding me, they danced with a spectrum of color that mirrored all that I contained within me. A smile flitted to my face as I beheld this infinite wonder, and I turned to Bryn to share this revelation.

He sat wreathed head to toe in a faint outline that shone with the myriad colors and startling brilliance of the Pool and reminded me of what Sam told me were spirits, cloaked in bright light. It constantly moved and shifted as he breathed, as he rolled his shoulders back and stretched. Unaware of the Ambience bathing him, tethering him with a thin line of power to me, he gazed into the flames, smiling and asking Sam when the food would be ready. Without looking up, Sam replied in a stern voice for him to wait.

As I gazed at him, the glow beckoned me, and I followed it without hesitation down the now visible tether between us. Bryn's mind sat open for me like in the forest, hunting alone in the dark. Every sensation from the rough bark beneath the fabric of his trousers to the heat on his face emanating from the fire nearby, I felt as clearly as I felt my own fingers flex in surprise.

His muscles tensed when he realized I was with him in his mind again. Fear coursed hot and strong through his veins, along with a feeling I couldn't place that flushed my cheeks. He turned his head, his hair golden in the firelight, his eyes the unforgiving and beautiful blue of the sea. The flush of his cheeks sent sparks of light racing along the shroud of Ambience encasing his form.

What is she doing? His thought sounded in my mind, a clear representation of the man and not just the sound of his voice. His sense of pride, of justice, and something deep within him that felt like loss and uncertainty flowed over me along with his words. His eyes watched my lips part in surprise and exultation at knowing him intimately and being able to trust what I saw.

Bryn? My voice, colored with the essence of all that made me who I am, rang as if I had spoken his name aloud.

Shock settled on his face and in his body. Gooseflesh prickled his skin, and his heart pounded against his chest.

Lila?! What's going on?

I shook my head. *I'm not sure.* His fear and confusion assaulted me, and I pulled back. *Don't be afraid,* I thought.

The wood groaned beneath his weight when he shifted away from me. His eyes flew wide, an angry breath escaped his lips. *How did you know I was afraid?* he asked.

I can feel it, like you can feel me. I can see and hear everything you do, and I can see you. My eyes roamed his entire frame, tracing the radiant cloak around him. *I can see Ambience around you, like an outline.* My eyes found his again, wary and confused, my face filling his mind. *It led me to you.*

Bryn continued to stare at me, as if he were trying to see *into* me. His thoughts assaulted me like a whirlpool; they swirled in a chaotic dance through his mind.

Can you stop?

My face fell for a moment before I regained control of it. Bryn frowned; my disappointment evident to both of us. *I think so,* I thought.

In the span of a moment, the Ambience responded to me, coming to my aid. As I would trust an old friend, as I trusted myself, I trusted the spirits to lead me. Unspoken question answered, it showed me the way to sever the connection between our minds.

I felt pulled toward Bryn, as if the spirits didn't want to close the channel between us. Dismayed by the impression of unease within him, I forced them to comply. Like stepping from a crowded room into the solitude of night, my mind cleared, my thoughts my own.

Bryn's shoulders sagged with relief. He looked down at his hands for a few agonizingly slow moments before he turned his face to look at me.

"Can you do it again?" he whispered.

A small smile lifted the corner of my mouth, and the clear path between us led me once more to share his thoughts. This time he looked prepared and only narrowed his eyes for an instant in response.

His thoughts and feelings were no longer a roiling mass. He felt calm and collected, and while I could still feel his reticence, he seemed to accept my presence.

We sat still for a time, looking at one another and examining each other's memories, guiding one another to experience the things we had only been able to talk about before. I saw his mother through his young eyes. She was beautiful, with golden tresses that flowed longer than my own, down past the small of her back. Her eyes shone the same clear blue as Bryn's. She was tall and slender, and he remembered her with a surprising strength.

Bryn in turn saw the hazy memories of my youth and people I had grown up with aboard the *Catherine*. He watched as Captain Morrig taught me the finer points of sailing, as Smitts taught me to read and write and later to treat the sick and injured.

Bryn seemed particularly interested in my memories of Hunter, examining him the first day I met him, during our lessons together and our sparring matches. Our friendship, my reluctance to start a relationship, and finally how much better everything was once I let our friendship become what we wanted it to be.

Once all our memories were shared we sat still, not quite sure how to proceed. It felt like much time had passed, but all of this happened in mere minutes. Sam still sat next to the fire, now finishing our dinner, unaware of what was happening between us.

You look different, Bryn thought.

How? I asked, and he looked into my eyes, holding my gaze with his.

They look brighter, but they aren't just hazel. They keep changing color. It's like there's a light just behind your eyes that's every color all at once.

That's what the Pool looks like to me, I replied.

Bryn hesitated, and I could sense excitement, eagerness, and a twinge of fear. *Can I see it?*

I frowned, unsure how to acquiesce. *I don't know, but I can try.*

Bryn's face disappeared when I closed my eyes, and I almost laughed at the image he showed me of my face screwed up in concentration. Rather than wait for me to figure out what to do, Ambient power rose up to meet us, hands of spirits surging outward to push us together.

His soft gasp sounded in the still air. *It's beautiful!*

Spirits danced around the pool, circling and sheltering us as we observed them. All parts of one whole now seemed to be assembled with an inaudible *click*, and something shifted in Bryn and me. The spirits' blazing cloaks flashed, sending a jolt through my limbs. The same sensation coursed through Bryn.

Ambience filled us, the power at our command larger than we could understand. With a touch or a look, we instinctively knew we could reduce the mountains to gravel and pull the stars out of the heavens to join us. Air rippled outward, the trees and plants shuddering as if afraid to see what we might accomplish. The stars burned brighter when we opened our eyes.

Where the faint cloak surrounded Bryn before, he now seemed to radiate with it. The energy encircling us undulated. Our hair waved about as if in a strong wind. The lines between us seemed to blur, and we were as one being. There was no longer a distinction between Lila and Bryn; a whole new entity took its place.

"What are you doing?" Sam demanded.

We turned our heads to regard him. His eyebrows rose far above his eyes, his forehead creased deeply as he gaped at us. His mouth suddenly closed to a thin line as his face turned from amazement to anger.

"Stop!" he exclaimed.

Power suffused his words, and ours instinctually shrank from it. Bryn and I separated the next moment and slumped as the Ambience drained from both of our bodies. I could no longer feel him, and I assumed he couldn't feel me. We were two individuals again.

My vision blurred as the last of the Ambience retreated deep within me. The colors were muted, and my surroundings became dark once more; I swayed at the loss.

I became aware of Sam rising to his feet and rushing toward me as I started to fall. Right before I faded, I felt Bryn's arms catch me, and then I knew no more.

CHAPTER THIRTY-ONE

Flickering light danced behind my closed eyes as I came to my senses. I blinked against the glare of the flames in darkness, my head pillowed on my wool cloak as I lay on my side. Bryn and Sam sat braced against the log near my head, and needles crackled beneath the heel of Bryn's boot when he stirred, seeing my eyes open. Sweat dripped from my neck and between my breasts beneath the smothering blanket, and I swept it aside to let the cool night air pierce through my shirt and bodice.

Two faces fixated on me when I lifted my head. A look of relief passed over both men's faces; while Bryn's grin heartened me, Sam's subsequent scowl made me want to melt into the ground.

"Good, you're awake," Sam grumbled.

"How long was I out?" I asked.

"A short time," Sam replied. "I saved you some of the stew and bread. I'll get it for you."

Sam rose to his feet and skirted around me to the packs, searching for a bowl and spoon. I watched his back for a minute before turning to Bryn.

Bryn shrugged at me when I turned a questioning gaze his way. Sam hadn't explained anything to him. As I pulled myself upright, a stab of pain lanced through my head and I grimaced, my eyes shut tight to dispel the sharp agony.

Bryn's hand grasped my shoulder. With a pained smile and a slow shake of my head, I tried to let him know that I didn't need help. His hand refused to retreat, and I opened my eyes to see concern etching lines around his mouth and between his brows. The pain passed, and I offered him a more genuine smile. With a nod and a gentle squeeze, he let go as Sam offered me a bowl and a crust of bread.

The stew smelled of herbs and fish and I placed a spoonful in my mouth. With a groan I sopped up some broth using the stale crust. In no time, my bowl sat empty, and I pushed a finger around the rim, savoring the last taste.

When I placed the bowl on the ground next to me, Sam spoke again with smoldering anger.

"Bryn told me some of what happened between you two. It was dangerous and reckless. What possessed you?"

"Instinct," I offered, quailing.

"I felt a large amount of energy from you, and it was the sort that can level a city," Sam said. "I've never heard of someone sharing the Ambience like that, transforming them into something...different. This must be because of the link between you; there's no other way it could have happened. Not like the others." He muttered the last as if to himself and scowled at me.

As the ache at my temples returned, I responded in kind. "I'm acting on instinct, Sam."

"*Instinct*," he snapped, "could have killed us all."

My anger began to build, and the Ambience coalesced in response. With a firm mental grip on the surge, I responded, trying to quell my emotions. "Neither of us knows what I'm capable of, Sam. You've made that clear. I appreciate your help, and I know I can't do this without you, but can't you understand that this is beyond what I can control? Can't you believe that I would avoid situations like this if I *could?*"

"Sam," Bryn pleaded, "don't push her. She's trying." I forced a grateful smile at Bryn through my frown. After what we shared, he knew me better than anyone had ever known me.

Sam sighed and rubbed his hands along his chin, fingers rasping in the long whiskers. "I know you are, Lila. I know."

"How did you stop us?"

"A trick I learned long ago to subdue wayward students," he replied. "I'm surprised I had the strength, considering the amount of power you two were using. You can't do this again. Not until we have a better understanding of what you can do on your own and know that you can control the outcome of anything you attempt."

"How am I supposed to know that I can control it if I don't try to use it?" I demanded.

"I don't know, Lila. But for now, you need to leave Bryn out of it." Opening my mouth to protest that I didn't intend to include Bryn, Sam silenced me with an angry wave of his hand and shouted. "Whether you meant it or not, I need you to restrain yourself! If an instinct grips you again, stop and ask me whether you should try it or not! You could have destroyed everything and everyone for *miles!*"

His chest heaved as he glared at me. I nodded, frustrated by the knowledge that I could ruin so much with so little effort and had no idea how to stop myself.

Sam sighed heavily and the anger faded from his face, his body sagging. "Just...continue your exercises for now, and nothing else. I need some time to think about what we should do next."

In tense silence, we cleaned the bowls and pot and made for our beds. While I gazed at the stars, now so distant and cold, I wondered if I would ever be able to take charge of my power. Sam's even snoring announced his descent into blissful sleep.

Bryn stirred in his bedroll, his head close to mine.

"I'm sorry, Lila. He can be...harsh," he whispered. I swiveled my head to peer at him. "He'll come around, and you'll figure this out."

I sighed, gave him an appreciative nod, and turned my gaze back to the sky. Hoping that Bryn was right, my eyes slid closed and I drifted off to sleep amid dreams of stars and the memories shown to me by the man at my side.

CHAPTER THIRTY-TWO

Dawn arrived as soon as I closed my eyes, yet not soon enough to wake me from a nightmare that left the tang of fear on my tongue. With a shake of my head, I dismissed the images of a land in destructive fire, my glowing body at the base of a mountain shrouded in dark fog. Sam's mood had lifted after a night of sleep, and it did much to dispel my irritation knowing he wouldn't be raising his voice every time he spoke to me.

The river followed a course through huge slabs of red granite, looking like so many boulders stacked atop one another, with no way to follow along its banks. The land rose in staggered peaks and steep valleys, leaving the foothills behind as they grew to mountains. Our path wound between those mountains, the sun peering out from behind one and disappearing beyond another, bathing us in light and warmth before plunging us into darkness.

As the sun reached its peak, the mountainous mounds of granite became a solid wall, halting our progress. Bryn and I stopped, panting in the thin air, but Sam continued in a straight line toward the jagged stones barring our way. With an incredulous look at the old man's back, Bryn and I darted after him.

"Sam," Bryn wheezed. But as he spoke Sam pivoted to his right and disappeared behind a tumble of boulders. Bryn followed in his wake and shouted my name the moment he vanished in front of me.

Rounding the nearest boulder, black specks dotting the gray of the cool and rough granite under my hand, I found myself in a cavern beneath the stone with the river roaring by. Rapids crashed over the rocks glistening beneath the surface in the little light that followed me through the opening, deafening in the small space.

Beyond Bryn, Sam shuffled along the narrow ledge that kept us above the surging water with one hand on the slick wall to his left and his eyes on his feet. A pool of light from an opening in the cavern ceiling illuminated his body for a moment and then he slid into the darkness beyond.

Bryn followed in Sam's footsteps; water splashed onto the ledge and Bryn's trousers. He considered each step before placing his feet, testing the slick rock.

The trek through the dank waterway passed quickly and within an hour we were back in the sunshine. We emerged into a grove of trees. The river surged past us out of the mountains, and a path overgrown with browning grass wound its way through small hills at the base of several mountains surrounding us.

All around, oak trees stood in blazes of ruby and saffron leaves and crimson berry vines snaked through fallen rock. Tall grass and leaves rustled and swayed in a cool breeze, carrying the scent of pine trees and the bite of winter cold. Sam set a brisk pace so Bryn and I followed, invigorated by our surroundings and the clear blue sky.

As I walked, I called the Ambience and let it embrace me. Considering Sam's warning, I did nothing but let it enhance my senses at first. The scurrying feet of small creatures fleeing our footfalls beneath fallen leaves and pine needles roared like the river through the granite walls.

The bright leaves all around paled in comparison to the cloak of Ambient light shifting around Bryn as he strode in the path Sam cut through the tall grass. Along the thread visible with my enhanced senses, I sought his mind. The spirits answered my call in the span of a heartbeat. Bryn's body tensed as he noticed my intrusion and shot a wry smile over his shoulder.

Sorry, I thought. *I didn't mean to surprise you.*

That's all right. He cast a furtive glance at Sam's back. *Should you be doing this? Sam said not to until you had control.*

He won't find out, I replied. *Besides, the power only grew when we...combined, so I won't do that again. Isn't this place beautiful?*

Yes, it is. I'm surprised no one else found it in all these years.

We shared every sound and sight, savoring deep lungfuls of damp and decaying leaves and the sweet smell of apple trees interspersed within the oaks and birches.

Another short hike over rocks hidden by brown moss and shrubs brought us to a valley between two hills, seemingly carved out of the rock itself. Sheer cliffs with outcroppings of rock rose over the path, blocking most of the afternoon sun and the cold breeze. Sam stopped a few paces ahead of Bryn, and in our distracted state of mind, each of us had to swerve around him to avoid crashing into his back. The abrupt change in focus made me lose my connection to the Ambience and Bryn's mind.

"We need to stop here," Sam said. "I left some...protections in place that should have kept out almost anyone who found this valley and made it this far."

Bryn and I glanced at one another. "Traps?" Bryn asked.

"Of sorts," Sam replied.

"What do they do?" I asked.

"They are a deterrent for Ambient and the rest."

"So, what do they do?" I repeated, squinting into the close space beneath the lip of the cliffs overhead.

"One will send any without the Ambience fleeing, and the other will disable anyone who may be able to bypass the first. The second is lethal to all but the strongest Tether. Or Conduit."

A look of astonishment settled on Bryn's face, and I could feel mine mirroring his. "You can do that?" I asked.

Sam paused. "In time, I'll show you. For now, I need a moment to disarm them. It'll take a short time, so why don't you two rest?" With that, Sam turned and moved to the entrance of the valley and bowed his head in preparation.

With outstretched arms, Sam concentrated on the invisible barrier. The strength of his conjuring assaulted me with a wave of pressure. My ears popped, and I swayed as another wall hit me. Bryn grasped my hand and turned me away from Sam, leading me back along the path.

We walked into a grove of tall oaks onto a bed of fallen leaves that crackled beneath our feet. Crisp and fragrant, I twirled one fallen piece of papery vermillion between my fingers. The distant clamor of rushing water drifted over birdsong and rattling leaves. According to Sam, the river ran underneath the grove into an underground cavern, flowing downhill from a lake near his cabin.

We sat at the base of a large oak with gnarled roots peeking through the bed of decaying leaves at its foot and a wide tangle of branches overhead in the shade of the leaves still attached. We removed our packs and Bryn dug through his in search of something to eat. His face lightened and he pulled out an apple, which he handed over to me. Another few seconds digging in his pack produced a wedge of cheese. He pulled his knife and sliced off a few pieces that he handed to me.

My teeth sank into the flesh of the apple, releasing a mouthful of tart juice on my tongue. The mild cheese cut the sour taste and I chewed in silence, savoring the meal and the beauty hidden between the forbidding mountains soaring above our heads. When I finished, I leaned my head back against the tree and looked at the clear blue sky. A sparrow wheeled about in the sky above, and the next moment Bryn shook my shoulder to wake me.

Sam strode toward our spot at the base of the oak. "It's done," he said. Bryn handed him a large slice of cheese. Sam nodded and gestured for us to follow him. Bryn and I rose to our feet, donned our packs, and made our way back to the path.

The valley dove between rugged granite walls and blocked our view of the grove a short way from the entrance where it veered to the right. A short distance from the abrupt turn, a chill racked me and my step faltered. The rock face continued unaltered, as did Sam in his relentless march toward his home, but fear rocked me back on my heels and stole my breath as the hairs stood out against my nape.

Bryn's hands found my waist and shoulder to steady me, my heart fluttering from the unseen force trying to repel me. Bryn showed no sign of distress when I searched his face aside from the obvious concern he harbored for me. My fingers ran along the surface of the stone in search of the cause for my unease. Finding nothing, I chose instead to rely on the Ambience to show me what I couldn't see.

Where my fingertip rested was a coalescing force that felt as if it were waiting for something. I recoiled, but the unease remained. Another shuddered step brought me back against Bryn's chest before he stepped back too. The wariness faded the instant I moved.

"Can anyone see your traps, Sam?" I called to his back.

"Only if they are Ambient and only if they know what to look for." Our voices echoed in the canyon, bouncing off the walls. "Describe what you see," Sam instructed.

"A small node, like a ball, against the wall. It's powerful, but it's not active."

"Do you feel anything when you pass beyond it?" he asked.

"Like I want to run in the opposite direction," I shuddered, and Sam nodded.

"The first shield evokes that instinct, calling on the body's response to fear. Chills, rapid breathing, pounding heart, and gooseflesh all combined to repel a person back the way they came."

"I don't feel anything," Bryn announced, his hands still holding me steady.

"I deactivated it, boy. The only reason Lila can feel it is through the Ambience." A frown danced across his face. "You *are* reacting strongly to a deactivated shield, Lila." He muttered something under his breath about me and then looked back to my face, a smile replacing his frown.

"You should be able to ignore it," Sam informed me. "Try walking to me."

Wary, I took a hesitant step forward. Bryn followed close behind, his hands still at my shoulder and waist. This time through, I steeled myself for the onslaught and stepped across the threshold of the shield with a shuddered sigh. My fear spiked, though not as it had a moment ago, and together Bryn and I strolled to Sam.

"I still only feel Lila's fear," Bryn informed us. Sam chuckled and Bryn's hands retreated, adjusting the straps of his pack while he rolled his shoulders.

"That's because you aren't Ambient. When they were active, you would have felt much like Lila does." Sam rolled his eyes with a smile and turned to me, gesturing in front of him. "Near the end of the canyon is the shield that will harm a person too resolute to stop at the first." Leading the way, Sam followed the curve of stone until a glimmer of sunlight on water became visible in the distance.

Sam stopped us with a gesture and waved his hand at the empty space before us.

"This is the last shield. Tell me what you see and feel."

I drew my focus from our destination to the surrounding walls. Dark red flecks suffused the lighter granite walls and in one spot at shoulder height I spied another node, larger than the last. As I approached, an intense spark coursed through me, and it became a struggle to move forward as the sensation increased. Bryn gasped behind me and once again offered the support of his body. Somehow amidst my own discomfort, I could sense the instinctual need to protect me emanating from Bryn. The moment his hand touched the fabric at my shoulder, warming the skin beneath, the discomfort eased and I was able to pass through.

Sam eyed us as we stood beyond the unseen and deactivated barrier, catching our breath and gazing at one another with relief.

"I've been close to lightning storms at sea and not felt a charge like that," I winced. "I saw another ball, bigger this time."

"This shield requires more power to fuel it. It's filled with a charge gathered from the energy all around us and would react exactly like lightning were you to pass through while active."

"Is this something you'll teach me?" I asked as Sam moved past me, emerging into the hazy afternoon light.

"In time I hope to teach you much more," he smiled, and a fine web of lines fanned out from the corner of his eyes.

We emerged from the shelter of the canyon to a wide, flat body of water lapping against a silt bank filled with tall reeds and grass. The surface of the lake moved in constant small waves from the mountains toward a small outlet a short distance to our right, no doubt leading underground towards the tunnel we had already passed through.

Mountains towered all around the lake, snowcapped and imposing in the sunlight. The far side of the water held a stand of trees to our left and a field to the right. A building stood on its own past the field, but it was too far away to clearly make out any details.

An island stood in the middle of the lake with a small, rock-strewn beach that gave way to forest covering the ground I could see. Part of it had broken away in ages past; jagged rocks jutted like teeth out of the clear blue surface. I released the Ambience and my vision faded back into the normal colors of reality.

On the near side of the lake, a small rowboat bobbed up and down against an old pier. Tall grass had overgrown the end of the pier some time ago and sprouted all the way down the bank to the water's edge. There was only a small strip of land on either side before the grassy hills overtook it and jutted out over the water, rising to form sheer cliffs.

"The boat is the only way across if you want to stay dry. And this close to the fall, the current is strong enough that I wouldn't recommend trying to swim," Sam said as we approached the pier.

He stepped cautiously, testing the boards hidden in the grass. A loud groan issued forth as he eased his full weight onto the wood, but it held beneath him.

When we all arrived at the end of the pier, Sam grasped the rope tying off the boat. Pulling it up out of the water revealed a large tangle of grass and algae that had gathered over the years.

Bryn stepped forward and grasped the edge of the rowboat to steady it so that I could step down. The boat rocked as I found my seat next to an oar, and a wave of nostalgia formed a lump in my throat as my hands gripped the splintering wood.

Sam made his way to the seat at the fore of the boat with his back to the water, and I reached up to grab the wood planks to steady us for Bryn. He sat next to me, and I shoved off.

For a moment, Bryn and I were out of sync as we rowed with one oar up and one in the water no matter how I tried to match his pace. Frustrated, I stopped and placed my hand on his arm to get his attention.

"It works much better if we row together," I told him with a smile.

"I'm sure I can figure it out," Bryn teased, but he followed my lead as I prompted each stroke of the oars.

Every stroke dragged us farther from the shore and weighed on my heart even as it lifted my spirits to feel the rocking comfort of water beneath the hull. I smiled, grief warring with the joy of gliding across a glassy surface on a clear day. The lake was large, and it took some time to cross.

The trip across the lake taxed muscles that I hadn't used for a while, and by the time we reached the opposite shore I was dripping with sweat, my cloak removed and piled between my feet, my sleeves and skirt hiked up to bare my arms and legs. My arms burned with each pull and I could see that Bryn struggled against every stroke the longer we rowed.

This side of the lake didn't house any sort of dock, so we came to a halt when we scraped against silt. Sam jumped out of the boat first, gripping the prow to keep it from sliding back into the water while Bryn and I vaulted over the rail behind. Together, we hauled the boat onto the beach. I doubled over, resting my hands just above my knees and panting.

"Warm day," I said between breaths.

"It is; thank you two for...." Sam trailed off as Bryn hit the water with a splash. I danced out of the path of the water, turning toward the field and house.

The trees I had thought part of a small stand were actually a sizeable forest that stretched out to my left, running into the distant mountain range. What I had assumed a small refuge was a sizeable tract of land hidden away in the shadow of the hulking, snowcapped behemoths.

To my right stood the field, about half an acre of weed-ridden flat land surrounded by a fence as tall as me, in considerable disrepair. Parts of the wire fencing sagged under the weight of toppled posts and one section near the beach had fallen altogether, swallowed up by a tangle of dried vines that seemed to reach out to us from everywhere and nowhere all at once.

The house on the far side of the overgrown field stood two stories high with a porch that wrapped all the way around. Wood siding, perhaps yellow in the days of its youth, sat faded and grimy. Many windows dotted the walls, drapes drawn against the world.

Sam started toward the field, muttering under his breath as he went. The splashing increased as Bryn waded through the water to the shore. I started after Sam.

He bemoaned the state of disrepair, shaking his head when he lifted a rotting post from the fence. He tossed it aside and stepped over the fallen planks of the fence to squat among the weeds and pull a handful up by the roots. With another disgusted shake of his head and renewed muttering, he tossed the weeds aside and strode toward the house again.

I turned my head to face loud, pounding footsteps. Bryn was soaked.

"Feel better?" I laughed.

"Entirely," he beamed. His head swiveled about as we walked, running his hands through his hair to shake out the water. "This place is great, Sam!" he exclaimed with exuberance. "I can't believe you ever left!"

Sam's lips tightened for a moment mid-grumble; if I hadn't been watching I wouldn't have noticed the brief change. Without a word, Sam strode off in the direction of the cabin, Bryn and I in his wake. At the edge of the trees, a wooden bench sat next to the trunk of a large pine. The feet of the bench sat buried under years of pine needles.

The remains of a swing hung from the lowest branch of the neighboring tree. One of the ropes had broken and the seat hung from the other, trailing along the ground as the wind pushed it back and forth. A track through the needles was worn away by the constant movement.

We came at last to the steps leading up to the porch. The lowest step had a hole through the middle, so Sam stepped over it and tested his weight on the next. When he was satisfied that it could hold him, he sprang up onto the porch, the wood creaking beneath him.

The front door was a faded green, with small strips of the paint peeled away. Large cobwebs clung to the corner of the frame and adorned every nook and cranny in the roof above the porch.

"It'll take me a moment to unlock the door," Sam grumbled, and placed his hand over the lock. To give Sam time to work, I wandered around the corner of the house. I waded through the tall grass and weeds, the plants swishing as they slid around my legs. Despite the disrepair, most of the structure appeared intact. At the back of the house I found a waist-high fence that extended out from the corners of the walls and formed a square. A table and chairs stood near the house, covered in dirt and leaning drunkenly to one side, worn by time and weather. A short distance away stood another swing, supported by an old wooden frame. The whole thing sagged to one side, giving it a forlorn and hopeless appearance.

My ankle turned as my foot descended on something hidden in the tall grass of the small yard. Sharp pain lanced through my ankle and up my calf, and I hobbled a step before falling hard on my behind. This close to the ground, I found my assailant; a ball, about the size of my closed fist with swirling blue lines, faded and cracked.

Nearby was a figurine of a horse, lying on its side, the dappled paint faded and chipped.

All the grumbling, the short temper, and the haunted looks he tried so hard to hide from us fell into place, and I wondered what had happened to the child that used to live here with Sam. What had happened to their mother? All my grief made me feel alone in this world; I hadn't considered how much pain Sam had amassed in all his years.

Standing, I winced at the jolt in my ankle when I tested my weight on it. Hissing, I hobbled out of the yard with my hand on the fence posts to support myself. I heard Bryn's approach through the tall grass; anxiety marked his features, and his eyes locked on mine as he rounded the corner.

"I'm fine," I called as he neared, trying to hide his own limp. "I stepped on something over there," I gestured behind me, "nothing serious."

Bryn stopped a few feet from me, watching as I struggled forward to stand in front of him. He looked me up and down for a moment, then nodded and turned, placing his right arm around my waist and pulling my left arm around his neck. His arms supported my weight, and the pain lessened.

"Thank you," I murmured. "But I can walk."

He snorted and shook his head. "It already feels better. Trust me, I know." My answering snort made him smile despite his grimace of pain.

"Door's open, and he had just gone into the house when you hurt yourself," Bryn said as we rounded the corner. Sam was nowhere to be seen, and the front door of his cabin stood ajar. When we reached the stairs, I started to reach for the rail when Bryn picked me up, slinging me over his shoulder. He made his way nimbly up the stairs and deposited me gently on the porch.

"Doesn't your ankle hurt, too?" I asked. His limp faded as we walked.

"Taking the pressure off of your ankle helped."

A flare of light from inside the cabin caught my eye, and I hopped my way through the door.

My first impression of the cabin was of darkness and dirt. Cobwebs hung from every corner and off every piece of furniture and decoration. A clear line of footprints showed that Sam had walked across the room and through a door to my left.

White linen sheets covered hulking shapes in the gloom of the sitting room. A cold fireplace set in the wall on our right seemed to draw the attention of the furniture. Dust, kicked up in the wake of Sam's entrance, floated through the air near my face and I coughed after breathing it in.

Sam appeared in the doorway and frowned as he watched me limp across the room. "What happened?" he demanded.

"I rolled my ankle." I grimaced.

Sam yanked a sheet from the nearest piece of furniture. Dust surged into the air, and the sofa underneath was revealed. It was made of some soft blue material, and the cushions appeared to be filled to bursting with stuffing. Sam beat the cushion a few times and gestured for me to sit.

Once seated, Sam knelt in front of me and gently picked up my ankle, laying it down on his knee. He bowed his head and closed his eyes.

In an instant, I reestablished my connection to the Ambience so that I could see Sam use it. I winced as he began to soothe the pain. It began as a sharp increase in the ache, and then warmed along bone and muscle. At the same time, a subtle glow emanated from his hands, now cupped around my ankle. Sam's channeling looked more precise than anything I had achieved so far.

Another moment passed and the pain was gone. Sam opened his eyes and peered up at me.

"Better," I confirmed, smiling at his grizzled face. "Thank you."

Sam nodded and stood.

Quietly, I asked, "Did you live here alone, Sam?"

Sam looked down at me. Profound sadness highlighted lines on his face I hadn't seen before, in moments showing every one of his hundreds of years. As if my words and his sorrow had been some sort of signal, a warm current suffused the air. My body relaxed, somehow assured of the comfort and safety of my surroundings and the love that once filled the halls. Sam gasped, and flashed a smile so full of love and joy that time couldn't diminish it, a tear escaping the corner of his eye to disappear into his beard.

"Looks like we have our work cut out for us!" Bryn called from the next room. His words broke the spell, and Sam and I were left reeling as the warmth ebbed, leaving us in the cool, musty darkness of the sitting room.

Sam shook himself and scrubbed the back of his hand against his cheek. His eyes closed, the vulnerability of the moment before locked behind the shield he held up to protect himself. Longing to ask him what had happened, I scooted to the edge of the couch. Before my question escaped my lips, Sam turned on his heel and fled the room in the direction of Bryn's voice. With a frustrated sigh, I rose and followed him.

Across a threshold sat a small kitchen with wooden counters and a large cast iron pot suspended on a bar above the ancient remains of a fire. Bryn stood leaning against a counter covered in a thick layer of dust, his eyes narrowed at Sam, and then me. He noticed the tension in Sam's shoulders, more pronounced after our encounter a moment before, but Sam interrupted his thought by speaking.

"It won't take so long, Bryn," Sam said as I strolled into the kitchen. "The three of us will make short work of the mess and make it livable before the snow starts in earnest. And in the process, I hope to teach Lila a bit more about how to use the Ambience for everything from cleaning and cooking to defense and battle."

"First things first," Bryn smiled. "We need to clear out a place for all of us to spend the night, have some food, and get some sleep. I'm not ready for anything more strenuous than that."

"True," Sam said. "There are a couple of bedrooms upstairs that you two can use. I have one down here. Why don't you go have a look?"

Bryn led the way through the sitting room to a large set of stairs constructed from pine half rounds with a thick handrail on either side. The staircase rose from one end of the sitting room to the upper floor, opposite the fireplace ringed in stones from along the beach. Wary of the steps, Bryn tested his weight on each before trusting that it would hold us. Each creaked in protest, but none fell apart under Bryn's feet. At the top, a narrow hall stretched along the length of the house with several closed doors on the left and right.

Through the drawn curtain, a single window let in stripes of light that reached down the hall in our direction. Bryn opened the first door on the right to a small room with a table and narrow chair in one corner and a shuttered window above it. Shelves lined the wall from floor to ceiling, containing multitudes of books and small objects.

Bryn shut the door and moved to the next on the right as I opened the first door on the left, directly across from what I assumed was Sam's study.

The room beyond my chosen door was furnished with a large bed in the middle of the wall to my right, a nightstand with ewer and basin and a large chair-shaped lump beneath a sheet flanking a window across from the door. A door on the left wall opened onto a small closet. I slid the sheets off the bed and chair and a dresser near the door; the air danced with specks of dust in the afternoon sun streaming through the window. I ran my fingers over the overstuffed, rich blue plush of the chair back. The pine bedframe matched the rest of the décor, and a down mattress topped the bed; every muscle in my body relaxed as I heaved a sigh and spread myself out in the bed.

My eyelids glowed red in the sun's light while I luxuriated in the feel of something soft beneath my body for the first time since Stalth. A sneeze wracked my frame as I inhaled some of the dust in the air, and I sat up, my moment's peace broken. I swung my legs off the bed and opened the window with a screech to let the cool breeze freshen the room and clear the air of dust.

I picked up my pack where it lay discarded by the door and heaved it onto the waist-high dresser; it settled atop nicks and gouges in the soft pine. Next, I unbuckled my belt and heaved Desire next to my pack, my fingers lingering on the copper-plated rose at the hilt. I smiled, picturing it flash in the firelight as I sparred with Bryn. My head shook in amazement; I hadn't smiled this much in a long time.

Sam poked his head through the door after a knock, holding a pile of blankets and a few rags.

"Good choice. This is the softest mattress in the house," he winked. A hand-sewn quilt with worn edges topped the pile, made from colorful patches of old clothing. One patch of silky blue caught my eye, and my fingers ran over the spot again and again. Thick, white flannel sheets accompanied the quilt and promised to keep me warm as the weather became colder.

"Thanks, Sam. You have a beautiful home. And thank you for helping me."

"Think nothing of it." He waved his hand as if dismissing the need for gratitude. "I'm going to start on something to eat. It should be ready within the hour. Bryn is going to get some water to clean the rooms out; he should be back any time now. There are pillows in the closet." He turned and left, his footfalls echoing in the narrow hall.

Small, flattened pillows were stacked on the lowest shelf of the closet along with another few itchy wool blankets. Crossing to the window, I leaned out and slapped each of the two pillows a few times to free them of dust and tossed them on the bed.

The edges of the flannel sheets tucked under the bed and the quilt thrown over the whole, I arranged the pillows at the head, next to the wall. As I stepped back to admire my handiwork, Bryn carried in a small bucket of water for me, the twin to another he held in his hand. He looked around at the room I had chosen.

"Nice," he said, moving to the window. I joined him as he whistled at the view. The window looked out on the field and the trees and the lake beyond. The small waves reflected the light, in perpetual motion from the current running through the lake to the fall at the east end. All we surveyed seemed serene, the branches of the trees to the west swaying in a sudden gust of wind.

"There's a broom in the hall," Bryn informed me, stepping back from the window to place my bucket of water on the stand with the ewer. "Sam said he would call us when the food is ready."

"All right," I said as he walked out of the room. I rolled up my sleeves, picked up one of the rags, and dunked it in the cold water.

Dust left the porcelain surface of the basin in streaks, the rag dragging the black grime away as I swept my hand around and around. I poured a small amount of water into the ewer and basin, swirled them around, and let the water drop outside my window to the ground with a splash.

The task of dusting took mere minutes, and I soon had all the dirt swept out of the room. My work was finished, and I took a minute to gaze at a space that was mine, and private. With a sturdy door and room to stretch, this small room was more space than I had ever claimed as my own. Aboard the *Catherine,* I had slept among the crew in hammocks suspended from the deck above, crammed in a small space amid many sleeping bodies. My adventures of late had proven no better; sleeping rough in the open with two men surrounding me offered little in the way of privacy.

Now I had a place to store my things and a place to rest my head at night away from prying eyes and constant danger, I hoped. Though I had, and now did, trust these men with my life, I relished the idea of having a space to distance myself from them so I could reflect on the turn my life had taken.

At that moment, all I wanted was to find a place for all my things. Food and supplies *thunked* onto the dresser when I upended my pack in a rush of movement, and I smiled again as I surveyed all that was mine in the world. A few apples and a small wedge of cheese wrapped in cloth, a packet of herbs I had cajoled Bryn into buying for poultices in case of injury or illness, my extra clothes, and a bundle of fine tools such as forceps used for healing sat in a heap. I smiled at the comb that Bryn had thoughtfully given me that rounded out my collection. Keeping my hair under control had gone a long way to making me feel less helpless in the past weeks.

The herbs crumbled as I unclasped the lid of the packet. Irritated, I resolved to talk to Sam about the plants in the area to see if I could replenish my supply. If the kitchen had a drying rack, I could gather handfuls of helpful herbs to store for use.

My folded pack found a place in the bottom drawer, my skirt, bodice and full-length chemise in the middle. In the top drawer I placed my food, herbs, and tools for easy use.

It felt as though a weight had been lifted from my shoulders, my immediate worry turning to the training Sam would put me through as I learned to harness the Ambience. Sam assured us that here in the mountains we were safe from the threat that followed us, and I allowed myself to hope that he could be right.

CHAPTER THIRTY-THREE

The next week we spent cleaning the inside of the house and making minor repairs. The whole time I spent awash in Ambience, never alone and never disconnected. Aside from allowing me to become comfortable with it in every way, it helped with the cleaning efforts, highlighting areas that I might otherwise have missed in my rounds of every room. Sam insisted that we start with this most basic lesson before tackling anything more complicated.

The cabin was larger than it seemed from the outside. Three bedrooms and the study dominated the top floor; the ground floor held two more bedrooms, the sitting room, kitchen, and a room for bathing. The large master bedroom on the ground floor had space for a massive bed and a spacious closet filled with clothes. It held a dressing table with a plain mirror. The pine table and frame were carved with intricate shapes of animals along the edges.

A few gowns of the same silky blue fabric as the patch in my quilt hung in the closet and I found myself admiring them any time I was in Sam's room. Sam caught me once and looked at me with that profound sadness that I often saw when he thought no one was looking. I decided not to press him, respecting his wish not to share details of his life.

My suspicions of a child were confirmed when I cleaned the room on the ground floor near the master bedroom. It had a small bed and a chest of toys under the window. A small desk was laid neatly with drawing materials and a child's interpretation of his family tacked to the wall above it. A child's signature told me the artist's name was *Sammy*. As I looked about the room, I thought that I could hear faint laughter around me. A spirit flitted into view with a stronger presence than most. It disappeared in a moment, leaving a sense of love and loss in its wake. The wind picked up and brought with it the creak of the repaired gate and distant trees and I left the room.

At the end of the week, we were all exhausted. There wasn't a spider web left in the whole house, and all the pieces of furniture and parts of the house gleamed. There were still repairs that needed to be done, but Bryn assured me that he could more than handle that while Sam taught me how to use the Ambience.

One chill morning, Sam led me on a walk around the grounds and out into the forest. Tall pines towered above us, their tops lost in a sea of green needles above. Deeper into the trees the air became still and close as the giants sheltered us from wind. Sam spoke as we walked.

He explained that at its core, one's power was an understanding of the world around us and an idea of how to shape it. Most Tethers needed that understanding in order to manipulate the forces of the world. What most people described as the gift was in fact a deeper connection to Celuthia and its forces and the lives all around.

"The Ambience allows me to change things around me, to use my will to alter what is there to make it into something of my choosing." He gestured at the trees above and the plants below. "In order to make something out of the wood of the trees, I must be able to access the energy within the tree and know how to change it. If I were to attempt to make plants grow, I would first need to understand what *makes* a plant grow, or I could have no hope of achieving anything. Do you understand?"

I nodded but frowned. "I understand what you're saying, but I don't understand how you gained this knowledge. How can you access the energy in a tree?"

"This is something that we will work on, and it will take some time. A Conduit's strength, the strength that you possess, is in *creation*, rather than alteration of the world around them. Where I can change the shape of a tree to make what I need, they were able to create the materials from nothing and form those materials into the shape required."

"That's incredible," I gaped. "How can you make something from nothing?"

Sam shook his head, bewildered and impressed. "I don't know. And I don't know how to teach you such a feat. All I can do is teach you what I know in the hopes that it will help you in the future. I'll keep studying the few books I have here, and hope that they can shed some light on how to proceed. Though it is often easier to manipulate the materials in front of you rather than create new materials, so my worry might be for nothing."

"It seems like it would be faster to make what you need," I replied.

"Faster, and more strenuous," Sam replied. He grinned. "You are using your own energy, augmented by the Ambience, to create something. It is by far the more sensible option to use what is already there than to use yourself as fuel."

"So, I was creating something from nothing?"

"Yes."

"The fire?"

Sam nodded. "That fire came from you, fueled by your fear."

"And when you make a fire...."

"I use what's around me. Heat created by rubbing my hands together can be transformed into a flame if you are practiced enough."

It was my turn to be impressed, and my eyebrows rose as we turned back toward the cabin and Sam began to explain how to interact with the world around me.

Over the next weeks, I despaired at ever understanding what Sam tried to teach me. Every day, from dawn to dusk and into the evening, Sam lectured me on the types of Ambient energy within different beings and objects, or had me pore through many of the tomes he had in his collection. It was thrilling to see so much information about the Ambience. I had spent so much of my life searching for books just like these, that gave me real-world experiences of Ambient like me. When he lectured, my eyes glazed and my mind wandered as I watched his hands move of their own accord, trying and failing to demonstrate a process that was second nature to him after all this time.

He explained that learning to understand the energy in something as simple as a blade of grass could be achieved through reflection and visualization of the thing itself. To augment my attempts, he produced ancient volumes filled with descriptions of things like plants, animals, and the elements. For centuries, Tethers had taken everything apart to see how it was made, including people passed from the world of the living. Some books had diagrams and drawings that proved gruesome but instructive, and my knowledge grew over the hours spent poring over them by candlelight, trying to decipher written and scribbled words on musty paper.

All the study proved worthless in aiding me to use the Ambience as Sam watched me trying to use my enhanced senses to channel it into plants around the cabin. Though everything seemed brighter and more vibrant to me, I couldn't grasp the concept of finding the energy in anything.

Sam moved on, frustrated that he couldn't help me to understand, but assuring me that everything he could find on the instruction of Conduits expounded the difficulty of learning what I failed to learn. All I could do was repeat to myself over and over the theory behind his instruction and hope that someday I would find a way to make it work for me.

One day Sam stood nearby in the field by the cabin, a small pinecone on his upturned palm, explaining how he was able to move things. My eyes strayed the field now clear of weeds and grass.

Sam recalled me to the moment. "Lila! Did you hear me?"

"Sorry, Sam." I grimaced, embarrassed to be found with my mind wandering. "Something about the weight of the pinecone."

My posture mirrored his; I stood straight with my palm upturned before me, holding an inert pinecone waiting to be lifted into the air.

"Yes," Sam huffed. "I can alter the weight of the object. I pull the air into a solid mass at the same time to make it move where I want it to go. After that, it is a simple matter to direct the mass of air. Observe." The pinecone rose from his palm to hover at the level of his eyes. After a moment of suspension, it gently settled back into his hand. He curled his fingers around it and let his arm drop to his side.

"Try it," he said.

No matter how I tried, mine wouldn't move. I could see the Ambience when he used it, attuned to it as I was, but I couldn't make things happen the way he wanted me to. For so long, I had wanted to learn about the Ambience, and now that I had the opportunity, I couldn't follow my instruction. It seemed useless to learn all of this if I couldn't put it into practice.

Tired of pushing for results that seemed unlikely to come, I just pictured the pinecone rising. The Ambience grew, the spirits came, and their hands lifted the pinecone above my palm. It hovered as Sam's had, and then I let go of the Ambience to let it fall.

Sam sighed. "Lila, that's not what we're trying to accomplish. Please, focus."

Now, I was getting angry. At myself, for not being able to use the skills Sam was teaching, but also at him, for not realizing that this wasn't something that worked for me. I wanted to destroy my pinecone. It crumbled in my palm, and I stared at Sam through the fine dust left behind, falling through my loose fingers.

"Another one, Lila," Sam said in his most patient voice that told me he was at the edge of his tolerance. He gestured to the ground, and I stooped to grasp another pinecone. "What I'm asking you to do isn't so different from what you can do innately. It just takes more control to find the essence of the world around you and tap into it. It might help if you visualize what you described to me about your connection to Bryn; a shroud of Ambient light around the pinecone."

My eyes slid closed and I heaved a heavy sigh. I tried to see the object in my hand surrounded by the Ambience, like Bryn. With that image in my mind, I tried to imagine it as an extension of the energy inside of it. My imagination wasn't enough to entice success, and my fingers curled into a fist and squeezed, the rough edges digging into my skin as I let my arm drop to my side. "I'm sorry, Sam, I just can't seem to make it happen."

"We'll keep trying, Lila," he replied.

I gave a curt nod and turned my eyes away from the cabin, toward the lake and the sunset. The sky was ablaze and the lake mirrored it, looking as though it were on fire, even dancing like flames. Movement at the edge of the forest caught my eye, and I turned my head just in time to see Bryn step out from under the trees. He had been chopping up a small tree, stocking the cabin with firewood while Sam was preoccupied with my training.

Bryn's chest was bare, his shirt tucked into the waist of his trousers. His muscles flexed as he lifted the axe in his hand to sling the handle over his shoulder. He ran a hand through his hair where the sun lit it, pulling his long locks off his face. Gold sparkled on the crown of his head while the ends shone with fiery red and orange. A thought came unbidden to my mind, something half remembered from the confines of Bryn's arms while my throat burned from smoke.

I think I would die if something happened to her. And I'm not sure if that's only because of the bond.

My pulse quickened and my cheeks flushed as I stared at Bryn, seeing him in a different light than I had before. Spirits swarmed to him, forming a massive cloak without any other effects. As soon as they did, I could feel the energy inside his body, the flow and ebb of it as he moved and breathed, flexed and relaxed his muscles. How had I ever considered him my enemy? How had I not noticed in all this time how beautiful he was?

"Lila!" Sam shouted. Startled, I turned to ask why he was shouting until I noticed the pinecone levitating about an inch from my open palm. My eyes widened and I felt my mouth drop open in shock.

"What did you do?" Sam asked, a smile growing on his face.

My cheeks reddened further as I realized that the only change had been Bryn's appearance. But I had caught a glimpse of what Sam was trying to describe to me, in someone that was intimately linked to me through the Ambience. So I used the embarrassment I felt at my appreciation for Bryn's body. It was deeper inside this lifeless piece of a nearby tree, but it was there. I could see it in the air around me as well, so I put both pieces together, as Sam had told me to, and the pinecone levitated above my hand.

It hovered higher above my palm for a few moments until Bryn stopped a few feet in front of me. Bryn greeted me with a grin spread from ear to ear, filled with more than congratulations. My cheeks reddened further, and the pinecone shot off into the air.

Bryn laughed and I joined him, the pinecone lost from view. Sam eyed me with suspicion, and then smiled at Bryn. "Well, whatever you did it seems to have worked. Remember that for your next lesson." Sam looked above me, and the pinecone streaked downward, stopping before it slammed into his hand. The next moment, he looked away from it, and it dropped gently onto his palm. "I think that's all for today. I'll go start dinner."

Sam walked away, and Bryn moved to stand in front of me. "That'll be handy when I'm ready to move all that wood! Nice job, Lila."

"Thank you," I beamed, gazing at his broad shoulders and square jaw. Rough golden stubble ran along his cheeks and jawline, glistening in the sunset.

"I know, I need a bath," he said, responding to my examination. "I'll be back in a while." With a carefree grin he turned and bounded in the direction of the lake. Despite how cold it was, it was still his favorite place to bathe. I stood for a time, watching as he splashed in the shallow water turned the color of blood by the fiery sky.

Aware of my intent to consciously draw on the Ambient Pool rather than reacting as I had in the past, I was able to harness it without relying upon Bryn to walk half naked in my line of sight.

As I repeated tasks Sam set for me again and again, I realized that my creation of natural forces mimicked the process that Sam described. Now that I understood both processes, I began to make leaps in my understanding of everything Sam taught me.

After more than a month failing to mimic Sam's way of harnessing the Ambience, I basked in the glow of pride and accomplishment my new grasp on his instruction afforded me. A stone teemed with the energy that had created it and altered it over many years to become such a smooth, smaller version of the stone it had been. All life around me, from the weeds on the ground to the towering pines above in the forest, teemed with energy flowing through every leaf and stem, and back into the ground to surge along roots and through the dirt that nourished other plants.

Animals, insects, and the three of us were filled to bursting with the energy required to sustain our lives. Every time I flexed my hand or even a finger, the Ambience sparked like the beginning of a forest fire.

Bryn also taught me to use his bow before the winter came. I spent weeks practicing until he was convinced that I wouldn't hurt myself or loose all his arrows into parts unknown. It felt a lot like my time learning to wield a sword; new muscles were sore, and I felt a surge of fierce pride whenever an arrow hit the target.

More and more, I noticed something that seemed to shadow our lives in Sam's cabin, especially after a long day spent learning how to harness the Ambience and use a bow or spar with swords. Like the first night, a warm gust of air touched my skin, but I saw a presence that seemed distant and intangible. It resembled the flow of Ambience I witnessed in Sam or Bryn, but it was muted as if in a fog.

Sitting with Bryn and Sam, teasing one another around the table at dinner, or sitting in front of the fire with a book recalling the adventures of some mischievous Tether from long ago, the flash would appear and then disappear just as suddenly.

Whenever I broached the subject with Sam, he would close himself off and become distant like the presence I felt, refusing to speak on the topic. Though curiosity burned in me to know what this was, I didn't push Sam to reveal something he wasn't ready for.

The more I began to understand the forces around me, the more Sam pushed me to try altering them in some way. In moments of exhausted frustration, my ability to create what I had intended to manipulate overcame my lessons. When I attempted to split a log using a focused, blade-like sliver of air and Bryn's arm brushed against mine as he passed, I blew the log into small pieces that ricocheted against the block and fence.

At night, when the only sounds were the creaking of the house and wind against the windows, I sat alone in my room with my thoughts for company. After the incident with the log, I felt confused by my reaction to Bryn. While I had experienced something like this with Hunter, I could discern a gradual change in my attitude toward him over years. Hunter had been my friend, and I trusted him from the moment we met. He grew to be a handsome man with a good heart, and he knew me as well as anyone had. A relationship with Hunter had been a natural outcome of our friendship and years together, no matter how hard I tried to push him away.

I inhaled deeply to curtail my depressing thoughts. My relationship with Bryn was complicated and confusing from the moment I met him. A vague recollection of his kindness and failed attempts to protect me while in his uncle's custody remained. And though our opinions differed in many ways and we argued for the first weeks together, I found myself enjoying his company now.

Knowing now where Bryn's life had taken him and his deep loathing for his uncle and everything the man stood for, months of traveling, the stress of running for our lives and the bond between us had brought us closer. Though strange at first, after our experience sharing memories and seeing into his mind, I knew that he was a good man at heart.

In the months here, with no immediate threat on our lives, all trace of tension between us had faded. Sam was an able teacher with the ability to keep me in check, which allowed Bryn to relax. His easy and dry humor spoke to me more than his physical beauty, and we connected in a way that I hadn't experienced with anyone else in my life. Now, the very thought of him made me excited and comforted, safe and terrified all at once. The fact that he inspired my ability to connect with the world as Sam saw it made me wonder at the depth of my feelings for him.

I pushed my circular musings to the back of my mind and picked up the journal Sam had given me to read from the pile of texts about the Ambience on my bedside table. Handwritten by someone named Lania, it described her study of the human form after death and the inferences she had drawn pertaining to the healing arts. Instructive as it was, it was dry enough for my mind to wander and my eyes to glaze. While rereading a section about the muscles in the forearm, a sudden realization hit me.

All that I felt for Bryn, beyond the appreciation of all that he had done for me, *could* be nothing but the bond, and thus not in my control or even entirely genuine. It could be a side effect of the tether literally pulling us toward one another that was visible any time I used the Ambience to see.

A weight lifted off my shoulders as I concluded that whatever might lie between us was secondary to my goal. I resolved to spend a bit more time examining our connection in hopes of finding a way to sever it, thereby releasing him from his forced guardianship of my health and safety and allowing a normal bond of friendship to form.

I had enough to deal with without a distraction, no matter how attractive and fun. With a firm nod of satisfaction, I pushed away my thoughts of Bryn and continued my study of the human form.

CHAPTER THIRTY-FOUR

My lessons progressed as the chill bite of winter descended upon us. No snow had fallen, but with every day, the temperature dropped in anticipation of its arrival. Having repaired the cabin, prepared the field for planting, and stocked us with supplies and the little amount of root vegetables he had found searching the surrounding area, Bryn took to exploring farther afield and building a smoking shed to preserve the meat he often hauled back after days alone in the forest.

To ensure that we had enough meat for winter and to teach me how to hit more than a straw target, Bryn took me hunting with him, deep into the woods. We set out at dawn with hoods drawn against the cold and packs filled with enough food to see us through the few days we planned to spend away from the cabin.

The valley was larger than I imagined, winding its way between the soaring peaks farther into the distance than I could see. We stopped on the top of a hill, level with the tips of the surrounding trees. We were about half a day's walk from the cabin and we intended to sleep rough tonight, both of us wanting to spend some time under the stars.

We talked a little as we walked. Bryn told me about his wanderings, and I updated him on my progress with my lessons. We shared almost everything about ourselves during our brief experiment with the Ambience. His dazzling, carefree smile stunned me, and I had to remind myself of my resolve to leave my feelings out of our interaction. The flush that rose unwelcome to my cheeks when he grasped my hand to help me over the trunk of a massive fallen tree served to illustrate how my body could betray me; the flush deepened when I wondered if he could feel it.

We stopped at another small hill and made camp that night. The sweeping valley below spread far beyond and into the base of the mountains in the distance, covered with a blanket of evergreens. The stars winked above our heads as we let our packs slide to the ground.

Bryn set a fire while I pulled a small amount of dried meat and fresh bread from my pack. We ate in silence, staring into the flames as we chewed. My hunger sated, I spread my bedroll out on a bed of dried pine needles close to the fire. Lying flat on my back, I looked up at the stars, trying not to think about the fact that Bryn and I were alone for the first time in months.

A few minutes later, I felt a slight stirring of the air next to my head. I turned to see Bryn placing his bedroll so that one end was next to my head, angled slightly to keep it near the fire. Bryn placed himself with his head near mine and looked at the stars alongside me.

"What have you been thinking about?" he asked me. "You've been anxious this whole trip."

Relief flooded through me; he couldn't interpret the confusion wreaking havoc on me.

"Nothing in particular," I answered, my voice even and unconcerned. "I'm excited about my first hunting trip, and nervous we'll go home with nothing."

Bryn chuckled. "You'll do fine, Lila. You have an *excellent* teacher."

"The best," I intoned, rolling my eyes. We fell silent, and many moments passed before Bryn spoke again.

"I've missed this," he blurted.

"What?" I asked.

"Lying under the stars," he replied with a sigh. "It's been too long. That's one of the reasons I left Stalth in the first place. I took a few jobs guarding caravans, sleeping rough, and I fell in love with it. I start to feel cramped after too long indoors."

"It's amazing you were able to live on a ship for any amount of time, then," I replied. "It's very cramped, sleeping in a hammock in the middle of a room with other people."

Bryn didn't respond, and my thoughts meandered back to conversations we had when we first broke off from Roglin's crew on our way to Stalth.

"Bryn? You said that you left Stalth because you had a falling out with a member of your gang. And just now, you said that not liking to be in cramped spaces was one of the reasons you left Stalth. Are there more? There were a few things I couldn't see when we shared our thoughts."

Bryn's reply came slowly. "I... *do* get restless and like to get outdoors. And I *did* have a falling out with one of the men I ran with. The reason I had a falling out...." He paused, and I heard him shift on his bedroll. "It was over a woman; his sister."

A sharp pang of jealousy twisted in my gut, and I tried to suppress it.

"When I was about seventeen, I thought my friend Douglas' older sister Maggie was the most alluring creature I had ever seen. She was so proud and beautiful that I followed her around wherever she went, trying to impress her.

"Douglas, another guy, and I started working as caravan guards, and I didn't see her for months at a time. I forgot about her for a while, to be honest. One winter when the caravans weren't running and I worked with Arthur and Maude, Maggie came in. We reconnected and spent a lot of time together.

"I started to follow her around again, becoming something like a slave to her every whim. I did anything she wanted and waited for her to give me permission to hold her hand or kiss her on the cheek; I was so nervous and shy around her and I still don't know why."

The picture Bryn painted was hard to reconcile with this confident and flippant man lying next to me under the stars.

"What I didn't know was that she was pulling this stunt with a few other men, and she wasn't withholding her affection from them," Bryn grumbled. "I confronted her about it, and she sobbed, insisting she made a mistake and it wouldn't happen again. When she told me she loved me, I was fool enough to believe her.

"I almost proposed marriage to her. Thankfully, I witnessed her coming out of the jeweler's, still lacing her bodice. Before I bought a ring. I was furious for a while."

Bryn paused; I flipped over onto my stomach and propped my head in my elbows to gaze at him. This was a memory that I had only seen parts of; he must have hidden them somehow, and I felt outrage on his behalf for the betrayal. The fire crackled while he clenched and unclenched his fingers and frowned.

"I told her I was done and told her brother what kind of woman she was. Douglas beat me mercilessly and tossed me into the street while Maggie looked on."

"That's awful," I scoffed. "I can't believe they did that to you."

"Well," he said, flopping onto his stomach to face me. "That's because *you* are a good person, and she is not." He smirked and mumbled, "I'd love to see the look on her face if she ever saw you."

"What?" I blinked, surprised and confused.

Bryn shrugged. "She's so vain," he stated. "If she could see you, I'm sure she would tear her hair out by the roots."

He turned his head to the fire, and I was grateful that he couldn't see the deepening flush on my face as he continued.

"Douglas forced me out of Stalth, spread rumors that I was stealing from the caravans so that I couldn't work. When I tried to work for Arthur and Maude, the bastard and his friends started to harass them in the street. That was why I decided to work for my uncle as hired muscle. But, after a few months with him, I knew I wouldn't be able to stay with him for long; the man is without shame or decency. Before I could find the courage to leave," he turned back to me with a smile, "you happened."

"And now you've had to run for your life and protect mine. And you're at the mercy of some strange form of Ambience that Sam and I can't undo." I snorted. "Vast improvement."

"What happened to thinking I was a scoundrel?" he smirked. "Not too long ago I would have sworn that you hated me."

"I thought the same about you," I retorted. He shot me a sardonic look, eyebrow quirked above narrowed eyes, and I shrugged. "I wondered the same thing for a while. One day, I trusted you. And after we shared that connection..." I shrugged again. "I was able to see *you*, and I know that I don't have any reason to fear you. I know that you would fight with me against your uncle if you were in that situation, even without the added incentive of the bond. It's in your nature."

"And I know that you weren't looking for any of this to happen to you either, Lila. And I think I trust you now, too. Can you tell me anything about your power?"

"It's part of me, but it's more than me. I've read references to Conduits, and I get the sense that I'm not normal, even for a Conduit. There's no experience that I can find that details anything like me. But Sam told me that his library is nothing compared to what used to exist, so...." I trailed off with a shrug.

"You're unique," Bryn stated. "Anyone can see that."

Bryn smiled again and turned onto his back with his hands under his head. After a moment, I followed suit. Stars glimmered in the inky black sky; one by one, crickets began their chirping serenade in the renewed silence. Two of the lights above seemed to burn brighter than the others, and when I let my eyes wander, I almost thought that they moved. I rubbed a hand over my tired eyes and sighed, drifting to sleep.

Our first hunt was successful; I took down a large buck with Bryn's bow and we dragged it to the cabin. Bryn seemed impressed, though he commented often on how well I had been taught. I rolled my eyes every time, reminded of another young man who once boasted the same.

My lessons that winter consisted of manipulating the elements. Sam had me start small fires in the fireplace in a controlled setting. Often, I would use the technique Sam had shown me, rubbing my hands along my arms to create a small amount of heat that I could focus into a flame directed at the logs and kindling.

We kept a small plot of vegetables habitable for growth through the cold months and protected ourselves from the same cold by heating the air around us. It was exhausting, but my endurance grew over time.

We continued in this way through the end of the season and into the next. One night I lay sprawled on the floor near the fireplace, a pillow under my head and the comforter from my bed beneath me as

I held a book high enough to read by the wavering light. Bryn was asleep on the nearby couch, his long legs hanging off the edge and his head propped up against the arm. I could hear Sam down the hall in his room, where he liked to hole up in the evenings to keep a journal of our progress.

I felt content and safe in this cozy home in the mountains. I lowered the book to my chest and tilted my head back to gaze upside-down at the flames. They flickered and the wood popped, throwing off an occasional spark and wafting hot air toward me. It took me a moment to realize that the warmth I felt wasn't entirely caused by the fire, and I lifted my head toward a presence in the room that I had felt before.

I nearly shouted, the book falling from my chest as I straightened with a start. A blue light hovered a few feet away in the middle of the room. Instinctively, I touched the Ambience, letting it flow through me to enhance my vision. The blue light seemed to waver, one moment looking like nothing so much as a star in the sky and the next shaping itself into the familiar shape of a person, and back again.

Rather than retreat, the presence tickled at my mind, using the spirits as a conduit. It felt akin to when Bryn and I were linked, but this was an entirely alien consciousness. It filled me with pain, longing, and sadness, but also a deep joy. Names and faces flashed behind my eyes, people and places that I had never seen. A laughing woman, a small child running across a field, a white tower in the distance; all these images and more came and went in an instant.

As suddenly as they began, the images faded, and I was left with a singular thought that was not my own. *Care for him.* A voice deep and female rang in my ears. An impression of longing and sadness came again, and my eyes sought Bryn's sleeping face before snapping back to the light. It coalesced into the figure of a woman more vivid than any other spirit. She had long black hair and kind eyes over a sad smile.

For a moment I heard a vicious cackle echoing outside and the woman turned to scowl at it. The sound vanished and she turned back to me with her arms outstretched. I stood and moved to her. I was drawn in a way I imagined a child would be to their mother. Her arms, while insubstantial, felt warm and welcoming. Her name came unbidden to my mind. *Penelope.* And then she was gone.

I padded softly down the hall, where a single candle cast a soft and wavering light on the table where Sam was bent over a leather-bound volume. He looked up when he noticed me, and the look of concentration morphed into one of concern as he peered at my face.

"Lila?" he murmured. "What's wrong? Bryn...?"

"He's sleeping," I replied, my voice flat in my ears as I struggled to comprehend what I had seen and experienced. Sam's brows furrowed as he stood, placing his hands on my shoulders.

"I just saw something...." I trailed off, gesturing toward the sitting room.

Sam's eyes widened, and his grip tightened. "What did you see?" His tone was urgent, and it drew me out of my fog of disbelief.

"A spirit," I said. "It...she...had long black hair. Penelope." Sam's arms dropped from my shoulders. For a moment he only stared at me, but then he began to speak.

"It's been a long time since spirits could be seen," he whispered. "They used to linger." He lowered himself to his chair, as if exhausted. He placed an elbow on his table and leaned his face into an upturned palm. "The magic that faded from Trylia with the ability to touch the Ambience caused the spirits to disappear as well. It's been years since I've encountered one I wasn't tethered to." He looked up at me with an unreadable expression. Was it hope, fear, or some mixture of the two?

"What happened?" he pleaded.

"I felt sadness, and longing," I said, and Sam's face fell. "But there was also joy, and what I thought was love. She showed me places and people that I've never seen before. I'm still a bit confused," I admitted, shrugging.

Sam buried his face in his hands. I reached out to touch him, but some instinct held me back, and my hand fell to my side.

"Do you know who the spirit is?" I whispered.

I waited for a few minutes in silence. When an answer wasn't provided, I backed out of the room, closing the door behind me.

CHAPTER THIRTY-FIVE

Sam and I didn't discuss the spirit again. Bryn's curiosity was piqued when I mentioned her to him; we argued for a long time about whether he should ask Sam for more information, but I convinced him that in this instance he should let Sam keep his secrets. The raw pain evident on my mentor's face was enough to convince me, and only when I shared that with Bryn did he relent.

I felt her more and more, like a friend come to visit. Often she lingered around Sam wherever he stood and reached out to touch him. He felt nothing, but I could feel the strength of her love for him. Whenever I struggled with a task that Sam set for me, I called out to Penelope first. She always answered.

When the weather changed and the snow melted, Bryn and I set out on a trip to Mountain's Shade. Large sections of the lake had thawed, but we maneuvered through tenacious floes on our way across the frigid water. Despite a few icy patches, we made it out of the valley and through the tunnel in a day.

A few brave birds had taken up their song of spring as we approached, but fell silent until we passed. Both of us had a spring to our step; despite our brief forays into the cold outdoors, we had spent far too long in the confines of the cabin. Sam said that he would rather stay at home. He preferred not to show his face any more than he had. Bryn and I were discussing what he meant as the small town came into view in the distance.

"I don't see what he could be afraid of after so many years," Bryn said.

"There's a lot he hasn't told us," I replied. "There's no way to know unless he opens up."

"We should make him tell us when we get back. He needs to stop keeping so many secrets," Bryn insisted with a frown.

"I think he's being cautious, and I think he's hiding deep pain." This was a point that I could sympathize with, and I tried to impress that upon Bryn again. "We can't force him to relive those memories. I can't say I'm any different."

Bryn shrugged, dismissing the topic. The chill air cooled my nose and cheeks, but bright sunlight helped to warm me as we strolled along the narrow path. Bryn's movements, as always, were measured and confident as if he had traveled this way countless times.

Bryn pointed out a few buildings from our earlier trip where we could buy what we needed, and we made our way to them. After a short time, our packs sat heavy on our shoulders, full of provisions for our retreat. In every shop we visited, the owners were brusque and disappeared into the recesses of the building before we were out the front door.

"Were these people like this when you were here last?" I murmured to Bryn as we stepped into the sunlight. "When we came through before, it felt different."

None of the townspeople were outside, bustling about as I would suspect they should this soon after a thaw. Spring thaw was a time for planting and repairs, a time to soak in the sun after long months indoors. A small dirt lane ran from where I stood to the river, and I couldn't see anyone working nets or poles to catch fish.

"No," Bryn replied, his hand grasping the hilt of his dagger.

A chill that had nothing to do with the weather ran down my spine. Here and there, drapes fluttered as a face disappeared behind them. In every direction, eyes peered at us from behind the safety of their locked doors.

"Bryn...." My fingers curled around the hilt of Desire, my hackles rising at the menacing pall over the town. My eyes raked over every surface, every shadow, in search of a threat.

Bryn grunted in response, the steel of dagger and sword ringing when they cleared their scabbards at a measured pace. His boots scraped against the dirt road as he turned in a slow circle, his back to mine.

My senses sharpened as the Ambience answered my dread. With more control and ease than I thought possible in this situation, I cast about the square for anything amiss. The faint flutter of energy from the plants and animals slid past my focus. The terrified frenzy in the people watching from their windows heightened my alarm. Desire sang in the quiet as I freed it and stood ready, my back to Bryn's. We mirrored one another, eyes roaming the empty streets.

A sudden flare of energy preceded the knife hurtling through the air toward Bryn. With a grunt I heaved him aside by his sleeve and the blade soared past at the level of his throat.

Before the knife clattered to the ground, I created a wall of air around us like what I used to contain heat, but solidified to stop further projectiles. Fueled by fear and mounting anger, it pulsed, sending jolts of pressure radiating outward. A moment later, an arrow came to a halt just in front of my face. I glared around it, toward the spot where it had been fired.

Three men streamed out from behind the blacksmith's shop following the arrow. One held a bow at the ready, and the other two held battered round wooden shields and shortswords. Light gleamed off the honed edges of the blades. All three moved with the grace of battle-hardened men; no sneers or taunts assailed us, they merely stood ready to attack. Bryn grunted, and I glanced past his shoulder at four more people emerging from behind buildings on the other side of the square.

With an enemy revealed, calm determination replaced anxiety. I scanned the area around our feet, watching out of the corner of my eye as a few more arrows skittered to the ground after being halted by my shield.

Logs stacked against the base of a nearby house gave me inspiration; a large pine round rose from the ground and hurtled through the air at the man closest to Bryn. I snarled while I conjured the necessary force, letting my instinct careen the solid stump into his side. He cried in pain and stumbled with his arms flung wide. The round rocked back and forth at the feet of two others who stood in awe and momentary fear.

Bryn craned his neck to glance at the men facing me while keeping an eye on the three still standing, surrounding him. All eyes in the square were fixed on the round as it rose and struck again, slamming into the side of the other man with sword and shield and throwing him sideways to land heavily on his shield arm. Either the shield or his arm cracked and broke the tense silence.

He moaned in pain, and the sword dropped from his hand. The remaining men paused, glaring at the two of us facing them as their fellow writhed on the ground, grasping his arm. Their leader, seeing that another arrow failed to reach its mark, flung the bow aside and drew a longsword from his belt. He bellowed a rumbling, feral growl, and spurred his men into action. Galvanized by the cry, the rest of them charged with swords drawn and angry screams resounding through the square.

The leader forced himself through my shield with a headlong rush through the pulsing air, ignoring the buffeting repellant. His steel met mine with a screech and my arms burned and shook with the effort of blocking his downward swipe. He screamed with rage; his spittle and foul breath assaulted me, broken and rotting teeth bared. I screamed back at him, calling the Ambience to answer my rage.

I shoved at my assailant, knocking him backward to give myself some room, and directed a surge outward along my arm toward him. Light and air coalesced into a shape mimicking my clenched fist; it hit his chest with a sound like a branch snapping, and his ribs caved in toward his heart. His eyes widened and his jaw fell slack as his hand groped toward his chest feebly, dripping with his blood. His other hand fell loose to his side, his sword clanging on a rock near his clumsy feet. Dead, he crumpled to the ground in a heap. I had time only to wince at the gruesome sight before another was upon me.

As I stepped back, I felt emptiness; Bryn no longer stood at my back. A shield bashed into my sword, the shock echoing along the blade and through my arms, numbing me. Without pause, my attacker thrust the shining tip of his blade at my exposed ribs. It missed me by a hair's breadth, and I slammed my pommel on the man's face, shattering his nose and spattering my face with his blood. He dropped to his knees and I stepped beside him with my sword tucked under his chin to pull my sword across his exposed throat.

I whipped my head around in search of Bryn, and found him on the other side of a man in dusty leather armor between us, while another two assailed him. Sunlight flashed off the swords as Bryn's attackers rained blows upon him. He danced out of their reach one moment to lunge forward the next, parrying one blade with dirk and another with sword.

The man between us spotted me and his companions bloodied at my feet, and rushed, his round wooden shield squared to me and his blade out wide to slash. I danced away from the shield in time to avoid another numbing blow and swiped low, trying to sever the muscles in his legs.

He proved too quick and brought his shield around to catch my blade. It stuck into the wood grain, and though I yanked with all my strength, it held fast. His blade swung in a tight arc toward my shoulder and I ducked away. He smiled with small yellow teeth haphazardly piled in his mouth. I closed my right hand into a fist and punched him over the top of his shield.

My knuckles caught his upper teeth and split as they buckled inward. A flash of searing agony coursed through my shattered hand, and we both grunted in pain. His shield drooped and the arm holding his blade sagged as his eyes popped open wide. With a grimace, I gripped Desire's hilt with both hands and planted my foot against the lower edge of the shield.

As the blade wrenched free of its prison, I stumbled backward and the man fell onto his rear in the dirt. Tears streamed down my cheeks when I adjusted my grip on the hilt and the bones in my right hand shifted.

Bryn's eyes found mine as he pulled his dagger free of a man's neck and blood splattered against his cheek. The deceased fell to the dirt heaped atop his fellow in a grisly pile. The expression on Bryn's face, blank determination and blood thirst, chilled me to the bone. His eyes softened when they strayed to my injured hand and his own flexed in response.

Another scream erupted from me as I thrust my sword at the last living man's throat. He tried to raise his shield in time but was a moment late. His blood ran in rivulets to join the pooled blood of his fallen comrades.

Footsteps pounded in the dirt to my left and my eyes sought the source of the sound. Another three men raced around the edge of the nearest building with bows drawn and murderous looks on their faces. All three aimed at Bryn when he turned to face them, dagger and sword ready and dripping with blood. Feral desperation consumed me, and my shield pulsed outward and shattered in the direction of the three men. Loose dirt puffed into the air in an arc as the shockwave hit. Slain foes' blood-soaked shirts rustled, and Bryn's hair blew back from his face as he squinted against the howling rush of wind.

The three men flew backward and slammed into the wall at their backs. The wood shuddered from the impact and they slid heavily to the ground in disordered heaps, their arms and legs at odd angles. My uninjured hand stretched outward, cupped as if I held something in my hand, and one of the men rose from the ground, looking like a puppet held aloft by its strings, to slam into the wall again with such force that the wood cracked.

I advanced in a fury, intending to smash them to pieces for daring to threaten our lives, when I felt a hand on my outstretched arm. Ready to strike, I turned my head to find Bryn, his expression grim but concerned. When I tried to wrench my arm free, he shook his head and tightened his grip.

"Stop, Lila," he said, and through my rage I knew that he meant to let go of the Ambience. More difficult than the insubstantial attempts to first harness it, I couldn't release my hold on the power it granted. I fought again to extricate myself from his grasp to make certain the last of our attackers was dead. I would not be haunted by any more thugs.

Bryn stepped closer, his eyes imploring. "Lila, it's over. We're safe now."

A shuddering breath I didn't intend to release escaped my lungs and I closed my eyes. One of the men on the ground groaned and the spirits strained to be free, to finish the task and end him.

As I opened my eyes, Bryn stepped forward and embraced me. I stood still for a moment, rigid with surprise. His hand strayed to my hair, stroking it as he had so many months ago to soothe me away from the grips of uncontrollable surges of Ambience. Against every instinct to destroy the last man living, my whole body relaxed at once and my arms dropped to my sides. Desire clattered to the ground and the broken body of the man in my clutches landed among the others with a thud and crackle of broken bones. My head tipped forward to rest against Bryn's bloody shirt above his heart.

The steady heartbeat soothed me further. I put my arms around Bryn, clutching the fabric at his back. My breath came out in ragged sobs, the fight draining from me and leaving me weak and shaking. Standing there, with Bryn's arms around me, I *did* feel safe despite the violence and stress of the past few minutes. It also left me shuddering with horrific guilt when my eyes found the open cavity of a ruined chest just beyond where we stood, our feet sticky with pooling blood.

Bryn pulled away and I let him, though I desired nothing but the safety of his embrace. He smiled at me through a mask of blood, and his hands slid down to my arms to give them a gentle squeeze. "Better?" he asked.

"You know I am," I mumbled through a weak grin and a small sob.

Bryn chuckled. "I do," he said. His eyes sought out the broken bodies littering the ground, and then turned back to gaze into mine, urging me to listen. "And their deaths are not your fault. But I think your hand might be broken," he said as he tried to flex his right hand. He stopped with a gasp and cradled it, glancing at my hand hanging limp at my side. He sighed and looked around the square.

Among the bodies of the dead, one man still breathed. The first to fall, he clutched one side of his chest and squirmed, the pine round still rocking near his feet. He struggled for each breath, and his face was ashen, his lips blue.

Bryn followed my gaze. "He doesn't have long," he grumbled, the frightening blank look filming his eyes again. "Let's find out who did this while we can."

He turned away, limping as he did so. "You're hurt?" I groaned, noticing the blood oozing from a gash in his thigh.

He stopped and smirked at me, the light tone of his voice doing nothing to dispel the cold calm that made my stomach clench with anxiety. "I think I'll live, Lila."

I followed him to the man on the ground. He seemed not to notice us for all the pain he was in. Bryn grunted as he knelt next to him, and I circled the man to stand on the opposite side.

"Who sent you?" Bryn demanded. When he didn't respond, Bryn grasped his collar and shook him. His chest flopped with every exhalation; his ribs were broken in several places. I had seen a wound like this once in my years with Smitts; that man hadn't lived long, and by the look of it, this man would die in minutes.

It was possible I could heal him, but this was a complicated injury, and I wasn't sure I wouldn't speed his death along, rather than help him. I wasn't sure I *wanted* to help him.

He tried to focus on Bryn, but his eyes kept wandering. Bryn shook him again. "*Who sent you?*" he roared.

"Don't know 'is name," the man wheezed. His body stilled but for the lopsided movement of his chest, and his eyes glazed and roamed. "Boss said a man with a scar over his eye was going to pay us for the girl with the red hair, alive if we could, but dead if she was too much trouble. He said we should kill *you*." He coughed as he glared at Bryn, blood falling from the corner of his mouth while his chest rattled. In the space of another gurgled rasp, his face and muscles slackened as he died. Bryn released his shirt to lay him gently on the ground.

Bryn's head dropped. "My uncle," he said, his voice a mixture of rage and resignation. "I should have known he wouldn't stop."

"How did these men get so close?" I groaned as I crouched to pick up my sword.

"They only just arrived." A man's deep voice boomed out over the square. We whirled around, ready for the next battle.

The man stood on the threshold of the two-story building that housed the smithy, filling the doorway with his tall and muscular frame. Intent gray eyes peered from beneath bushy black brows. His arms, thicker than my legs, were crossed over a barrel chest covered with a thick leather apron. His eyes flicked to our weapons but showed no hint of fear.

"They asked after you, asked whether we had seen a girl with long red hair pass through here. When we didn't answer, they threatened to kill us." His gaze and tone accused us.

Bryn straightened, wiped some of the blood from each of his blades, and replaced them in their scabbards with deliberate care. His stare matched the blacksmith's, refusing to be cowed. I was less than stalwart and felt my cheeks flush with a small amount of shame and guilt at being the unwitting agent of distress for the innocent people here.

"We empathize with your trouble, but we are not the cause of it." Bryn glanced over at me, pointedly fixing his eyes on my sword before turning back to the smith. I straightened as well, and Desire hissed into the scabbard.

"Perhaps," the smithy nodded, "but you've made quite a mess of our town."

Doors creaked open all around the square as people stepped out into the light, hesitating at their doorsteps while craning their necks to hear what we would say. I imagined we looked a mess, covered in gore, surrounded by bodies.

"Again, we are sorry for the trouble, but we didn't send these men to your town. We are victims, as surely as you." Bryn's words were gentler this time as he glanced around at the faces peering from the safety of their thresholds.

The blacksmith chuckled, a rumbling, pleasant sound despite the incredulity on his face. "I wouldn't call you victims, sir. You and your lady seem capable enough, and after seeing what you did to those men, I have to wonder whether you brought this on yourself."

"My lady and I have done nothing but wish to live our lives in peace, and these men were sent to ensure that we are unable to do so. Speculate on our intentions all you like, but that is the truth."

The townspeople stood, assessing the veracity of Bryn's words. Most seemed to believe him; some were nodding as if to vouch for him with their spokesman, which gave me a modicum of relief. The blacksmith stood silent, his eye gauging first Bryn, and then me. I stood still, as tall and proud as I was able, given my exhaustion and pain, meeting the gaze of anyone that looked me in the eye.

While they seemed to agree with Bryn, most wouldn't look at me for long; they seemed to fear me, and I couldn't blame them after what they had seen. A few curled their left hands into fists and placed them over their hearts.

After a moment that seemed to stretch into eternity, the smith nodded and unfolded his considerable arms. He stepped away from his shop and strolled across the square to stand in front of Bryn.

"We appreciate what you did here, and while we're grateful, my people are also frightened." When his eyes darted to me and back to

Bryn, he made it clear that I was the cause of that fear. His voice dropped to a murmur.

"There are people here who need coin. I wouldn't be surprised if some aren't already preparing to leave. To head to the next town to see if they can collect the bounty. And we don't want anything to do with curses. We need you to leave."

Bryn's mouth fell open and his brows drew down into a frown. "You see the state we're in?" he hissed, matching the volume of the smith.

"I do," the smith nodded, his eyes once again darting to my face and back. "But what we saw...." He shook his head. "I don't know what your lady can do, but it's not natural. We don't want that in our town."

Bryn backed a step, limping and leaving a trail of blood in his wake. A small puddle had formed at his foot as his wound oozed. My hands twitched, wanting to bind his leg before he lost too much blood, but I dared not interrupt the hushed battle of wills.

"You admitted that we have done you a service, and you throw us out of your town?" Bryn's voice rose to a bellow, and the men and women all around flinched. The smith stood firm and crossed his arms again. Before Bryn became more enraged, I stepped forward and placed a hand on his shoulder. His angry gaze turned to me, but his eyes softened as he clenched his pained fist.

"Bryn, we need to leave. We need to get home."

His scowl melted as I spoke, and he nodded in agreement. When he turned back to face the smith, he scowled anew.

"We're sorry for the trouble," Bryn snarled.

He turned his back on the man and held his arm out for me. I hooked my arm through and walked with him toward the tree in the center of the square where our discarded packs waited. With the straps in place on our shoulders, we started our slow, halting march out of town. When we reached the edge of the square I glanced over my shoulder, locking eyes with everyone I could see before settling on the blacksmith.

"I hope no one was hurt, and I apologize for the trouble. The Six protect you."

The blacksmith's stern countenance faltered for the first time, a small smile twitched his lips. Bryn tugged on my arm and I walked with him, my arm nestled firmly in the crook of his elbow as the sun set sank behind the peaks of the mountains in our path.

CHAPTER THIRTY-SIX

Wind howled through the countryside, bending the branches of the trees and whipping the surface of the river into a frenzy as the light faded all around us. Cold seeped into my body to weigh down my limbs and stiffen my fingers and toes. With a small trickle of Ambience, I altered the air around us to keep the cold at bay. Even that small effort left me panting in the wake of such a strenuous afternoon. Every step was a battle to remain upright, and I could feel Bryn shaking beneath my arm.

I knew that Bryn wouldn't stop and let me tend to his injured leg until we were out of sight, so I pushed ahead and supported his weight as best I could. We followed the river until the town was no longer visible. I struggled to remain on my feet and knew Bryn wasn't faring any better, so I halted and tugged his arm.

"We need to stop, Bryn." The leg of his pants was soaked through with blood, and I blanched at the sight, noticing now that his skin was waxy and pale.

I gasped, and pulled on his arm again, forcing him to the ground. He collapsed with his legs splayed out in front of him, and I dropped to my knees. My broken hand fumbled with the clasp on my bag and I cursed and spat until it clicked open. Bryn gasped, my pain adding to his, and I cursed again.

Fresh bandages sat tucked inside a small pot, and I pulled both out and set them aside. Bryn stretched out on the cold ground, letting his head fall into the dirt. His breathing slowed, and I let out a sob.

"Please," I groaned, not knowing if I was begging him not to die or begging the spirits to help me save him. In either case, he groaned when I shifted his weight off his sword belt and pulled it free. Dried blood stuck his dagger to its sheath and held it fast, forcing me to grasp the sheath with my broken hand. I sobbed at the searing pain when my fingers curled around the wood, but I gritted my teeth against the grinding bones and pulled.

When it wrenched free, I swept through the sodden fabric of his ruined pants just above the wound, sawing at the material with my left hand and gritting my teeth as I held it taut with my right.

The pant leg gave way and I stumbled back with the sudden release, tears coursing down my cheeks. With my fumbling grasp, I tied it around Bryn's thigh, and the oozing blood slowed to a trickle. A weary, relieved smile broke out on my face.

"You're going to be fine," I assured Bryn, whose head lolled on the ground. He groaned again; I pulled a blanket from my bag to drape over him against the cold, then I rose to my feet with the small pot grasped in my good hand.

The river roared along its banks and splashed up in my face when I knelt at the edge to fill the pot. A few branches sat strewn along the shore and I collected those, balancing them in my elbow as I tried not to spill the water.

When I reached Bryn, I set the pot aside and stacked the wood. In short order, I had a fire crackling. My vision blurred, and my head drooped as I pulled on what little strength I had to force the wood to catch through sheer will. I searched for other injuries on his body; a few scratched and bloody knuckles marred his skin, and a fresh bruise looked to be blooming under his left eye, but nothing explained why he looked like he might die aside from the wound on his thigh. I decided it was more serious than I assumed at first, and that the only way to ensure his survival was to use the Ambience to heal him. My bottom scraped against the dirt as I scooted closer, pulled the blanket back and spread my hands over Bryn's thigh. His skin felt cold even to my frigid fingers. The edge of his skin pulled back from the wound as if recoiling from the insult to his flesh.

Armed with a recollection of diagrams of the human form and a longing to bring Bryn from the edge of death, I whispered a silent prayer to the Elder Livette, as Smitts had so many times, and to Penelope to guide me. I envisioned the muscles and vessels severed, their ends pulled away from one another. The Ambience answered my call and surrounded Bryn, appearing as a prismatic glowing cabal of blurred figures I assumed were spirits all reaching out to place their hands upon him. I focused on the wound and saw the energy severed along the gash. My hands moved to the leg and I began knitting every torn part back together to leave him whole. The figures flashed and released him, and his blood flowed through his veins again to add color to his skin and flush his cheeks.

His eyes popped open as I sagged against him, my head in his lap when he lifted his torso off the ground. Panting, I curled into a ball while he pulled me to his chest and cradled me.

"Thank you," he whispered. "But you're going to kill yourself."

"Worth it," I mumbled, the renewed heat from his body seeping into my cold skin to warm me. He shifted closer to the fire and pulled the blanket around his shoulder to fall over me. As he did, my broken hand tapped his chest and I moaned.

"Lila, your hand."

I managed to nod against his chest.

"What happened?"

"Punched one," I mumbled. "Sword got stuck in his shield."

His chuckle bounced my head against his chest. "Did you punch his forehead?"

"Teeth," I murmured, and he chuckled again.

"I'll teach you how to fight with your fists, Lila. There are ways to avoid breaking your hand." I shrugged, and he clutched me tighter. "You fought well. You're so brave." His head lowered, and he kissed the top of my head. A shiver of excitement ran through me and pushed some of my exhaustion aside.

My heart pounded, and I tilted my head back to see the firelight dancing in Bryn's eyes, limning his hair with fire and gold. He smiled his lopsided grin down at me.

"I want you to tell me something, and I want you to be honest with me, Lila." He waited, and I nodded my assent. "Something's changed between us, hasn't it?"

My eyes widened and I nodded, not sure which change he was referring to. So many things had changed over the months we had been together. Another spark surged through me as his eyes searched my face. My heart beat faster, and I would have flushed with embarrassment or possibly hope, if my body had the energy. Bryn's eyes narrowed.

"That, right there, is what I mean. You're flustered right now, and I think it's because of me." Not knowing what to say or do, I remained silent and stared into his eyes. I felt a thrill of fear and longing, not as suppressed as I hoped, bloom in my chest and knot my stomach. When I didn't speak, he smiled, unleashing the radiance of his full smile through the blood on his face. "You don't need to say it, Lila. I can read it on your face."

In a last attempt to deny my feelings, I said, "We almost died, Bryn. Why are you bringing this up *now*?"

"*Because* we almost died, Lila. I've been waiting for months for you to say something and wondering if I was imagining it. One minute I can feel your heart race, and the next minute you're cold like you were in the beginning. When I was lying there and you were cursing and trying so hard to help me, it hit me that I might not get the chance to tell you that you are the most beautiful woman I have ever seen, and I am amazed at how strong you are.

"There is no reason you should have survived everything that you have, but through all of it, you became stronger. And you didn't let it change you or make you bitter. You should hate me for the part I played in my uncle's plans, but it's not in you. You see all of me, including my faults, and look past them. If the Ambience hadn't tied my life to yours, I would still follow you to the ends of the earth and consider myself lucky just to be near you."

Tears fell from the corners of my eyes. I reached up to caress his face, and the Ambience surged of its own accord to link us. The sincerity of his words and depth of his feeling flooded me, and I sobbed. My feelings for him, ignored and dismissed in pursuit of harnessing my power, flooded both of us, and he gasped.

"Why didn't you say anything?" he beamed. "You should have said something."

"I was trying to focus on what Sam's been teaching me. And after what happened to Hunter...." I trailed off, not wanting to sour his mood. He understood, despite my lack of words, experiencing my grief and worry that expressing my feelings for him would end in disaster as it had the only other man I thought I loved. He nodded.

"I understand." My eyes closed, and he leaned forward to kiss my forehead. Gentle and sweet, his lips ignited every part of me. I felt him smile against my forehead. Our thoughts swirled, awash in pleasure and excitement. He reached out and grasped my injured hand. When I shrieked, he recoiled and held me at arm's length.

"Your hand!" he groaned. Shame and guilt colored his thoughts, and he berated himself for forgetting and wished that he could heal me.

The Ambience surrounded him, pulling at something deep within me. It felt like a chasm filled with more power than I could understand and reminded me of the brief time that Bryn and I had considered pulling the stars from the sky. My glimpse at this deep well ended, as if a door had been shut, and the trickle followed Bryn's desire and coursed across our link to take root in him. Arms of a spectral form surrounded and illuminated him; the figure grasped his wrist and lifted his hand to touch my swollen fingers.

My hand warmed and I experienced a momentary jolt of pain as the bones repositioned themselves into their natural state, and then knitted themselves back together.

The warmth died away and Bryn released my hand, sagging away from me while keeping his arms locked around me. I felt the spirit smile, pleased with itself and Bryn, and then disappear. Our eyes wide, we stared at one another, our shock evident across our link.

"What just happened?" Bryn whispered, his chest heaving as though he were still in the heat of battle. My weariness and the deep chill abated, leaving a warm tingle throughout my body. My right hand closed on Bryn's blood-stained shirt, appearing as if it had never been broken.

Bryn shook his head slowly. "I have no idea. Are you all right?"

"I feel great." I smiled, bewildered and grateful.

Bryn's hands curled and stretched along my arm, testing it for any trace of pain. He took my hand, turning it over to examine it, and ran a finger along my knuckles. The contact sent shivers of pleasure throughout my body. "That was amazing." He looked up at me. "*You* are amazing."

"I think it's amazing that we can do so much together."

He pulled me closer, my body flush with his, and placed his lips on mine, soft and insistent.

Tingles of pleasure and excitement spread from my lips through the rest of my body. Warmth blazed in my chest, threatening to ignite and consume me. Bryn responded, able to feel my reaction, emboldened by it. His kiss deepened, became more urgent.

My hands fisted in his hair, pulling him to me. He moaned against my lips. His hands roamed my back and my legs, my face and my hair, trying to touch every part of me at once. Wherever his hands touched, my skin burned.

We parted and I eased back from Bryn's chest, both of us panting and gazing into the other's eyes as if seeing them for the first time.

"This feels right," Bryn breathed. His hand swept a lock of my hair behind my ear, and I leaned into his cupped palm. Callused fingers rasped across my cheek. "I've never wanted anything so much as I've wanted this."

"It scares me to say it, but I feel the same way."

"Why does it scare you?"

My response tumbled out in a breathless rush of longing and fear, excitement and dread. "Because I don't know how it happened! One minute you're making sure I don't escape, the next we're running from your uncle, at each other's throats, and then we became friends. Everything I've known is gone and I don't recognize myself. I've spent so much of my life trying to figure out who I am and where I belong. I didn't think there was time for romance, and the one time I let myself believe I could love someone, he died." I shrugged again. "I don't know how to do this, Bryn."

"You don't have to know how; I don't think there *is* a right way. Just be with me." He paused and flashed me a shy grin. "I know what you're thinking, but you haven't said it."

"The Six help me, Bryn, I'm in love with you."

"The Six help us both," he replied, and kissed me again.

CHAPTER THIRTY-SEVEN

Movement at my back woke me, and I blinked against the glare of sunlight.

"Good morning," Bryn murmured, nuzzling the back of my head. His right arm cushioned my head and his left clasped my hands across my chest, my back snuggled tight against his front. Weariness had claimed us swiftly after our conversation, and we were lying in a cocoon of the blanket draped around us, Bryn refusing to let me out of his grasp. My face felt tight and stiff with gore that hadn't been washed away.

"Good morning," I sighed. "Sleep well?"

"I did," he groaned, stretching. I lifted my head to free his arm and rolled over to face him. Blood caked his brows and hair, and I grimaced at the sight of him smiling through the mess. His eyes widened when he saw my face. "You could do with a wash, Lila."

"I'm not the only one," I said with a grimace of distaste. My stiff clothes crackled as I stood and stretched.

"I'll make something to eat. Why don't you go wash first?"

"All right. Don't get any of that mess in the food."

He grinned and nodded, and I stooped to pick up my pack. Heaving it onto my shoulder, I wandered toward the river a short way from where we had slept, behind a boulder. The events of last night replayed through my mind, and Bryn's satisfaction and amusement played across our unbroken link while he dug through his pack for some cheese and dried meat. With a playful mental slap, I severed the link, and my mind became my own again. If I was going to get clean, I didn't want him watching me do it.

A brief and thorough scrub of my entire body and clothing left me feeling invigorated and frozen in the early morning chill. A small trickle of heat spread through the fabric of my shirt and pants, allowing them to dry faster than they would have over a fire so I could dress. Back at camp, I found Bryn chewing and staring into the fire, lost in thought. A wistful smile played on his lips, and I stopped to gaze at him. His hair sat slicked back on his head, doused in the nearby river and dripping down his back. Cheeks and forehead had been scrubbed clean, his skin pink and raw.

Even with his clothes a mess, he looked like happiness itself. His smile widened when his eyes found mine, as they always did, and the brilliance of his smile made my heart flutter.

"How are your clothes dry?" he demanded when I joined him.

"Talent," I replied with a smirk. "I can do the same for you after you've washed them."

"One kiss and you're ready to take my clothes off?" My cheeks flushed while he shook his head in mock horror. "Miss, I don't think I'm ready for such a step in our relationship."

My embarrassment gave way to flustered annoyance when he began to laugh at me. And when I threw a stick at him, he ducked and ran for the safety of the trees. I laughed at Bryn's easy humor.

Alone again, I began to pack our blankets, tucking them beneath the straps at the bottom of our packs. I shook my head, thinking how easy it was to communicate with someone over the bond that we shared; it would have been a lot easier with Hunter this way.

My hands stilled in the middle of tying a knot as I considered our bond. Sam and I had found no information about anything like it in ages past, and we had no idea how complex it might be. It had allowed Bryn and I to become friends, to share our histories with one another. Though there was no denying he was a gorgeous man,

I couldn't help but circle back to the idea that our tether could be the entire reason we were attracted to each other.

I peered over my shoulder at the spot where Bryn had disappeared, trying and failing not to obsess about my doubt. We both felt out of control where our love was concerned, but that seemed to be the case for anyone in every story I had read or heard on the subject. My brow furrowed as I wondered, *am I insane for wanting this?*

Branches snapped and swayed, in Bryn's wake as he rushed through the trees. My anxiety was stamped on his face, and his eyes roamed the campsite before settling on me.

"What's wrong?" he demanded. He bounded to my side.

"It could be Ambience," I replied. My inward reflection left my tone flat.

"What?"

I gestured back and forth from Bryn to myself. "This could be because of what I did to you."

He sighed and relaxed. "I considered that," he admitted. "Believe me, I've considered it. Since this started, before you destroyed the ship, my world seemed to revolve around you. But I didn't like you at first, especially because of the bond. In fact, you terrified me, and all I wanted was to be rid of you and find somewhere to live in peace. That's changed now. Does it matter why?"

"I think it does," I insisted. "If this is nothing more than the product of unintentional use of Ambience designed to protect me, I don't want both of us to end up heartbroken."

"Would that happen?"

I shook my head. "I don't know. But I still intend to find a way to free you. If something happens to me, I don't want you hurt."

He grasped my hands and pulled me to my feet. His eyes blazed intensely. "And I'm not going to leave your side for anything, so let's worry about it if the time comes. If this *is* the Ambience, at least it's brought us together. I can live with the possibility of the lie if it means we can be together. I love you, Lila." He took a deep breath and searched my eyes, willing me to believe that his words weren't influenced by anything more than true love for me. "I've survived for most of my life. I didn't know what it was like to *live* until I found you. I don't want to lose that."

I pulled my hands from his grasp and cupped his cheek. "I don't want to either, Bryn. But I can't accept the possibility that we're being forced into this."

"Don't worry about me." He paused and nodded, as if coming to a decision. "Sam said something to me after we left Stalth, the night you had the nightmare and he told us about the Ambience. He told me that it looked like there was more between us than whatever you did to me. I didn't believe it at the time, but now I know it's true."

We dropped the subject, unwilling to talk in circles while we finished breaking camp and started walking home. My thoughts swirled with dark thoughts of having no control over myself, one of my worst fears, and Bryn often glanced at me with worry clear on his face. The day turned to night as we reached the edge of the forest and decided to camp in the shelter of the trees. I took first watch. After waking Bryn for his turn, I fell asleep with the vision of his intense gaze watching over me.

Bryn did his best to drag me from unceasing worry and doubt for the rest of the day, engaging me in conversation and regaling me with stories of his youth. Most were small moments of mischief and fond memories of his mother, and I felt some of the weight ease from my shoulders bit by bit.

The lake was beautiful, reflecting the sunset peeking between mountaintops in the still water. Our trip across was quick this time, since Bryn finally had the hang of rowing. He splashed into the water to pull the boat onto the shore for us and lifted me out, setting me on the shore after kissing my forehead. We were laughing when we entered the cabin that evening.

Sam wandered out of the kitchen, smiling when he heard our voices. He watched us banter for a minute, looking back and forth between us and listening to Bryn's description of a pile of dung one of the other children had thrown at his face.

"How was your trip? I hadn't expected you would be quite so long."

"We ran into some trouble, and we stayed the night down the mountain," I said.

Sam's eyes narrowed. "What trouble?"

We relayed the details of the ambush and told him that Roglin had sent them to track us down and capture me.

"Were you hurt?"

"All healed, thanks to Lila." Bryn beamed at me. Sam quirked an eyebrow.

"You managed to heal both of you after such a brawl?"

"I healed the gash in Bryn's leg, but he helped me to heal my hand and his."

"Explain." Sam's scowl passed over both of us.

"We were connected..." Sam heaved an exasperated sigh, and I rushed to explain, every inch the student frightened of disappointing her teacher. "I don't know what happened. Bryn used the Ambience to heal my hand, and it felt like he was using something...more than that. I watched a spirit guide him, I think."

"I *told* you I didn't want you two doing this. You could have destroyed that whole village! But you knew that, so I won't scold you like children. What exactly happened when he did it?"

I explained the sensation and the result, and Bryn told Sam what it had been like for him. Sam looked lost in thought as he processed our words.

"I haven't heard of someone being able to use another person's connection. You keep pushing the limits, Lila." He sighed again and scrubbed a hand over his face. "I'm glad you escaped relatively unharmed, and I'm glad that nothing disastrous came of your actions. We will talk about this more at length, but it seems that we are running out of time where your uncle is concerned, Bryn."

"As long as I'm connected to the Ambience I'll always be running, won't I Sam?" I asked.

"The time may have come to deal with this, though I wish we had more time to finish your instruction, Lila. Especially since you seem to be making up your own rules and using the Ambience in ways that haven't existed before."

"We should find him and anyone following him, and make sure that they can't terrorize anyone. Ever again." Bryn's cold certainty brought a worried frown to my lips, and though I shared the sentiment, I reached over to grasp his hand, trying to pull him from his dark thoughts. His eyes sought mine, and the desperate pain and rage faded.

Sam cleared his throat, and we turned our heads to look at him. He looked pointedly down at our hands. "When did this happen?" he asked, amused.

"You know very well that it's *been* happening, old man," Bryn said with a lopsided grin. "You were the one that told *me* that it was happening. So stop acting surprised."

Sam chuckled. "So I did. I didn't know if Lila felt as you did, but I could certainly see it in *you*."

"We may have bought ourselves some time," Bryn said after a few moments of silence, "but I'd rather not wait and wonder when they'll find us."

"Even if they send someone looking for the mercenaries, the people in Mountain's Shade don't know where my cabin is," Sam said. "And the way isn't without its defenses. Derth can't track you, so we can wait as long as we need to prepare for a confrontation."

I was already shaking my head before Sam finished. "Bryn's right, Sam. We can't let this stand. What if Roglin and Derth send people – or come themselves – to terrorize the people of Mountain's Shade for information about us? They don't have much to give, but that won't stop them from suffering. Then we have their pain on our consciences, not to mention nowhere to go for supplies that won't take a week or more. I couldn't live with anyone being hurt on my account." I looked at Bryn, thinking of what he'd endured since he met me. "Not again."

Sam nodded. "If that's how you both feel, I think we should prepare to leave in the next few days. With those men dead, it will take some time for your uncle to learn what became of them unless someone from the town is on their way to inform him. We can use the time to find him before he hears what became of the people he hired."

"That's decided," I said, "but where do we start? We don't know where Roglin is."

"I think we should start in King's Port," Sam said. "It's the nearest city, and we should be able to get some information there."

"My crew's families might be able to help with that. They're resourceful; they'll have been listening for any word of us when we didn't come home." Bryn squeezed my hand while I fought the usual wave of grief.

"I think you and Bryn should take a couple of days to rest after your ordeal, Lila. And there are some things that I would teach you before we have the possibility of another confrontation."

We stayed for another week. Sam asked me to describe in detail every aspect of my use of power during combat and seemed impressed by my adaptation of the shield as a projectile. When I described thrusting the man into the wall of the building, he frowned but remained silent.

He honed my skill in directing heat and air into weapons until I could form a jet of flame and thrust it as I would a blade, with precision and dexterity. That was the only thing I accomplished with enough regularity to say I mastered it. Sam gave me brief instruction on a variety of feats over the next few days, such as how to conjure images of myself to confuse enemies.

The illusions were meant to mimic the subject, with the complexity of a living being moving about. Sam's copy of himself followed his every move, but my conjuration looked a pale, still version of myself. He implored me to practice with any spare time while we traveled, if it was out of sight of strangers.

Bryn and I also sparred in the evenings, and I forced Bryn on the defensive by the end of several of our matches. On our last night, I wanted a last chance to bathe in comfort before setting back down the road, so it was a short match before I hurried to fill the bath with water from the well. Once the tub brimmed with frigid water, I pulled heat from the nearby fire, increasing the temperature by increments until it steamed in the cold air.

I slid under the water, relaxing from head to toe; my mind wandered without focus. Lavender-scented soap, gifted to me by Maude in Stalth, coated my skin and foamed in my hair. Just cool enough not to scald me. I felt serene, letting the worry, doubt, and violence of battle drift away with the lathered soap. I suffused myself with the Ambience while I bobbed in the full tub. My eyes roamed over the ceiling, tracing the whorls of knots in the wooden beams.

My eyes lost focus of the wood grain, and Bryn's hands came into view, packing his belongings in the leather bag on his bed. His hands stilled and he looked up in the direction of the stairs. In my relaxed state my mind had reached out for him, and I severed the connection between us as my naked arms came into view.

His footsteps thudded on the stairs while I rose from the tub, grabbing a towel and throwing it around myself. A hesitant knock sounded on the door to the washroom.

"Lila?" Bryn called, trying and failing to suppress a laugh.

"Don't you *dare* come in here!" I shouted, halfway between mortification and laughter.

"I won't," Bryn said, chuckling. "Was that intentional?"

"Yes," I replied, my voice dripping with sarcasm. "I think it's a *very* good idea to do that while I'm bathing."

"So do I," Bryn replied, a little too smoothly. "It was a nice surprise." He moved away, his laughter trailing behind him.

"What was that about?" Sam asked.

Bryn laughed harder. "I think she might kill me if I told you, Sam." Bryn ran up the stairs, laughing all the while, and closed the door behind him with a click.

Just before dawn the next morning, we locked up the house and set off. After rowing across the lake, we made our way slowly up the path. Sam and I set shields at increasing intervals to protect the cabin while Bryn wandered ahead, bored by the learning process. I observed Sam's process for infusing the furthest with the same terrible energy held by lightning strikes; he used a small handful of lake water to form tiny storm clouds that began to flash in the space where the shield shimmered, and as the charged bolts arced from the miniscule storm, they bounced through the curtain of air and force before settling into the node in the side of the wall. We finished just past midday and emerged from the path to find Bryn waiting with a meal spread out on a faded green blanket in the shade of the nearby trees.

With a broad smile, I sauntered toward him, content to allow myself a moment to be happy. He stood and caught me in his arms, spinning around once. I giggled as my hair flew out behind me, my head against his shoulder. He set me down and gestured to the food. "Ladies first," he said with a bow.

"Thank you, good sir," I said, and sat down with exaggerated care.

"This is going to get old quickly," Sam grumbled as he sat down near us.

"What is?" I asked innocently, an apple suspended in midair near my mouth.

"The two of you," he said, wagging his finger back and forth between Bryn and me.

"You don't have to look, old man." Bryn leaned over and kissed me on the cheek as I chewed a bite of my apple. I smiled at him and tried not to meet Sam's eyes.

We ate our lunch quickly, Bryn and I chatting while Sam made exasperated noises and tried to hide his smile.

We traversed the slick passage in the tunnel and the path through the base of the mountain with haste and exited into the open air just before sundown.

Bryn set up our bedrolls side by side next to the banked fire and took his place on one, his arms held wide to invite me to lie down. I curled up next to him, my head in the hollow between his arm and chest. Together, we pulled the cloaks and blanket over ourselves to protect against the early spring chill in the air. It was an effort to force the doubt from my mind and relax into Bryn's embrace, but I resolved that until I could change the bond, I had enough to worry about without torturing myself.

With the sound of the river rushing nearby and Sam's sigh from his place on the other side of the fire, I fell into a deep sleep.

CHAPTER THIRTY-EIGHT

Our trip was uneventful for the first week, and Sam continued to tutor me as we traveled. His topics ranged from diversionary tactics to devastating explosions to feeling out people, animals, and objects around me.

We avoided the town of Mountain's Shade, preferring not to involve them further with knowledge of our departure.

The closer we came to King's Port, the more people we encountered. Having abandoned the idea that we could entirely conceal ourselves, we followed the rise and fall of the hilly road as it led south. I kept the hood of my cloak pulled over my hair during the day and Sam affected his hunched, shuffling gait. Bryn alone remained unchanged, and he kept a keen watch for us in the more populated areas, trailing behind as our silent sentinel.

We came within sight of the city gates nine days after leaving the cabin. Anxiety and excitement rose in me as I considered what I would say to all the people waiting with no news of our ship.

Bryn noticed my agitation, so I let him into my mind.

What's bothering you? he asked.

What am I going to say to them? That I alone survived?

With everything I've seen, they love you like they loved their people. They'll be happy that you survived, not angry with you for not doing more. Remember, they don't know you're a Conduit. And if they did, they would understand that you did all you could.

I smiled, taking comfort in his words. He smiled back, feeling my tension ease.

Thank you, Bryn. You always know how to make me feel better.

It's hard not to, he thought. *I don't have a choice.*

My face fell, his words stoking my guilt and doubt.

I love you, Lila. Don't forget that.

We camped by the side of the road, the gates a beacon of light in the distance. The land sloped down to the sea before us, the ocean spread wide and far to the horizon. It beckoned to me with memories of the pitch of the waves beneath the deck at my feet, the smell of salt in the air all around. My nose twitched as a faint breeze carried that scent of home.

We ate in silence, each lost in thought. In our case, Bryn and I were lost in each other's thoughts. I tried not to dwell on everything I thought could go wrong and Bryn distracted me by telling me stories and asking questions about sailing.

I fell asleep in his arms, his body keeping me warm and his thoughts of gallant heroes rescuing distressed maidens calming me into oblivion.

The road sloped down from where we stood in the morning, changing from packed dirt to paving stones just before the city entrance. The ocean glittered in the sunlight beyond the city. Smoke rose from chimneys dotting the steep rise. The castle stood like a beacon atop its hill, standards of the king just visible as they flapped in the ocean breeze.

Judging by the number of people marching along the road to King's Port, it must have been market day inside the walls. Wagons and carts, people carrying their goods on their backs, and families with children young and old filed through the gates. We were swept up in the crush of people, just another few faces among many. As we neared the city, our procession slowed; the gates were not large enough for everyone to pass at once. The deafening clatter of horses, wagons, and people assaulted my ears, and I huddled close to Bryn to keep from being separated as the crowd propelled us forward.

I wound through the city easily, picking my way from memory to the street where Lottie lived. My footsteps clicked on the stones below my feet, quickening with every turn of a corner. Her house was the same faded yellow of the other homes on the street, but she had always maintained a colorful garden year-round. Though the bed was slightly overrun with weeds, the flowers were starting to bloom.

Gauzy curtains swayed in the open windows astride a green door. My fist rapped the hard surface three times and I waited with my heart in my throat for her reply.

"A moment please!" Lottie called. My stomach flipped with anticipation when I heard her familiar voice through the door.

It opened, revealing a face I hadn't seen in almost a year. She looked much older; her back hunched and her eyes sunken. She was over sixty years old, but she had always radiated such a sense of vitality that it broke my heart to see her this way.

"What...?" she asked, looking only briefly at me and then past to Bryn and Sam behind him. When I pulled back my hood, her eyes widened. "Lila?" she whispered.

"Lottie...." My voice died in my throat, choked by grief and longing.

Tears fell from her eyes and streamed down her cheeks, the color of burnt umber, as she put her arms around my waist and pulled me close. Stooped as she was now, her head came to my chin. I hugged her back, putting my head on top of hers.

"We all thought you were dead, or worse!" she sobbed. "When those men took you, we thought we would never see you again!"

My body stiffened with surprise. "How did you know I was taken?" I asked.

A large man stepped out into the hall and stopped when he saw me hugging Lottie. I stared at his tall, muscular frame. He had aged, and lines and scars marred his once smooth face, but the warm brown eyes held me fast.

"*Roy?!*" I cried.

Lottie stepped back and pushed me forward with a warm hand on my back. Roy looked just as stunned as I felt, and I stopped in front of him, staring up at his wide eyes.

A hesitant hand reached out to touch a lock of my hair. He recoiled, as if surprised that I could be real. His face crumpled the next moment and he swept me into his arms with a sob.

My arms circled his neck, and I wept with him. I wept in memory of our fallen ship and our fallen family. And I wept with joy that this one man had survived.

Lottie ushered Bryn and Sam inside and closed the door behind them. They stood awkwardly in the entryway as Lottie joined us, placing her hands on either side of my face once her son set me back on my feet.

"We thought you were gone," Roy croaked. "They took you and destroyed the ship and left us for dead."

My mind focused on one word. "We?"

"Well, the captain...."

"Captain Morrig is *alive?*" I shrieked in disbelief as new tears fell from my eyes and rolled down my face. *"Where is he?"*

"He's staying at the inn up the street...."

I turned and ripped open the door, letting it slam into the wall behind me. My feet flew up the street with speed I hadn't known I possessed. Bryn shouted my name, but I would not turn or slow.

Caution forgotten, my hair streamed out behind me as I ran. I came to an open market selling fabrics and clothing, armor and arms, and picked my way between the vendors, trying to get through the throng of people.

I darted around a woman and stopped short before wheeling into her three children spread out across the narrow lane. Looking for another way through, I backtracked and turned around a corner, slamming into the solid frame of a man that grasped my arms to keep me upright.

"Thank you," I panted, and looked up.

The deep green of his eyes, the loose tumble of his brown hair was too familiar. *Hunter.*

"Are you all...?" He stopped mid-sentence and stared. His eyes darted from my hair to my eyes, to the rest of my face and all down my body before darting back up. *"Lila?"* he breathed.

"Hunter," I murmured, and then I was folded in his arms, crushed against his body. He pulled back and started to run his hands over my face and hair, trying to force himself to believe that I was standing in front of him. Tears surged unheeded from his eyes and he pulled me to him again.

"Why aren't you dead!" I cried, too overwhelmed by shock and joy to keep my voice down.

Hunter pulled back, smiling. At that moment, I heard thundering footsteps come to a sudden halt behind us.

"Lila!" Sam exclaimed, sounding winded. Bryn's presence pulled at me and I turned my head against Hunter's chest to find him.

He recognized Hunter from my memories and a look of wonder spread across his face. Bryn's thoughts were churning, but with surprise that we had now found two men from my ship alive when he had thought everyone was dead. There was no trace of anger, no jealousy; he felt only genuine pleasure that I was reclaiming so many people that I loved.

I smiled with tears in my eyes, letting him feel how grateful I was for his unconditional support. His eyes settled on mine and he smiled back.

Hunter hadn't missed the silent communication between Bryn and me. He wiped an unhappy look from his face.

"I'm so glad you're alive. Where's Captain Morrig?"

"I'll take you to him," he said with a smile. He glanced at Bryn again before he slid his hand down my arm to clasp mine.

I looked back at Bryn. *He's taking us to Captain Morrig.*
We're right behind you.

Hunter led us through the market and onto another street. Hunter sensed my anxiety and set a brisk pace.

Made of stone and two stories tall, the largest building on the street sported a sign above the door with a sword and shield and proclaimed itself to be the 'The Barracks.' Windows dotted the front of the building, letting the smell of roasting meat and the sound of men laughing out into the street.

Hunter pushed the heavy door inward on well-oiled hinges and I followed him inside. A bar ran along the length of the right side of the main room. Small round tables and several long rectangular tables were scattered about with boisterous patrons seated among them.

I searched the faces at the tables for Captain Morrig, but Hunter tugged on my hand, leading me through a door to the left of the bar.

I caught a glimpse of a familiar face with silver piercings gaping in surprise as I rushed by. The door opened onto a long hallway lined with doors at regular intervals on either side with a staircase at the far end. Hunter climbed the steps quickly, my hand still clasped in his as I matched his pace.

Our destination was the first door on the left. He knocked, and I heard the creak of a chair as someone rose to answer. Hunter pulled me behind him as the door opened.

"Hunter," a deep, familiar voice rumbled; a sobbed breath escaped my lungs as his voice triggered memories of him comforting the small girl I had been. "Who do you have there?" he asked. Hunter stepped aside, and I looked up into the face of Captain Morrig.

I had surprised my fair share of people today, but none reacted as strongly as the man before me did now. He staggered back a step, his sob answering mine. A large hand stretched out in my direction and hesitated. Shock and relief warred on his face until I stepped forward and touched his hand, and he crumpled to the ground in a heap.

He pulled me away from Hunter and into his arms, cradling me in his lap on the floor. He pulled my head to rest sideways against his shoulder and stroked my hair repeatedly while tears began to fall from my eyes. He sobbed, murmuring into my hair that he had me back and wouldn't let anything happen to me again. He promised that I would be safe, and I believed him. Every suppressed emotion, from joy to grief, spilled out of me as I nestled into his embrace.

We spent the rest of the afternoon in his room; Hunter closed the door to give us some much-needed privacy. Every experience and trial I had faced over the last months came pouring out of me in a rush when the captain asked me what happened. He blanched when I described what Derth put me through and how I had escaped his clutches. He growled at every mention of Roglin and applauded my grasp of the Ambience.

My link to Bryn still held, and while the captain and I reconnected, I watched through Bryn's eyes. He sat at a scarred and sticky table with Hunter and Sam. Apart from a few muttered comments, the three men spoke little as they waited. Hunter looked reluctant to ask any questions of the two strangers, and I could see his suspicion of Bryn in the frown on his face.

He seemed to be appraising Bryn with every glance and muttered comment. Though Bryn tried to be civil, I could feel his ire rising with each pointed question Hunter directed at him. Every one of the questions revolved around me.

The captain was very interested in Bryn and the bond between us. I held nothing back and told him of our blossoming relationship and every sparring match, every fight between the two of us and every attempt on our lives. When I mentioned the mercenaries in Mountain's Shade, he grilled me for more information about them and the man that sent them to find me.

"This Bryn is important to you, dear one."

I blushed. "He is, sir. He has been my friend and my savior and pushed me to keep going after everything that happened. I can't imagine how I would have survived without him."

I paused, and then urged him to tell me what happened and how any of them had survived. We moved from the floor to the small table, sitting on the two wooden chairs facing one another, both of us composed.

"We fought in a frenzy when we saw you unconscious and hauled belowdecks," he began. His black and gray eyebrows drew down as he frowned. "It didn't matter that we were outnumbered; all that mattered was that our Lila was in danger.

"I suppose those murderers thought you were worth more than what we had left in the hold, because that hunched man of theirs threw fire down the hatch, and it blew the ship apart. I was thrown into the water, and they disappeared as quickly as they came.

"Most of the men were dead; I found Roy trying to pull Marl onto a section of the hull, but he was already dead, with a piece of the mast through his neck. I had to convince him to leave his brother and help me lash together as many of the barrels and pieces as we could to keep afloat. We floated for about a day before a merchant vessel found us. I had to pay dearly for the few of us that they found.

"They only found us because Hunter was on board. He was well clear of the ship by the time it exploded, was so disoriented that he swam away from us and toward the other vessel. He said he snapped out of it by the time the sailors pulled him up, and he led them to the rest of us."

"Who else made it?" I asked.

"Not many," he replied, shaking his head. His once proud shoulders seemed hunched from the weight of so much grief. "Aside from those you've already seen, only a few of the new crew made it. Kai was one. They decided to leave when we reached King's Port." His eyes filled with tears again. "I was able to bring Walter's body back to his mother."

I gasped, thinking of the boy's bright eyes and the endless questions. Tears rolled down my cheeks again and I covered my mouth, shaking my head in fierce denial. My heart broke anew. I cried until I had no more tears to shed and listened as the captain continued.

"I haven't wanted to find another ship, nor could I afford one. And with most of the crew gone..." he shrugged. "There was no point."

"I am so sorry for all of this."

"It's not your fault, Lila. We could have fallen victim to any number of men like this Roglin, and you had nothing to do with that."

"At first, that was true. But now *I* am his target, and I'm putting the few of you I have left in danger. All I want to do is get to him before he can get to me. I don't know if I'll survive it, but I need to finish this. If he's gone, he won't be able to hurt the rest of the family I have left in the world."

"You won't be alone, girl. If he had only destroyed my ship, I could live with that. If he had stopped when he killed all but a handful of my men, I would have killed him quickly. Now that I know he's after you, I will make sure that he bleeds slowly for all that he's done."

Bryn growled his appreciation for the captain's words. Sam and Hunter both looked at him, confused, but he directed his thoughts to me, confirming his desire to help the captain end his uncle's life.

I shook my head, intending both to see my fear. "I don't want to lose you again, sir. I don't think I could live through that."

Captain Morrig placed a hand on my cheek. My hand covered his, holding it to my face. "You would be surprised what you can live through, dear one. The trick is to find something that keeps you going until you can find something to live for again."

CHAPTER THIRTY-NINE

We met the others in the tavern downstairs, surrounded by different faces just as rowdy as the previous crowd. Bryn stood and offered me his chair, grabbing two from the next table and placing them on either side of me. With a gesture to the chair on my left for the captain, Bryn sat at my right.

He searched my face, taking in my tear-battered appearance with concern. Hunter stared at Bryn, whose gaze was fixed on me. When I glanced over Bryn's shoulder, Hunter flashed me a tight smile and looked away.

Introductions were made all around, and Roy strode in a short time later and leaned against a wall behind his captain. He nodded at Sam and Bryn, and smiled warmly at me.

"Thank you both for taking care of my girl," Captain Morrig said. "It's such a relief to see her unharmed and happy. *And* you've helped her with her gift. There is no way I can ever repay you for this."

Sam shook his head. "She's as much a part of our family as she is a part of yours now. There is nothing to repay."

Bryn took my hand and nodded in agreement. Across the table, Hunter frowned.

"There *is* the problem of Roglin and Derth, however," Sam said, leaning forward. "From what Lila told us, Roglin has more to lose than his ship. He *must* either deliver her as promised – to whom, we don't know – or he will face something worse than what Lila can do to him. Otherwise, why would they pursue her after she's shown that she can protect herself? I can't imagine anyone who could inspire such fear in such men is someone we'd like to come across. Knowing what she can do, they must be confident in the ability to control her. And, if someone can take control of her, we could all be in tremendous trouble."

"What do you mean?" Hunter murmured, drawing himself closer to the table.

"Lila is an incredibly talented young woman. And she's only just beginning to understand her strength. If someone were to capture her and use her for their own purposes, she could decimate anything and anyone in their path."

"She wouldn't do such a thing," Roy insisted. "No one could do that to our Lila."

"You didn't see what happened to me last time," I murmured. All eyes focused on me, and I gazed at all of them in turn. I shuddered as I recalled my time under Derth's manipulation. "One man was able to turn me into a husk with no control over myself. I followed every instruction without hesitation, simply because I didn't have a reason not to. It was my body, but it wasn't me. Imagine if that were to happen now. When I have some control over my...gift. They could make me do terrible things, and I would never think to challenge it."

"That was the gift," Hunter protested. "Only you and that monster have it."

"That you know of," I argued, glancing at Sam. "But even without using the Ambience, there are ways to break a person. People can be made to do terrible things when they're forced past the limits of their endurance."

"True," Captain Morrig said. "But all of this is just a conversation. No harm is going to come to you again while I'm near you."

I smiled a sad smile. "You can't promise something like that, sir. He's chased us across Trylia to fulfill his obligation, and if he's involving more people, he's probably getting desperate. He said he'd have to kill *anyone* who knew he had me, and that includes all of you, now. I need to end this, but I'm not going to put all of you in danger to do it. And no matter how many mercenaries he can hire, Derth is the real threat. The only reason I can see for his continued involvement is that he's under the same obligation. But there's something terrifying about the way he looks at me. Like he wants to take me apart. When it comes time to deal with him, it might take more strength than I have, and I don't want to destroy any of you if the gift destroys me."

A chorus of angry grumbling erupted from the men around the table, and every one of them assured me that they wouldn't let me face him alone, if at all. Bryn's thumb traced circles on the back of my hand and the captain placed his large hand on my shoulder. Smiling at each of them in turn, I nodded, resigned to let them help me. They seemed satisfied by this, and sat back in their seats, more relaxed.

"What made you come to King's Port, if you know that he was following you to Stalth?" Roy asked.

"It's the closest city to where we were staying, and large enough to get lost in the crowd while we searched," I replied. "And I wanted to find the families to let them know what happened."

"Thank you for thinking of my mother," Roy murmured to me, shuffling his feet. Sam and Captain Morrig continued their conversation about Roglin in the background of my hearing. "When I told her about Marl, I thought I was going to lose her. When she recovered, all she wanted to know was what happened to you, Lila."

"I'm so glad you made it home to her, Roy." He smiled, and we joined the conversation again.

"...stands to reason that he would find a place in a port like this, try to find another ship. I haven't heard of any trouble in the city, or of anything strange."

"*I've* heard something," Hunter interrupted. "I heard that someone was paying good money to find someone. Some sailors waiting out the winter at the docks were talking about it. It was a few weeks ago, and they told me that the man gave them half of the money up front as incentive. Good amount of silver and gold, from the looks of it. He was at one of the taverns on the edge of the city, and I went to find out what the work was. When I saw him and the crew he was with, I decided I didn't need money badly enough to try to sign up."

"What did the man look like?" Bryn asked.

"Hunched, with nasty teeth and dirty light hair."

"That's Derth," I said, turning to Bryn. "I suppose they're recruiting more people to look for me."

"They must not be telling them much," Bryn replied. "When you were hurt on my uncle's ship, Derth said that they were supposed to deliver people like you to someone. And that they needed to follow through or kill you to make sure no one knew you existed."

Hunter stiffened and Roy stood straight, pushing away from the wall. Malice and anger rolled off each of them in waves. Roy's eyes locked on the back of Bryn's head, and Hunter scowled from across the table. "Your *uncle?*" Hunter seethed. "The man hunting Lila is your *uncle?*"

Bryn stilled, and his free hand twitched in the direction of the dirk on his belt. From the corner of my eye I saw Roy's hand slide to the hilt of his sword.

"Don't," I warned, and Hunter pulled his eyes from Bryn's face. "You can trust him."

"His uncle is hunting you, Lila. How can *you* trust him?"

"I don't work for Roglin anymore," Bryn asserted. Hunter's jaw fell, his eyes widening in shock.

"He used to *work* for the man?" Hunter shouted. A few heads turned in our direction, and I tried to hush Hunter.

"I will tell you everything when we have time," I hissed, irritated and worried that he would attract more attention after my display in the market. "For now, trust *me*. *I* am telling you that you can trust him, and that's all you need to know."

Roy relaxed against the wall, satisfied by my assertion. Hunter scoffed until the captain demanded his silence. His eyes remained locked on Bryn, who returned the stare with quiet confidence.

"I think we should go back to the tavern you were in, Hunter," I said, trying to draw him back into conversation. He reluctantly pulled his eyes away from Bryn. "Which one was it?"

"It's down by the harbor. The Crow's Nest."

"I've never been," I said. "Can you take me there?"

"You shouldn't be seen there, Lila," Bryn said as he squeezed my hand. He shook his head when I turned to look at him. "I'll go.

Derth or Roglin may be there, and I don't want you to stumble into a trap."

"Neither of you should go," Sam said. "They know both of you by sight. We need someone they won't recognize to ask around."

"I'll go," Roy said. All eyes turned to him. "I doubt they would recognize me."

"I'll go with you," Sam said. "We'll do some digging and come back."

Sam rose from his seat, pulling his cloak on, and followed Roy to the door. They slipped out into the daylight, leaving the rest of us to sit and wait among the chattering crowd.

"Lila?" Hunter asked. He cocked his head to bid me follow him when he rose from his seat. With a glance at Bryn, I nodded and followed him into the hall. Bryn's eyes bored into my back as I retreated from his sight.

Hunter stopped just beyond the doorway leading to the inn and turned to face me. His eyes held uncertainty and longing, and he reached out to grasp my hands in his.

"What happened to you, Lila? And are you sure you can trust that one?" He lifted his chin and sneered in Bryn's direction.

"A lot has happened to me, Hunter. And Bryn has been a big part of that. He kept me safe when no one else could." I felt touched by his concern. For a moment I wondered what would have happened if we hadn't fallen victim to Roglin.

"What did he do for his uncle?"

"He was with him for a few months, and he was in charge of making sure nothing happened to me."

"You mean he was the one that kept you from escaping?" he growled. I frowned at him.

"Yes," I retorted, angry for having to defend Bryn. "And since I escaped, he has been *keeping me safe!*"

Hunter sighed and shook his head. He closed his eyes, and his face fell from a mask of anger to one of defeat and sorrow.

"When you were lost, I thought I had nothing to live for," he whispered. "And now you're back, and I see you with that..." His mouth closed, his lips tight, and waved his hand toward the tavern. "I love you, Lila." He caressed my face, flooding me with the memories of his hands touching me before everything went wrong.

"Hunter..." At a loss for words, I shook my head and gazed into his eyes. Bryn's attention pushed at my mind, straining to react to

Hunter's admission. With gentle insistence, I pushed Bryn away and closed myself off from him. My lost love stood holding me, imploring me with his expression to return his hushed words to him while the man I had grown to love with more intensity than I thought possible waited to see what I would do.

To avoid the conflict warring within me, I gave Hunter a brief explanation of the past few months. He listened intently, but with disappointment evident on his handsome face. A long piece of his soft brown hair flopped onto his face and my hands longed to brush it back for him. I resisted.

"You sound certain about Bryn. In more ways than one." He released me and thrust his hands in his pockets, likely with a white stone in one of them. Without another word, he slid past me and walked back into the main room, his shoulders hunched in defeat.

The moment he disappeared, I let out a sob of frustration and ran my own hands through my hair, pulling the thick strands away from my face. No matter what I decided to do, someone would be hurt. Could I live with myself if I broke Hunter's heart again? Or Bryn's?

Bryn's eyes locked onto mine when I stepped into the tavern again. The look on his face was unreadable, and that shook me. I hadn't thought it possible for him to hide anything from me.

"Where are you staying?" Captain Morrig asked me.

"I guess we'll stay here," I replied. "I know Lottie has the room for all three of us, but she's been through too much to put her in harm's way. If Roglin *is* here, and finds us there, she could be hurt."

"That's a good idea. Do you need to arrange rooms?"

"I have that taken care of, sir," Bryn interjected. "Lila is in the room next to yours, and Sam and I are across the hall."

"You can set your things in your rooms and meet me in mine," Captain Morrig said, rising from the table.

We followed him up the stairs and found our rooms. Similar to the captain's room, I had a small bed with white linen sheets, a small table with two chairs, and a stand holding a basin and ewer for washing. Thick linen curtains covered the small window. Pulling them aside, I was able to see the cobblestone street beyond, filled with citizens rushing in different directions. I scanned the faces, worried that I might see Roglin or Derth, but I saw no one I recognized.

Past a few rows of buildings, the white canvas canopies of the open market dotted the area like clouds in the sky. And beyond the city walls, the water in the harbor glinted between hulking ships that bobbed on the waves. Their sails furled, the masts reached into the sky like bony fingers.

Captain Morrig was seated on his bed when I entered the room, and he patted the space next to him, beckoning me to sit. Hunter and Bryn sat in the two chairs, spaced as far apart as they could in the confines of the small room. Hunter and the captain chatted with me about inconsequential things until Roy and Sam returned a short time later. They shuffled into the crowded room and closed the door.

"We found the man you were talking about, Hunter," Roy announced.

"Your uncle was in the tavern, as well, boy," Sam informed Bryn. Bryn gripped the arms of the chair; his knuckles turned white from the strain. "He was raging at some people asking why he hasn't heard anything about Lila yet."

Bryn let out a growl and I rose from the bed to stand at his side. He stared up at me when I placed my hand on his shoulder. Bald fury had a grip on him again, and it chilled me as it had before.

"Calm down, Bryn," I said. Bryn sighed heavily and loosened his grip on the chair.

"Did you hear what he's planning?" Captain Morrig asked.

"It's not good," Roy said. "It seems like he's given up on keeping her in one piece. He told the hunched fellow that he wants her alive so that he can break her himself. And he mentioned you, Bryn." Bryn's back stiffened. "He wants you alive, too. And as much as he wants to make our girl suffer, he wants to make you watch even more."

The blood drained from my face as Roy spoke. There was no doubt that Roglin, along with Derth, could do terrible things to me. But the thought of what it would do to Bryn when they tortured me frightened me more.

"He underestimates you, Lila," Sam mumbled through a grim frown. "If they think it will be easy to subdue you now, they're wrong."

"I think it would be dangerous to underestimate *him*," I told Sam. "What's to stop him from separating me from the Ambience again?"

"Me," Sam said. All eyes focused on him, and Captain Morrig nodded with grim appreciation.

"There are ways to guard against the kind of attack Derth used, and I will teach them to you when we have time," Sam said. "But now that we know where Roglin is, we have the advantage."

"I agree," Bryn said. "We should strike before he realizes we're in the city."

Everyone but Sam and I nodded in agreement. "We can't attack them here," I insisted. "There's nothing to stop them from hurting innocent people. And if Derth gets involved, he could destroy the whole city. Not to mention being thrown in prison for starting a fight within King's Port. There are strict laws about that."

"True," Sam replied. "But we can't wait too long or we'll lose the element of surprise. Is there a way we can lure them out of the city?"

"We would need to let him know that I'm coming here, but it needs to be of my own free will. If he thinks someone will deliver me to him, he'll hole up somewhere and we won't have a way to reach him."

"You can't just wait outside the gates and yell his name, Lila," Bryn said. "He'll know something is wrong, and he won't respond unless he thinks he has no chance of losing." He turned to the other men in the room.

"My uncle is ruthless, and he is the most calculating man that I have ever had the displeasure of knowing. If we underestimate him, we won't stand a chance. He considers every outcome and is always a few steps ahead."

Sam nodded. "We'll have to make him think the men he sent after you never found you, and that you have no idea he's in the city or even looking for you. If we can leak the information to him, make him think that *he* is setting a trap for *you,* we can get him outside the walls and take him by surprise."

"Wouldn't he just wait until I was walking down a street and ambush me in the dark?" I asked.

Bryn shook his head. "It's too risky to attack in the open. He may have paid the guards here, like in Stalth, but an open confrontation is hard to explain away. We don't know how high his influence goes, but if there's a way to get to you without involving the guards, he'll take it." Bryn paused, a pensive look on his face.

"What if the men he sent *did* find us?" Bryn asked. "You can make illusions of yourselves, right?" Sam and I nodded. "Can you use illusions to make someone look and sound like another person?"

Not confident enough in my own ability, I turned to Sam.

"I think we could, Bryn. What do you have in mind?"

"If you disguise one of us to look like one of the men sent after us, he could warn Roglin that we were on our way back to the city."

"Why would one of them come back on his own?" I asked, skeptical. "They were sent to capture me. If they hadn't, they would have all come back."

"We could say that he was sent back to report that they had a new lead to our whereabouts. Since my uncle seems riled by the fact that they haven't gotten back yet, it stands to reason that he gave them a time limit to find us. On his way, he could have seen the two of us and decided to rush back to warn Roglin."

The men around the room smiled; even Hunter looked impressed by Bryn's idea.

"We could say that Lila and I are about two days behind him, traveling slowly. That would give him time to arrange an ambush far enough along the road to be out of sight of the gates and soldiers."

"Meanwhile," Captain Morrig said. "We follow him out of the city and take *him* by surprise. Clever, Bryn."

"Thank you, sir."

"How many men will he bring with him?" I asked. "What if we find ourselves outnumbered?"

"He would bring Derth, and however many people he can pay for this kind of work. I don't know how much money he has access to, but I wouldn't be surprised if he has enough to buy an army. He'll let them trickle out of the gates to avoid suspicion, but he'll want to ensure victory. With Derth at his side, he may decide that a small force will be enough. Derth is powerful, from what I've seen him do." His eyes shone with hard determination when he turned to me. "I don't think you should come with us, Lila."

Hunter protested before I could.

"She was a good fighter *before* she learned how to use the gift," he argued. "She's not weak, and she shouldn't be treated that way."

"I know how well she can fight, Hunter. I've fought alongside her and you're right, she's not weak. But that doesn't mean that she needs to confront my uncle. No matter how prepared we are, there is *always* a chance that something could go wrong. If she's out of sight and we fail, at least she won't be delivered directly into his hands."

"I am coming," I insisted. "When he sees me, Roglin may become so incensed that he makes a mistake." Hunter and Roy nodded, and I could see the hurt beneath Hunter's grim expression.

Roy clapped me on the shoulder before walking to the bar. Hunter flashed me a sad smile before he joined him, as Captain Morrig squeezed my hand on the table. Bryn's cold determination still nagged at me. My touch on his arm did nothing to stir him, and I withdrew it.

We discussed our plan and anything we thought might go wrong until the sun set. Roy and Bryn lit candles to stave off the darkness and the captain opened the small window to let fresh air in.

It was decided that Sam and I would act as defense for the group. We would use whatever we could to distract Derth to allow the rest of the men to fight off Roglin's mercenaries. If their number was too great for our small company to handle, we would try to kill Roglin and retreat. We could scatter if needed and designated a spot in the foothills to the west to meet if that happened.

While there seemed to be too much relying on luck, I could see no alternative unless we involved the city guard. The captain and Sam argued against that possibility, saying that it would be almost impossible to persuade the guard to get involved without evidence of Roglin's crimes. Also, as Hunter pointed out, a man like Roglin might have arrangements with some of the guard. He *had* been vocal about his intentions and hadn't been arrested so far.

We decided that Hunter would pose as one of the mercenaries on his way to inform Roglin of our whereabouts. To be sure he wasn't recognized, Sam would rely on a description provided by Bryn and me of one of the men that had attacked us in Mountain's Shade. Sam assured us that the illusion would hold long enough for Hunter to accompany them out of the city so that he could be among them when the time came for us to attack.

When we had said everything that could be said, the room fell silent. Hunter broke it by regaling the room with stories of my blunders as a child. I retaliated by telling an equally embarrassing story about Hunter and an incident involving his defeat teaching Walter how to use a sword.

"It was the first time he had even picked up a sword, and you were cocky," I said through my laughter. Hunter denied the whole thing, and we continued to reminisce.

I laughed more than I had in months, sitting in that room with Hunter and the others. As we talked, we slipped into the easy rapport we had once shared. Some of the burdens I had acquired over the past months slipped from my shoulders as we chatted and quipped. His charm and wit soothed me and reminded me of the girl I had once been.

Well past sunset, I yawned and bid the men goodnight. If we were to put all of this in motion in the morning, I would need to get some rest. After the excitement of the day, I felt drained.

Captain Morrig embraced me, telling me again how glad he was to have me back. I got a smile and a nod from Roy as he slipped into the hall on his way back to his mother's house. Sam exited the room behind him. The two remaining men followed me out of the captain's room and escorted me the few feet to my own.

Hunter and Bryn stood waiting, expectant as they gazed at me and pointedly ignored one another. Their words sat unspoken on their lips, and I could imagine every one of them as if they had been spoken aloud. I tried and failed not to compare them as I searched each one of their faces in turn. Hunter spoke to my past and the feeling of family, while Bryn filled me with excitement and hope for the future.

I took a deep breath to steel myself, and then turned to Hunter. "I'm so happy you're all here. And safe. For now, at least. I'll see you in the morning." I leaned forward and kissed his cheek. He sighed and nodded, and I could see his disappointment in the sad smile he gave me.

Watching him as he walked away I wanted to go after him, to comfort him. But I knew that wouldn't help either of us. Time would.

"Are you all right?" Bryn asked.

I turned to him and wiped a tear from my cheek. "I will be. It's hard to disappoint him. He's so important to me, but we can't be the same. Too much has changed. Will you come in so we can talk?"

He nodded and waited for me to open the door. Inside I grasped his hand and led him to the table, motioning for him to sit with me. He reached out and took my hands in his, resting them on the cream tablecloth.

"I'm sorry I've been such a mess today, and that you've had to just sit by and wait for me."

"There's nothing to apologize for," he said.

"Thank you. Seeing Hunter again, it made me wonder about a few things."

Bryn sat up straight and let his face go blank. "I figured that's why you haven't let me in for a while."

As his body tensed I realized my mistake. "No no no," I blurted in a rush. "Not about us. Not about whether I should be with Hunter, or let you go." Bryn's shoulders relaxed and I slumped with a laugh. "Oh, I'm so bad at this," I mumbled. With a sigh I sat up and looked him straight in the eye. "I've been wondering whether it wouldn't be better to take a bit of time to separate us. If it's possible."

"Do you think now is the time? Couldn't it be something to give us an edge?"

I nodded. "Possibly. But if something happens, if I'm injured, or if I lose control and destroy myself, you'd be gone too. And if Derth can sever my emotions again, would the same happen to you?" I shook my head and looked down at our clasped hands. "I don't really want to take the risk. And I don't want you hurt if I am. That sounds like the least practical thing we could do in this situation."

"Plus," Bryn added, pulling on our hands to make me look at him. "There's something telling you that you need to make sure that our feelings are real. That we aren't being pushed by the spirits or the Ambience."

"That's part of it too."

"I understand. How do we do it?"

We'll start with this, I said as I established our link. Bryn blinked and smiled. *I think we should start with the tether.*

We examined the link of Ambience between us. Nothing was different about it now and it didn't give any clues about how to break it.

What if we go to the Pool? Maybe with enough Ambience you can just decide *to break it?* Bryn asked.

That could work, I said. *Come with me.*

It took just a moment to visualize the veil that separated us from the Pool. We stepped through to the waiting spirits and stood at the edge. Once again, the tall figure rose from the center and floated toward us.

You came, it said. Its voice was like tinkling bells and the roar of thunder. I felt it in my chest and shivered as it slid across my skin.

I want to free him, I said, pulling Bryn closer.

You have but to make it so. The spirit nodded and pointed to each of our chests above our hearts. *It is within your power, if that is your true desire. Your soul is yours to share.*

I looked to Bryn, his eyes glowing with the radiant light of the Pool.

He was part of me and part of the Ambience now. The Pool reverberated with ageless depth and strength and seemed drawn to Bryn. Would that change when I broke our bond?

I don't want to lose this, Bryn said. *I want to be able to feel you, to know when you need me. But I understand why it needs to happen. It won't change how I feel. I love you.*

I love you too, I answered. I kissed him with our toes lapping in the wellspring of power for our world. Spirits danced and the Pool sparkled. I felt something pulling at the edge of my soul. I felt like grabbing Bryn and diving headfirst into the Ambience to be consumed.

He pulled away and squeezed my arms. With my eyes closed, I told the bond to break.

The large spirit grasped the tether between us and tore. The next moment Bryn and I were shunted from the Pool and left sitting at the table with our hands together.

Sweat trickled down my forehead and neck. My breath came in ragged gasps and Bryn looked the same.

"I can't feel you," he said. Tears fell from his eyes and I realized that I was crying too. "I feel like I just lost something important."

"Me too," I said. "But at least you're safe."

"Until we find Roglin, anyway."

"You were right," I whispered. Bryn frowned, confused. "I still love you."

His frown transformed into the brilliant smile that made my heart race. "I love you, too."

Bryn pulled me to my feet and lifted me into his arms. He placed me on the bed and crawled beside me, pulling the quilt over us. Lying face-to-face, I gazed into his beautiful eyes. They were so full of love and pain, mirroring mine, that I wanted nothing more than to open his mind and share in it with him. To make sure that he knew I felt the same without resorting to the feeble nature of my fumbling words.

Bryn leaned forward, kissing me with an urgent need that I felt, too. I kissed him, trying to express the depth of my love and desire. It overwhelmed me, and I pressed myself against him.

Our clothes hit the floor, and we were left with nothing between us, a different intimacy than what we'd had, but now that we were here, it felt just as important. He laid atop me, pulling the quilt up again. When he searched my eyes, I could read the question in them, asking me if this is what I wanted. I nodded. I didn't know what would happen next, but at least we were together.

CHAPTER FORTY

The next morning, I awoke in the bed alone. There was no trace of Bryn in the room, or in the hall when I poked my bedraggled head out. There was no answer when I knocked on the door to his room.

I frowned and padded back to my room. *Where is he?* I thought.

A note was on the table when I sat down.

I'm going to have a look around. I'll be back by breakfast.
I love you.
Bryn

A quick glance out the window showed me the light of early morning, and I wondered how long he'd been gone.

After a quick wash and change of clothes, followed by a battle against tangled hair, I was presentable enough to head downstairs. Captain Morrig and Hunter were sitting at a table with plates of breakfast food and looked up when they heard my boots on the stairs.

"Good morning, dear one," the captain said. He smiled through the thick salt and pepper beard. "Did you sleep well?"

"Yes," I replied. "Have you seen Bryn?"

"He left before dawn," Hunter said with a scowl. "Doesn't seem right to leave you alone after spending the night in your room."

"I'm sure he had a reason for it," the captain said. He gently smacked Hunter on the shoulder, a familiar admonishment that made me smile for a moment.

"He has an incessant need to keep a lookout," I said, sitting opposite the two of them. I gestured to the bar to get the attention of the woman there and pointed at the plates on the table, and then myself. She smiled and nodded and walked into the kitchen. "I'm sure he's doing that. Maybe getting some air. We had a strange night."

"I don't want to hear this." Hunter stood and walked to the door. He leaned against the frame and looked out into the street.

I watched him go with a frown. Did he really think I was going to discuss something intimate in front of them? "Still an idiot, then." The captain chuckled at my grumbled words. "I was going to say that we figured out how to break our bond. It was the right thing to do, the logical thing, considering what we're planning. But it made us both feel empty, somehow." I shook my head, at a loss for how to describe what we experienced. "I don't know how to explain it any better."

"And has it changed anything else?" he asked. "You told me you weren't completely certain your relationship was genuine."

A smile crossed my lips. "That's the one consolation. We still love each other. As much as we know what that means. But I *miss* him in my head. It was wonderful having someone understand me so well. There's only so much you can share of yourself with words."

He nodded, and not for the first time, I saw grief on his face. He lost his family before he found me, and I always suspected I filled a void for him.

"Well, I think it's a good idea," Sam interrupted. He pulled the chair next to me out with a screech. "Makes it harder to find him, though. You're sure it's gone? No lingering traces?"

"I'm sure. I can't hear him." My mind cast outward to search for him, but there was nothing to find. We weren't connected.

"Tell me what happened." Sam watched as my food was delivered and asked for his own.

In between mouthfuls of eggs and buttered bread, I recounted the process of the previous night. Sam scowled as he always did when I mentioned the power we shared, but by the end he was nodding.

"This larger spirit that you keep describing is strange. I wish I had my books with me." He pulled a small notebook from a pocket on his belt and scribbled until his food arrived.

I waited for Bryn to return. Anxiety rose every time someone passed the doorway and it wasn't him. I paced outside in the street for a while until Sam called me inside.

"It's reckless for you to be in the open. If one of Roglin's people sees you —"

I interrupted him. "He shouldn't be gone this long, Sam. Something is wrong."

"Let's send your friend to look around then," he said.

"I'm not going to sit here and wait!" My voice echoed in the tavern. The woman behind the bar turned to stare at me.

"If you want to find him, let's do it our way while Hunter searches."

Hunter stalked out into King's Port and I followed Sam upstairs to my room. He sat in one chair and I took the other, clutching the note from the table.

"We can try to find him. We know him, we can see the Ambience in everything. Let's find Bryn's light in all the rest."

My eyes closed and I stepped back through the veil to the Pool.

Spirits, Penelope, I need your help. My worry and love poured unchecked into my plea. The spirits at the Pool turned and put their hands on my shoulders, infinite ethereal figures bathed in prismatic light surrounding me. I felt the familiar sorrow and love and knew that Penelope was there. And the large spirit stood behind them all, arms outstretched to the sky.

Bryn! I called. Ripples of my power echoed out from me, and washed over the surrounding neighborhood.

"Lila, be careful," Sam said, his tone full of warning.

I ignored him and pushed farther. Up the steep hill toward the palace, out across the homes and shops, down toward the ocean. And I felt something stir outside the city, well beyond the gates.

There. I followed the sensation and found him walking, surrounded by others that weren't as distinct. I couldn't see or hear, but I *felt* the light that was Bryn. He still had an echo of the

Ambience that drew me like a beacon. I gasped as I felt the pain he was in. Broken ribs, bruises and cuts, one eye swollen shut. And beside him, I watched the roiling dark mass of twisted Ambient power that infused Derth turn in my direction.

He waved a hand toward me and I was shunted back into my body.

"Sam!" I reached over to grab his hand as the door burst open.

"He's been taken!" Hunter exclaimed.

Roy followed, limping, with a cut across his cheek and lip. One of his eyes was swollen shut. "I saw Bryn in the market this morning, and I didn't think anything of it until I realized someone was following him. When he turned into an alley, his uncle was waiting for him. They beat him to make him talk, and when I tried to stop them, a few of them did the same to me. They were herding him, Lila, like dogs herding a sheep. That man, Derth, pointed at me, and I–I, couldn't move," he said apologetically. "I could only watch as they dragged him away, and then Hunter showed up."

I dashed to my feet, the chair sent tumbling onto the ground behind me. I raced down the steps toward the entrance to the tavern. Captain Morrig's large hand grabbed my arm and held me in place. As I whipped around to tell him to let me go, Sam stepped forward to place his hand on my other arm.

"Lila, you are about to lose control. Take a deep breath."

"Getting yourself caught won't help him, Lila," the captain added. When I tugged against the grips on my arms, Sam interjected.

"Maintain your control, Lila."

"I am in control of myself, Sam," I growled, though I knew that fear and rage were fighting to the surface. "But I will not stand by and wait to hear that he's been killed. Let me go."

"I don't think he'll kill him," Roy said. His eyes implored me to stay, and he added his hand to the growing number restraining me. "He seemed to think that finding Bryn meant that you weren't far behind. Roglin started barking orders about gathering weapons and moving out of the city."

My eyes turned to each of the men holding me. "We need to move," I demanded. "They've had him too long already. He's in pain. We need to get him out of their hands as soon as possible."

"They were moving toward the gate the last time I saw them. It took a while for Hunter to get me up, and then I couldn't move fast enough. They may have been able to get out of the city by now."

"They are," I said. The captain frowned as Sam moved to Roy and put a hand on his leg, drawing on the Ambience to heal his injury. "Sam and I were searching for him, for his light. And I know what they did to him. We have to *go*." Roy smiled at Sam, his eyes wide with wonder. Sam patted his shoulder.

A pointed look at the captain secured my release from his grasp. My strength would have to be enough to save him; my grasp over the Ambience would have to be absolute. With my sword belt fastened around my waist, I burst back into the tavern below and out into the sunlight.

Hunter sprinted ahead, slipping through the crowd like a spirit to warn us if he saw any of Roglin's men left behind.

When the rest of us caught up with him, he gestured to the guards on the walls.

"They spotted Roglin and Derth leading a group of men out of here a while before I arrived. They were heading east," he pointed into the mass of rolling hills stretching across the land in a sloping rise from the port.

I heard the whisper of many voices, as if from far away, all urging for their release in the tumult of my roiling anger. In the glare of sunlight from shining metal shields of guards atop the gate, I watched incorporeal figures of hundreds of spirits coalescing around me, stretching out their shrouded arms to touch me. I suppressed the urge to unleash them and instead forced them to wait, letting their number grow. They obeyed, fed by my fear and stoked to frenzy by my anger. "Let's go," I said, and started forward as I passed beneath the glaring light and the images of the spirits faded.

Sam stepped up next to me, matching my stride. It took gargantuan effort not to break into a dead run and leave my friends to catch up once we were free of the crush of people. Each footfall crunched forcefully on the packed earth beneath me, kicking up dust.

Sam's voice rose as he chased me. "If we have any chance of succeeding, we need to take them by surprise. Once we're clear of the city we should create an illusion around everyone to hide them from view."

My long strides carried me up the crest of a few hills and down again until we were hidden from view of the road to our left and the city behind us. Sam stopped and I reluctantly followed his lead, my skin crawling at the delay. When our group assembled around us, Sam explained his plan.

"Lila and I are going to alter the light around each of us to conceal us from sight of Roglin and his men," Sam started. Impatience for action drowned out Sam's words, overwhelming my sense of caution. A sense of detachment settled over my shoulders, like the touch of dozens of cold hands, and I flung my hand around in an arc toward my friends, disregarding Sam's careful instruction and letting the spirits loose to follow my specific purpose.

Our skin shimmered, and for a moment, we looked like wisps of fog. We solidified again, and I felt my skin tingle from head to toe. Sam was glaring at me, shaking his head.

"You're being reckless!" he growled. He took a deep breath and held his hand up to forestall another attempt as I raised my hand again. "I can imagine how you feel, and those emotions aren't conducive to precise tasks like this."

Sam raised his hands, the spirit around him flared, and every one of us vanished from sight in an instant. All was silent but the birds and Hunter's squeak of surprise.

Sam's scolding tone, designed to shame me into submission, only incensed me. The outline of every man shone with the faint radiance of a spirit draped around them like cloaks.

"I can't see anyone," Captain Morrig said. "How will I know where everyone is?"

I sighed heavily at this delay. Sam and I could see them, I knew, but the others didn't have the advantage of being able to see the spirits. Their souls weren't linked to the Ambience like ours.

It reminded me of the spirit I'd met the night before, who had told me that my soul was mine to share. It had given me my bond with Bryn, so why couldn't I do the same with the rest of my family?

We need your help, I called. *They need to see, and I want to give them that gift to help Bryn.* Spirits holding a small portion of the Ambience and the deep well I now knew I possessed draped over the others; this allowed them to see as I did, though perhaps not the defined forms of the spirits. They all gasped, and Sam leveled me with a look which would have cowed me on any other occasion.

"Everything is so much more...." Roy started. He fell silent, unable to think of a way to describe it.

As an unexpected side effect of my hasty action, each of their thoughts became as clear to me as Bryn's had been. Rather than having full access to their minds, though, it only allowed me to see what passed through their thoughts in the instant that I centered my attention on it. When I let my focus slip, their voices became a faint whispering in the back of my mind, a confused jumble of impressions. Without waiting to see if they would follow, I took off in the direction Hunter had indicated.

My feet bounded along the ground. I slid down most of the hills, and with every rise my breath caught as I expected to see Bryn's blonde mop of hair shining in the sunlight.

I cast my eyes and the Ambience about in search of Bryn. Energy surged from life all around, and a faint glow in the distance urged me onward in hopes that this was the group we sought. With every step my thoughts centered on Bryn.

Bryn! I shouted in my head, but received no response except the impression of agonized thoughts and pain. My mind singled out that spark, and for an instant I was able to feel Bryn. My feet stumbled beneath me; such was the force of agony that emanated from him.

Standing still atop the next rise, I gazed in the direction of his pain. As if through a fog, all that I experienced from Bryn's perspective became muffled and distorted. Whether he witnessed his surroundings as I did, I couldn't tell. His uncle paced ahead of him with the fury of a storm at sea. Bryn staggered in his wake.

When Bryn stumbled and a flash of searing pain tore through his leg, the connection strengthened.

That witch certainly got her hooks into you. You're pathetic. Roglin sneered over his shoulder at Bryn. His eyes exuded cold fury in the shadows cast by the hill in front of him. *There was a time that I thought you could be my legacy, boy. But she ruined that.*

Fresh burning pain exploded from Bryn's side, just below his ribs as his attention was focused on Roglin. A gasp burst out of me and I clasped my hand to my side, feeling a blade slide through his skin. The knife ripped out, leaving a shallow gash in his back, and

Bryn cried out through gritted teeth. Cold fury to match Roglin's drenched me in a horrible calm. Calm that accompanies certainty of purpose. Spectral spirits began to move in Bryn's direction and my mind moved with them to encompass him, overtaking his conscious mind. His lips moved as I spoke, and a feral grin spread across his bleeding mouth.

"I am coming."

Roglin stood stricken, his eyes wide and filled with fear. *His eyes,* he said. *They're glowing.* Roglin's fist swung toward Bryn's face; my head snapped back, and my eyes watered as something cracked in Bryn's cheek. The spirits retreated from Bryn, and I growled as I took off at a dead sprint.

Dusk descended upon the countryside as I crested another hill. My arms prickled with gooseflesh in a sudden cold breeze and my eyes turned to the valley falling away from my perch. Roglin led his men, who formed a ring around Bryn, as they trudged up the side of the next hill. More mercenaries than I'd expected, at least a dozen, but Derth was conspicuously absent.

"They're here," I whispered over my shoulder. The footsteps ceased as my friends halted alongside me.

One bastard tripped Bryn and laughed. A feral snarl ripped from my lips. As he stumbled upright, I waved my hands in front of me, pulling the air together to form a wall on all sides of Roglin's position, leaving only a gap wide enough for two nearest my position. While they waited for Bryn to regain his feet, I sprinted into the valley.

"Lila!" Sam whispered at my back. I paid no heed to his frantic admonishment.

My friends followed in my wake; they ran on the balls of their feet, their movement a whisper in the grass and dirt. Sam calmed and summoned shields around each of us, leaving me to do what I would.

We reached the floor of the valley as Roglin strode face first into the solid wall, stumbling back a step and shaking his head. He held his hands out in front of him, feeling along the wall as he moved from side to side. He turned to his men. "Something is wrong. On your guard."

I closed on the wall, illuminated for us by the spirits projecting the Ambience as a soft glow. We slipped inside, silent compared to the ring of steel clearing sword belts and worried grumbles from our targets.

I halted several feet from Bryn. Spirits rushed to enshroud him, bending the light in the valley to hide him from view, while another harnessed the essence of lightning to deter anyone from nearing him using what Sam had taught me on our first trip to his cabin. One brute yelped and stepped back when Bryn disappeared. The others turned to see that he was gone, and Roglin bellowed with rage.

"She's *here!*" He glanced behind him, murmured, "Find her," and stomped closer to where his nephew had disappeared. The broad man behind him nodded, and I noticed that there was darkness enshrouding him like the spirits surrounded me. Derth's darkness.

A broad-shouldered man wielding a club extended his arm to the space where Bryn had disappeared. As he touched the shroud, it shimmered and the man dropped to the ground, writhing. His eyes didn't perceive the spirit as its touch receded to enclose Bryn. Where the air shimmered, a blurry vision of Bryn's surprised face could be seen for the space of a heartbeat. Before he disappeared, his eyes sought mine through my invisibility and locked on my face as they always did, drawn to me as I was to him.

I pulled Desire from its scabbard and darted forward. Before any heads could turn toward the thudding of my feet, I attacked. My sword thrust forward and ripped into the nearest thug, extruding through his lower abdomen. As I wrenched the sword free and the others rushed forward, driving their weapons into a few other thugs, I felt a pulse of darkness from behind Roglin. The man standing there faltered as he started to walk forward, but the darkness remained behind.

It rushed forward, engulfing me, wracking me with waves of dizziness. I fought to stay upright as Derth's laugh echoed through my mind. His darkness smothered me, threatening to come between me and the Pool. A lone spirit stepped forward, reaching its large, taloned fingertips in my direction. As I reached out, Ambient light swelled inside me, and the darkness pooled and rolled away, like oil repelled by water.

Derth snarled, and I felt Sam at my side. Seeing the shroud of darkness as I had, he pointed in its direction and sent a burst of energy in that direction. The energy recoiled, narrowly missing Sam, and my limbs tingled as his concentration moved to shielding us from a gout of fire. The rest of our friends materialized behind me, and Roglin's mercenaries turned to face us with angry shouts.

Roglin's eyes found mine, and he stalked forward with a grin. "So, I've found you at last. You won't get away from me this time, little girl."

"I am going to kill you," I said, suffused with cold calm. Roglin's grin faltered while swords clashed around us.

I felt the touch of a spirit in my mind. It was familiar, as if some part of me knew who they were. A memory pulled at me, a flash of bright red hair, a man wielding the Ambience with finesse. Training for battle. His voice was muted when he smiled, and I heard *"Watch this, little flame."*

Captain Morrig's, Hunter's, and Roy's swords screeched and clanged against four of the brutes as Sam hurled a volley of fire at the other two. My attention called back from the red-haired man, I snarled at Roglin. Another of his thugs lunged, attempting to sink his sword into my side. The spirit whispered a warning in my ear and my palm thrust out to bat the flat of the blade aside. My assailant stumbled to my right, following the momentum of his thrust.

I glanced over my shoulder as he turned, and a narrow jet of spiraling flames coalesced from my fingertip to sear through his chest through his heart. He screeched as the scent of burning flesh filled the air, and then the flame subsided.

A malevolent chuckle sounded from behind Roglin, and I could hear Derth's delight in the violence. Shadows dripped from him like rain from leaves, revealing him, his eyes wide and hungry, his smile wide. He sneered at me, and my body rose into the air for the length of a startled grunt and then I slammed onto my back in the grass to slide down the slope. Bryn's muffled cry rose above the cacophony of the battle.

I struggled to my knees, hurling a gust of wind into the ground to kick up dirt that I flung at Derth's eyes. "Stay there, Bryn!" I shouted.

Sam thrust his hand toward Hunter and the others. Two of their opponents slammed into one another and stumbled into their fellows in a heap of limbs. Hunter, Roy, and Captain Morrig pounced, their blades flashing in the fading light.

Sam advanced on Derth, throwing wave after wave of air and fire and raw Ambience. Derth swatted each away like so many flies.

Sam persisted, and they became ensconced in a heated battle; a constant shockwave shook the ground and vibrated in my chest as if amplifying the pounding of my heart.

Roglin stood still, weapon drawn as he waited for me. I circled around the separate battles in my path, hair blown back from the pressure created by Derth and Sam's efforts. Cries from people battering one another with naked steel roared in my ears as a metallic spray of blood dotted my jaw and lips. My attention narrowed to the malevolent man awaiting my arrival.

Roglin bellowed over the clamor while I stalked forward. "I knew Bryn would betray me the moment he laid eyes on you. I saw the disgust on his face. He's always been soft, like his mother."

"Then you brought this on yourself!" I yelled. Hunter darted to my right, his blade slicing past a man's defenses faster than I could track. His opponent grunted as a spray of blood hit Hunter's shirt, and the two tumbled out of sight.

"I thought I would make him squirm," Roglin sneered. "The look on his face when I told him what I would do to you!" His laughter rang over the small space, echoing off the walls, his eyes locked on my progress all the while. Each slow step carried me closer to him while I considered my options. I molded a fine point of air and hurtled it toward Roglin's throat. Derth's eyes flicked to Roglin as it dissolved against a shield.

"Derth assures me that your gift will be useless against me, girl," Roglin sneered.

"I've heard something similar before. And he turned out to be wrong."

I unleashed more spirits, and a whirlwind of fire engulfed Roglin. It battered the shield encasing him with no visible effect. With the intent of taking Roglin's life, the Ambience urged me to loose more, threatening to overwhelm me in a conflagration of fiery rage if I failed to heed it. Derth flinched from the heat of my assault as if feeling the searing flame himself.

Behind the column of white-hot flames, I lost sight of Roglin. I waved my hands, coaxing more of my cadre of spirits to form several illusions of myself, each face contorted into a bloodthirsty mask. The Ambience urged me forward and I obeyed, relishing the sense of power.

I sprinted to Bryn while my copies scattered, one remaining in the position I vacated. The barrier vibrated against my palm, and

Bryn's hand reached out to touch the spot where I stood. Roglin laughed again as he stood unscathed behind the flames. Longing and fear washed over me from Bryn's touch, galvanizing me as I willed the illusions to mimic my movements. To my amazement and satisfaction, they stalked toward Roglin's location in unison with me, their swords ready to strike.

I released the flames around Roglin; his eyes flicked from one to another of the illusions, trying to make sense of what he was seeing. He focused on the copy I had left in my original position. "Do you think your tricks are going to help you?" he screamed. "You can't best me. If you surrender now, I'll let these men go. Even my traitorous nephew can leave."

Roy leapt at a man behind Roglin, his knife finding a home in his opponent's throat. In one deft movement, Roy flicked his wrist and laid open the windpipe beneath his blade. As the man fell gurgling to the ground, clutching his throat, Roy ran to his captain's aid.

One of my copies reached Roglin and lunged, sword point leveled at his belly. He flinched but she disappeared in a blast of thunder erupting from the shield, and he sneered at another that sidled up to him. While he cast about for his real opponent, I closed the gap between us. He leveled a withering scowl at the illusion he assumed to be me.

"Is that the best you can do? Try to scare me to death?"

Another illusion lunged at Roglin, and he parried a blow that never hit. His shield destroyed her, and he swung around in a stumbling arc. When one thrust at his middle, he deflected another strike that never landed and growled as another lunged, aiming at his head. He swung around and angled his blade to catch hers, but she again disappeared as soon as my conjuration hit Derth's.

Roglin screamed as I lunged at him before he could recover from the last assault, so my blade sliced through the flesh of his arm. My remaining copies vanished as my focus changed from maintaining my grip on the Ambience to swordplay, and Roglin's sword swung in a deadly arc toward me. I parried, but the force of his swing left my arms ringing with numbing pain, and I was forced to dance back a step to avoid his next lunge.

I fought with all the ferocity I could muster and all the skill I possessed. Stabbing and swinging with all my might, parrying and dodging his blows, trying to keep in mind all that Bryn, Hunter and the rest had taught me. The grimace on Roglin's face belied his easy movement with the sword, and I poured all my remaining strength into an attempt to slide my blade through him.

He danced aside and pressed his advantage, using his lifetime of skill and his muscled fury to force me into defensive postures and darting movements to dodge away from the point of his sword.

A sensation of the Ambience being drawn from me drew my attention to Bryn. His hands moved past the barrier holding him in place. He had used some of the Ambience that coursed through me to dismiss it. He grimaced through the blood and bruises and moved in my direction.

That was the moment that Roglin used the hilt of his sword to crack the base of my skull.

I heard a sickening crunch that reverberated through my entire body, and I hit the ground. Bright points of light danced in my eyes before being engulfed behind a dark fog. The cool grass matted beneath my bleeding skull soothed the burning sensation spreading across my face, and the breeze whispered across my skin. My mind wandered through a haze of agony, trying to remember why I was on the ground.

My gorge rose when I tried to lift my head, and I flopped back into the grass and dirt. My chest heaved, trying to gasp enough air into my lungs, but I could not remember how to breathe.

Roglin moved into my field of vision and gazed down at me dispassionately. He spoke, and his words came to me as if he stood at the opposite end of a long tunnel.

"Keep breathing, girl," he growled. "I have plans for you."

A furious cry wrenched his glare from my face, but not fast enough to prevent something from slamming into him, carrying him away from me.

I tried and failed to rise, the agony in my head sharpening to an unbearable level that stole my vision and left me puddled in the grass. Somehow, I managed to turn enough to see Roglin in a tangled heap of grappling limbs a scant ten feet from me. I saw a flash of dark blonde hair, and I whimpered.

"Bryn..." I whispered. My arm twitched on the ground, my attempt to reach for him thwarted by my lack of control over my body. *Not again,* I thought.

The dark fog at the edges of my vision spread as I felt my vitality wane. I cried out for the Ambience, for any spirits with the ability to help. For Penelope and the Elders and the Founders. Cool, spectral hands on my brow stemmed the flow of blood and attempted to heal my wound. The pain receded inch by inch until my eyesight returned, but my mind wandered and my grasp of the Ambience slipped; it was not enough to force my recalcitrant limbs to move.

Bryn and Roglin had struggled to their feet, each holding a sword. Sudden fear lanced through me. I begged the spirits to protect Bryn, to give him the strength to defeat his uncle. One reached out to grasp Bryn, to follow my command. Bryn staggered as he felt the change, and his attack fell short. Roglin sensed an opening and lunged.

Bryn blurred before my eyes, and he reappeared behind Roglin. His fist connected with his uncle's face as it turned. Blood sprayed from Roglin's crumpled nose and Bryn replaced his hand on the hilt of the sword. He chopped at Roglin's feet, but his uncle dodged to the side. I cried out with voice and intent, calling spirits to heal me again. My skull burned as shards of it were extracted from within to reform, and my hold slipped again, the spirit vanishing.

Roglin's eyes watered. Blood ran in streams down his mouth and dripped from his chin. He struggled to block Bryn's blows. His eyes flashed to me, and he abandoned his nephew to lunge at my prone form.

Roglin fell to his knees, positioning the edge of his blade at my throat. I smiled through a mouthful of blood; no matter if my life would end, I had taken control of the Ambience and he couldn't take that victory from me. Bryn could survive, because of what I had done to stop his uncle.

"You'll die first," he smirked. His face hovered mere inches from my own, and bloody spittle struck my cheek.

If he hadn't stopped to gloat, he would have been right. Desire burst through the front of his chest, spraying me with hot blood. Bryn's face appeared over Roglin's shoulder, and he twisted the sword first one way and then another with a sound that reminded me of stepping through mud before ripping it out of his back.

"*No!*" he screamed. He jerked back as Bryn wrenched my sword from his chest. He started to turn, one hand on the ground and the other braced on his knee so he could stand. Bryn stumbled back and struggled to hold his arms up.

Roglin spat blood and heaved his sword in Bryn's direction. I lunged at him, grasping his belt and ripping Bryn's dirk free. When he looked down at me I threw myself up and lodged the dirk in his neck behind his windpipe.

Roglin hovered for what seemed an eternity before crumpling to the ground, his face inches from mine. His eyes widened, his face frozen in a grimace, and I couldn't move my eyes from his as the light in them died.

I felt myself being lifted, and I whimpered when a hand touched my head. With the movement came the darkness again, and I started to fade.

Cobalt blue eyes accompanied me into oblivion.

CHAPTER FORTY-ONE

I flitted in and out of consciousness. Voices sounded above my head in varying degrees of urgency, fading in and out as they moved. My eyelids fluttered in vain to find their source.

My arms and legs refused to obey my wishes, lying limp despite my fervent desire to scratch an itch above my eye. A hand smoothed hair away from my forehead, and stabbing pain lanced through from the gentle caress, driving thoughts of the itch from my mind. I longed to groan or whimper, but my body remained still and silent.

When I *did* manage to open my eyes, gauzy curtains fluttered in the breeze from a window in the blue wall of a bedroom. Darkness dominated all but the far corner where a single candle's flame flickered in a silver candlestick. A single hair twitched back and forth to irritate my heavy eyelids. Arms and legs still disobedient, I could only blink in a vain attempt to dislodge it from my eyelashes.

I wondered for a moment why my limbs wouldn't move and how I came to lie in this bed. Recent events were a hazy dream, and my mind drifted. Movement near the bed caught my eye, and I tried to turn my head to find its source. Agony blossomed from a point above my right ear and I whimpered, unable to muster a shriek in response. Tears ran from my eyes as the world narrowed to a small point of light amid sudden darkness.

As the agony subsided, my eyes cleared. A pale, handsome face hovered above my bed; dark hair flashed with gold in the candlelight, and blue, worried eyes searched my face.

"Lila?" Bryn murmured. "Can you hear me?" Surprise and relief carried his words on a whisper. Creases marked his forehead and a frown tugged at the corners of his mouth, showing the extent of his worry.

"Bryn," I croaked. "Are you hurt?"

Bryn let out a sigh. "You've been lying in a bed, unconscious for days, and you ask if *I'm* hurt?" His head shook in disbelief and chuckled, his eyes never leaving mine. His hand found mine, little sparks radiating through me from his touch.

"How did I get here?" I croaked.

"You don't remember?"

I began to shake my head and gasped while Bryn reached out as if to stop me. His eyes left my face for a moment, the worry lines on his face deepening while he looked at the spot on my head that seemed determined to incapacitate me.

"Roglin found me and tried to make me take him to you. You and the others came to rescue me," he paused and fixed me with a scowl, "which you shouldn't have done. It was close, but we all survived, and Roglin and his men didn't."

The memories came back as Bryn spoke. "Was anyone hurt? What happened to Derth?" A fit of coughing ripped from my dry throat; each one added pressure to my pounding head, making me moan.

Bryn leapt for the door in a rush, wrenching it open with a shriek of the hinges. Bright light poured into the room, and I squinted. "Sam!" Bryn called. "She's awake!"

Many footsteps pounded on the floor like thunder, and Sam rushed into the room. "Oh, thank the Elders," he panted.

"Hi, Sam," I croaked between gasps. "Were you hurt?"

"No, dear girl, I'm fine. It's *you* everyone has been worried about. We thought you were dead. Bryn was sitting there, holding your limp body with blood running down your face and the rest of you splattered with gore. I could barely get him to let go of you long enough to heal what I could." He spared an angry look for Bryn, who had moved around to the side of my bed nearest the window. He took my hand in his and gazed down at me, not acknowledging Sam's words in the slightest.

Sam's face fell in a rare moment of chagrin. "I'm sorry I haven't done more for you before now. It was all I could do to drag myself back here after dealing with Derth and healing you as best I could with the little strength I had left. It took everything I had left."

"I think I did a bit of that for myself," I said, suppressing another cough.

"It's a good thing you did; he caved in your skull. There was so much blood, if you hadn't healed yourself, you would have bled to death before I got to you. I almost couldn't stop the bleeding after that."

"The Ambience almost took me, Sam."

At that moment Lottie bustled into the room with a tray, pushing past the congregation of men I hadn't seen in the doorway. They moved aside grudgingly, all eyes fixed on me. I flashed a weak smile their way but the high-pitched chime of dishes clinking together sunk like knives into my throbbing head.

"Poor dear," Lottie said anxiously. "Can you do anything for her?" she asked Sam.

"I'm still a bit weak, but I will do everything I can." Sam placed his hands on either side of my head, not quite touching me.

Pain eased as the Ambience coursed through me. Sam's hands began to shake, the strain evident on his haggard face. Soothing warmth spread from his hands to my wound and through my skull. As the pain ebbed, Sam shook more until he broke away from me, sagging under the weight of his effort. Large hands supported him from the doorway until he could push himself upright under his own power.

Bryn spared an anxious glance for his friend, but his focus couldn't be drawn from me for long. "How do you feel?" he asked, looking to my hairline and back. "It looks better now."

"It feels better," I replied. My limbs moved when I demanded it; fingers curled in toward my palms and out again, and my legs stretched and pointed beneath the quilt. With Bryn's help, I was able to scoot myself up into a sitting position with my back braced against the wall. The excruciating agony was replaced by a dull aching throb, and I turned my head with a wince.

Bryn tucked the ends of the quilt around my waist and propped a pillow behind the small of my back to make me comfortable. He then took the tray from Lottie and placed it at the foot of the bed before handing me a small glass of water.

Though I grasped the glass with both hands, I nearly dropped it. Bryn had to steady it enough for me to take a welcome sip of the cool water. With a small smile of gratitude, I thanked him. His answering grin steadied me even more, and together we lifted the glass again.

When I drank my fill and my throat felt soothed, he took the glass and placed it back on the tray. His eyebrows rose in question when he touched the bread.

"Not yet. But thank you so much, Lottie," I smiled at the old woman hovering between Sam and the bed. "How is Roy?"

"Nothing but a few scrapes," she informed me with a smile and glance over her shoulder at her tall son. "He's had much worse. Don't worry about anything but getting well. We love you, sweet girl." She blew me a kiss and excused herself from the room, shooing my friends away from the door in the process.

Sam pushed himself upright to follow her. "Sam!" I called. "Please, take the food. I can't eat, and you look like you need it." Bryn rose to carry the tray for him after my pointed glance. "Thank you again. I owe you my life many times over."

He smiled shakily at me. "Think nothing of it. But try not to use the Ambience for a while. Overexertion likely added to your state, and you're still healing." He shuffled out of the doorway with one hand on the wall to steady himself.

Bryn paused beyond the door while someone spoke in a murmur. He glanced at me, his lips tight with disapproval, and then nodded once before smiling back at me and following Sam away from my room. Hunter, with a gash above his eyebrow held together by a few stitches, sidled in and took a seat in the chair by the bed.

"That looks bad," I said, weakly pointing to his head.

"Yours is worse," he replied with a smirk.

"You aren't wrong. How is the captain?"

"I'm well enough," he grumbled, limping into the room. "I'm glad you're awake, Lila. I thought we'd lost you again."

"I'm fine," I assured him. "Are they all dead?"

Hunter shook his head. "We lost track of the gifted one, Derth, in the fighting. Sam is sure that he didn't kill him. Pulled the same stunt you did and we lost him."

"We need to find him," I said. "Even without Roglin to guide him, he's dangerous."

"We'll worry about that when you're well, dear one." Captain Morrig patted my arm. "For now, you rest and mend. All other things will keep until you're back on your feet."

Captain Morrig limped out of the room, but Hunter lingered. For once in his life, he seemed unable to speak and studied his hands in his lap.

"He loves you," he blurted.

"I know he does," I replied. "He's the best man I know. Like a father."

Hunter shook his head. "Not the captain...Bryn."

"Oh." A blush crept up my neck to warm my cheeks.

"When he thought you were dead, he looked like he would die from grief. I loved you, once. But I don't know if I'm even *capable* of that kind of love. It scares me."

"It scares me, sometimes," I admitted. "But I love him that way, too."

Hunter nodded, almost to himself, as if I had confirmed something.

"I won't get in your way, then. If I thought there was even a chance that you could still love me, or that you would come to love me again, I would hound his every step. But I can see now that that would make you unhappy, and I won't do that to you."

"Thank you for caring about me so much, Hunter. I hope we can be friends again."

"You won't be getting rid of me, that's for sure," he grinned. He patted my hand and rose from the bed to saunter into the hall. Before he could cross the threshold, Bryn appeared. Hunter clapped him on the shoulder and slid past him. Bryn turned to watch him walk away with a confused grin.

The chair next to the window creaked beneath him as he settled into it. He took my hand in both of his, running his thumbs back and forth across my skin in a gentle caress. Small jolts of pleasure coursed through me from his touch, even in my current state, and my heart started to pound in my chest.

"It's been said over and over again," he whispered. "But I thought I lost you. You were so still... And I...." He dipped his head and grief choked off his words. He took a shuddering breath and looked up at me, eyes red and rimmed with tears.

"I'm sorry I left. I'm sorry my uncle found me, and that you were forced into that before we were ready. I should have stayed here." His words came out in a rush as he apologized, and I stretched my fingers out to touch his tensed arm.

"When I found you battered and being dragged along behind your uncle, and then that man stabbed you..." I trailed off, starting to shake my head and stopping as the pain flared. "More than any time in my life, I was afraid. I love you, Bryn, and I can't lose you."

"I feel different without our bond," Bryn said. My face crumpled with my disappointment and heartbreak. Seeing my expression, he shook his head in anxious denial. "The bond *was* affecting me. It made me obsessed with your safety, and I think it was clouding my judgment. But it didn't have any effect on my loving you. That was all me." He smiled his impossibly sweet, lopsided smile, which broke the last of my defenses and I started to cry, letting my fear and desperation leave me in a rush. At that moment, I was a little girl again. Stranded with no idea where she was, hopeless and afraid.

"What's wrong, Lila?"

"I've been so worried," I sobbed. "When I woke up, I was worried when you didn't come back. And then I was worried that your uncle would kill you. And after I did everything I could to keep you safe, you attacked him, and I couldn't help...."

"Stop crying, love. You don't have to worry about that anymore. I love you, we're both alive, and I'm not going anywhere."

Seeing that I couldn't stop the jarring sobs, Bryn climbed under the sheets, wrapping his arms around me without shifting my head. The bedsprings screeched in protest beneath our combined weight.

My tension eased in a flood as he embraced me, and I touched my forehead to his chest as my sobbing slowed. He cupped his hand to the back of my head with extreme care; finding that I didn't cry out in pain, he stroked my hair, lulling me back into a deep sleep with his gentle rhythm, cradled in his strong arms, blissful and unafraid.

CHAPTER FORTY-TWO

Early morning light filtered through the curtains to cast a blazing glow on my closed eyelids. My eyes opened to blink at the clear blue sky beyond Bryn's shoulder.

Bryn still slept, his face relaxed and his long dark eyelashes fanned out above his cheeks. I reached up, my arm obeying me more readily this morning, and stroked his hair. He murmured something unintelligible as I did, and then settled again.

Without moving him, I slid off Bryn's outstretched arm and pulled the blankets off myself. My head swam when I planted my feet on the floor and stood. I swayed for a sickening moment before the sensation passed. When I recovered, I shuffled to the table where my clean clothing waited in folded piles. With one hand on it, I stepped into my skirt. The bodice gave me more trouble as my fingers fumbled to tighten the laces, but after a few minutes' silent struggle I succeeded.

After I had managed that small miracle, I located my comb and started in on my tangled hair. Yanking the tangles out as I would normally do proved very detrimental to my fragile head, so I continued with much more care. With a small, soft cloth soaked in cool water from the basin, I washed my face. The cold invigorated me, and my thoughts cleared.

Once I had put myself to rights, I moved on silent tiptoe out of the room, closing the door behind me with a soft thump, and padded down the hall and stairs to the kitchen.

Lottie stood at the counter, drizzling honey over fresh bread. My mouth watered as I sat at the empty table and inhaled the sweet scent.

She cried out when she turned around. "Lila! My goodness, I wasn't expecting anyone to be up and about! You scared the wits out of me!" She clapped a hand to her chest and smiled.

"Sorry Lottie. Where is everyone?"

"Still asleep if I know men. And I do." She gave me a knowing wink. "Would you like something to eat? You must be starving."

"Yes, please," I said eagerly. She set a plate of the sweet bread in front of me with a steaming cup of tea and a plate of fruit. I devoured each morsel with zeal.

As I finished my meal, Roy and Hunter stumbled out of the hall and plopped down on the chairs opposite me. They blinked through sleep-swollen eyes for a moment before realizing that I was out of bed.

"Feeling better, I see," Roy said smiling.

"Finally out of bed," Hunter said. "Took you long enough!" His head jerked suddenly forward with a loud crack as Lottie smacked the back of it.

"You leave her be," she scolded. "Now eat." She placed plates piled with food in front of them, and they quickly lost interest in me.

Lottie supplied me with another mug of hot tea, and I moved to the empty sitting room. Mismatched chairs and couches of all shapes and colors filled the room at odd angles as if a giant hand had scooped up the lot of them and let them tumble out in a mess to settle where they would about the large room. The heavy red drapes let only a sliver of light make its way through a gap.

A green overstuffed armchair that I loved the most sat next to a large window that looked out on the street. I had spent many hours watching people as they strolled past, or reading in the natural light. I pulled back the heavy curtain and secured it with a tasseled rope on the wall before I climbed into the chair, tucking my legs beneath me and facing the window. I closed my eyes, basking in the warm sunlight as the heat from my mug dissipated the chill in my fingers.

Soon, urgent footsteps thudded in the hall and Bryn halted at the entrance. He looked wild-eyed and afraid. He spotted me curled in the chair the next moment and his shoulders sagged with relief. He crossed the room in a few long strides and sank to the floor in front me, his knees thudding on the rug.

His hair stuck out at odd angles, matted in some places and hanging over his eyes in the front. Red creases marked his cheek where it had rested on the pillow.

"You weren't there," he mumbled. "I had the worst nightmare that you died in your sleep, and you weren't there when I woke up...." He shook his head, trying to clear it of images that haunted him. I removed my hand from the mug and ran it through the hair at the top of his head, trying to smooth it for him. I pursed my lips in concentration.

"I'm all right, Bryn. I just thought you could use more sleep. I'm sorry I didn't wake you."

"That's fine," he said blearily. He placed his head in my lap as he knelt in front of me, and I continued to run my fingers through his hair.

He nodded off for a moment, his breathing evening out from the hectic rhythm caused by fear. I gazed at his profile while my fingers scratched his scalp and wondered how I could love someone so much. Bryn started when Sam came into the room and bid us good morning. With a grunt, Bryn rotated to sit in front of me with his back against my chair and rubbed his face vigorously with both hands.

"Morning, Sam," he grumbled.

"I see all is again right with the world," Sam said, his voice full of glee. "Both of you up and about and back to your constant proximity." He fell silent under our gazes. "I'll just go and see what Lottie's made for breakfast," he drawled, and sidled out of the room in the direction of the kitchen.

Bryn and I turned to one another.

"What's gotten into him?" I asked. Bryn shrugged as Sam's voice drifted down the hall.

"My good woman, you have outdone yourself!" he exclaimed with more exuberance than I had heard before.

Bryn and I broke out in laughter while our old friend continued to expound on Lottie's many fine qualities.

After a morning spent eating Lottie's wonderful food, we assembled in the sitting room at Captain Morrig's insistence.

"I met with the King's man yesterday," Captain Morrig announced from his perch on one of the couches. "It seems that his soldiers took notice of Roglin's group leaving the city. They've been watching him for some time, suspecting that he had a hand in the slave trade and hoping to finally catch him in the act when they heard he was assembling groups to abduct someone. When they saw Bryn, they decided to send someone along after we left."

Still in my favorite chair as the men settled around me, a freshly washed and clothed Bryn sat at my feet with his legs drawn up to his chest and his arms draped around them. My hand rested on his shoulder and the muscles tensed beneath it at the mention of his late uncle's name.

Purple bruises marred his lovely face beneath his eyes and along his jaw. Bryn had informed me that he refused to let Sam attempt to heal any of his injuries so that he might treat mine.

The other men had escaped with minor wounds. Captain Morrig sustained a nasty gash on the back of his thigh; an attempt to hobble him had been turned aside by a timely lunge, and though the wound still caused him pain, he insisted that it was better than losing his leg. He had also refused Sam's offer of help, urging him to tend to me, since Sam hadn't been able to recover his strength fully. He winced when he shifted his weight.

"The soldiers found the site of our little scuffle and saw that their prey was already dead," he said. "When they questioned the gate guards, they remembered Hunter's questions and found us at The Barracks. The King requested our presence tomorrow morning."

"Why do they want to see us?" I asked. "Are they going to arrest us?"

"I doubt it," Captain Morrig replied with a shake of his head. "If they wanted to do that, they would have. What worries me is the King asked to see you specifically, dear one."

Suspicion settled like a blanket over me. "Why me?"

"I couldn't say," the captain replied. "But it would be unwise to refuse. If you don't come with us, he'll only find a way to force you."

"I didn't fight free of Roglin's influence only to end up in the hands of the king," I grumbled.

"You won't be," Bryn assured me.

"I don't think it wise for me to accompany you," Sam said. All eyes focused on his tense form leaning against the wall by the door, but he would offer no explanation and shrugged when the captain asked him why.

"The king asked for all of us," he insisted. "And you would rouse more suspicion if you stayed here."

With an exasperated sigh, Sam nodded, and I wondered again about the past that he refused to share with us.

Captain Morrig finally allowed me to heal his leg the next morning. It was lucky that I insisted, because the wound was inflamed. A few more days untended and he could have lost the leg altogether.

My first attempt to call on the Ambience failed, feeling like falling from a step I hadn't known was there. My stomach dropped and I gaped at the emptiness within me. Bryn calmed me with a few words, and Sam reassured me that after such a test of my strength it was common for the spirits to need a rest as well. It would take patience and determination, he told me, to reestablish my grasp on it and wake it from its slumber.

After a few minutes of meditative breathing, I searched for that spark within me. Bryn clasped my hand, and for a moment, I felt the immeasurable wealth of power beckoning as it had on several occasions. The moment passed and I was reunited with the brilliance of the Ambience and gentle touch of spirits. It flowed through me, restoring the last of the strength that had flagged in my journey near death.

The captain grimaced as spirits and I pulled his torn flesh together. A heartbeat later, he smiled in wonder and watched the glow fade from his leg and my hands to leave his skin whole again.

Roy, Hunter, Lottie and the captain all praised my abilities and chatted about the wonder of the gift.

Sam was able to finish my journey to health as well. It felt like water trickling over my scalp, an intense itch, and then I was whole.

I found myself on the streets of King's Port shortly thereafter, on our way to the palace all too soon for my liking. I walked hand in hand with Bryn, surrounded by the rest of our group.

The streets curved and turned between buildings on their way to the palace. The palace grounds spread out in a solitary square that separated the marble edifice from the rest of the city, positioned on a lone hill to watch over its subjects. Well back from the harbor and the land approaching the city gates, it sat protected by a high wall of stone. Thicker than any boundary I had seen, it rose well above our heads to shield it from invaders and keep it separated from the common folk in the streets.

The wall also blocked the view of the extensive gardens and arbors littering the expansive grounds that greeted us as soon as we passed through the iron gates. Gardeners buzzed around the flower beds like bees, tending the growth of older flowers and planting scores of new bulbs and seeds to add to the beautiful collection. Even this early in the season, some of the flowers bloomed in a spectacular vision of yellow, purple, red and pink that fluttered in the ocean breeze.

Two armed guards wearing uniforms emblazoned with the king's standard escorted us along the cobblestone lane that led from the gate to the impressive entrance. Uniform stones larger than my feet supported us while we wandered among young and old birch trees that punctuated the space between the flower beds lining the lane. Shadows cast by the moving leaves shifted among our feet.

The palace itself towered above us, rising to heights that seemed to rival the distant mountains. Sculpted from blinding white marble, the building sported large double doors atop a wide, sweeping staircase. Its many windows were trimmed with gold accents, and the roof was dotted with stoic marble gargoyles.

The doors swept out at our approach. We ascended and stepped inside the entrance hall. Large paintings of past monarchs stared down at us from gilt frames. Polished tables held various trinkets and breakable objects painted dazzling colors, propped up for display by golden brackets.

The guards departed as the doors closed, plunging the hall into darkness broken by candles glittering in golden candelabras at intervals along the walls. A stiff man in the spotless uniform of a butler appeared in the doorway to our right. The top of his balding head came to the level of my chin. His face was drawn in a pinched scowl as he pivoted on his heel and walked away along the hall, expecting us to follow.

We walked past room after room without pause. I glanced in a few, catching a glimpse of a large table with a burgundy runner under a dark chandelier in one, and a grand piano surrounded by chairs and sofas in another. One massive room held nothing but a raised dais at one end and a large, polished floor that stretched from the hall to what I assumed was the other end of the palace itself.

Something strange stirred the air as we passed yet another open doorway. It felt at once comforting and frightening, familiar and alien. Half-heard whispers slid past my ears, nudging something in my memory that I couldn't quite place, and then vanished.

Again, I felt a warm presence all around me, though it was stronger than what I had experienced in Sam's cabin. This presence seemed to call to me as if it knew me. I stopped in the middle of the hall, the others flowing around me as they took in the sights. I peered into a doorway where I had heard someone whispering, just out of sight.

An overwhelming sense that I should know this place drew me into the room, which looked like a large study under a shroud of darkness. As I poked my head inside, the butler called to me, breaking my concentration. The feeling of being called faded, and I faced the group. All of the men were gazing after me, and as I turned to leave, I thought I glimpsed a flare of light. When I turned back, nothing had changed. The butler cleared his throat, and I left the room behind.

After a long walk to the other side of the palace down this straight hall, we turned into a doorway on our right that opened onto the throne room. The dark wooden throne with a deep blue plush seat sat upon a dais at the far end, and columns of white and gray marble surrounded it. Tapestries lined the walls, depicting landscapes from throughout Trylia. The polished dark marble floor glittered with snaking gold lines. Light reflected off its surface from the series of chandeliers above our heads. Small crystals tinkled softly as we made our way across the room. A wide burgundy carpet stretched directly from the door to the dais and muffled the sound of our footsteps until our guide halted us near the edge.

The butler disappeared behind the throne, and I leaned to the side to see the tapestry against the wall swinging in place over a hidden door. Minutes passed in which we stood waiting for the King to arrive. Bryn's hand warmed mine.

The butler reappeared in the company of several well-dressed attendants and soldiers. One man's coat held several shining medals and ribbons, and I guessed he was Commander Falich, leader of the King's armies.

Shortly thereafter, the King himself arrived. He stood tall and lean and moved with the grace of a dancer when he climbed the short steps of the dais. His sharp gaze surveyed our group when he took his seat; he sat erect with his hands on the arms of the throne, his face carefully blank.

He looked to be in his forties. Dark brown hair with streaks of gray at both temples was combed back from his tawny brown face in artful waves. His striking gray eyes bored into mine when they settled on me and stopped his roaming gaze of my friends. His full lips twitched amidst a trimmed mustache and beard streaked with gray.

"So, you are the people that caused so much trouble outside the city yesterday." His surprising deep, rich voice held a tone of disapproval that ran a chill down my spine. For some reason I recoiled a step, as if I were a frightened child about to be punished.

"Well done, I say, for ridding the world of that terrible man and his influence!" he exclaimed, his tone changing, becoming warm and congratulatory while his mouth bloomed in a radiant white smile. Roy sighed with relief. Bryn remained stiff at my side, not disarmed by the sudden change in the monarch's attitude, but more wary than before.

"We've been watching him for some time, but he never left enough evidence behind for us to act. Thanks to you, I am relieved of that duty."

Sam snorted, drawing the king's eyes to his face. King Demetrius leaned forward on his throne. "I know you, sir," he drawled, as if trying to place Sam. His eyes widened, and he straightened. "Your name is Samuel, if I'm not mistaken. You served the throne long ago. How is it that you are still alive?"

Sam shifted his feet and ducked his head. "My name is Samuel, sire, but I am no one of import. Just a humble teacher, schooled in the myth and lore of Trylia."

"Peter," the King called. One of the men leapt forward for the King to whisper in his ear. Peter dashed around the dais and disappeared behind the tapestry. The King pulled his gaze from Sam with some reluctance and looked over the rest of us again.

"Well, you all seem to have survived your encounter with the notorious Captain Roglin, but I heard that it was a near thing for you, miss." His eyes came back to mine, and I nodded.

"Yes, sire, it was. But my friends were there to assist me." My glance at Bryn made the king smile.

"Yes, I had heard that you had a dashing fellow looking after you while you were unconscious. Good work, sir, saving the life of such an important young woman."

Bryn nodded, and King Demetrius beamed.

"Sire, if I may ask a question?" I asked. At his nod, I continued. "Why am I here?" Sam and Captain Morrig sighed, no doubt thinking my question lacked diplomacy, but Hunter snorted and Bryn's impassive façade was broken by a brief grin.

"What a direct question!" King Demetrius exclaimed. "How refreshing!" He clapped his hands together. "You are a very special young woman...Lila." He hesitated before speaking my name. "I have spies all throughout Trylia and beyond. Though we are largely unsuccessful, my people and I attempt to halt the trade of Trylia's citizens as slaves. When word reached my men of a young woman being sold for an outrageous price, they investigated. Their investigation led them to believe that this young woman possessed something unheard of in the past few centuries."

My heartbeat quickened, pounding against my ribs. The king's direct gaze told me that he knew of the Ambience, and my ability to use it.

"My family has passed down stories of a time when the Ambient flourished for generations." My stomach turned with dread. "Since their disappearance, the rest of the population has dismissed these as tales of fancy, but the monarchy knows that they are rooted in fact." The king settled into the cushioned backing of the throne and rested his elbows on the arms. Sam stood still as stone, despairing as I was that our secret had been revealed. I wondered what would become of us as the king continued.

"While the Ambient flourished, the kingdom was an altogether safer and more harmonious place. Since they have faded from the world, people have reverted to their baser instincts, to kill and steal, rightly thinking our power to stop them has faded with the passing of those with powerful means to stop them. We cannot be everywhere at once and I have few enough soldiers to patrol the coast, let alone the rest of Trylia."

At that moment Peter reappeared, holding what looked like a frame in his hands. He showed it to King Demetrius, who smiled broadly and looked back and forth between what he saw and Sam.

"I *knew* I had seen you before!" he exclaimed. He waved Peter away in our direction, and the man walked down the steps and turned the frame around.

It was a portrait of a young man around fifteen years old. He bore a striking resemblance to King Demetrius with his gray eyes, complexion, and chocolate-colored hair. Standing behind him, with a protective hand on the young man's shoulder, stood Sam.

I gaped at the painting. The Sam depicted within was younger, with no lines on his face and a rich brown head of hair. His formal posture and high-collared jacket gave him an air of confidence he didn't seem to possess any longer. Bryn leaned forward to stare at the portrait as well.

Sam, meanwhile, stepped to the back of our group, his face revealing nothing. King Demetrius descended the steps and moved to stand in front of him, and the rest of our group respectfully parted.

"The young man in that portrait was my great-great-great grandfather," he told us while not taking his eyes from Sam's face. Sam returned the stare with a blank countenance. "He found that he possessed some small talent for the Ambience, and the best tutor in the kingdom was summoned. That tutor was you, sir."

"It seems that I can hide no longer," Sam replied evenly.

The King looked taken aback. "Why would you be hiding from us?" he asked. "What threat did we ever pose to you? My family treasured your advice and treated you as an honored guest!"

Sam nodded. "That was always the case, Your Majesty. I had no quarrel with the ruling family, and I was not hiding from you. I was hiding my existence to protect myself from those that would do me harm, in the event that the Ambient made their return to Trylia. To do that, I had to cut all ties."

King Demetrius nodded sagely. "Yes, that *would* have been prudent. I understand, Samuel."

"I don't," Hunter said.

Sam sighed. "The Ambient were hunted to near extinction hundreds of years ago. Anyone that had a connection to the Ambience, anyone who had produced a child with such ability, or anyone even related to someone with the ability, was killed one by one over the course of several generations. It was an attempt to wipe us from the face of Trylia, and it nearly succeeded. We will speak more of this later. For now," he said, turning to the King, "I would like to know what you intend to do with us."

The King moved back to his throne and sat as Peter took up his place to the left with the other attendants. "I intend to ask for your assistance," he said gravely. "I do not wish to detain you or to use your talent to my own ends," he said, looking at Sam and me. "But I would ask that you might consider helping the people of Trylia."

"How would we do that?" I asked.

"You know that we have been having more and more trouble with inhabitants of Vortheim in recent years. They are becoming more daring, abducting and killing more and more Trylians every year, and my soldiers cannot be in every city at once. I would ask that you help to patrol our waters between Trylia and Vortheim, in hopes that you might be able to combat this rising threat before it ever reaches our shores."

Captain Morrig cleared his throat. "That seems like a monumental task for so few to undertake, Your Majesty. And I lost my ship when Roglin took my Lila. How can we accomplish this for you?"

"My good Captain, I would like to supply you with a new ship and help you to choose a new crew. And as I'm sure that your Lila would love to accompany you, you would have the advantage of her talent on your side." He smiled at Captain Morrig. "I have heard of you, good sir, and your abilities in commanding a vessel with such dangers as exist to those that brave the open water. I can think of no man more qualified to command our renewed naval defenses."

Captain Morrig's face lit like a sunrise over a calm ocean. "Thank you, Your Majesty! I will get to work straight away." He bowed again and clasped Hunter on the back. Hunter and Roy smiled at him, as eager to get back to the sea as he.

"Lila, can I count on you to assist Captain Morrig in this endeavor? Your skills would be of great use to him, I'm sure."

I hesitated, considering with longing the life I once had on the ocean, the deck of a ship carrying and sheltering us day and night. Though I had reservations about my ability to aid in halting the advance of Vortheim's ships, a part of me thirsted for the chance to try. Only the thought of living without Bryn at my side gave me pause. My decision would affect him, and I didn't want to make it alone.

My eyes turned to Bryn, who smiled. "Whatever you decide, I'll be with you," he murmured.

"My place is with you, as well," Sam added from behind Bryn. "We will continue your training, and I can do that wherever you choose to go. I haven't spent much time on the ocean. A new experience."

I beamed at them, elated by the knowledge that my decision wouldn't break apart the bond of friendship we had forged over the past months. I turned back to the King.

"I will do what I can to help," I smiled.

King Demetrius clapped his hands together in delight. "Wonderful!" he said. "We will begin work on your ship immediately. If you have any opinions on the design, Peter will introduce you to the men in charge. Now, I have a lavish feast prepared to celebrate the return of Ambience to the kingdom."

He rose and gestured for most of his attendants to lead the way to the banquet hall. Sam cleared his throat.

"Your Majesty, if I might suggest something?"

"Certainly, Master Samuel," he replied.

Sam was surprised by the title. "I would suggest that we keep secret the knowledge that a few of the Ambient are present. If word were to get out...."

The King waved his hand dismissively. "My men have been sworn to secrecy already. I would trust anyone that was just in the room with my life."

"I have a few more questions," I interrupted.

The King descended the steps and placed a hand on my shoulder. Inexplicably, it reminded me of Captain Morrig's fatherly gestures.

"You seem very eager to help us, and I would like to know why."

"I believe I asked *you* for aid, my dear," the king insisted. "Anything I can do to assist you in your efforts on behalf of my people is in reality a selfish gesture."

"Have your family's ties to the Ambience been sustained over the years?"

"To a certain extent," he replied. "You remember that my great-great-great grandfather was Master Samuel's pupil?" I nodded. "Well, those responsible for the extermination of the Ambient in centuries past found it exceedingly difficult to get close to the royal family.

"Over the years we have kept that part of ourselves secret. Since most of the people with the potential were killed, strength with the Ambience has weakened with every generation. As a result, *I* have a connection to it, but it manifests itself in a much different way than it does in you."

"How does it manifest?" Sam asked.

King Demetrius smiled, a handsome and devilish grin. "I am *very* persuasive," he replied.

"You seem eager to give us a lot of freedom and power. How do you know you can trust us?" I demanded. Pressure from the king's arm moved me along the carpet, leaving the rest to fall in step behind us.

"No, my dear Lila. I have a suspicion about you, and I am relying on my abilities to judge a person's character more than anything else. You have a good heart, and I know that you will do all you can to prevent events like those that haunt your past to haunt anyone else if it is within your power to do so."

"You're hiding something," I informed him, and he chuckled in response.

"Many things, in fact," he quipped. "Rest assured I will share some of that information with you when the time comes, but for now let's enjoy the feast. Tomorrow, you can start gathering all that you need to protect Trylia."

CHAPTER FORTY-THREE

King Demetrius made good on his word, and within a year, *Catherine's Revenge* was ready to sail. Master shipwrights repurposed a ship already in production that matched Captain Morrig's specifications. She was built long and low, made for speed and maneuverability. She sported three masts with square sails and had a single deck for crew's quarters.

The only change the captain requested was to the cabin specifications. Aside from the Captain's cabin, there was the galley and a guest cabin that Sam was to use. Captain Morrig sacrificed some of his own space to allow for a larger cabin for me.

He excused my protests and insisted that I would also serve as ship surgeon, having studied under Smitts and possessing a talent for healing using the Ambience. Hunter and Roy exchanged significant glances with me after hearing about my increased living space aboard the new ship. They both suspected, as I did, that he was also trying to accommodate my blossoming relationship with Bryn.

Summer had just begun in earnest when the six of us gathered on the docks, looking out to the harbor at *Catherine's Revenge*. She was anchored with a few other ships and she put them all to shame.

It was late morning, and we borrowed a rowboat to visit her. Bryn and Hunter volunteered to man the oars, so I sat in the single seat at the bow, facing the ship. I inhaled the sea air, pulling it into my lungs. At no time in my trek across land had I felt as comfortable as I did with the waves rocking beneath me and the salty water splashing against my forearms where they rose above my grip on the rail.

Bryn followed Hunter's lead and they pulled us with swift strokes to our destination. Once we reached the ship, Captain Morrig and I threw lines above the rail. There were a few people on board, including Kai, part of the team that had put her together. They made fast the lines and lowered a rope ladder for us to climb.

My hair whipped free of the leather tying it behind my head. I felt invigorated, more alive than I had since the day our ship had been destroyed so long ago. My boots hit the deck with a thud, and I strolled about fore to aft. When the rest joined me, I shot them a mischievous grin, kicked off my boots and stockings, and took to the rigging.

Bryn shouted my name while Hunter, Captain Morrig, Kai, and Roy laughed at the familiar sight. I left them as I climbed higher and higher. Muscles I hadn't used in so long screamed with the effort of pulling me to the heights. When I reached the yard of the main topmast, I took a much-needed break and locked my legs beneath the beam.

I shook out my arms to relieve the burning sensation and looked around the harbor at the other ships. From my vantage point, I spied people scurrying around the decks, tying lines and repairing sails. One schooner was anchored nearby, several carpenters hanging by ropes to repair a section of the hull. The hammers pounding nails into the wood echoed over the water. Feeling as though I had stalled long enough, I finished the climb. I arrived in the Bird's Nest, as Roy had named it, and pulled myself over the rail onto the platform.

It was bigger, with space to walk around the tip of the mast without having to squeeze through. I smiled and leaned back against the mast to bask in the sunlight and salty breeze. The wind was stronger up here, and the movement of the ship rocking on the waves greatly increased.

Looking down to the deck, I pictured hands scurrying about the myriad tasks required to sail. I had spent the past few months with what remained of my crew, interviewing potential hands. After a few were weeded out, based upon the captain and Hunter's uncanny ability to read people, and Roy's skills in searching out their past associates, we put together a solid crew. All seemed to share some of the same basic principles that drove us. A fair few of these were sailors by trade and a good number of them had known the grief of loss of their crew at the hands of slavers and pirates. We were able to recruit a decent number of fighters as well; people that had experience as soldiers or mercenaries who occasionally found work guarding merchant vessels.

When we explained our task to those we favored, almost all of them were on board even before we mentioned that this was a mission King Demetrius himself had given us. With the possibility of more pay than they ever had before, we were met with overwhelming agreement to join.

We decided not to mention the Ambience to the recruits. We planned to take *Catherine's Revenge* out for a few months to train them in our ways and teach them to work as a group before we engaged in any hostilities. We didn't want to run the risk of the information getting to the wrong people, and we didn't know if we could trust everyone yet. Now that I was standing on the ship, I started to feel hopeful about our prospects. We would get back to the life we knew, and we would protect Trylia in doing so.

I moved to the rail and back over the edge, making my way down to the deck. A few feet from my destination, strong arms gripped my waist and pulled me back, spinning me around once before setting me on my feet.

Bryn's hair ruffled in the breeze, his cheeks full of color and his lean muscular frame brimming with excitement. His exuberant smile matched mine, and he kissed my forehead.

"Does it feel good to be back on a ship?" he asked me.

"It does," I sighed. "How does it look?" I asked.

"Captain Morrig seems incredibly pleased. He keeps running his hands over every surface and smiling."

"I'm glad he's happy," I said and stepped close, circling my arms around his waist. He laid his head against mine and put his arms around me. I wondered if Bryn genuinely wanted to come with us, or if he was just doing it to please me, and for a fleeting moment I longed for the connection we had once shared.

Not having the bond between us proved disheartening for both of us. We reminisced when we were alone about the ease with which we had once shared our thoughts.

"Bryn, I want to try something. But I need your consent to do it."

"Whatever it is, I'm sure I'll agree. But for the sake of that stark comment, maybe I should hear about it first.

"I miss what we had with the bond. Not the danger, but being able to hear and feel you, to talk to you without speaking. And I want some of what you had. I want to know where you are in case something goes wrong. I want to be able to feel what you feel for the same reasons."

"I miss it too," he said. He kissed me, soft and insistent. Warmth tingled through my body. "How do we do it?"

I reached out to Bryn with a tendril of Ambience. My will was answered with a flood of spirits so strong that the air began to vibrate around us. This was not only *my* intent, but the desire of that deep font of power that existed only between Bryn and I, and I gasped as it tore away from my control. Bryn pulled away from me too, and the next instant his pupils dilated as the Ambience hit him with massive force; he spasmed, his arms flung out to either side. He grimaced, and then his mouth dropped open.

"Bryn?" I pleaded. He gritted his teeth and grunted. *"Bryn!"*

My focus followed the flow of Ambience inward, trying to see what was happening to him. It seemed to be coursing throughout his body, unable to settle. In place of the small connection between our minds as I had intended, it seemed to be embedding itself into every fiber of his being.

"Sam!" I shrieked, terrified and searching for help. Seconds felt like hours as I watched Bryn struggle. Finally, Sam appeared from below decks, fearful confusion on his face.

"Lila?" he asked as he jogged over to us. He took one look at Bryn and his fear turned to panic. *"What happened?"* he cried.

"I was trying to give him a bit of the Ambience, like I did with all of you. But it was different, more powerful! Something is wrong!"

Sam closed his eyes and held his hands out to Bryn. He frowned as he concentrated, no doubt sensing the torrent racing throughout Bryn's body.

I focused my attention on Bryn as well, seeking some understanding of what I had wrought. The Ambience seemed to be working its way inward, after suffusing every inch of Bryn's body with something more than he had been, to some hidden core that I had not been able to access before. I could see every bit of Bryn, all his experiences, all his memories, his hopes and his fears, his spirit.

It was the most beautiful thing I had ever seen, and tears filled my eyes. All the Ambience I had poured into Bryn coalesced there, and he screamed.

I reached out along the wave of Ambient power to what I thought of as his soul and tried to soothe him. The spirits working to root the power there reacted strongly, pulsing outward, and I was wrenched away from Bryn to fly a few feet from him and crash onto my back.

When I regained my feet, I saw Bryn crumpled on the deck, writhing. I sprinted to his side as he stilled. His eyelids fluttered when I knelt next to him, lifting his head to cradle it in my lap.

"Bryn," I whispered. "Are you all right?"

Bryn's eyes opened suddenly and focused on mine, and he placed a hand on my cheek. A jolt passed between us, and his voice echoed in my head.

What did you do? he asked.

I tried to give you some of the Ambience, so that I could have this *again.*

I guess it worked, he replied. He seemed to draw his focus inward while amusement coursed through him. He inspected himself from head to toe, drawing on the spirits like I would if I were attempting to heal.

The spirits called me to watch his examination, and I found myself immersed in the essence of his private self. Power coursed through him as it did in me, but altered. Rather than an active connection to the Ambience and the spirits who allowed my will to shape it, Bryn's body seemed to have absorbed the essence of my connection without the ability to consciously control the spirits. They followed his direction in relation to our connection and bolstered his physicality.

I think I've changed, Bryn thought wryly.

This is amazing! Does it hurt?

No, it doesn't. In fact, he paused, and jumped to his feet, startling me. *I feel better than I have ever felt. Like I could move mountains!*

Sam had struggled to his feet during our silent exchange and was staring at Bryn. "Are you all right, boy?"

"Great, Sam! Never better!"

He held his hand out, and I took it. Before I could get my feet under me, Bryn scooped me from the deck in a blur of movement to hold me against his chest with my feet dangling above the ground.

He kissed me thoroughly, and everything else faded. I was lost in his embrace, in the feel of his lips, his arms around me, his tongue in my mouth....

As suddenly as it began, it ended, and I was left standing in front of him, my mind jumbled and incapable of coherent thought. I heard the others talking and shook myself, trying to interpret what they were saying.

"...thought something happened," Hunter was saying. "We heard both of you scream and Sam went running."

"Everything is fine, here. Wouldn't you say, Lila?" Bryn looked down at me with a wolfish grin on his face.

"Uh huh," I slurred.

Captain Morrig raised an eyebrow as he regarded what I assumed was a very blank look on my face.

"How is she?" I asked Captain Morrig, trying to collect myself and gesturing at the ship to distract him.

"She's exactly how I pictured her. Not the same, but she'll be better for what we need. You should look around. I think you'll be impressed."

I nodded and the men dispersed, leaving Bryn and me alone on the deck.

We need never doubt each other again, Bryn thought.

That's true, I replied. *I'll never have to ask what you're thinking. And you were able to initiate it this time. I've been the only one who could make that happen.*

He shrugged, unconcerned. *I just wanted to hear what you were thinking, and I did.*

Can you do it again? I asked, mimicking his words from the first time I connected our minds as I pulled away from him. A moment later, I felt his presence again as it nudged the edge of my thoughts.

Yes I can, he thought. He felt triumphant, excited.

My answering smile was full of hope and joy. I couldn't think of anything to say, so I started for the hatch to explore the ship. The main berth and the galley were as I pictured them and remarkably like what I had seen on the *Catherine.* What surprised me was the cabin Bryn said was ours.

It was as large as the captain's across the hall, with a bunk built into the hull that was large enough for two. A small table adorned the corner with four chairs situated around it, and that was where Sam, Hunter, Captain Morrig, and Roy sat praising the work that had been done.

Captain Morrig smiled at me over Sam's head. "What do you think?" he asked.

"I think it's too much," I replied.

"After your description of your room at Sam's cabin, I don't believe that. Living on a ship isn't as comfortable as I'd like, but I thought I could improve upon things a bit."

I sat on the bunk, surprised at how soft the mattress was. It was nowhere near as comfortable as my mattress in the cabin, but it was far removed from the small hammock I had once used.

The men left while I inspected the contents of my new living space. A small chest housed herbs, bandages, and many of the small instruments to dress wounds. There was also a small chest of drawers that would be more than adequate to hold what few material things I possessed.

The sun lit my face when I emerged on deck again. Captain Morrig clapped Hunter and me on the shoulders and beamed down at us. "Welcome home."

The Story Continues In

PROVENANCE OF POWER

Book Two of The Ambience Series

Coming Soon!

ACKNOWLEDGMENTS

I've worked on this book for a long time. It was the product of whim and a dream, and has changed so much since it began. I have to thank my husband, Quinn Brentson, for being my sounding board and writing partner, as well as a person to talk at so the ideas could flow over the years. And my beta readers, Rhiannon Brentson, Beth Waymire, Alex Fisher, Trinity Cunningham, Mark Gellis, Paul Brentson, and Sherrie Brentson, for giving me your insight. I didn't know how much I needed it, but Woody Johns of Copper Coin Editing, my wonderful editor, you made this a much better story. I am so grateful to all of you for your insight.

I have so many people that encouraged and supported me along the way, Tim and Holly Fisher, my parents, thank you for introducing me to fantastical worlds and an ability to love and create things with excitement. To one of my early influences in writing, Jon Alston, for imparting your knowledge. It has stuck with me all these years. To Alex Fisher, my brother, I hear your voice when I'm plotting. To Rhiannon Brentson, my sister, thank you so much for your enthusiasm about this book. To my kids, Kaylee, Carter, and Ellie, I love you, and I'm grateful for your patience when I needed to write and edit.

For this finished product, I have nothing but gratitude for the people who helped me get it done. Rebecca Guyton, thank you for the map for this, and my other books. Marybeth Modok, I love the cover, it's so beautiful.

And thank you to you, the reader, for giving this book a chance. I appreciate you coming on this journey with my characters. Hopefully, you'll accompany them as they find more adventure.

Extras

Meet The Author

DANA C BRENTSON has been enjoying fantasy storytelling since she was small, whether in books, movies, or video games. As an adult, she began to create her own stories, which blossomed when she started to explore tabletop gaming.

Find out more about her and her other works by subscribing to her newsletter at www.dcbrentson.com

If you enjoyed
HER LATENT CHARM
Check Out
DESOLATE SEASONS
The Ambient Series: Sam
By
Dana C Brentson

1

The man was shivering and shaking, steam rising from his skin as he lay at Sam's feet.

"Where are they?" Sam was shaking too, but his tremors were the product of rage. The Hunter at his feet suffered from the effects of Ellen's alterations. And he was about to be consumed by them.

He chuckled, the whites of his eyes slowly turning red from the ruptured blood vessels. "Inside. Didn't you see them?"

"All I saw was ash. Where is Penelope's family?" His voice broke at his lost wife's name.

"That's the point. Ash is all that remains." The man coughed up steaming blood.

Sam growled. "I remember you. You were in the class behind her. One of her followers when she had free rein in Salvation." Sam knelt next to him. "Parson, right?"

The Hunter blinked in recognition. Sam smiled, feral rage seeping to the surface.

"It's a shame you became one of her puppets. You were bright."

"We were victims!" Parson shouted. "We didn't want this!"

"Unfortunately, there's no going back," Sam whispered. "There's nothing I can do to help you now. There was nothing I could do for any of you. No matter how long I've looked for an answer over the years it always ends the same way. Any of the Ambient that cross your paths trigger you, and you do what she designed you to do."

"I don't want to die," Parson whispered. His tears evaporated on his cheeks. "Please."

Sam frowned, his rage smothered by a blanket of grief and regret. "I'm so sorry. I'll take the pain away."

Sam called on the Ambience to give him strength. He reached out, grasped the burning skin at Parson's cheeks, and wrenched his head around his neck. After a grunt and a snap, he fell back onto the loose pine needles. His skin cooled instantly, his bloody eyes staring at the canopy of pine trees above them.

Sam sighed and sat down next to the body. After countless months wandering the wilderness with no destination in mind, he hadn't expected to stumble on a Hunter. Or to find that his late wife's family was dead.

He felt like his last connection to his past was gone. It left a hole in his chest that throbbed with the beat of his heart.

What's the point of this? He thought.

There was no one left in the world like him. His elders had sacrificed themselves to prolong his life. They had tasked him to guide the next generation of Ambient in Trylia. To teach them how to harness the force at the heart of their world that would allow them to change it with a thought. But he couldn't fulfill his purpose until they were born with the connection to the Ambience. And he had no idea how long that would take.

Am I doomed to live forever? With no one and nothing to care for?

In the shadow of the northwest mountains, he walked through dense forest. These were familiar paths from a time when he stalked his prey as a ruthless hunter. And he shuddered when the leaves whispered in the canopy above. He felt eyes watching him from the gloom.

He retraced his steps for weeks to the hiding places of his people, where they huddled in fear of the Hunters. All he found were bodies and empty spaces. He piled the corpses of friends and enemies alike and burned them in hot Ambient flames so that they could return to the Pool.

Every time he searched he found nothing but disappointment. All hope faded. He was truly alone.

Several months of walking found him along the East coast of Trylia. The ocean air revitalized him. It was a new scent, a new experience for him. He had never been further southeast than the central city of Stalth and was excited to see what else this continent had to show him.

Sam walked through the wooden palisades of a small town with a packed dirt street and a small main thoroughfare. It had one general store and one small inn. The rest of the buildings were houses barely large enough to have two rooms. A crowd milled around in the open to chat, barter, and chase after children.

Sam listened to the town gossip. Guards with rustic spears complained about a group of bandits in the area scaring away traders. Mothers following the chaotic journey of several children through the streets complained about a teacher leaving. The rest mentioned the lack of Gifted visiting over the past few years, wondering what happened to them and whether they would see a healer soon.

In the decades since the Hunters killed so many Ambient like him, Sam had heard more people adopt 'Gifted' to replace the description for his people. In their absence, it seemed the citizens of Trylia had already forgotten much of his culture.

The path through the town was short. In a matter of minutes, he passed through and found himself at the cliff's edge that marked the end of town. He gasped as he looked out at the wide expanse of ocean.

More marvelous than the mountains he grew up with, vaster than any countryside he had seen in his many years of wandering. Almost as radiant as the Ambient Pool. The ocean evoked more feelings from him than had pierced his hard shell of apathy in years. When he walked through town again he listened to all that these people needed and worried about. And he decided that he needed to take control of his life. If he couldn't find meaning in a purpose that may never come, he would find meaning elsewhere.

In the tavern that evening Sam sat at one of seven tables. They were rectangular and communal, and he was between groups of rival caravan operators.

"My three need schoolin'," one said. She was a slight, wiry woman with pale skin and golden brown hair. Her low voice was hard to hear over the conversations echoing in the room. "My wife can't teach 'em all they need."

"Used to be we had an Ambient to do all that. Or Gifted, if that's the word." The man who spoke up across the table was tall and burly. He frowned, wrinkling the deep brown skin at one corner of his mouth. "They were the ones who did all the learning. This far from the capital or the big cities, anyway."

"An' what happened with them? They just left? Hidin'?"

"I heard they's all dead," said the person to the woman's right. Their blonde hair flopped to one side when they shook their head. "Killed by they own kind."

Sam sighed and continued to eat his fresh bread, swishing it around in the broth from his stew.

"Well, we need someone," said the man.

"Excuse me," Sam said. Everyone at the table looked at him. "If there's a need for a teacher here, I have some training."

"Where you from?" asked the blonde. They narrowed their brown eyes at Sam. "Haven't seen you here before."

Sam shook his head. "This is my first time on the coast. I came east from Stalth."

"Ah, one of the big cities. Like I said." The man flashed a smug smile at the table and took a drink from his mug.

"Just so," Sam replied.

"Well, you can speak wit' the steward. In the house at the cliff's edge. Biggest one, can't miss it." The woman stood and walked with her plate and cup to the bar.

Sam nodded in thanks as he stood. "Thank you. Much appreciated."

Tucked in his room for the night Sam thought about how much he could give to this community if the steward allowed him to teach the children. And he thought of the children that had been lost before. Perhaps he could begin to heal here.